COURTROOM SHOOTOUT

"Marshall Irvin," he intoned, "I order you to remove yourself and those men from my court. If you refuse—"

A strangled scream echoed off the walls. Bud Wilson leaped past Irvin, his Remington six-gun extended at arm's length. The pistol roared and Proctor staggered backward into the defense table. In the next instant gunfire erupted throughout the courtroom.

Ryan acted on reflex alone. He saw the Light Horse sergeant's carbine aimed directly at him. Ryan's arm moved in a blurred motion. The Colt appeared in his hand and spat a sheet of flame. The slug impacted beneath the sergeant's breastbone and jerked him sideways . . . .

A hail of lead whistled across the room as the Light Horse Police exchanged shots with Wilson and the Cherokees. The ranks of both sides were winnowed as though chopped down by a giant scythe. Three of the Cherokees were hurled backward. Another dropped, and finally Wilson staggered . . .

Through a haze of gunsmoke, Ryan sensed all around him the carnage of a bloodbath. He was vaguely aware that he'd been wounded himself . . .

INDIAN TERRITORY

MATT BRAUN

St. Martin's Paperbacks

The story which follows is fiction, based on the true facts gleaned from musty newspaper archives and the chronicles of men who were there.

INDIAN TERRITORY

Copyright © 1985 by Matt Braun.

ISBN: 0-312-94853-0
EAN: 9780312-94853-5

Printed in the United States of America

Pinnacle edition / August 1985
St. Martin's Paperbacks edition / September 1999

St. Martin's Paperbacks are published by St. Martin's Press, 175 Fifth Avenue, New York, NY 10010.

10 9 8 7 6 5 4 3 2 1

To Leslie, Nicole, and Darren

CHAPTER
ONE

The town took shape like a wintry mirage. On a wooded creek bank Ryan reined his gelding to a halt. He sat studying the distant buildings.

A light February snowfall covered the plains. Located in the southeastern quadrant of Kansas, the town stood framed against an overcast sky. It was called Parsons, the latest in a line of railheads advancing across the prairie. As yet, it appeared on no map.

Somewhat bemused, Ryan slowly inspected the layout. Only last spring he'd ridden through here on his way to Abilene. From Fort Smith, where he served as a deputy U.S. Marshal, it was a five-day trip by horseback. At the time there had been nothing along Labette Creek except a vast expanse of prairie grassland. But now, bundled in a mackinaw against the cold, he saw a bustling little metropolis. He was impressed, and all the more curious about the man who had summoned him.

Parsons was the offspring of the railroad. Chartered several years ago, the Missouri, Kansas and Texas had begun operations in Junction City. The company name, too cumbersome for everyday use, had been shortened by natives to the "Katy." Last year, the summer of 1870, the line had laid track to the border of Indian Territory. Then, some miles above the border, the Katy turned eastward and began laying track toward Sedalia, Missouri. The juncture, situated on a fertile prairie, was only a stone's throw from Labette Creek. Here, seemingly overnight, Parsons sprang from the earth.

Windswept and sprawling, the town was a beehive of activity. Along the main thoroughfare was a collection of stores and businesses, clapboard buildings wedged side by side. Immense piles of trade goods, offloaded at the Katy depot, were stacked in snow-crowned mounds. Beyond the main street board shanties and canvas tents were rapidly being replaced by newly built houses. The population was approaching two thousand, and the inhabitants seemed charged with the galvanic energy peculiar to boom towns. Parsons had assumed a look of permanence.

Gathering the reins, Ryan kneed his gelding forward into the creek. A short distance beyond the opposite bank, he skirted the train depot and the rail yards. The main street was jammed with wagons and a noonday throng crowded the boardwalks. As he rode past, he noted that everyone, even the farmers, seemed in a hurry. Farther uptown he spotted the Belmont House Hotel directly across the street from a bank. At the hitch rack he stepped down from the saddle, then loosened the cinch. He left the gelding tied out front.

Inside the hotel he took a moment to shrug off his mackinaw. The lobby was furnished with a horsehair-and-leather sofa and several easy chairs. The room clerk behind the desk was painfully frail, with a pursed smile and round moist eyes. He nodded as Ryan crossed the lobby.

"Good afternoon, sir."

"Afternoon," Ryan replied. "I'm looking for Colonel Robert Stevens."

"Oh, yes sir! Colonel Stevens is in room two-oh-one. Just take the stairs and turn left."

The clerk's snap-to-attention reaction amused Ryan. But it was hardly more than he'd expected. Colonel Robert Stevens was, after all, managing director of the Katy railroad. Upstairs he turned left and proceeded along the hallway. He idly wondered if Stevens' rank was from wartime service or simply an honorary title. On second thought, he decided it wasn't worth asking. He rapped on the door.

The man who opened it was attired in a broadcloth coat, with matching vest and trousers. He was of medium height, with brown hair receding into a widow's peak and nut-brown eyes. Something about him gave an impression of raw vitality, an air of enormous confidence. He smiled cordially.

"May I help you?"

"Colonel Stevens?"

"Yes."

"I'm John Ryan."

"Well, do come in, Mr. Ryan. I'm delighted to see you."

Stevens thrust out his hand. Ryan pumped his arm a couple of times and moved through the door. The room was a combination bedchamber and parlor overlooking the town's main street. A brass bed along with a dresser and washstand were positioned off to one side. Nearer the windows were a small desk and two overstuffed armchairs.

"Allow me to take your coat."

Stevens hooked his hat and mackinaw on a hall tree. Then, leading the way, he motioned Ryan to one of the chairs. After seating himself, his eyes flicked over Ryan in rapid assessment. He noted the leather vest and and boots, and his gaze touched briefly on the Colt .44 strapped to Ryan's hip. He settled back, crossed his legs.

"You come highly recommended, Mr. Ryan. Oliver's letter was nothing short of a testimonial."

The reference was to Oliver Logan, U.S. Marshal for Western Arkansas and Indian Territory. Ryan shrugged off the compliment. "Oliver tells me you're old friends."

"Indeed we are," Stevens acknowledged. "We met some years ago in Washington. That was before his appointment west, of course."

"And before you got involved with the railroad."

"Exactly." Stevens was silent a moment. "I understand you've resigned as a deputy marshal. May I ask why?"

"Oliver must have explained it in his letter."

"I would prefer to hear it from you."

"Why not?" Ryan said equably. "Last month the President appointed Joseph Story as judge of the Western District Court. Story is a crook and an incompetent, and I won't work for either. It's just that simple."

"What do you mean by 'crook'?"

"Well, for one thing, he's appointed his cronies as chief prosecutor and court clerk. For another, the word's out that payoffs will buy leniency in criminal cases. I don't hold with corruption, so I quit."

"Why doesn't Oliver resign?"

"I guess he's too old to start over."

"And you're not?"

"Judge for yourself."

Stevens had already rendered judgment. He knew that Ryan had served with distinction in the Union Army. Following the war, he'd drifted westward, working at a variety of jobs. Then, at the age of twenty-eight, he had been hired by Oliver Logan. That was four years past, and by all accounts he had found his true vocation as a lawman. He had been assigned to Indian Territory the entire time and lived to tell the tale. He'd also killed nine outlaws in wilderness shootouts.

And now, scrutinizing him closely, Stevens understood why he came recommended so highly. He was whipcord lean, lithe yet broad through the shoulders, perhaps a shade less than six feet tall. His manner was deliberate and steady, somehow assured beyond his years. But it was his eyes, curiously pale and very direct, that set him apart. The effect of his gaze was striking, as though he looked at nothing and saw everything. His weathered features and sandy hair in no way dispelled the impression.

"Tell me," Stevens said at length, "how much do you know about the railroad business?"

"Not a whole lot."

"You're aware we intend to build through Indian Territory?"

"So I've heard."

Ryan actually knew a great deal about the Katy. Through

Oliver Logan, he'd learned that Stevens was an influential man with influential friends. The Department of the Interior had ruled that the first railroad to lay track to the Kansas state line would secure the exclusive right to enter Indian Territory from the north. Last summer, in a dead heat with other companies, Katy construction crews won the race to the border. As an added prize the Katy was awarded 1,300,000 acres in federal land grants along its Kansas right-of-way. Only two days later Congress passed a bill opening government lands in southern Kansas to settlement.

The Katy reaped a sudden windfall. Homesteaders and immigrants were pouring into Kansas, more than sixty thousand settling there in 1870. The virgin soil, along with a favorable climate and abundant streams, made it appear the promised land. In the months that followed, the Katy easily disposed of its federal grant. The price was ten dollars an acre, generating cash revenues in the millions of dollars. Quite clearly, Colonel Robert Stevens had friends in Washington.

Still, the largest prize of all was on the horizon. By federal grant the Katy would be awarded five alternate sections of land per mile on each side of its railway through Indian Territory. The purpose of the grant was to provide sufficient incentive for a company to spend the millions involved in construction costs. And in the case of Indian Territory, the incentive was very great indeed. The Katy grant, similar to that awarded for the first transcontinental line, would be ten square miles for each mile of road constructed. In total, the prize would represent 3,064,390 acres.

"I'm curious," Ryan said quietly. "How do the Indians feel about it? Won't a railroad through there open the Nations to settlement?"

"The price of progress," Stevens remarked. "Indian Territory is the key to a railway system throughout the entire Southwest. Here, let me show you."

Twisting about, he took a rolled map from the desktop. Then he leaned forward and unfurled it between them. His finger stabbed at the map.

"The shortest route to Texas is through the nations of the Five Civilized Tribes. A straight line between the Kansas border and Colbert's Ferry on the Red River."

"And after that?" Ryan asked.

"An empire!" Stevens said expansively. "We already have a grant to extend our road from Indian Territory through Texas to the Rio Grande. We'll eventually link Old Mexico and the Far West to the eastern markets. Just think of it!"

"Sounds like you've been burning the midnight oil."

"We have indeed. But what we're after now is to win the race to the Texas border. Then we'll connect with our Missouri division and establish an outlet to St. Louis and the East."

"What do you mean by a 'race'? I thought you had right-of-way through the Nations."

"Only the north-south route," Stevens advised him. "The Atlantic and Pacific has east-west right-of-way, and they're building from Missouri right now. We have to shut them off from the western markets by extending track to the Red River."

Ryan's expression revealed nothing. Yet he understood that Stevens was talking about establishing a monopoly of trade with Texas and the Far West. After a moment he shifted in his chair.

"How does all that involve me, Colonel? Your letter to Oliver wasn't too clear about what you have in mind."

"Have you ever seen a camp at end-of-track? Where we establish our supply depot until the next leg of the road is built?"

"Not that I recall."

"Well, it gets rough, very rough. There's always lots of money at end-of-track. Usually a settlement of some sort springs up as well. So it attracts whiskey peddlers and gamblers and prostitutes. What some people call the sporting crowd."

"I'm familiar with them," Ryan noted.

"You're also familiar with Indian Territory. Which in itself adds considerably to our problems. So I'd like to offer you the job of special agent.''

Ryan looked at him without expression. ''What exactly does a special agent do?''

''Keep the peace,'' Stevens answered. ''Hold down violence and make the sporting crowd toe the mark. Enforce the law.''

''Whose law?'' Ryan rocked his hand, fingers splayed. ''In the Nations, there's Indian law and there's white man's law.''

The problem he alluded to was essentially one of bureaucratic bungling. Of all the legal tangles created by federal government, law enforcement in Indian Territory was perhaps the most bizarre. White men, whatever their crime, were subject to arrest only by federal marshals. On the other hand, federal marshals could not arrest an Indian unless it involved an offense committed against a white. Light Horse Police, who enforced tribal law, were unable to arrest whites regardless of circumstances. The situation oftentimes became confusing and dangerous.

''To be quite frank,'' Stevens said, ''I'm not worried about Indians.''

''You should be,'' Ryan observed. ''There are still some savages in the Five Civilized Tribes. They just don't like *tibos*—white men.''

''Perhaps so. But my main concern is with the sporting crowd, or perhaps I should say with the safety of my construction crew.''

A moment elapsed while the two men stared at one another. Then Ryan spread his hands. ''What legal authority would I have?''

''I'll arrange to have you appointed a deputy sheriff here in Kansas. That should suffice until we reach the Texas border.''

''Sounds pretty thin.''

Stevens smiled. ''Any badge is better than no badge at all.''

''How much does the job pay?''

"Five hundred a month plus a bonus when we cross the Red River."

Ryan whistled softly. "That's a lot of money."

"You'll earn it."

An instant of weighing and calculation slipped past. Finally, with a tight grin Ryan nodded. "Colonel, I guess you've just hired yourself a special agent."

"Excellent! I'm delighted to have you on board, John."

There was a rumbling knock at the door. Then it opened and the entryway seemed momentarily blocked of light. The man who entered was tall and burly, with massive shoulders and a cannonball head. His hair was wiry and red, and his ruddy features were complemented by bushy ginger eyebrows and a ginger mustache. He lumbered across the room.

Stevens rose, motioning to Ryan. "John, I'd like you to meet Tom Scullin, our construction superintendent. Tom, this is John Ryan, our new special agent."

Scullin stuck out a gnarled, stubby-fingered hand. "Pleased to meet you. By your getup, I take it you're not from the old country?"

"A ways back." Ryan quickly extracted his hand from the big man's crushing grip. "My folks came over in 'thirty-nine."

"Aren't you the lucky devil. Most of my boys are fresh off the boat, and there's a fact."

"Your boys?"

"Our construction crew," Stevens interjected. "Tom has dubbed them the Irish Brigade."

"So now," Scullin went on bluffly, "you're to be our guardian down among the red heathens. Have you had experience at it, then?"

"Some."

"Some!" Stevens echoed. "John's too modest by far. For the past four years, he's served as a deputy U.S. Marshal. And all of it spent in Indian Territory."

"You don't say." Scullin wagged his head appreciatively. "Well, John Ryan, I'd think you'll do very nicely. Very nicely indeed."

Stevens resumed his seat. "Enough of your blarney, Tom. Why aren't you on your way to end-of-track?"

"Would you have me leave without sayin' good-bye? The construction train's loaded and we'll pull out within the hour."

"Which brings us back to the question you keep avoiding. Our plans for Indian Territory are delayed until we have a direct link to Missouri. So I ask again—how soon will you reach Sedalia?"

"By the Jesus!" Scullin said in a booming voice. "A mile a day, and there's my word on it. You'll have your connection in thirty days, no more."

"Good. I'm pleased to hear it. And I'll hold you to your word, Tom."

"You'll have no need! Trust an Irishman to deliver every time."

Scullin winked at Ryan and walked toward the door. When he was gone, Stevens laughed and shook his head. "It's like pulling teeth to get a commitment. But Tom hasn't failed me yet. He always delivers."

Ryan appeared thoughtful. "I heard him mention thirty days. Are you planning on me starting then or now?"

"Consider yourself on the payroll as of today, John."

"You mean to let me loaf for a month?"

"Hardly. We leave for Indian Territory tomorrow morning."

"Any particular part?"

"The Cherokee Nation. You can act as my guide."

"You've never been there?"

"No, never."

Ryan smiled. "You're in for a shock, and then some."

CHAPTER
TWO

Ryan and Stevens rode out of town shortly after sunrise. They were trailed by a packhorse loaded with victuals and camp gear. Where they were headed accommodations for travelers were virtually unknown.

Their route southward was along the Texas Road. Originally blazed by traders, the trail began on the Red River and meandered northward through the nations of the Five Civilized Tribes. At the Kansas border, it made a dogleg northeast and terminated at old Fort Scott.

Only a few years ago the Texas Road had been a major trade route. Herds of longhorn cattle were driven to midwestern railheads and quickly shipped on the hoof to eastern markets. Then in 1867 the Kansas Pacific Railroad laid track to Abilene. Located in central Kansas, Abilene cut time and distance to the Texas border. Cattlemen quickly switched to the Chisholm Trail, which bisected Indian Territory some miles west of the Nations. Abilene boomed and longhorn herds along the Texas Road became a thing of the past.

As Ryan and Stevens rode south, they steadily moved backward in time. Where the railroads ended, the borderlands of the frontier began. Squatters were homesteading the Cherokee Strip, which extended along the border and acted as a buffer between Kansas and Indian Territory. But settlements were often a day apart, connected by flinty backcountry trails. Some freight wagons, drawn by mule or oxen, still plied the Texas Road. An occasional stagecoach hauling passengers between Dallas and Kansas City clattered past, but Ryan and Stevens pretty much had the road to themselves. White men seldom ventured on horseback into Indian Territory.

Upon crossing into the Cherokee Nation, Stevens became quietly attentive. He scanned the terrain with a railroader's eye, measuring grade and topography. Kansas was composed largely of windswept plains and offered no particular obstacle to laying track. But the Nations were a land of rolling hills, and farther south, certain parts were distinctly mountainous. The rainfall was also heavier, and dense woodlands covered much of the terrain. Spongy bottomland along the Neosho River was choked with canebrakes and vast thickets of blackjack. Mulling it over, Stevens concluded that Indian Territory presented a formidable challenge. Both the people and the land were decidedly inhospitable.

Yet for all its drawbacks, the Nations were unquestionably a wildlife paradise. While the buffalo herds had migrated westward, there was still an abundance of game. Great flocks of turkey swarmed over the woodlands; at dusk the timber along the creeks was loaded with roosting birds. Deer were plentiful, and grouse and plover, pound for pound the most toothsome eating imaginable, were everywhere. Fat, lazy fish crowded the streams and river shallows, eager to take a hook baited with grasshopper or worm. It was truly a land where no man need go hungry.

Every night Ryan pitched camp along the riverbank. Stevens was strictly a tyro outdoorsman, more hindrance than help. But Ryan was amused rather than critical and gladly undertook most of the chores. After staking out their horses, he would walk off into the woods with his shotgun. He would return shortly with a young turkey or a bag of grouse and kindle a fire. By sundown a spit loaded with wildfowl would be roasting to a golden brown. A quick trip to the river produced catfish or trout, which were soon simmering in a skillet. With the coffeepot bubbling, there was nothing to do but wait and savor the rainbow of aromas.

On their second night out Ryan took a seat before the fire. Stevens, who was lounging nearby, watched silently as he swabbed out his shotgun. The weapon intrigued Stevens, for it wasn't a run-of-the-mill scattergun. An expensive double-barrel Greener, it had mule-ear hammers with a single trigger, and the barrels had been trimmed to half their normal length. Until now Stevens had restrained himself from prying. Tonight his curiosity got the best of him.

"Tell me, John," he asked in a casual tone, "why do you carry a shotgun? I thought everyone out here preferred a rifle or a saddle carbine."

"Most folks do." Ryan paused, peering through the barrels from the open breech. In the firelight the twin bores looked big as mine shafts. "Lawmen generally stick to a scattergun, though. I reckon I just got in the habit."

"What makes a shotgun preferable?"

"Well"—Ryan glanced up at him—"when you shoot a man, you want two things to happen. You want him to go down, and you don't want him to get up. That's what ends fights."

"I see. But don't those short barrels put you at a disadvantage? You're awfully limited on range."

"You'd be surprised. I've never yet tangled with a man at any considerable distance. Seems like it always happens fast and too close for comfort."

Stevens was tempted to ask still more questions. Like most easterners he'd never before encountered an authentic mankiller. Ryan's sidearm, which was a Colt Army .44 converted to metallic cartridges, was no less intriguing than the shotgun. But the railroader sensed that Ryan would indulge his curiosity only so far. He wisely changed the subject.

"How much farther to Boudinot's?"

"Couple of days. Maybe a little less."

"You're not altogether keen on the idea, are you?"

"I'm not being paid for my advice."

"I'd still like to hear your reason. What do you have against Boudinot?"

"Let's just say I don't trust turncoats. Anyone who sells out his own people won't think twice about doing it to a *tibo*."

"I disagree. Boudinot is widely respected in Washington. And I might add he's one of the few Indians who is."

Ryan shrugged. "I think you just made my point."

Ostensibly the purpose of Stevens' trip was diplomacy. He planned to conduct negotiations with William Ross, principal chief of the Cherokee Nation. But he had also arranged a secret meeting with Elias Boudinot. Some months ago in Washington, they had concluded a business deal known only to themselves. He meant to assure himself of Boudinot's support before calling on Ross.

The delicacy of the situation was compounded by tribal politics. William Ross and Elias Boudinot were avowed enemies, leaders of rival factions. A dedicated Unionist before the Civil War, Ross had nonetheless approved the Cherokees' alliance with the Confederacy. Circumstances, and the proximity of Confederate troops, left the Cherokee Nation no alternative. Ross, who considered it a white man's war, sought only to preserve his people.

Elias Boudinot, on the other hand, was something of an opportunist. Casting his lot with the South, he had served in the Confederate Army throughout the war. Afterward he'd been instrumental in forming the Southern Party, which stood in opposition to Ross' Union Party. In 1865, following the cessation of hostilities, federal commissioners were appointed to negotiate treaties with the Five Civilized Tribes. As spokesman for the Southern Party, Boudinot had actively courted the favor of the commissioners. He had also formed alliances with railroad companies lobbying to acquire right-of-way through the Nations.

The upshot of the negotiation was a victory for Boudinot. The treaty proclaimed a general amnesty and restored to the Cherokees their confiscated property. But it also required them to grant future right-of-way to railroad companies, as well as providing for the erection of military posts within the Nation. Still, it had represented something of a Pyrrhic victory. In the aftermath neither Boudinot nor the Southern Party had been able to gain control of the tribal government. These days Boudinot spent a good deal of his time hobnobbing with Washington politicos.

All of which dovetailed neatly with Stevens' own goals. Watching Ryan clean his shotgun, he decided to press the issue. "Why do you consider Boudinot a turncoat?"

"For one thing, he wants to do away with tribal ownership of the land. Parcel it out to individuals in lots of a hundred sixty acres. For another, he believes the Nations should be placed under a territorial governor appointed by Washington. None of that would work to the benefit of the Cherokees."

"I didn't realize you were an advocate of Indian rights."

"I'm not," Ryan informed him. "I just don't like turncoats—red, white, or polka dot."

"Well, I still think you're wrong about Boudinot. He wouldn't dare pull a fast one on me."

"It's your railroad."

Ryan loaded the shotgun with double-ought buckshot. He snapped the breech closed and laid the Greener across his saddle. Then he took the spit off the fire and began dissecting grouse with his knife. He glanced up at Stevens with a wry smile.

"What's your pleasure, Colonel? White meat or dark?"

On the fourth day they sighted Fort Gibson. There, deep in the heart of the Cherokee Nation, the road veered off to the southwest. At the Arkansas River crossing they turned southeasterly onto a rutted wagon trail. Toward sundown they passed through the settlement of Webbers Falls.

Their destination was the farm of Stand Watie. A leader in the Southern Party, Watie was also the uncle of Elias Boudinot. Yet unlike his nephew, he chose to use his Indian name. Boudinot's father, some years before his death, had adopted a white man's name. For the most pragmatic of reasons the son elected to follow his father's example. As Elias

Boudinot he found a warmer reception among Washington power brokers.

Stand Watie, while not so flamboyant as his nephew, was nonetheless a man of considerable prestige. During the Civil War, Watie had risen to the rank of brigadier general in the Confederate Army. It was a military honor accorded no other Indian and stemmed from his command of the Second Regiment Cherokee Mounted Rifles. After Lee's surrender at Appomattox, he had continued to lead his cavalry on guerrilla raids for almost three months. By holding out, he'd earned a singular distinction in the prolonged and bloody conflict. He was the last Confederate general to surrender his sword.

Watie's farm had been purposely selected for tonight's clandestine meeting. The area around Webbers Falls was an enclave of Southern Party members, all former Confederates. The chance was therefore slight that there would be any loose talk about two white men visiting the farm. Stand Watie still commanded the loyalty of his wartime comrades, and a certain military code prevailed even now. No one who valued his life would risk being branded a traitor.

Stevens and Ryan rode into the farmyard shortly after nightfall. The front door opened and a shaft of lamplight spilled across the porch. Stand Watie stepped outside, waiting for them to dismount. He was tall and portly, with a ramrod-stiff bearing that belied his age. His greeting was civil, though somewhat restrained.

Inside they were ushered into the parlor. Boudinot strode forward, clasping Stevens' hand with a show of warmth. He was a full head shorter than his uncle, somewhat stocky in build, and attired in a dark, conservative suit. When they were introduced, Ryan noticed that his hand was damp with sweat. Boudinot invited them to be seated, commenting that the women and children had retired for the night. Their discussion would not be interrupted.

Stevens came straight to the point. "Day after tomorrow I'm scheduled to meet with William Ross. I thought it worthwhile that we review our agreement beforehand."

Boudinot frowned. "I understood we were in accord when we met in Washington."

"We were, and I trust we still are. However, since then a new element has entered the picture."

"What might that be?"

Extracting a cigar from inside his coat, Stevens struck a match. He lit up in a wreath of smoke. "I've decided to propose a bond issue. It's an accepted procedure whenever a railroad builds through an area. The purpose, of course, is to help defray construction costs."

"With one slight difference. White communities want a railroad and they're willing to raise a bond issue to ensure they aren't bypassed. The Cherokees, by and large, have been opposed to the project from its inception. A bond issue would simply stiffen their opposition."

Stevens rather enjoyed jousting with Boudinot. He thought of the other man as an educated redskin and took amusement at his fancy manner of speech. Fixing Boudinot with a look, he puffed importantly on his cigar.

"Elias, the matter isn't open to debate. I prefer to have the Cherokee Nation committed by way of hard cash. And I expect your Southern Party to support it in the tribal council."

Boudinot and his uncle exchanged a quick glance. Stand Watie's features were unreadable, and there was a moment of oppressive silence. Then Boudinot threw up his hands. "Very well. You are assured of our support."

"Good," Stevens said easily. "Now on to other matters. Are you familiar with White Oak Creek?"

"Yes, of course," Boudinot replied. "It flows into Neosho maybe thirty miles below the border."

Stevens nodded. "I have information that the A&P survey line will run through there. I suggest you plan your town site for that general area."

For the next hour or so Stevens and the two men huddled around a map of the Cherokee Nation. Ryan sat quietly off to one side, solely an observer. Their discussion centered on an elaborate scheme to force the Atlantic and Pacific to detour around White Oak Creek. The purpose, insofar as Ryan gathered, was to delay construction of the rival railway. While it was unstated, Ryan discerned still another element in the conspiracy. Boudinot and Watie, in payment for their support, would be allowed to organize a major town site. The Katy would guarantee its success by establishing a terminal on the location.

To Ryan there was a certain irony about their secretive intrigue. Some thirty-five years ago Boudinot's father had been involved in a similar conspiracy. The elder Boudinot, along with others, had signed a secret treaty which ceded the tribe's ancestral southeastern lands to the federal government. Yet ancient Cherokee law exacted the death penalty for unauthorized land cessions by members of the tribe. Following removal of the Cherokees to Indian Territory, there had been a settling of accounts. The elder Boudinot and his co-conspirators were executed in unceremonious fashion. All in all, Ryan thought it was perhaps a case of like father, like son. It seemed there was a trace of conspiracy in the Boudinot blood.

When the meeting ended, there was another round of handshakes. Stevens appeared pleased with himself, nodding and smiling all the while. Stand Watie walked them to the door, his nephew trailing a pace behind. Outside the three men paused for a last word as Ryan moved toward the hitch rack. Halting beside his horse, he stooped down and tightened the cinch. As he straightened up, he saw Stevens wave and turn away from the house. Boudinot and Watie were framed in a streamer of lamplight from the doorway.

The night suddenly erupted in gunfire. Almost in unison the sharp crack of two rifles sounded across the yard. Stand Watie cursed, grabbing his left arm, and tumbled off the porch. Stevens flung himself to the ground, scrambling toward the hitch rack. With surprising agility, Boudinot dove headlong through the doorway. He kicked the door shut as he rolled into the house.

All thought suspended, Ryan reverted to sheer instinct. He pulled his shotgun from the saddle scabbard, stepped around his horse, and thumbed both hammers to full-cock. The buttstock was seated against his shoulder as the rifles cracked again, showering Stand Watie with dirt. Silhouetted against the fiery muzzle flashes, Ryan saw two men materialize from the dark not thirty yards away. He aimed high, triggering both barrels with a double tap of his finger. The scattergun exploded with a thunderous roar.

Buckshot sizzled across the yard in a deadly hailstorm. One of the men reeled sideways in a strange haywire dance. He lost his footing and went down in a tangle of arms and legs. The other man buckled from the impact and dropped his rifle. He slumped forward without a sound. Tossing the shotgun aside, Ryan threw his Colt and slowly walked forward. He circled the men, watching them closely under the faint starlight, alert to any movement. At last, one at a time he rolled them over with the toe of his boot. They were both dead, chopped to pieces by buckshot.

Ryan struck a match and inspected the bodies. In the flare of light he saw that they were both Indian, and doubtless Cherokee. As he turned away, Stand Watie crawled to his feet, clutching a nasty arm wound. The door opened a crack and Boudinot cautiously peered outside. Approaching the house, it occurred to Ryan that all the shots had been fired at the two kinsmen. There seemed little question that someone was aware of the conspiracy and had invoked ancient tribal law. The dead assassins merely underscored the point.

Elias Boudinot and Stand Watie were marked for death.

CHAPTER
THREE

Tahlequah was the capital of the Cherokee Nation. Set among gently rolling hills, it lay some eighty miles south of the Kansas border. To many, it was considered the hub of progress in Indian Territory.

It was midmorning as Ryan and Stevens rode just south of Tahlequah. For the last hour they had passed magnificent baronial homes, with colonnaded porches anchored by towering Grecian columns. The setting was one of antebellum plantations transplanted from a more gracious era. The lavish estates were outnumbered by log cabins and unpretentious frame houses, but it was obvious that wealthy Cherokees lived on a scale befitting their position. Some were farmers, and others, clearly, were gentleman farmers.

Stevens, much as Ryan had predicted, was somewhat awed. The tales he'd heard about the Five Civilized Tribes were far exceeded by reality. While he knew that the Cherokees maintained plantations before the war and were slave owners as large as any in the South, he was dumbstruck by the extent of their progress along the white man's road. He expected to find advanced savages a step above the nomadic Plains Tribes, who had evolved into tillers of the soil after being pacified by the federal government. Instead he found a people who cultivated the land with something approaching reverence. Theirs was a thriving agrarian society that rivaled even the most prosperous midwestern farm community.

William Ross lived five miles south of Tahlequah. Like many prominent Cherokees, he and his family operated a sprawling plantation prior to the Civil War. His home, which was reminiscent of Old South mansions, was a two-story structure with tall columns and a wide veranda. The house commanded a sweeping view of the countryside, and split-rail fences bordered its mile-and-a-half-long driveway. Outlying the main grounds was an orchard with over a thousand apple trees.

Upon sighting the house, Stevens began revising his strategy for dealing with Ross. He reminded himself that William Ross was the most influential man in Indian Territory. A graduate of Princeton University, he'd been groomed from youth to assume leadership of the Cherokees. Before he had taken over, his uncle, John Ross, had been principal chief of the tribe for more than forty years. Since 1866, he had, if anything, surpassed the stature of his late uncle. Above all others, he'd been elected president of the Intertribal Council, which was working a coalition of the Five Civilized Tribes. And judging by his baronial home, he was something more than a blanket Indian with a fancy education. Stevens thought to himself that diplomacy rather than demands might better suit the moment.

A stable boy took their horses as William Ross greeted them on the veranda. He was a dignified man, with strong, angular features and piercing eyes. His bearing was straight and square-shouldered, a posture of austere self-assurance. He wore a frock coat with dark trousers and a somber black cravat. He welcomed them with something less than warmth.

The inside of the house was, if anything, even more imposing than the grounds. The ceilings were high and the staircase facing the entrance rose like an aerial corridor. Large wall mirrors flanked either side of the hallway, and double French doors opened on to a room appointed with ornately carved furniture and an immense piano. Opposite was an informal parlor, and beyond that, a tall-windowed study. The study was quite masculine, paneled in dark wood with leather wing chairs set before a broad mahogany desk. The bookcases occupying one wall were lined with history tomes and works of literature.

Ross indulged in small talk for only a short while. The meeting had been arranged by letter, at Stevens' request, and there was a certain protocol to be observed. But after his visitors were seated, Ross quickly dispensed with preliminaries. He ignored Ryan, whom he took to be an aide of some sort. His full concentration focused instead on Stevens.

"Your letter was somewhat vague, Mr. Stevens. May I inquire the exact nature of your business?"

"Of course," Stevens said pleasantly. "First, I wanted to personally advise you that the Katy will begin construction quite shortly. We plan to start laying track the first week of March."

"So, our respite ends."

"I beg your pardon?"

"The Cherokee Nation, Mr. Stevens, does not want your railroad. We look on it as an invasion of our tribal lands—nothing less."

"But unavoidable, Chief Ross. And I might mention, sanctioned by the treaty of 1866."

"A regrettable fact, but nonetheless at odds with the interests of my people."

"Progress won't be denied," Stevens intoned. "However, there's no reason your people should suffer in the process. With your assistance, they might profit very handsomely instead."

Ross eyed him keenly. "Are you selling or buying, Mr. Stevens?"

"Oh, I'm buying! And paying hard cash, I might add. The Katy is in a position to pump upwards of a million dollars into your economy. Sound interesting?"

Stevens went on to explain the proposition. Railroad ties were laid at a rate of 2,600 to the mile, and the Katy had some 250 miles to traverse to the Texas border. Simple arithmetic indicated that nearly 700,000 ties would be needed, and Stevens was willing to pay the generous sum of a dollar a tie. He thought the contract would best be administered by the tribal governments.

Ross was a skilled negotiator. He deferred judgment on the ties and shrewdly waited to hear the next proposal. Somewhat nonplussed, Stevens raised the matter of trailing longhorn herds to railhead. By long-standing practice, each of the Five Civilized Tribes had always charged a per-head tax for the privilege of trailing through Indian Territory. The Cherokees, whose land abutted Kansas, charged the most, seventy-five cents per cow. Stevens outlined his plan to resurrect trailing along the Texas Road while the Katy was building south. But to stimulate trade, he wanted the Cherokees to set the example by reducing their tax to twenty-five cents. Everyone, Indians and railroad alike, would benefit.

Once again Ross deferred any decision. Outfoxed, Stevens was forced to move on to the next topic. He reluctantly broached the matter of a bond issue. Though it was unstated, he clearly wanted the Cherokees to set a precedent for their Indian neighbors to the south. He reviewed the benefits to the tribe, which would include more backcountry depots and a major terminus located in Tahlequah. His suggestion was that an equitable bond issue would be something on the order of $500,000.

"I think not," Ross said with a querulous squint. "In Kansas you could bludgeon communities into paying such extortion. The Cherokees are under no duress to meet your demands."

Stevens gave him a dull stare. "How would you like it if the Katy bypassed Tahlequah altogether?"

"Very much," Ross said crisply. "In fact, I urge you to bypass the entire Cherokee Nation. We would be much happier if there were no stopovers at all."

Stevens took a deep breath, let it out slowly. "Would you at least put the question to the tribal council?"

Ross' tone was clipped, incisive. "The bond issue is a dead issue, Mr. Stevens. You need pursue it no farther."

Their eyes locked. Stevens boiled inwardly, but he knew he was beaten. After a long silence, he spread his hands in a bland gesture. "What about the other proposals?"

"Would you and Mr. Ryan care to join me for noontime?"

"Well, yes, thank you. We would enjoy that very much."

"Fine." Ross stood. "I'll just send for Major Tappin. He's our tribal treasurer, as well as commander of the Light Horse Police. I'd like him present when we resume negotiations."

Ross walked quickly from the study. When the door closed, Stevens turned and looked at Ryan. His voice was tinged with exasperation.

"Any idea what he has up his sleeve?"

"Tell me," Ryan said, deadpan. "Have you ever been between a rock and a hard place?"

"I'm not familiar with the expression."

"It's a form of the old squeeze play. I think you're about to get educated—by the redskins."

The negotiations were suspended for lunch. Shortly before the noon hour they were joined by Major David Tappin. He was swarthy, somewhat darker than the usual Cherokee, with marblelike eyes and sleek, glistening hair. His manner was one of ill-disguised mistrust, guarded contempt.

Ryan was on speaking terms with Major Tappin. Previously, as a deputy marshal he'd had occasion to work with the Light Horse Police. He knew that Tappin, whose principal responsibilities were tax collection and law enforcement, wielded considerable power within the Cherokee Nation. Some said he was second only to William Ross, and no man to have for an enemy. Ryan never doubted it for a minute.

Still, lunch was not altogether an ordeal. At the table they were joined by Ross' daughter, Elizabeth. She was an exquisite young woman, with dusky golden skin and dark raven hair. Her eyes were extraordinary, emphasizing her high cheekbones and delicate features. She relieved much of the tension around the table by simply being there. Her presence precluded any discussion of business.

After lunch there was yet another surprise. Ross suggested that his daughter would be happy to show Ryan around Tahlequah. The offer was made in such a way that it would have been impolitic to refuse. Stevens looked chagrined, for it was apparent that Ross and Tappin wanted him to themselves. Ryan, on the other hand, wasn't the least bit offended. He thought the girl a welcome, and very attractive, alternative.

A horse and carriage were waiting outside. Ryan helped Elizabeth into the seat, then took the reins from a stable hand. The sky was a perfect cloudless blue, and a warm sun offset the chilly air. The unseasonably pleasant day somehow eased a potentially awkward situation. After getting acquainted, Elizabeth deftly turned the conversation to her people. She was proud of her heritage and quite well-versed in the origins of the Cherokee Nation. On the way into town, she told him things known to only a few white men.

In old tribal language, she noted, the word for Cherokee was *Tsalagi*. The ancient emblem of bravery was the color red, and bravery was believed by her people to originate from the east where the sun rose. So in essence *Tsalagi* meant "Red Fire Men" or "Brave Men." While most Cherokees had been converted to the Christian faith, tribal lore had not disappeared entirely from everyday life. Even today, the people still thought of themselves as the *Tsalagi*. The Cherokees' ancestral homeland was once in the Southeast. What was known now, Elizabeth observed, as Tennessee, Alabama, and Georgia. In 1830, under pressure from white frontiersmen, Congress passed the Indian Removal Bill. A legalized form of larceny, the legislation granted western lands to the Five Civilized Tribes in exchange for their ancestral birthright. Over the next several years, a total of 18,000 Cherokees were herded westward over what became known as the Trail of Tears. Of that number, more than 4,000 men, women, and children perished before reaching Indian Territory. The Cherokees still honored their memory by resisting all things white.

In Tahlequah Ryan continued to act the rapt listener. Though he was familiar with the inner workings of tribal government, he gladly allowed Elizabeth to go on with her guided tour. Their first stop was the capitol building, which dominated the town square. All governmental offices as well as the council chambers were housed in the two-story brick structure. The building was only slightly less stately than the capitol in Kansas, and there was an air of bustling efficiency about the place. Ryan was once again impressed by the fact that the men who governed here wore swallowtail coats and conducted themselves like seasoned diplomats. It occurred to him that they were far more dignified than their counterparts in Washington.

The Cherokee Nation, Elizabeth explained, was virtually an independent republic. White men were not allowed to own property except through intermarriage, and unlike western Plains Tribes, the Cherokees accepted no annuities or financial assistance from Washington. For practical reasons their form of government was patterned on that of the white man. A tribal chief acted as head of state, and the tribal council, similar in structure to Congress, was comprised of two houses. Issues were closely drawn, and the two political parties, the Union and the Southern, were bitterly hostile toward one another. Seldom was an accord reached until the pressure of events forced a compromise.

On another note Elizabeth commented that Tahlequah was recognized as a symbol of progress throughout Indian Territory. While they drove around the square, she pointed out the supreme court building, a sturdy brick hotel, and several prosperous business establishments. Her voice took on an added note of pride when they passed the offices of the *Cherokee Advocate*. The newspaper was printed in both English and Cherokee, the two languages side by side. She went on to relate that the Cherokees, of all the Indians in America, were the only ones with an alphabet. Their language could therefore be written, books and newspapers printed. No other tribe was able to preserve its culture so completely in the ancient tongue.

By now Ryan was aware of her in the way of a man seated beside a bonfire. There was an air about her, something in her carriage and poise that he found captivating. Then, too, there was an aura of innocence mixed with sensuality. The silk of her teal-blue gown and the hat perched atop her head merely enhanced the image. Her figure was breathtaking, with a stemlike waist, rounded hips, and firm, youthful breasts. Her voice, which was proper, was at the same time warm and somehow intimate. He'd known many women, but none with such verve and sultry beauty. The combination was irresistible.

Upon leaving town he finally got her to talk about herself. Elizabeth told him she had attended the Cherokee female seminary and afterward gone east to a finishing school. She'd returned only last year, shortly before her mother died. Since then, she had acted as hostess for her father's many social functions. She made no mention of suitors or plans for marriage.

Elizabeth was no less intrigued by Ryan. She knew of his reputation as a marshal, and like most Cherokees, she had little sympathy with the white man's law. Yet when he looked at her, she was aware of an elemental force such as she'd never experienced. She felt strangely drawn to him, and she sensed she could trust him. Still, she pushed the impulse aside, kept herself under tight control. Her father had ordered her to question John Ryan. To find out, subtly, why he'd gone to work for the Katy.

"And you?" she inquired innocently. "Fair's fair, after all. Tell me something of yourself."

"What would you like to know?"

"Well, let's start with where you're from."

"Fort Smith, most recently. Until last week I was a deputy U.S. Marshal."

"Last week!" she repeated. "You mean you've just joined the railroad?"

"To be precise, six days ago."

"Imagine that. And what is it you do, your position?"

"Troubleshooter," Ryan said with a slow smile. "I keep the peace for the railroad."

"Are you talking about trouble with Indians?"

"No, ma'am. I'm talking about gamblers and whiskey peddlers, the construction crew. They'll give me all the trouble I can handle."

"Then you weren't retained because Mr. Stevens expects problems with the Cherokees?"

"Not unless I was hired under false pretenses. And if that's the case, Stevens will have to get himself another man."

Surprise washed over her face. "Why do you say that?"

"I've always thought the Cherokees do a pretty good job of policing themselves. So far as I'm concerned, it ought to stay that way."

"I wish more people shared your views."

She threw him a quick, enigmatic glance. Then her eyes suddenly shone and she smiled. Ryan had the impression that he'd just been subjected to some sort of test, and passed. He laughed without quite knowing why.

Some while later, he parted with Elizabeth on the veranda of the Ross home. A moment after she went through the door, Stevens stepped outside. His features were set in a scowl of barely contained rage. As the stable hand brought their horses around, Ryan decided it would be wiser not to ask. But then on the way into town, Stevens let it out in a rush of anger.

The price of railroad ties had been doubled over what he'd offered. The Cherokees wanted two dollars each and there was no choice but to go along. As William Ross had pointed out, all the trees belonged to them!

Ryan tactfully smothered a laugh. He thought Stevens understood little about Indians and even less about the Cherokees. The Red River suddenly seemed a million miles away.

They rode in silence toward Tahlequah.

CHAPTER
FOUR

The sky was like dull pewter. Heavy clouds hung ominously overhead and the Texas Road stretched northward toward the border. A flock of crows took wing from a stand of timber along the river.

Stevens' mood was abstracted. Tahlequah was two days behind them, and he'd maintained a thoughtful silence since departing the Cherokee capital. Ryan sensed that the railroader was nursing wounded pride, but he welcomed the respite, for he was absorbed in thoughts of his own. His mind, as though playing tricks on him, conjured fleeting images of Elizabeth Ross. Not surprisingly, he liked what he saw.

Late that afternoon they crossed into Kansas where the river made a sharp dogleg to the northwest. Some miles ahead lay the frontier settlement of Chetopa. While sparsely populated, no more than an outpost along the Texas Road, it was the first sign of approaching civilization. Of still greater consequence, the Katy tracks ran through Chetopa on the way to the border. A thin ribbon of steel extended magically onward to the horizon.

Upon sighting the rails, Stevens seemed somehow revitalized. His glum mood evaporated as they crossed the border, and he sat straighter in the saddle. He motioned toward the broad expanse of prairie.

"All this was once Osage land."

"I know," Ryan said, wondering what prompted the remark. "Whiskey smugglers used to run wagons from here into the Nations."

Stevens nodded absently. "The damnable Cherokees would do well to heed the lesson. Otherwise they might go the way of the Osage."

The statement required no elaboration. The Osage had once been one of the most powerful tribes on the western plains. Warlike, they terrorized every tribe within striking distance, including those resettled in Indian Territory. Then during the Civil War, the Confederacy pressed the Osage into service against the Union. As a result of this unfortunate alliance, the Osage were compelled to cede vast amounts of land to the federal government following the war. Only last year, after one-sided negotiations with Washington, the Osage were forcibly removed to a reservation in Indian Territory. Their ancestral lands, encompassing some eight million acres, were then opened to settlement by an act of Congress. The Osage were now reduced to subsisting on government handouts.

"There's a difference," Ryan said at length. "The Osage tried to hang on to the old ways. The Cherokees tend to bend with the wind. They're red, but they know how to think white."

"Do they, indeed?" Stevens grunted. "You certainly wouldn't know it from their attitude. And unless they change quickly, they'll find out how the game is really played."

"What game?"

"The only game that counts—politics!"

"I don't follow you."

Stevens was silent a moment. Then he gestured with his cigar across the prairie. "Last summer all this—the Osage lands—went on the auction block to settlers. You recall that?"

"Yeah."

Stevens gave him a crafty look. "A month before the public announcement, I bought a fifty-thousand-acre tract north of Chetopa. The price was seventy-one cents an acre."

Ryan stared at him. "Got it sort of cheap, didn't you?"

"I got it cheap and sold it dear. So you see, it pays to have friends with political clout."

"Like the Secretary of the Interior?"

"Please," Stevens said lightly. "I never divulge a source. But suffice it to say I do have some rather well-placed connections."

"And you think those connections will help you with the Cherokees?"

"John, there are no ironclad guarantees in politics. But when the time is right . . ."

Stevens' voice trailed off. He grinned and wedged the cigar into the corner of his mouth. Ryan was left to draw his own conclusion, and it took no great effort. He thought Stevens was telling the truth, probably understating it to some degree. The Cherokees were in for rough sledding.

An hour or so later they spotted Chetopa. The settlement was a crude collection of buildings, seemingly scattered at random beside the railroad tracks. As they rode nearer, Stevens glanced around at Ryan, and the railroader jerked his head toward the ramshackle buildings.

"We're being met in Chetopa."

"How do you know?"

"I arranged it before we left Parsons. George Walker, our chief surveyor, should be waiting there now."

"What's he going to survey?"

"The Cherokee Nation," Stevens said. "I delayed until now in the hope we would have William Ross' cooperation. We don't, but that's neither here nor there. We'll proceed with our plans anyway."

"I gather you didn't mention it to Ross?"

Stevens merely nodded. "I want you to act as guide for Walker and his survey crew. Your knowledge of the country will speed things along."

"Guide," Ryan asked, "or bodyguard?"

"I see no reason to anticipate trouble."

"Maybe, maybe not. But you ought to understand something. I didn't sign on to be the Katy's hired gun against Cherokees.''

"As I recall, you dispatched those two at Stand Watie's place without any great qualms."

"They started it," Ryan said flatly. "When somebody opens fire in my direction, I've got this peculiar habit. I shoot back."

"I ask nothing more," Stevens countered. "Just protect Walker and his men, bring them back alive. I daresay you won't find it any problem at all."

"And if I do?"

"Handle it however you see fit. I trust your judgment implicitly in such matters."

Ryan lapsed into silence. He felt he'd been snookered, for it was obvious that Stevens had purposely delayed mentioning the assignment. But it was a reasonable request, and one that fell within the bounds of his job. Short of quitting, he saw no practical way to refuse. He decided to go along.

"When do we leave?"

Stevens smiled. "Tomorrow morning should be soon enough."

Later after supper, Stevens called a meeting. While there was no depot in Chetopa, construction crews had built a supply shack near the tracks. There beneath a lantern, he huddled with Ryan and Walker around a map of Indian Territory. He traced a line southward from the Kansas border.

"George, your survey line should generally follow the Neosho River. From what I've seen, it's fairly decent topography."

"How are the grades?"

"Not as steep as I'd expected."

"Anything special I should look out for?"

"Only the rivers and streams. We may encounter a problem with eroding banks. So select your approaches very carefully."

Walker was short and squat, thick through with muscle. His face was moonlike and he was bald except for tufts of hair curled over his ears. He knuckled back his hat, staring at the map.

"There's the original line we marked. Straight south from the border, then angle off toward Tahlequah and Fort Gibson. Any changes since we talked last?"

"Just one." Stevens indicated a spot north of Tahlequah. "Survey a line from there due southwest to the Three Forks area."

Walker looked astounded. "You plan to bypass Tahlequah and Fort Gibson?"

"Let's call it a contingency plan."

Stevens stood there a moment longer. Then his gaze slowly moved from the map and fixed on Ryan. The corners of his mouth lifted in a sardonic smile.

"The contingency being our reception by the Cherokees."

The survey party resembled a small caravan. Apart from George Walker, there were two assistant surveyors in the crew. Their gear and equipment required three packhorses, with the tripod-mounted surveyor's level lashed tight onto the gentlest animal.

Four men and seven horses quickly attracted attention, and Ryan knew from the outset that secrecy would be impossible. There was simply no way to hide so many white men on a trek through the Cherokee Nation. Nor was it possible to disguise their purpose with the surveyors constantly plotting a north-south line.

Their first day out Ryan spotted a lone Indian observing their activities from a distance. The rider, who was mounted on a black-and-white pinto, trailed them until they pitched camp. There seemed little doubt that word of their presence would reach Tahlequah by morning. Ryan kept his suspicions to himself, for there was nothing to be gained in bothering the other men. But his vigil became more watchful, constantly alert.

Ryan found the surveyors better trail companions than Stevens. They were accustomed to sleeping on bedrolls, with no complaints about hard ground or chilly nights. Even better, one of Walker's men was a master cook over an outdoor fire. With the abundance of game, Ryan easily supplied several tasty choices for the evening meal. Everyone pitched in with the camp chores, and by the end of the first day they'd fallen into an easygoing routine. They were comfortable with one another in the way of men who thrived on wilderness travel.

After supper Ryan took the first watch. To protect against horse thieves, a guard would be posted throughout the night. Before dawn each man would take his turn. The two assistants quickly crawled into their bedrolls. Walker, who had drawn the dawn watch, joined Ryan at the fire. Hands to the flames, he was silent for a time, as though lost in thought.

"You expect trouble, don't you?" he asked.

Ryan sat cross-legged, the shotgun cradled over his knees. He studied the question a moment. "What makes you say that?"

"You're a little on edge. Waiting for something to happen."

"Never hurts to be careful."

"I get the feeling there's more to it than that. Is there something Stevens didn't tell me?"

"Let's just say we're not welcome here. The Colonel and William Ross didn't exactly see eye to eye on things."

"Small wonder," Walker said with a low chuff of mirth. "Stevens is used to getting his own way—especially with Indians."

"What's the story on the Atlantic and Pacific?" Ryan asked. "The Colonel seems to think they could still bollix his plans."

"No doubt of that. The head of the A&P is a fellow named Andrew Peirce. He plays rough, very rough."

"How so?"

"Well, for one thing, Peirce and his backers are trying to get control of the Missouri Pacific line. If they do, then we'll have lost our connection to St. Louis. They'll just close the door."

"And that would block the Katy from the eastern markets."

"Exactly," Walker affirmed. "The Missouri Pacific would join with the A&P to create a direct route from the southwest. To put it mildly, we'd be left out in the cold."

"So Stevens has to beat the A&P through Indian Territory. Otherwise he loses all the marbles."

Walker nodded. "That's why he needs cooperation from the Cherokees. A construction delay of any type could turn into a disaster."

"Well, George, just between you and me, he's no diplomat."

"What do you mean?"

"I mean he doesn't understand Indians. They get stiff-necked and stubborn when a white man treats them like inferiors. And that goes double for the Cherokees."

"Is that why you think we'll have trouble?"

"Hard to say if we will or we won't. I wouldn't give odds either way."

Ten days later they halted on the southern boundary of the Cherokee Nation. They were four miles below Fort Gibson, on the banks of the mighty Arkansas. Across the river lay the Creek Nation.

Ryan led the survey crew north from the river. As Stevens had directed, he retraced their route to Fort Gibson and they proceeded along the Texas Road. Not far north of the military post, three mounted Indians approached them, riding south. The riders were light-skinned, apparently Cherokee half-breeds, and one was mounted on a black-and-white pinto. All three had carbines laid across their saddles.

Ryan watched them closely. His scrutiny centered on the one who rode the pinto. No great believer in coincidence, he was convinced he'd seen the horse before. A gut hunch told him the pinto's rider was the man who had shadowed the survey party their first day out. The man was still on their trail and no longer alone. As they passed in the road, Ryan stared hard at the man on the pinto. The rider glanced at him, then looked quickly away. In that instant Ryan knew his instincts hadn't failed him. He'd seen a peculiar glitter, something cold and deadly, in the Cherokee's eyes.

A mile up the road, Ryan reined his horse aside. He motioned Walker and the surveyors on, ordering them to ask no questions. Twisting around, Walker saw him dismount and lead his horse into the woods. Some moments later he reappeared with the shotgun cradled across the crook of his arm. He took up a position behind a tree at the side of the road.

Still looking back, Walker's eyes suddenly narrowed. He saw the three Indians ride into view perhaps a half mile to the rear. As the survey party rounded a bend in the road, he lost sight of the riders. His last impression was of Ryan pressed against the base of the tree, waiting. He wondered why the Indians were following them; he wondered what Ryan intended to do.

The crack of a rifle shot sounded in the distance. No more than a beat behind came the dull roar of a shotgun blast, followed instantly by another. A deafening silence followed. Walker reined about, halting his men in the middle of the road. He was torn between staying put and going back when he heard the thud of hoofbeats. A lone rider appeared around the bend in the road.

Ryan took his place at the head of the column. He said nothing, ignoring their stares. His features were set in a grim scowl, eyes pale and stony. No one asked any questions.

CHAPTER
FIVE

A week later the survey party rode into Parsons. George Walker and his crew went straight to their hotel rooms. With suppertime approaching, they were looking for a hot bath and a civilized meal. Walker seemed in no hurry to deliver his survey report.

At the hotel Ryan was informed that Robert Stevens had moved into a private railroad car. He stabled his horse and walked down to the Katy supply depot. Dusk fell as he crossed the main tracks and approached the private car, which had been shunted onto a nearby siding.

Ryan was in a foul mood. For the past week he'd done little but dwell on the shooting incident. Since accepting the job of special agent, he had killed four men. Which was almost half the number he had buried during *four years* as a marshal. At that rate, the number might jump to a score or more before the Katy traversed Indian Territory. He had no intention of allowing that to happen.

Unlike some lawmen Ryan was not a killer by nature. He believed certain men were fated to be killed, and he thought that others, by the viciousness of their crimes, deserved the ultimate penalty. Yet he was an advocate of reason and law over the rule of the gun. He preferred to bring lawbreakers, even murderers, to justice before the courts. A legal hanging, in his opinion, was by far the greater deterrent to outlaws. So he killed only as a last resort.

Tonight he intended to voice that very thought. All the way from the Cherokee Nation, he'd been preoccupied by the latest shootout. While he had pulled the trigger, he in no way faulted himself. He had fired only after being fired upon; in that sense, the killings were unavoidable. The fault, in his mind, fell instead on Robert Stevens. The latter's motives were murky, and he couldn't put his finger on the exact cause of the bloodletting. But something about the whole assignment stunk.

Mounting the steps, he climbed to the rear platform of the car. Through the door window, he saw Stevens seated in an armchair, smoking a cigar. A manservant lighted the last of the overhead lamps, then disappeared into the kitchen up forward. Ryan knocked on the door, three hard raps. Stevens turned, looking somewhat irritated, and rose from his chair. A moment later he opened the door.

"Well—John! Where did you come from?"

"Just rode in," Ryan replied.

"Excellent! I've been expecting you for the last day or so. Please, come inside."

Stevens ushered him through the door. Entering along a narrow companionway, Ryan noted that the bedroom door was closed. Moving into the main room, he saw that it was lavishly appointed. To the rear was a parlor area, with paneled walls and ornately carved furniture. Toward the front was a dining area, with a candlelit table, fine linen, and an array of bone-white china. Ryan saw that two place settings were arranged on the table.

Still smiling, Stevens motioned him to an armchair. Ryan sat down, dropping his hat on a nearby table. The luxurious surroundings made him all the more aware that he was covered with grime and trail dust. It occurred to him that the Katy's general manager lived in the style befitting a man of wealth and influence. Stevens took a chair opposite him.

"Where's George?"

"Up at the hotel," Ryan observed. "He said he'd write up his report tonight."

"Then I'm doubly glad you dropped by. I'm anxious to hear how things went."

"If you're talking about the survey, it went fine. Walker and his boys got it done just the way you wanted."

"And the new route," Stevens inquired, "bypassing Tahlequah and Fort Gibson? Any problem with that?"

"No," Ryan said tightly. "No problem with that."

Stevens arched one eyebrow in question. "From your tone, I take it something went wrong."

"Wrong as it could go. I had to kill two men."

"Damn!" Stevens muttered. "Who were they?"

"Cherokee breeds."

"Why did you kill them?"

"No choice," Ryan said in a low voice. "They trailed us all the way down to Fort Gibson. Whether or not they meant to do us harm is anybody's guess. I never got a chance to ask."

"What happened?"

"I braced them just north of the fort. Before I could ask their business, one of them took a shot at me. I killed him and another one who tried to make a fight."

"Are you saying there were more than two?"

"Yeah," Ryan acknowledged. "The third one took off and never looked back. I let him go."

"Were George and his men involved?"

"Not directly. I'd sent them on ahead."

"How about the Army? Did you notify anyone at the post?"

"No."

"And the Cherokees? Did you report it to anyone in Tahlequah?"

Ryan shook his head. "I figured the wisest thing was to let well enough alone. No telling who sent them."

"Sent them?" Stevens repeated, frowning heavily.

"Well, they damn sure weren't robbers. Not the way they trailed us for ten days."

"You think they were spies?"

"Or worse."

"Oh, come now! Aren't you exaggerating slightly? Why would anyone want to kill our surveyors?"

"You tell me."

"How would I know?"

"You must've known there was a risk."

"I knew nothing of the kind."

Ryan searched his eyes. "Then why'd you send me off to bodyguard George and his boys?"

Stevens met his stare. "Are you accusing me of something?"

"Not yet. I'm just asking you a simple question."

"You asked me the same question before you left. And I'll tell you now what I told you then. Walker needed a guide."

"You're a liar," Ryan said bluntly.

There was a long pause as the two men examined one another. Then Stevens rose and moved to a window at the side of the car. He stood there for several moments, a cigar clenched between his teeth, staring out at the darkening sky. Finally he turned back, his features set in a somber expression.

"All right," he conceded, "I wasn't altogether frank with you. I suspected something might happen."

"Why?"

"Well, after all, an attempt was made on the lives of Boudinot and Stand Watie."

"That's tribal business, between the Cherokees."

"Yes, but quite obviously someone ordered it."

Ryan gave him a narrow look. "What's that got to do with the survey crew?"

"I can only hazard a guess. It seems rather apparent that the someone—whoever he is—doesn't want a railroad built."

"So the place to stop it was before it got started—the surveyors."

"That seems a reasonable explanation."

"Only one man could issue that kind of order."

"I agree."

"And you think William Ross sent three breeds out to kill us?"

"How could I think otherwise? Particularly when I'd informed him only days before that we plan to start construction next month. The timing of it squares too neatly to be coincidence."

Ryan pulled at his earlobe, thoughtful. "Ross doesn't strike me as an assassin. It's not his style."

"Indeed?" Stevens countered. "Nothing happens in the Cherokee Nation without Ross' tacit permission. You should know that better than I."

"Maybe so. But my instinct tells me different. And I'm generally not wrong."

"I suggest we stick to deductive reasoning. I wouldn't care to wager my life on instinct."

"You wagered my life, not to mention the surveyors'. Even after you'd already *deducted* all this."

Stevens admired the tip of his cigar. "You have a point. I've no real excuse except to say that there was no alternative. Without a survey line, we can't lay track."

"What about the truth? You could've told me what you suspected."

"To be quite honest, I couldn't take a chance on losing you. I was concerned you might quit rather than lead the survey party."

"I don't scare that easy."

"No, I daresay you don't. The way you challenged those half-breeds proves that."

"There's something else I don't do."

"Oh?"

"I refuse to work for a man who won't level with me."

"Suppose we write it off as an error in judgment?"

"You lied to me," Ryan said in a measured tone. "Do it again and we're all through—then and there."

"I understand."

"Fair enough."

Ryan stood and collected his hat. As he turned to leave, the bedroom door opened. A compelling, attractive woman in her late twenties moved into the parlor area. She was blond and tawny, rather statuesque, with inquisitive, bold eyes and a vivacious smile. Stevens stretched out his hand and drew her forward.

"John, I'd like you to meet Sally Palmer. Sally, this is the fellow I was telling you about, John Ryan."

"Oh, yes," Sally said in a throaty voice. "You're Bob's special agent."

Ryan nodded. "Pleasure to meet you, Miss Palmer."

"Please, just call me Sally. Everyone does."

Ryan thought it an understatement. Up close, there was something common, almost bawdy, about the girl. She wore a velvet gown, her rounded shoulders were bare, and rather too much of her cleavage was exposed. He found it amusing that Stevens, who was a married man, had himself a camp follower. Sally Palmer, to all appearances, was not too far removed from the oldest profession.

She looked at his dusty trail clothes. A wise smile brushed the corner of her mouth. "Bob said you've been to Indian Territory. How was life among the savages?"

"About like usual."

"You've been there before, then?"

"Off and on." Ryan took a step back. "You'll have to excuse me. It's been a long trip and an even longer day. Colonel, I'll see you in the morning."

Nodding to Stevens, he turned and walked from the car. Outside, through the window he saw Stevens seat the girl at the dining table. The manservant materialized from the kitchen and began pouring wine. Ryan chuckled softly to himself.

Stevens clearly intended to live the good life while building his railroad.

Ryan took his time next morning. He figured he'd earned a respite, however brief. Nor was he in any great rush to resume talks with Stevens.

Shortly before nine, he walked in the direction of the rail yards. His mind almost reluctantly turned to Stevens. He wasn't entirely satisfied with their conversation of last night. He considered it a toss-up as to whether or not Stevens would level with him in the future. The railroader was clearly unaccustomed to taking others into his confidence.

Even more worrisome was the matter of William Ross. Ryan still wasn't convinced by Stevens' argument. He found it difficult to believe that a man of Ross' stature would stoop to conspiracy and assassination. The fact that Ryan was attracted to Elizabeth Ross did nothing to color his opinion. He simply felt that her father was an honorable man, above resorting to murder. His gut hunch told him that the answer lay somewhere else.

All that left a very large question mark. If not William Ross, then who? Someone had engineered a rather elaborate scheme, involving secrecy and cold-blooded murder. Whoever was responsible clearly had many dedicated men under his command. Four Cherokees had already lost their lives; that number in itself indicated a conspiracy of some scope. Obviously then, the leader had to be someone of importance within the Cherokee Nation. But the *who*, at least for now, remained a mystery

On one point there was no doubt. In less than a month Ryan had killed four members of the conspiracy. So the leader of the group had, in all likelihood, added Ryan's name to the death list. Wherever he traveled in Indian Territory, he would now be a marked man. He reminded himself not to get careless.

At Stevens' private car, he knocked on the door. Footsteps sounded from within, then the door opened. The manservant greeted him with a polite nod.

"Good morning, Mr. Ryan."

"Morning. I'd like to see Colonel Stevens."

"Sorry, sir, he's out."

"Any idea where he went?"

"I believe you'll find him at the surveyor's office."

"Much obliged."

As Ryan turned to leave, Sally Palmer suddenly appeared in the companionway leading to the main room. She was attired in a gauzy peignoir worn over a nightgown.

"Well, hello there!" she called. "Come on in."

"No, thanks," Ryan said. "I'm looking for the Colonel."

"I expect him back in a few minutes. Hang around. I'll give you a cup of coffee."

"Don't go to any bother. I'll just—"

"No bother!" She waved to the manservant. "Henry, get Mr. Ryan a cup of java."

"Yes, ma'am."

Henry disappeared into the kitchen. Ryan allowed himself to be led into the main room. Following Sally, he noted that her peignoir was quite sheer and very revealing. The fabric, like curves in melted ivory, clung to her long, lissome legs and voluptuous figure. She took a seat across from him at the dining table.

"So tell me. How's it feel to be back among civilized people?"

"All right," Ryan said without inflection. "Not that I've got anything against the Cherokees. For the most part, they're pretty decent."

"Do tell?" She gave him a glance full of curiosity. "Bob told me you barely escaped with your scalp. He said those surveyors owe you their lives."

Ryan looked uncomfortable. "That's stretching it quite a ways."

"Oh, c'mon! Don't be modest."

Henry emerged from the kitchen. He set a cup and saucer in front of Ryan, then poured from a steaming coffeepot. Finished, his gaze shifted to Sally.

"If that's all, ma'am, I have errands in town."

"Sure, Henry, you run along. I'll hold down the fort."

Henry departed with a perfunctory nod. As the door closed, Ryan took a sip of his coffee. He was aware that Sally was looking him over with more than casual interest. She had enormous hazel eyes that seemed to dance with secret laughter. She smiled warmly.

"Bob tells me you were a deputy marshal."

"Yeah, I was."

"Maybe we have mutual acquaintances."

"Where from?"

"Abilene," she responded. "I got to know Tom Smith before he was killed. Everybody liked him lots."

"Doesn't surprise me. He was a damn fine lawman."

"Have you heard the latest? The town fathers are all set to offer Wild Bill Hickok the marshal's job. Isn't that a riot?"

"It's liable to be a riot and a half. I understand there's no love lost between Hickok and the Texas drovers."

"He won't last long in a cowtown, then. Texans are there in swarms the whole summer."

Ryan studied her over the rim of his cup. "Way you talk you must have left Abilene just recently."

"You might say that." She returned his look without guile. "I met Bob there last summer. We kept in touch and he finally made me a proposition. As you see, I accepted."

"Nice work," Ryan remarked dryly, "if you can get it."

"Well, he's sweet to me and it beats working in a parlor house."

"Yeah, I suppose it would."

She gave him a puckish smile. "You weren't fooled, were you? I saw it in the way you looked at me last night."

Ryan grinned. "I've seen the inside of a few parlor houses in my time."

"See there, I knew it! We're birds of a feather."

Sally suddenly stood. Her look was at once sensuous and humorous, somehow bold. She moved around the table with catlike grace and stopped beside his chair. Her voice was sultry.

"Do you like me, John?"

"Why?"

"Because I like you. And I'm not exactly a one-man girl."

"Stevens would be sorry to hear it."

"What he doesn't know won't hurt him."

She laughed and cupped his face in her hands. The scent of her perfume and the warmth of her body seemed to envelop him. She bent lower and kissed him fully on the mouth. Her lips were moist and inviting, and her tongue performed an artful mating dance. Ryan sat perfectly still, not responding. At last, pulling back slightly, she stared down at him with earthy wisdom.

"Don't worry. Henry won't be back for at least an hour."

"What about Stevens?"

"I lied!" She laughed gaily. "He told me he'd be gone all day."

Ryan moved her hands from his shoulders. He stood, collecting his hat off the table, and moved out of reach. She gave him a puzzled frown.

"What's wrong?"

"No sale," he said evenly. "But don't take it personal. I never mess around with the bossman's lady."

"Foolish man. You don't know what you're missing."

"I've got a pretty fair idea."

"C'mon, be a sport—take a chance!"

"Guess I'm not much of a gamblin' man."

A vixen look touched her eyes. "It's a long way through Indian Territory. And nothing but squaws till we cross the Red River."

Ryan shrugged. "I reckon it's my loss."

"Well, there's always another time. You'll be around and I'm not going anywhere." She paused, lowered one eyelid in a slow wink. "The offer's always open."

"I'll keep it in mind."

"Oh, I know you will . . . especially at night."

Her musical laughter followed him out the door.

CHAPTER
SIX

On March 7 the Katy entered Indian Territory. It was a Monday morning, and there was still a nip of frost in the air. The spot chosen to cross the border was known as Russell Creek Valley.

Colonel Robert Stevens and Tom Scullin stood at the end-of-track. Their eyes were directed southward, and for a moment neither of them spoke. Behind them some fifty cars loaded with construction supplies stretched northward. The Irish Brigade, Scullin's construction crew, were gathered a short distance away. At last Stevens looked around, and stuck out his hand.

"Tom, let's build a railroad."

Scullin pumped his arm. With a nutcracker grin, the construction boss turned to the Irish Brigade. He raised a mighty forearm and pointed them toward the Cherokee Nation.

"Awright, me boyos! Lay track!"

The Irish Brigade, some two hundred strong, belted out a lusty cheer. The sun, edging over the horizon in an orange ball of fire, lighted the valley as they surged forward. A mile of roadbed had already been graded in preparation for the first day's track laying. At Scullin's command a mule-drawn wagon pulled up beside the grade and men began offloading rough-hewn ties. Not far behind, the iron men dumped a load of rails.

Stevens watched them in silence for a short while. He was aware that Scullin preferred he not linger at end-of-track. The construction boss was something of a benign tyrant, driving the Irish Brigade with equal doses of curses and encouragement. He boasted that he could whip any man on the payroll, and he stood willing to prove it at the slightest provocation. But he preferred to work his men in his own way, without anyone looking over his shoulder.

Still, there was something special about today. Stevens risked overstaying his welcome for a final word with the massive Irishman. When he could delay no longer, he finally motioned southward.

"How long to reach Big Cabin Creek?"

"God's blood!" Scullin huffed. "You've asked me that no less than a hundred times."

"Then one more time won't matter, will it?"

"I'll tell you what I've been tellin' you. Thirty miles in thirty days, God willing. I cannot do better."

Big Cabin Creek was Stevens' initial objective on the drive south. It lay thirty miles beyond the border, where the military road from Fort Gibson split off from the Texas Road and angled northeast. Stevens was determined to reach the fork of the trail no later than early April. Otherwise there would be no railroad in place when the spring cattle drives trailed north out of Texas. He was counting days and a fortune in freight charges won or lost.

"Thirty days," he mused out loud. "That would put us across Big Cabin Creek on April sixth."

"Aye," Scullin agreed. "Unless there's heavy spring rains, or God forbid, a flood. We've a bridge to construct before we'll be crossing the creek."

"Yes, but our engineers always precede the tracklaying crew by at least a day. Surely we won't be delayed more than a day or so completing the bridge?"

"Maybe. Maybe not. As I said, it depends on the rain."

"All right, let's assume the worst. We'll suppose it rains the second Flood. I could always build stockyards *this* side of the creek."

Scullin looked at him, puzzled. "Why would you do a foolish thing like that?"

"Simple economics," Stevens said quickly. "You've never understood that there's more to building a railroad than just laying track."

"It's the cattle drives you're talkin' about?"

"Indeed it is! No less than a hundred thousand beeves will be trailed out of Texas this summer. And right now Abilene is the closest railhead."

"Which means the Kansas Pacific would profit handsomely."

"Profits," Stevens added, "that would defray a large percentage of our construction costs. But only if we lure the cattle trade away from Abilene."

"So you've no choice but to establish a railhead, and soon."

"No choice whatever."

"But you've still not answered my question. Why build stockyards this side of the creek? Would a few more days make so much difference?"

"A few days might turn into weeks, even a month. Spring floods are unpredictable."

Scullin shook his head. "Aren't you being a bit pessimistic?"

"I prefer to plan for contingencies. I'd call it realism, not pessimism."

"I say it makes no sense. The stockyards belong on the south side of the creek, not the north."

"No, Tom," Stevens corrected him. "The stockyards belong wherever they can be built in early April. Only then can I send agents into Texas with word of a new railhead. And closer than Abilene by two weeks trailing time!"

"Why not wait until we're farther south? A railhead on the Arkansas would cut the time in half."

"I want the cattle trade now—not later."

"Have you heard it said, a man's reach should never exceed his grasp?"

"What's your point?"

Scullin lifted his hands in a shrug. "Perhaps you're over-reaching yourself, Colonel. You want everything, and you want it fast. Some would say too fast."

"And what would you say, Tom?"

"Well, to quote some wise man, Rome wasn't built in a day."

Stevens laughed. "I'll settle for thirty days to Big Cabin Creek. A deal?"

"By the Jesus," Scullin muttered. "Will that get you out of my hair and back on your fancy car?"

"Yes, gladly."

"Then it's a deal."

"I knew you wouldn't let me down, Tom."

"Go on with you! I've work to do."

Still chuckling, Scullin turned to leave. He stopped suddenly and Stevens' eyes followed the direction of his gaze. A short distance uptrack Ryan reined his horse past a work crew. His hat was tugged low against the morning sun and his shotgun was balanced across the saddle. He looked armed for bear, and his features did nothing to dispel the impression. As he approached, he nodded to them.

"Morning, Colonel. Tom."

The two men returned his greeting. Without stopping, he rode past them, eyes fixed on the distance. They watched as he continued on to a point beyond the graders. There, halting his horse on a low rise, he sat staring off into Indian Territory. After a moment Scullin whistled between his teeth.

"I've not asked," he said to Stevens, "for it was your own business. But now my curiosity has the best of me."

"About what?"

"About John Ryan. What was your reason for hiring him?"

Stevens gave him a sideways glance. "We needed a special agent, and Ryan was the best man available."

"All the same, I understood his job was to maintain order at end-of-track."

"And so it is."

"Then suppose you tell me"—Scullin paused, nodding

to the solitary figure on horseback—"why has he killed four men, and scarcely a month on the payroll?"

"Four Indians," Stevens noted. "There is a difference."

"Indian or white, the question still holds."

"Ryan did what needed doing. It's as simple as that."

Scullin was silent a moment, considering. "There's a rumor around that someone intends to stop us from building a railroad. Any truth to it?"

"Tom, I never deal in conjecture. After all, why borrow trouble?"

"You've not said yes or no."

"Well, anything's possible. At the moment we're considered intruders by the Cherokees, but there's nothing to worry about."

Scullin motioned toward the construction crew. "Those boys are loyal to me because I look out for 'em. I'd like to keep it that way. You're sayin' my boys are in no danger?"

"I'm saying you need not concern yourself. John Ryan will attend to any . . . problems."

Stevens grinned and slapped Scullin across the shoulder. Turning away, he walked off alongside the construction train. Some distance uptrack an unloaded supply train stood waiting with his private car coupled to the rear. He strode toward it with a purposeful air.

Scullin stared after him only a moment. Then his gaze swung back to Ryan and the uncased shotgun. His brow furrowed in a dark scowl.

Off to the southwest, a treeline marked the path of Russell Creek. Like a sentinel, one hand resting on the shotgun, Ryan studied the trees. He had the prickly feeling he was being watched.

After several minutes, he looked away. There was no movement in the trees, nothing that appeared out of the ordinary. Still, something told him there was more to the feeling than imagination. For the moment, though, he decided to play a waiting game. He turned his attention to the tracklaying operation.

The lead element was the grading crew. With picks and shovels and mule-drawn scrapers, they transformed rough earth into a level roadbed. Behind them another crew laid the ties and leveled each one with the roadbed surface. Next in line were the iron men, five men to each five-hundred-pound rail. After they dropped the iron in place, the spikers moved up and quickly anchored parallel rails to the crossties. Ten spikes to the rail, three blows to each spike kept the air ringing with the metallic whang of sledgehammers.

Farther back the screwer crew finished spiking rails and screwed down fishplates to secure the rail joints. Following them were the gandy dancers, who levered up ties by wedging a shovel blade beneath the tie and bouncing up and down on the shovel handle. The filler gang moved in then and finished bedding the loosened ties with stone ballast. The last crew in the operation was the track liners. Their job was to check the alignment of the rails and inspect ballast underneath the ties. The final step was a close once-over by the tracklaying boss.

Uptrack from the work gangs was the construction train. Every mile of track laid required forty carloads of supplies, plus food and water for the men and animals. So the construction train, for all intents and purposes, was a self-contained town on wheels. Hauled by one locomotive and pushed by another, the train was a ponderous collection of freight cars and flatbeds, several three-decker rolling bunkhouses and one entire boxcar devoted to the mess kitchen. Scullin's quarters were in one end of a car near the front of the train. The opposite end was his office, complete with desks and a telegrapher-clerk.

Observing the operation, Ryan was struck by the efficiency of it all. On the surface it looked like a madhouse flung into chaos. But upon closer examination it became apparent that there was a synchronized chain of events not unlike a finely balanced clock. The parts, operating with seeming independence, ultimately meshed together and brought about a frenzy of construction. It was clear to him, watching them now, that Scullin and the Irish Brigade had earned their reputation. No one built a better railroad or built it faster.

Ryan's attention was suddenly drawn back to the treeline. He saw four Indians ride out of the heavily wooded grove and halt beside the creek. Their horses began swizzling water, but he wasn't fooled. They'd been there all the while, secreted in the trees. Despite appearances, the Indians weren't simply watering their mounts. They wanted him to know the railroad was being watched.

Tom Scullin, who had also seen the riders, walked forward. He stopped beside Ryan, gazing for a moment at the four Indians. Then, reining their horses about, the men rode south along the creek bank. When they were some distance away, Scullin finally looked around.

"Cherokees?" he inquired.

"Nobody else."

"Have they some mischief in mind?"

"Yeah," Ryan laughed. "I'd say that's a safe bet."

"What is it they might try?"

"Blow up the tracks. Set fire to the supply cars or wreck equipment. Hard to say where it would start—or end."

"You being the special agent, what do you suggest?"

"We ought to post guards, especially a night watch. You pick the men and I'll assign them to shifts. Sundown to sunrise."

"I'll see to it," Scullin agreed. "Of course, my boys aren't gunmen. They're more experienced with their fists or pick handles."

Ryan smiled. "Want me to give them a few pointers?"

"I'd think you're the one to do it."

There was an awkward pause. Scullin held his gaze a moment, then looked down at the ground. "Do you mind if I ask you a personal question?"

"Go ahead."

"Understand, I'm not judgin' you. It's just—"

"Curiosity."

"Of sorts, yes." Scullin glanced up, cleared his throat.

"The Colonel tells me you did what needed doing. I'm talking about the four men you killed."

"So what's your question?"

"Was the Colonel tellin' me the truth?"

"You think he'd lie?"

"I'm askin' you."

"No." Ryan looked at him without expression. "You're asking me if Stevens hired himself a professional killer, aren't you?"

"Since you put it that way, I suppose I am."

"I'm going to make an exception in your case."

"Exception?"

"Normally, any man who asked me that would pay a stiff price."

Scullin tensed, somehow standing taller. A muscle pulsed in his jaw and his great hands knotted into fists. Then, looking closer, he saw no animosity in Ryan's face. What he saw instead was sardonic amusement, a hint of laughter. His hands slowly unknotted.

"What makes me the exception?"

Ryan shifted in the saddle. He seemed to weigh his words before he spoke. "It's a long haul to the Red River. I've got a feeling we'll both need a friend before we get there."

"Because the Colonel never lets the right hand know what the left hand's doing—is that it?"

"Close enough," Ryan said. "Where I'm concerned, I think he knew he'd get a fight of some kind from the Cherokees."

"So he purposely went out to hire himself a gunhand."

"That's about the size of it."

Scullin looked at him questioningly. "Why do you stay on, then?"

"In a way Stevens was right." Ryan motioned off into the distance. "Somebody out there means to stop the Katy— no matter who gets killed."

"And I take it you mean to stop this somebody?"

"Last time out," Ryan said stonily, "his men tried to kill me. That tends to make it personal."

"Well spoken," Scullin rumbled. "So tell me now, would you care to join me for supper tonight? I might even offer you a drink."

"I'd like that, Tom. Thanks."

"One thing, though."

"Yeah?"

"Would you not bring your shotgun? I promise you'll find no red heathens at my table."

Scullin walked off with a booming laugh. Ryan stared after him a moment, chuckling softly. Then his eyes shifted to the treeline, and all humor melted from his face. The prickly sensation returned and with it his unease.

He still felt watched.

CHAPTER
SEVEN

Sam Irvin showed up unexpectedly. The Katy was some six miles into the Cherokee Nation, having spanned Russell Creek with a timbered bridge. The track-laying crew had so far delivered on Scullin's promise of a mile a day.

A deputy marshal, Irvin worked out of Fort Smith. He'd worn a badge most of his adult life, serving as a federal lawman for the last five years. He was on the sundown side of thirty, with a bulge around his beltline and flecks of gray in his hair. Yet no one, least of all the men he hunted, was fooled by his fatherly appearance. When crossed, he was a dangerous man.

Ryan and Irvin were old friends. Over the years they had teamed up on several assignments in Indian Territory. On occasion each had saved the life of the other, which engendered a very special sort of kinship. In a gunfight Ryan knew of no one else he'd rather have as a partner. Many men were what he tended to categorize as toughnuts; they thrived on rough-and-tumble fisticuffs and eagerly invited trouble. But a man like Sam Irvin was another breed entirely. When words failed, he never resorted to fists or a contest of physical strength. He pulled a gun.

Irvin rode into camp late Sunday afternoon. The construction crew was quitting for the day, having just completed the sixth mile of track. Ryan, as he'd done every day, had stationed himself some distance ahead of the graders. He grinned upon spotting Irvin, genuinely pleased to see an old comrade. Still mounted, they shook hands warmly.

"Long time no see," Ryan greeted him. "How the hell you been?"

"Fair to middlin'," Irvin allowed. "No need to ask about you. Any fool could see you're in hog heaven."

"Yeah, sure," Ryan laughed. "All I've got to do is wet-nurse a whole railroad through the Nations. It's a cushy life."

"Beats chasin' a bunch of hard-ass badmen."

"I take it you're on the hunt."

Irvin nodded. "Ed Garrett was killed four days ago."

"Where?"

"Creek Nation," Irvin said. "Outside of Okmulgee."

"How'd it happen?"

"Ever hear of a robber named Jack Spainyard?"

"I recall the wanted circulars."

"Well, him and a couple of other hardcases went on a spree. Started out, they robbed a Texican horse buyer just north of Okmulgee."

"And Ed Garrett went after them?"

"Caught 'em too," Irvin said dourly. "Only he must've got a mite careless. They killed him."

"Damn shame," Ryan said, tight-lipped. "Ed was a better peace officer than most."

"It gets worse. Spainyard and his gang hightailed it into Cherokee country. They took a farmer and his family hostage and holed up night before last."

Ryan waited, knowing there was more.

"Then the bastards," Irvin went on, "raped the farmer's wife. All three of them took turns—all night."

Irvin avoided his eyes as though embarrassed by the words. Like many lawmen, he was hardened to murder and the ways of cold-blooded killers. Yet he was acutely uncomfortable with the thought of a woman being violated, forced to perform indecent acts. Ryan finally broke the silence.

"Was the woman Cherokee?"

"Yeah," Irvin affirmed. "But Garrett's murder takes precedence. So Oliver Logan ordered me to bring 'em in—or kill 'em.''

"By yourself?" Ryan asked, surprised. "Seems like Oliver would have sent along some help."

"We're damned shorthanded, John. Since Judge Story took over, he's fired about half the deputies. Told everybody the money had to be appropriated to 'court costs.' Which means it'll wind up in his own pockets.''

"Jesus Christ," Ryan muttered. "That'll double every marshal's workload."

"Doubles the territory we've gotta cover too."

Irvin's statement underscored an already critical problem. Law enforcement in Indian Territory was a grueling business, conducted under the strangest circumstances ever faced by men who wore a badge. With the advance of civilization, a new pattern of lawlessness began to emerge on the plains. The era of the lone bandit gradually faded into obscurity, evolving into something far worse. Outlaws began to run in packs.

Local peace officers found themselves unable to cope with the vast distances involved. Gangs made lightning strikes into Kansas and Missouri and Texas, terrorizing the settlements, and then retreated into Indian Territory. These wild forays, particularly bank holdups and train robberies, were planned and executed with the precision of military campaigns. In time, due to the limitations of state jurisdiction, the war became a grisly contest between the gangs and the federal marshals. But it was hide-and-seek with a unique advantage falling to the outlaws.

Once in the Nations the gangs found virtual immunity from the law. And by any yardstick, they enjoyed the oddest sanctuary in the history of crime. While each of the Five Civilized Tribes maintained Light Horse Police, their authority extended only to Indian citizens. However heinous the offense, white men were exempt from all prosecution except that of a federal court. It was the marshals who had to pursue and capture every wanted white man. The Nations quickly became infested with fugitives from justice. Curiously enough, the problem was compounded by the Indians themselves.

All too often the red men connived with the outlaws, offering them asylum. Few in the Nations had any respect for white man's law, and the marshals were looked upon as intruders. So the job of ferreting out and capturing lawbreakers became a herculean task. Adding yet another obstacle, even the terrain itself favored the outlaws. A man could lose himself in the mountains or along wooded river bottoms and live outdoors for extended periods of time in relative comfort. Tracking badmen into the Nations was a dirty, dangerous business. It was no job for the faint of heart.

Judge William Story merely intensified the problem. With his reduction in the number of federal marshals, the outlaws' advantage suddenly became a deadly edge. The favorable terrain and a general atmosphere of sanctuary were now improved by too few lawmen chasing too many desperadoes. The Nations swarmed with killers and robbers and dozens of small gangs like the one led by Jack Spainyard. Outnumbered and outgunned, marshals were forced to ride alone into Indian Territory. Sam Irvin clearly was faced with the specter of his own death. That was the thought Ryan expressed now.

"Aren't you playing into a cold deck?"

Irvin smiled. "Oliver Logan figured it the same way. He told me to drop by here and ask you to lend a hand."

"Lend a hand! Hell, I'm a civilian now."

"I got the authority to deputize you."

"What about my job here? The Cherokees are on the warpath, and no bones about it, I can't just walk out."

"John, I need your help," Irvin said solemnly. "We go back a long ways or I wouldn't ask. Course, you don't owe me nothin'. . . ."

"Don't soft-soap me," Ryan cut him short. "You know damn well you meant to put me on the spot."

"A man does what he has to."

Ryan pondered it a moment. "How long you figure it'd take?"

"Couple of days. No more'n three at the outside."

"Any idea where Spainyard and his bunch are holed up?"

"Nope," Irvin admitted. "But I thought our first stop ought to be Tahlequah. Major Tappin might've heard something."

"While we're there, why not ask him for the loan of a few Light Horse? You said the farmer and his wife are Cherokee."

"Maybe," Irvin said doubtfully. "I just don't want any argument about jurisdiction. Spainyard killed a federal marshal, and that makes him ours—not Tappin's."

"By 'ours' I assume you mean you and me."

Irvin grinned. "You as much as said you'd come along."

"Yeah, but it'll take some powerful explaining to Tom Scullin. He's the Katy construction boss."

Irvin motioned toward the tracklaying gangs, who were trooping back to the supply train. "All the men look full-growed to me. You'd think they could wet-nurse themselves for a couple of nights."

"If they can't," Ryan noted, "I'm liable to be an un-employed special agent."

Irvin eyed him with a crafty look. Shaking his head, Ryan reined about and gigged his horse. They rode off in search of Scullin.

Late the next afternoon Ryan and Irvin entered the Cherokee capitol building. Upstairs they were ushered into Major David Tappin's rather monkish office. The furnishings consisted of a desk and chair and a lone file cabinet. The tribal treasurer apparently believed in the brisk conduct of business.

Forced to stand, Ryan and Irvin planted themselves in front of the desk. Tappin finished signing a letter and carefully returned the pen to the inkwell. Then he sat back in his chair, hands flat on the desk, and stared at them. His mouth was razored in a polite smile.

"Gentlemen," he said civilly. "What brings you to Tahlequah?"

"Jack Spainyard," Irvin told him.

"Of course," Tappin said matter-of-factly. "I understand he killed one of your marshals."

"After which," Irvin said, "him and his men raped a Cherokee woman. We have reason to believe he's holed up somewheres hereabouts."

"Indeed?"

"We thought maybe your Light Horse might know where—just exactly."

Tappin sat perfectly still for a moment. Then his gaze shifted to Ryan. "Have you resigned from the railroad, Mr. Ryan?"

"No," Ryan said. "I've been deputized on a temporary basis."

"Too bad," Tappin remarked. "Your work with the Katy seems a little beneath you. Some people might even call it a gun for hire."

Ryan ignored the barb. "We're not here to talk about the railroad. We're looking for Jack Spainyard."

"And welcome to him!" Tappin said shortly. "We're already overrun with your outlaws and gunmen."

"Glad to hear it," Irvin interjected. "You won't argue about jurisdiction then?"

"No, not this time. Take him back to Fort Smith and hang him."

"In that case let's go back to my first question. Any ideas as to his whereabouts?"

Tappin spun around in his chair. He opened the top drawer on the file cabinet and riffled through a folder. Extracting a sheet of paper, he consulted it briefly and closed the drawer. Then he turned back to them.

"Spainyard and his men were reported camped on Blackgum Creek."

"How long ago?"

"Day before yesterday."

"And you made no effort to notify Fort Smith?"

Tappin smiled. "You seem to forget, Marshal, we Cherokees are a very backward people. We haven't the benefit of the telegraph."

"Would it make any difference if you did?"

"Perhaps," Tappin said equably. "Perhaps not."

"Well, thanks for your time anyway."

"You're entirely welcome."

"One more thing," Ryan said, almost as an afterthought. "We were wondering if you could spare a couple of Light Horse. It would improve the odds some."

"Spainyard is your responsibility. I couldn't jeopardize my own men, not under the circumstances."

"You've got a funny way of looking at things, Tappin."

"Do I?" Tappin said pleasantly. "Well, no matter. I understand you thrive on long odds."

"What's that supposed to mean?"

"A passing comment," Tappin said, nodding to Irvin. "Good day, Marshal. Always a pleasure to see you."

Outside, Ryan led the way along the corridor. He was quietly seething, but he said nothing as they went down the stairs. Finally, as they emerged from the front door, Irvin chuckled and shook his head.

"You know something, John? I don't think that son of a bitch likes you."

"He especially doesn't like who I work for."

"What was all that about you thrivin' on long odds?"

"Hard to say, Sam. Tappin talks in riddles about half the time."

Yet it was no riddle to Ryan. He'd understood perfectly what the remark meant. Tappin was talking about the four dead Cherokees, the ones he'd killed.

As of today, he'd been put on warning.

Dawn tinged the skyline. Blackgum Creek, flowing swiftly from winter melt-off, wound through a tangle of hills and wooded undergrowth. Nothing stirred where the stream made a sharp dogleg and gurgled off in a southeasterly direction. A deafening stillness hung over the land.

Ryan and Irvin were crouched behind trees on the slope of a hill. Below them, just past the bend in the stream, there was a small clearing where three horses were tied along the treeline. Around a smoldering campfire, the outlines of three men in bedrolls were dimly visible. In the dusky light, a tendril of smoke drifted skyward.

The lawmen had approached from the northwest shortly before dawn. They had hidden their horses in a stand of trees some distance upstream and slowly and with great caution had catfooted through the woods. Upon spotting the clearing, they had crouched down. Now, their eyes fixed on the sleeping figures, they spoke in whispers.

Irvin, who was armed with a Winchester carbine, nodded toward the clearing. His lips barely moved. "What d'you think?"

"Looks good," Ryan said. "I doubt they'll roll out before sunrise. So there's no need to rush it."

"You figure we ought to separate?"

Ryan understood that the older man was offering a suggestion. He studied the terrain a moment, estimating time and distance. On the opposite side of the creek, the woods were thick and brushy, skirting the shoreline. He judged the stream itself to be eight feet wide, studded in spots with large stones. The ground underfoot was still damp with dew, and therefore quiet.

"I'll cross over," he said softly. "You cover me till I'm on the other side. Then I'll work through those trees and come up directly opposite the camp. We'll have them in a crossfire."

Irvin nodded. It was the very plan he'd had in mind himself. Once Ryan was in position, there would be no need to delay further. His own field of fire already enabled him to cover the clearing from woods to creek bank. He glanced at the younger man.

"Don't take no chances."

"It's your show." Ryan shrugged. "How do you want them—dead or alive?"

"I'll give 'em one chance to surrender."

"And if they don't?"

"Kill 'em," Irvin said flatly. "Save the trouble of hangin' them anyway."

"Whatever suits. I'll wait for you to make the first play."

Ryan climbed to his feet. Angling downslope, taking it one step at a time, he drifted toward the dogleg. There, like a wraith he moved clear of the treeline and forded the creek, hopping from boulder to boulder. On the far side he quickly took cover in the brushy undergrowth. Quiet as wood smoke, he slipped through the shadowed timberland. Within ten minutes he was positioned immediately opposite the campsite. He waited behind the broad trunk of an oak tree.

Jack Spainyard suddenly awoke. Reacting to a faint noise or some instinct, he went from deep sleep to a state of instant alertness. He sat up in his bedroll and looked around the clearing. Then his gaze shifted to the woods.

Ryan froze. On the opposite side of the creek, Irvin went still as a stone monument. Hardly breathing, they held themselves motionless as Spainyard scanned the trees. For a long moment they were like partially hidden hunters who had inadvertently spooked their quarry. They waited in the deepening silence.

Finally Spainyard crawled out of his bedroll and stood. As he stepped from the blankets, he pulled a pistol from his waistband and peered warily into the trees. His eyes flicked to the tethered horses, then moved back to the woods. His look was at once guarded and puzzled, and he hesitated only briefly. He rapped out a sharp command to the other two men.

"Lem! Chuck! Haul your ass outa there. Let's go!"

Irvin reacted instantly. As the two outlaws scrambled from their bedrolls, he threw the carbine to his shoulder. He centered the sights on Jack Spainyard's chest.

"Hands up!" he yelled. "Do it, goddammit! Now!"

Spainyard snapped off a hurried shot. He fired in the general direction of the voice, already moving toward the woods as he pulled the trigger. Irvin levered three quick shots from the carbine. The slugs pocked crimson dots on Spainyard's shirtfront and he lurched sideways in a grotesque reeling dance. He went down, arms and legs akimbo, firing another shot as he fell. He dropped to the ground in a lifeless ball.

At the first shot the other two men sprang to their feet. Guns drawn, they seemed intent only on escape. One of them backed across the stream, firing wildly at the muzzle flash of Irvin's carbine. As he turned to the creek bank, Ryan stepped around the tree and triggered one barrel of his scattergun. The fist-sized load caught the outlaw in the brisket, splattering bone and gore. Legs pumping crazily, he stumbled backward into the creek. He hit the water with a loud splash.

The sound of the shotgun stopped the second man. Sprinting toward the horses, he halted in midstride and turned to fight. His pistol leveled as he spotted Ryan across the creek, and he fired. The slug shaved bark off the trunk beside Ryan's head and whistled harmlessly into the woods. Ryan let go with the shotgun, and in the same instant Irvin touched off another round from the carbine. Struck by a load of buckshot, the outlaw clutched his stomach as a carbine slug plowed through his rib cage. Like a puppet with his strings gone haywire, he collapsed to the earth.

A stillness descended on the clearing. Irvin started downslope, and Ryan waded across the creek. They met beside the campfire and stood for a moment staring down at Spainyard's body. The ground was puddled with blood, and the stench of bowels loosed in death filled the air. Irvin wrinkled his nose, slowly wagged his head. His voice was somehow rueful.

"Dumb bastards never seem to learn."

"What the hell," Ryan told him. "It beats hanging."

"Yeah, I reckon it does."

Irvin walked off to inspect the other two bodies. Ryan broke open his shotgun, extracted the spent shells, and reloaded. He started upstream to collect their horses.

The stench of Jack Spainyard followed him. His pace quickened, but he knew he'd never walk fast enough. It was a smell no man ever outran.

CHAPTER
EIGHT

The delegates began arriving on a sunny March afternoon. Their attendance at yet another Intertribal Council gathering marked a worsening situation. The Katy was now twelve miles into Indian Territory.

The meeting had been called in Muskogee, capital of the Creek Nation. Not quite ten miles from Fort Gibson, the town was located south of the Arkansas River. It was situated roughly in the center of Indian Territory, and therefore accessible to all the delegates. The Five Civilized Tribes, as well as several smaller tribes, were represented.

Hastily convened, the purpose of the meeting was to devise a united strategy. Ancient tribal animosities led inevitably to squabbling and a breakdown in solidarity. But a mood of compromise prevailed as wagons and groups of horsemen made their way into town. Today the council would discuss encroachment by the railroad and various land-grab schemes. And it would address as well an even greater threat—the federal government. Finding some means of staving off the devious tactics of white politicians was a matter of critical urgency.

Nearly two hundred delegates gathered in the local meeting hall. While allied, they represented separate peoples and divergent interests. Yet beneath all the jealousy and bickering, they were nonetheless brothers in blood. There was a businesslike air about them, the somber dignity of those faced with mutual peril. They met to consider the onrush of white domination.

John Ryan was the only *tibo* present. He rode into Muskogee shortly after the noon hour and dismounted outside the meeting hall. Officially, he was there as the emissary of Colonel Robert Stevens and the Katy railroad. While he could not address the council as a whole, he'd been ordered to work behind the scenes. His ostensible goal was to present the railroad's position in the most favorable light.

For all that, Ryan was still very comfortable. Stevens, though he never actually stated it, clearly expected him to spy on the proceedings. The council members crowding into the hall resented that their actions would be scrutinized by an uninvited white man. The looks they gave Ryan were laced with hostility. He felt like the worst sort of interloper simply because he was a *tibo*, and as far as the Indians were concerned, an enemy.

Yet the truth was something altogether different. Ryan was sympathetic to the Indians' cause and their long list of grievances. His years as a marshal had taught him that the Nations were another world, one that mystified most white men. And he understood that men were generally compelled to destroy what they failed to understand. So human nature, abetted by railroad barons and power-hungry politicians, represented a formidable threat to the Five Civilized Tribes, which were now confronted with the specter of their own dissolution.

At root was the fact that so many people coveted Indian lands. Choice homesteads had already been claimed by a flood of immigrants and settlers. The clamor to open all public lands to settlement had intensified as the westward migration gained strength. With the scarcity of good farmland, one of the primary targets of this movement was the Unassigned Lands. Ceded by the Creeks and Seminoles as a home for tribes yet to be resettled, the Unassigned Lands embraced some two million acres of well-watered, fertile plains. White settlers were also eyeing the Cherokee Outlet.

Spawned by federal bureaucracy, the Cherokee Outlet was one of the government's more bizarre creations. Earlier in the century, when the Cherokees were resettled in Indian Territory, they were granted seven million acres bordering southern Kansas. At the same time they were also granted a westward corridor, providing a gateway to the distant buffalo ranges. Comprising more than six million acres, roughly 150 miles in length, it was designated as the Cherokee Outlet. The legal status of this strip was confounding from its inception.

While the Cherokees held title to the Outlet, they were forbidden to dispose of it in any manner. Their lands to the east were sufficient for the entire tribe, and as a result they seldom ventured into their western grant. The upshot was a huge land mass that had remained unoccupied for the past thirty years. All that changed when the Chisholm Trail was blazed through Indian Territory. Texas cattlemen discovered a lush stretch of graze watered by the Canadian and Cimarron rivers. The Outlet made a perfect holding ground for long-horns, where cows were fattened out before the final drive to railhead at Abilene. For the last two trailing seasons, vast herds were halted a week or longer in the Outlet.

Word of this grassy paradise spread and quickly drew the attention of homesteaders. In short order, a public outcry arose over both the Unassigned Lands and the Outlet. The settlers were backed by several influential factions, all of which had a vested interest in the western expansion. Politicians and merchant princes and railroads, all looking to feather their own nests, rallied to the cause. Alone in their opposition to settlement were the Five Civilized Tribes. Their dealings with the government over several generations formed a chain of broken pledges and unfulfilled treaties. They saw settlement as a device for the enrichment of white farmers and greedy politicians.

In Washington those same politicians were holding out a wide array of enticements. Efforts were under way to convince the Five Civilized Tribes that their best interests would be served by abolishing tribal government. They were told that full citizenship within the Republic would afford them equality before the law, voting rights, freedom of speech and worship, and improved schooling. Still, based on their experience with *tibos'* promises, they had good reason to doubt the faith of the government. So all of them—Cherokee, Creek, Choctaw, Chickasaw, and Seminole—were unwilling to exchange independence for the dubious privilege of citizenship. Indian leaders, as well as the lowliest tribesman, preferred the old ways to the white man's road.

For all their resistance, however, the Indians were weighed down by a sense of fatalism. Educated men such as William Ross knew that their people were in the process of slow but certain absorption into the white culture. Once the railroad was extended to Texas, pressure would mount for the settlement of Indian Territory. The Five Civilized Tribes numbered less than fifty thousand people, and much of their land lay untilled. The movement to gain control of those millions of acres would ultimately put the tribes in an untenable position. So their leaders sought to forestall the inevitable by devising some bolder delaying action. The Intertribal Council would meet today to consider that very question.

Inside the council hall, Ryan paused at the rear of the room. There was no sanction against whites attending, but he was under no illusions. The men crowding through the door eyed him with a mixture of loathing and outrage. His presence was an affront, for he represented their most visible threat, the railroad. He reminded himself that the journey back to end-of-track would require unusual caution. Another attempt on his life seemed a distinct possibility.

The noise inside the hall was deafening. Knots of men scattered around the room were involved in loud and sometimes heated discussion. It occurred to Ryan that whites had a general misconception about Indians. Contrary to popular belief, the stoic red man with never a flicker of expression rarely existed. Indians were prone to play the part around whites, but in private they were as talkative and expressive as other men.

A familiar face down front caught Ryan's eye. He saw Major Tappin huddled in conversation with several men. By their dress and features, he took the other men to be of the Creek tribe. Tappin appeared to be lecturing them, emphasizing some point with a sharp, chopping gesture. The listeners nodded, seemingly convinced, their attitude one of absolute respect. With hardly a pause for breath, Tappin went on in a windy monologue.

Watching him, Ryan was struck by an ironic twist. The council hall might well have been a legislative chamber or a congressional assemblage. Except for their color, the men here today were scarcely different from a gaggle of white politicians. Some talked and others listened, and only a very few provided leadership. The art of persuasion was everywhere in evidence, typified by Tappin lecturing the attentive Creeks. The politician's standbys—compromise and trade-off—were equally apparent, and some tribes would fare better than others in the exchange. Ryan found the similarity to whites somewhat disappointing, almost sad. He thought the Indians had learned all the wrong things.

"Well, Mr. Ryan! We meet again."

Turning, Ryan found William Ross in the doorway. As principal chief of the Cherokees and president of the Inter-tribal Council, Ross was the most influential man in the hall. He was slated to give the opening address, and his speech would set the tone of the meeting. The council, in effect, was an instrument of his will.

Ross was scrupulously polite. Yet he regarded Ryan with casual interest, as though their meeting were a trivial event in an otherwise memorable day. He pointedly made no offer of a handshake.

Ryan pretended not to notice. "Quite a crowd," he said. "Looks like the Nations are well represented."

"And the railroad too," Ross noted. "I assume you're here at Colonel Stevens' direction?"

"Strictly as an observer."

"Naturally the Colonel had pressing matters elsewhere. Otherwise I've no doubt he would have been here himself."

The statement was delivered in a wry tone just short of mockery. Ryan smiled, sensing that the barb was not directed at him personally. He lifted one hand in an empty gesture.

"Tell you the truth, Mr. Ross, I don't think Stevens would be caught within ten miles of Muskogee. He places too high a value on his own hide."

Ross appraised him with a shrewd glance. "Are you implying that Colonel Stevens would not be safe here?"

"Maybe he would and maybe he wouldn't. I'm just telling you how he looks at it."

"And how do you look at it, Mr. Ryan?"

"Well"—Ryan hesitated, still smiling—"let's say he was wiser to send me."

"A diplomatic reply, indeed. Your tact does you credit."

"A man tends to mind his p's and q's when he travels alone."

"Which reminds me," Ross said with a calm, judicial gaze. "I understand your friends won't be here today."

"What friends?"

"Why, Elias Boudinot and Stand Watie, of course."

Ryan was momentarily taken aback. He recalled quite vividly the assassination attempt on the two kinsmen, but he was amazed that Ross would make any reference to their conspiracy with the railroad. However indirect, it seemed a damaging admission.

"What makes you think they're friends of mine?"

"You disappoint me, Mr. Ryan. One minute tactful and the next evasive. Are you denying that you know them?"

"No," Ryan said vaguely. "I'm just saying we're not what you'd call friends."

"Would you say the same for your employer?"

"I don't speak for the Colonel. You'll have to ask him."

Ross allowed himself a reserved smile. "I daresay his reply would make interesting listening. Don't you agree, Mr. Ryan?"

It occurred to Ryan that he'd been given a message. Or perhaps a warning. Ross clearly intended for him to pass it along to Stevens. He inclined his head in a faint nod.

"I'll tell the Colonel you asked."

"Yes, do that," Ross said agreeably. "You might also tell him that Boudinot and Watie make poor allies. Their reputation for double-dealing is well-known."

"Is that why they're not here today?"

"I suspect their reasons are the same as Colonel Stevens'."

There was an implied threat in the reply. Ryan started to pursue it, then changed his mind; there was nothing to be gained in pressing the matter. Better to let things take their natural course. He decided to switch to neutral ground.

"How's Elizabeth these days?"

"Quite well, thank you."

"Give her my regards. I hope to see her again before too long."

Ross examined him with a kind of bemused objectivity. "Would you care to stop over tomorrow night? As our houseguest, of course."

"Well, sure." Ryan sounded surprised. "I'd like that."

"I trust it won't compromise you with Colonel Stevens?"

"If it does, I reckon that's his worry."

"In that event, why not travel with me tomorrow? I have my coach here."

"I don't mind horseback."

"Yes, but why ride alone—on a lonely road?"

Ross' expression was unfathomable. Yet there was no doubt that he'd extended a warning. Once again the deeper purpose was unclear. And once again Ryan decided not to press the issue. Not now.

"Sounds like good advice," he said. "I'll plan on riding with you."

"Excellent."

Ross stuck out his hand. He smiled and shook Ryan's hand warmly. The gesture was hardly lost on the men crowded around the doorway. Nor was Ryan unaware that a message had been passed. The handshake guaranteed his safety while in Muskogee. He pumped Ross' arm once for good measure.

With a nod, Ross walked off. He made his way to the front of the hall, exchanging greetings with several men along the way. Mounting a speaker's platform, he moved directly to the podium. The hall quieted as he took up a gavel and hammered the delegates into silence.

For a long moment Ross just stood there. The silence thickened. Finally, when the crowd was absolutely still, he raised his arms in greeting. His voice flooded the hall.

"Brothers! Delegates to the council. I welcome you as we unite once more in a noble cause. One people, undivided—red men all!"

The crowd responded with a thunderous ovation. Someone loosed a shrill war whoop, and the delegates roared their approval. In that instant every voice there was fused into a single voice. By unspoken agreement all their past differences and the pettiness of tribal politics were set aside. They joined in a confederation of mind and spirit, proudly defiant.

William Ross spoke for nearly an hour. He talked of the railroads and the audacity with which they planned to exploit the Nations. He railed at the conspiracy of white politicians—and certain Indians—who sought to gain control of the red man's domain. He addressed himself to Congress and the federal bureaucracy and their unholy alliance with white power brokers to bring about settlement of Indian lands. His arguments struck to the very marrow of present and future dangers.

And at last, his voice alive with rage, he flung down what was both a challenge and a warning. He predicted an effort to bring about the allotment of their lands in severalty, forcing each of them onto the same 160 acres awarded to homesteaders. When that happened, he promised, there would soon follow the dissolution of tribal governments and Indian Territory as they had known it. Finally, calling the railroad a "greedy cormorant," he warned of a day when 23,000,000 acres of tribal land would be engulfed by a white tide. All that, he concluded, unless the council acted now—today!

Following his speech, Ross opened the floor to debate. Members of each tribe spoke at length, voicing their own concerns. But there was no debate, for every speaker agreed that action—an act signifying resistance—was imperative. By late afternoon a resolution had been drafted to President Ulysses S. Grant. In it the council expressed satisfaction with their own governments and the tribal ownership of land and urged Washington to abide by the provisions of existing treaties. There was nothing in the document to indicate open defiance.

Looking on, Ryan realized that it was all whitewash. The resolution was meaningless, another piece of paper to be ignored by both the President and Congress. But William Ross' speech had nonetheless inflamed the other tribes, incited them to act. Unable to challenge Washington, the Indians would instead strike a symbolic blow. And there was no question as to the closest enemy at hand.

They would attempt to stop the railroad.

CHAPTER NINE

A morning mist slowly burned away under the brassy dome of the sky. The coach trundled northward, drawn by a matched pair of carriage horses held to a steady pace by their driver.

Ryan occupied the front seat inside the coach. His horse was hitched to the rear, his saddle deposited in the luggage boot. He was unaccustomed to traveling in style and was impressed by the plush comfort. He thought it befitted an aristocratic Cherokee.

Ross and Tappin were seated opposite him. Earlier, before their departure from Muskogee, Tappin's greeting had been civil but cool. Aside from small talk, there had been little conversation and no reference to yesterday's council meeting. The three men had ridden in complete silence for the past half hour.

Ross appeared preoccupied. He was staring out the window with a faraway look in his eyes, as if toward something dimly visible in the distance. He was clearly pondering a matter of great complexity and seemed unaware of his traveling companions.

Watching him, Ryan was absorbed in thoughts of his own. He wondered why he'd been invited to share the coach. It was entirely possible that Ross wanted to protect him from an assassination attempt. By any estimate most of those attending the council meeting had viewed him as their mortal enemy. And as Ross had implied, a lone horseman on the Texas Road presented a tempting target. Yet that raised a question in Ryan's mind to which there was no ready answer. Why would Ross want to protect him?

No reasonable explanation occurred to Ryan. He had to assume that Ross was responsible for the violence to date. Certainly two assassination attempts had not gone unnoticed by the principal chief of the Cherokees, and it was reasonable to assume that the tribal leader had, at the very least, tacitly sanctioned the attempts. Great men, by their silence, often consigned lesser men to death.

Protection was ruled out, and Ryan was left to ponder exactly why he was jouncing along in the coach today. The obvious conclusion was that Ross wanted something from him. Ryan waited for Ross to make an overture.

Only the leathery creak of the coach broke the silence. As they forded the Arkansas, Ross finally stirred from his spell. Unfolding an oilskin tobacco pouch, he produced a pipe and started to fill it. He glanced at Tappin, who was staring out the opposite window. Striking a sulphurhead, he puffed a billowy cloud of smoke. He at last looked across at Ryan.

"Are you a student of government affairs, Mr. Ryan?"

Ryan shrugged. "Politics never much interested me."

"You're fortunate to have that option. No Cherokee could afford such a luxury."

"No, I reckon not."

"Be that as it may, you're hardly an uninformed man. So perhaps you'd indulge me. I have a question."

"I'll do my best."

"Call it idle curiosity . . ." Ross hesitated, puffing a wad of smoke. "As an observer, what was your opinion of the council meeting?"

"In what respect?" Ryan asked cautiously.

"Quite simply, do you believe we accomplished anything worthwhile?"

"If you're talking about Washington, I'd have to say no. The resolution you drafted won't hardly cause a ripple."

"Another piece of paper to get lost in a blizzard of legislative paper. Is that it?"

"Pretty much."

Ross considered a moment. "Are you aware there's a movement in Congress to force territorial status on the Nations?"

"How's that different than what you've got?"

"All the difference in the world, Mr. Ryan. We would then be a unified territory—with *one* territorial government, not five independent republics."

"Wouldn't that give you a stronger voice in Washington?"

"Hardly," Ross said firmly. "The President would appoint a governor and all the judges. Congress would have veto power over all territorial legislation. And eventually, of course, it would lead to statehood."

"I take it," Ryan said with a smile, "you're not interested in becoming just another state."

Ross laughed without mirth. "Territorial status and statehood would require the dissolution of the Five Civilized Tribes. It would also violate every treaty we have with the United States government."

Ryan rocked his hand from side to side. "Maybe your treaties aren't as ironclad as you thought."

"On the contrary," Ross said. "Our sovereignty was guaranteed for 'as long as water shall flow, as long as grass shall grow.' Hardly equivocal language, wouldn't you say?"

"Sounds permanent, all right."

"Indeed it does. Of course, the coming of the railroad changed all that. As Colonel Stevens once remarked, progress will not be denied."

Ryan nodded. "Even at the cost of a few treaties."

"Let me be frank, Mr. Ryan. You seem reasonably sympathetic to our cause. Am I mistaken?"

"No," Ryan said slowly.

"Then perhaps I might ask a favor. I assume you will deliver a report on the council meeting. Is that correct?"

"Yes."

"When you do, be so kind as to consider something. We might very well strike an accommodation with the railroad if there were a quid pro quo. Some assurance that the railroad would assume a neutral stance—not oppose us—in our struggle for sovereignty. Would you relay that message to Colonel Stevens?"

"I'd be glad to."

"And perhaps," Ross asked pointedly, "argue the merits of such an arrangement for all concerned?"

It sounded to Ryan like an offer to cease obstructing the railroad, but also as though Ross was trying, very subtly, to enlist him as an ally. Or perhaps plant a spy in Robert Stevens' camp. He phrased his reply with care.

"I think cooperation would be to everyone's benefit. That's what I'll tell Stevens."

"What sort of reaction would you anticipate?"

"I doubt he'll go for it. He'd have to burn a lot of bridges in Washington."

"A pity," Ross said ruefully. "Where power and money are concerned, there are no reasonable men. Only winners and losers."

The statement seemed to Ryan a prediction of sorts. He thought the best the Cherokees could hope for was a delay of the inevitable. Stevens would never adopt a position of neutrality where the Nations were concerned. The Katy, as well as the federal government, had everything to gain by the dissolution of Indian Territory. The Five Civilized Tribes were slated for the chopping block.

The coach rolled past the turnoff to Fort Gibson. Tappin, who had taken no part in their conversation, suddenly found his voice. He gestured out the window.

"Up the road is where two Cherokees were killed just about a month ago."

Ryan looked at him, fully alert. Tappin's composure was monumental, and he studied Ryan with an expression of open appraisal. Ross seemed unaware of the byplay. He glanced at Tappin with casual interest.

"Have you determined who was responsible?"

"Not yet," Tappin said, still staring at Ryan. "But whoever it was, he used a shotgun. It's not a common murderer's weapon—among Indians."

"Indians!" Ross repeated sharply. "Are you implying it was done by whites?"

Tappin shrugged, a sourly amused look on his face. "Why not ask our guest? He's a former marshal, and reputedly quite a manhunter." He paused, staring hard at Ryan. "What's your opinion, Mr. Ryan?"

Ryan gave him a wooden look. "Hard to say, Major. Were there any witnesses?"

"No." Tappin eyed him with the same disquieting stare. "Not to my knowledge."

"I never had much luck proving murder without a witness."

"Well, no matter," Tappin said with ominous calm. "Someone will come forward sooner or later. It's only a matter of time."

Ryan sensed the threat. He was suspect and he was being warned that the killings were not forgotten. He kept his features devoid of expression.

Tappin smiled and resumed staring out the window.

Dinner that night provided still another riddle. As an overnight guest, Ryan was treated with great cordiality. The meal, complemented by suitable wines, centered around imported oysters and a haunch of native venison. Afterward, a fine Napoleon brandy was served to the men.

All through dinner Elizabeth seemed elusive. She was obviously pleased by Ryan's visit and extended herself to make him feel welcome, but her attitude, while gracious, was distant.

Ryan pretended to notice nothing, but underneath he felt as though he was involved in some sort of charade. Compared to the last time, when they'd toured Tahlequah, Elizabeth was not herself. Her natural vivacity was muted, and she seemed on edge, curiously tense. He wondered if her father's presence was inhibiting her. He concluded instead that it was attributable to his presence.

Later that evening she confused him even more. Following dinner, Ross engaged him in conversation in the drawing room. Their discussion ranged over a variety of subjects, but they didn't talk of politics and the railroad. Elizabeth listened quietly, rarely offering a comment. Then as she excused herself for the night, she seemed to do a complete turnabout. She invited him to stay over another day on the pretext that he'd not yet seen all of the Cherokee Nation. Her manner was so charming that he readily agreed.

Early the next morning they drove off in an open carriage. Elizabeth wore a fashionable dark blue dress trimmed with gray piping and bone buttons. Her hair was drawn back sleekly, accentuating the contours of her face, and atop her head sat a jaunty little hat. She was animated and sparkling, chattering gaily, her eyes shining like black pearls.

Elizabeth's feelings veered wildly. In Ryan's absence, she'd found herself lost in long reveries about their last ride together. She knew it was witless and silly, for they were separated by his continuing loyalty to the railroad. But now, seated beside him, she was unable to control herself. She felt dizzy with happiness.

Elizabeth took him to see Park Hill. Some five miles south of Tahlequah, the small community was known as the "Athens of the Cherokee Nation." Here were two elegant brick churches, one Methodist and one Presbyterian, both fashioned along the lines of a New England meetinghouse. But most impressive was the Park Hill Mission, which was funded by religious donations. A printing shop operated by the mission produced schoolbooks that were distributed throughout the Nations. Elizabeth was quick to tell Ryan that some books were also printed in the Cherokee language.

Sequoyah's invention of a tribal alphabet had stamped out illiteracy among the Cherokees. In the years that followed, all schools in the Nation were mission operated, sponsored by religious organizations. Then in 1841 the tribal council established a formal educational system, with eighteen elementary schools. Trained schoolteachers were engaged, log schoolhouses were built, and every child was assured an education. The program, Elizabeth pointed out, marked a milestone in Cherokee progress.

Ten years later a system of higher education was established. Seminaries, one for boys and another for girls, were constructed outside Park Hill. The buildings were brick and stone, three stories high, with massive columns on the front veranda. Here, among other subjects, the older children were taught Latin and algebra, grammar and science. While their schooling was conducted in English, they were also grounded in their mother tongue. The most promising students were later sent to colleges and universities back east. In effect, the Cherokee Nation was looking to the future, building from within. The best of each generation was trained in business and law and medicine.

Elizabeth was justifiably proud. She was also somewhat chauvinistic about her people and not the least bit ashamed of it. She boasted that the public schools, particularly the seminaries, surpassed white institutions in both Kansas and Texas. Ryan accepted the statement, for he found himself impressed by the tribe's vision and far-reaching planning. He saw now that these same qualities had been brought to the Cherokees' struggle for sovereignty. William Ross was already planning a generation ahead.

As they turned from Park Hill, Ryan's thoughts took on a personal note. He sensed she was attracted to him, but it was hard to tell with educated women. Particularly one whose moods were so damnably mercurial. A wrong move too early might easily scare her off.

The point quickly became moot. Elizabeth's mood underwent a transformation. Out of the corner of his eye, he saw her expression change. The gaiety was replaced by a troubled look, and her shoulders seemed to tense. Her hands were clenched in her lap.

"John?"

"Yes."

"Would you mind . . . ?" She faltered, then hurried on.

"Before we get back to the house, may I ask you something?"

"Of course," Ryan said. "What is it?"

"Father told me about your talk on the way from Muskogee. He said he thought you were unusually sympathetic toward the Cherokees."

"I suppose that's a fair statement."

She gave him a searching look. "Were you sincere with him or just being diplomatic?"

"I'm no diplomat," Ryan said, glancing at her. "Either I say what I think or I don't say it."

"Then you meant it?" she asked anxiously. "When you agreed to speak with Colonel Stevens?"

"I'll talk to him. But as I told your father, I doubt it'll change anything."

"It could . . . if you tell him the right thing."

"What's that?"

"Convince him," she said quite intently, "that he will never build the railroad unless he accepts my father's offer. There are men who mean to halt the construction—at any cost."

"You're talking about Cherokees, aren't you?"

"Yes."

"Who are they?"

"I have no idea."

"Does your father?"

Her chin tilted. "No, he doesn't. But he knows they exist, many of them."

"So he put you up to telling me about them—"

"No!"

"—and asking me to pass it along to Stevens."

"Please believe me," she implored, "he has no idea I've told you, and it would make him very angry if he knew." She paused and her voice dropped. "He's ashamed of what they're doing, going back to the old ways. He's trying to stop them."

"How can he stop them if he doesn't know who they are?"

Her voice was barely audible. "I'm afraid he will find out, afraid for him."

Ryan looked deep into her eyes. He read no guile there, and some inner voice told him to believe her. He popped the reins. It seemed important that he return to end-of-track, and quickly.

He had to have a long talk with Stevens.

CHAPTER
TEN

Track laying slowed to a virtual halt by early April. Heavy rains turned the prairie into a quagmire, making it impassable for days at a time. End-of-track was scarcely fifteen miles from the Kansas border.

With construction at a standstill, Stevens ordered the supply depot brought forward. A siding was built off the main roadbed, and trains began chuffing back and forth. In a matter of days a mountain of construction supplies and equipment was unloaded on the soggy prairie. The Katy had established its first terminus.

Over the next two weeks the terminus was transformed into an anthill of commerce. Word went out that the Katy had shifted its supply depot, and the race was on. Gamblers, cutthroats, and harlots—all scenting fast money on the wind—arrived by wagon and horseback. Sprawling over the prairie, a shantytown went up as the horde descended on end-of-track.

A squalid, ramshackle affair, the town was constructed of poles and canvas. The street, such as it was, consisted of saloons, dance halls, and gaming dens. The lone hostelry, large as a circus tent, reeked of stale sweat and filthy blankets and charged four bits a night for a rickety cot. Where a grove of trees towered over the prairie, there was a dingy collection of one-room shanties. Among the sporting crowd it was known as Poonville, for it was where the whores practiced their profession. The ladies operating these dollar-a-throw brothels were an enterprising breed, offering something to suit the tastes of any man. Yet they were a ragtag bunch, unkempt and coarse, the lower rung of whoredom. Only the fact that their customers were blinded by lust kept them in business.

On any given night the town was crawling with renegades—bandits, cardsharps, wanted killers—a fraternity of rogues seeking sanctuary, whose chief goal in life was to put distance between themselves and the law. Brawls were a sporting pastime. Among men who prided themselves on being ornery as well as tough, any dispute was an excuse for kick-and-stomp. On a nightly basis, cock-of-the-walk squared off against bull-of-the-woods, and blood flowed.

Tonight, with the street axle deep in mud, the town resembled an unholy carnival. Huge Studebaker wagons piled with freight and pulled by triple spans of mules clogged the street. Hitch racks outside every shanty were jammed with saddle horses, and raucous laughter from indoors left small doubt that firewater was being dispensed in liberal doses. From dance halls came the sprightly wail of fiddles, and an occasional banjo twanged strident chords. Hundreds of men joined in a rowdy jostling match as they made their way from one dive to the next.

The shantytown was a lure for a particular breed of men who roamed the western plains, men whose appetites ran to fast women, popskull whiskey, and games of chance.

Ryan's job here was a monumental task, and constantly dangerous. For all practical purposes, he was the law at end-of-track. Day and night he was required to maintain order among outcasts and outlaws gathered from across the frontier, and thus far, only his reputation had prevented a serious outbreak of violence. He'd not yet been forced to kill anyone.

When the sporting crowd arrived, Ryan had quickly laid down a code of conduct. Fisticuffs, even rough-and-tumble brawls, were permissible as long as an altercation did not lead to killing. Theft and robbery, whether by whore or penniless drifter, would result in swift justice. Gunplay, whatever the provocation, would not be tolerated. Anyone who killed or resorted to a gun would be called to answer for it. And it was known that Ryan would exact harsh payment.

Still, throughout the town there was a prevailing attitude of devil take the hindmost. The sporting crowd was comprised of fly-by-night operators, rootless vagabonds. Their interest was in fleecing the railroad workers, not settlement of the land or legitimate business. In fact, any attempt to settle on Indian land was punishable by a federal fine of $1,000. The single exception was for a white man who had intermarried within the Five Civilized Tribes. Such an individual was exempt from normal restrictions and could not only claim land, but found it considerably easier to obtain tribal license for certain types of businesses.

There was no license, however, for trading in whiskey. By federal law spirits in any form, whether liquor, wine, or beer, were illegal in Indian Territory. For selling or bartering, there was a $500 fine. Smuggling or attempting to transport alcohol into the Nations brought a $300 fine. Operating a still for the manufacture of spirits carried a fine of $1,000. Yet no one paid any attention to the law. Popskull and rotgut were stable commodities of trade throughout the tribes.

The crux of the problem was enforcement. Federal marshals were few and far between, due to the reduction in manpower ordered by the Fort Smith court. Whiskey smugglers risked small chance of arrest, and nowhere was the fact more obvious than at end-of-track. Freight wagons loaded with barrels and wooden cases rolled into the shantytown on a regular schedule. All of this compounded Ryan's problem, particularly after dark. Drunks, like vampires, were more active at night.

On only one front had Ryan been allowed a respite. Hampered by the rains, railroad construction was proceeding at a slow crawl. In the last week the track-laying crews had advanced less than a mile, and with the Katy stalled, the threat from the Cherokees had momentarily disappeared. Weather had seemingly accomplished what the Indians wished for most. The white man's iron horse was stopped cold.

Ryan completed his early evening swing through town. He generally made the rounds three times a night, with a break for supper. Tonight there was the usual orderly chaos, with every dive packed to capacity. Off toward Poonville, where red lanterns hung outside the tent bagnios, he saw lines of men waiting their turn. A knot of men gathered outside a saloon fell silent as he walked past. He felt their eyes on his back and imagined what they were thinking. Lots of men would like to be known as the man who killed John Ryan. He wondered how long it would be before someone tried.

Slogging toward the railroad siding, he headed for a meeting with Stevens. Their dealings lately had been very much that of boss and hired hand. Upon returning from Tahlequah, Ryan had presented William Ross' proposal. As he'd expected, Stevens turned it down flat, refusing all discussion. It was obvious that the railroader wanted things his own way. A truce with the Cherokees, at the cost of angering white politicians, was not to Stevens' liking. He clearly believed in leaving his bridges unburned.

Stevens had been angered, too, by what he saw as Ryan's meddling. He failed to understand why Ryan had spent the night at Ross' home and stayed over still another day. Nor was he pleased that Ryan had taken it upon himself to act as a negotiator. While never stating it, he had implied that Ryan had been disloyal. The matter had been dropped, but Stevens plainly hadn't forgotten it. Over the ensuing weeks, he'd treated Ryan with stiff formality.

A conference was under way when Ryan entered the private railroad car. Tom Scullin and Otis Gunn, the construction engineer, were seated while Stevens paced back and forth in front of them. Scullin glanced around at Ryan and rolled his eyes in a gesture of resignation. Stevens caught the byplay and halted, his face screwed up in a frown. His gaze shifted to Ryan.

"Have a seat, John," he said curtly. "I'll be with you in a minute."

"Saints preserve us," Scullin moaned. "Don't you believe it, Johnny m'boy. He's set to talk the whole night, and never a pause for breath."

"Spare me your humor!" Stevens' voice was peevish. He stabbed a finger at Scullin. "I fail to see how you can joke when we're so far behind schedule. And falling farther behind every day!"

"Would you have me wail and gnash my teeth? It's hardly of my choosing."

"Well, it has to improve. No two ways about it, Tom."

"Talk to God," Scullin muttered.

"I beg your pardon?"

Stevens looked as though he couldn't have heard correctly. Scullin shook his head, crossed one massive leg over the other. His eyes were hard.

"You understood me, Colonel."

"Don't get on your high horse with me!"

"Then lower your voice," Scullin grated. "I'll not be talked to in that manner."

A strained silence fell over the car. The two men were locked in a staring contest, glowering at one another. After several moments, Stevens broke eye contact. He massaged his forehead as though he had a headache.

"I didn't mean to snap at you, Tom. It's just that we're running out of time."

"All the same, God's the one who makes it rain. I've no control over the weather."

"No, of course you don't," Stevens agreed. "But that doesn't change our predicament. We have to reach Cabin Creek by the end of the month. That's our absolute deadline."

Scullin pursed his lips. "We'll never make it."

"We must!" Stevens declared loudly. "Otherwise we'll lose the cattle trade for the entire season."

"Would we now? I've always heard that the Texans trail through the end of September. It seems we've still got a bit of leeway."

"You don't understand. Once they start trailing to Abilene, they'll continue throughout the summer. Texans are like sheep—they follow the leader!''

''I know it's a loss—''

''*A loss!*'' Stevens cut him short. ''We're talking about tens of thousands of dollars. And keep in mind, we won't get a nickel from the Indians in bond issues. It's a loss that may well drain us financially.''

Scullin made no reply. He looked down at his hands with a sorrowful expression. The worry lines on Stevens' forehead deepened, and he seemed at a loss to continue. After a moment he turned to Gunn.

''Otis, you're the engineer. Isn't there some way around the damnable rain?''

Gunn looked pained, as though his teeth hurt. He ran a hand through his thinning hair and shot a glance at Scullin. At last he drew a deep breath.

''No, sir, there's not,'' he finally answered. ''As quickly as the graders get the roadbed leveled, the rain washes it away. We're lucky if we lay track four hours out of the day.''

''On top of which,'' Scullin added, ''half the ballast on track we've laid gets washed away. We've got ourselves a hell of a patch job once the rain stops.''

The discussion hobbled on awhile longer. None of the men was struck by inspiration, and the rain seemed the clear winner. Several minutes later Scullin and Gunn trooped out of the car. Stevens just stood there a moment, staring dully into space. He finally became aware of Ryan.

''Yes, John,'' he said absently. ''What is it?''

''No idea, Colonel. You sent for me.''

''So I did.'' Stevens slumped into a chair. ''How are things going in town?''

''Pretty tame,'' Ryan said. ''Usual fistfights and a couple of stabbings. But nothing too serious.''

''I understand Red Baird showed up. Is that true?''

''Yeah, he's here.''

''Why didn't you advise me?''

''No need,'' Ryan told him. ''Baird's just another gambler.''

"I have it on good authority that among other things he's killed a dozen men," Stevens said shortly.

Ryan smiled, but there wasn't a trace of amusement in his eyes. "Don't believe everything you hear. These gunmen like to boost their reputation by several notches. It makes other hardcases leery."

"The fact remains he's a killer. And he's the sort of man who attracts violence. I want to know how you're going to handle it."

"I've already handled it. When he pulled into town, I had a talk with him. We understand one another."

"Do you, indeed! And what happens if he kills one of our men?"

"He won't."

"What makes you so sure?"

"Because if he does," Ryan said, a touch of irony in his voice, "he knows he'll have to deal with me."

"And you believe that will stop him?"

"Has so far."

"I would prefer something a little more final."

"What'd you have in mind?"

Stevens idly waved his hand. "I suggest you run him out of town."

"Won't work," Ryan said. "If I run Baird off, I'd have to post half the men in town. We'd need an army to make it stick."

"Perhaps it would serve as an object lesson for the others. By posting Baird, you would serve notice."

"Only one problem. Unless he causes trouble, I've got no reason to post him. Not just on his reputation anyway."

"I see," Stevens remarked stiffly. "What if I ordered you to do it?"

Ryan gave him a stony look. "I don't tell you how to run your railroad." He paused, slowly stood. "Don't tell me how to do my job."

"You seem to forget," Stevens growled, "you're working for me."

"No, I haven't forgot."

Ryan walked to the door and let himself out. On the back platform he filled his lungs with air, then let it out slowly. He'd almost lost his temper, and he took that as a bad sign. A damn bad sign, he told himself, for a man in his line of work.

Heading uptown, he realized it was past suppertime. He normally took his meals with Scullin in the car where they both bunked. But tonight he wasn't interested in further talk about the railroad or Robert Stevens. He decided instead to try one of the tent cafés near the center of town.

The street was relatively quiet for midevening. Wooden planks, which were priceless in a tent city, served as a crude boardwalk. As he passed a saloon, Ryan came upon three men standing on the plank byway. The customary practice was for idlers to vacate the boardwalk in favor of passersby. As Ryan slowed, his attention directed to the men, a gunshot sounded from within the saloon.

Turning back, Ryan stepped through the entrance to the saloon. He pulled his Colt and held it alongside his leg, his thumb hooked over the hammer. He stopped just inside the entrance, assessing the situation and those involved at a glance. A man was sprawled on the floor, arms flung wide, blood staining his shirtfront. Standing over him, gun in hand, was a man dressed in a flannel shirt and a battered slouch hat. Beside him was a youngster, similarly dressed, who appeared to be in his late teens. Their backs were to the door.

"Drop it! You're under arrest!"

Ryan's command splintered the silence like a thunderclap. The spectators, who were fanned out away from the killing, froze in a still tableau. The roughly dressed man hesitated for only a fragment in time. Then, crouching low, he whirled and brought his pistol around. All in a split instant Ryan identified the man as Indian and thumbed the hammer on his Colt. A corner of his mind registered amazement; until now, not one Indian had ventured into the shantytown. In that same instant, suppressing conscious thought, Ryan reverted to instinct. The Colt roared, spitting a streak of flame.

The Indian staggered up against the bar. A bright red dot

widened on his chest, and the pistol dropped from his hand. He buckled, folding together like an accordion, and slumped to the floor. The youngster, standing not a foot away, reacted even as the older man fell. He stooped low, scooping up the pistol in a swift movement. There was a metallic click as he cocked the hammer and spun back toward the door. His face was contorted with a mixture of rage and fear.

"Don't try it!"

Ryan shouted the order too late. The youngster was already turning, arm extended, the pistol level. Their shots cracked almost simultaneously, indistinguishable twin roars. A slug nicked Ryan's waistband, ripping a belt loop off his pants. Opposite him, the youngster lurched backward, struck dead center below the sternum. Arms windmilling, the Indian youth lost his footing and went down. He fell between the two older men, the pistol still clutched in his hand. His eyes stared into a sightless void.

A leaden moment slipped past. Then Ryan walked forward and stopped before the three bodies. He stared down at the youngster, whose boyish features were set in a rictus of death. His own face went ashen and his stomach knotted in a queasy sensation. The bitter taste of bile flooded his mouth as the truth struck home.

He'd killed a kid.

CHAPTER
ELEVEN

The shootings created a momentary sensation. Word of the incident swept through town within the hour. Three dead in itself sparked only minor curiosity; violent death was no stranger to those who worked the frontier. It was the dead men themselves who generated such sharp interest.

The victim was an itinerant cardslick. Something of a loudmouth, he'd objected to the presence of an Indian in the saloon. When he became abusive and put a hand on his gun, he had paid for it with his life. The other man, who was Cherokee, shot him dead. Later it was determined that the Cherokee had wandered in with his son, looking for a drink. The bartender never had a chance to inform him that Indians were not served whiskey. Upon entering the saloon, he'd been braced by the gambler.

There was little surprise generated by the outcome. The sporting crowd knew Ryan to be a man of his word. He had threatened swift reprisal for those who resorted to gunplay, and he'd delivered on the promise. No great importance was attached to the fact that the dead man was an Indian. Everyone agreed that Ryan would just as quickly have tangled with a white man. Nor was there any stigma associated with the killing of a Cherokee boy. Opinion on the youngster, who looked to be about seventeen, was fairly uniform among the sporting crowd. He shouldn't have made a try for the gun.

Ryan was somewhat less charitable about himself. He saw no way to have avoided killing the Cherokee man, and he agreed that the boy had been foolish to take up the fight. But all that failed to absolve him in his own view for killing a kid. He mocked himself for not having faster reactions or greater foresight. He thought he could have handled the situation differently, far more wisely. If he had, the boy would still be alive.

He knew that he was being harsh with himself. His regret was prompted basically by the youngster's age, and by hindsight. Given the circumstances, his reaction was inevitable. Anyone who tried to kill him, man or boy, foreclosed all other options. When the choice was kill or get killed, there was no choice at all. Still, however much hindsight kindled his regret, he couldn't entirely accept the reality. He wished that it had somehow ended differently.

The only positive note to the whole affair was that in the two weeks since the shooting, the town had become almost civilized. The sporting crowd, drifters, and outlaws were on their best behavior. A triple burial of the dead out beyond Poonville had proved highly persuasive. There was even talk that the cardsharp had saved time and trouble by getting himself killed by the Indian. Had he lived, according to local wits, Ryan would probably have shot him anyway. The dark humor contained a moral that escaped no one. Don't start trouble.

Several days later, shortly before sundown, Ryan was on his way to see Stevens. He'd been summoned earlier in the afternoon, but he saw no need for urgency. Since the shootout, he'd been left pretty much to his own devices. Apparently Stevens thought the killings proved his ability to maintain law and order. Ryan considered it ironic that men had to die before he was judged to be doing his job.

Neither Stevens nor the manservant was in evidence when Sally Palmer let him into the private car. He thought about leaving but changed his mind. The railroader's mistress was not his worry and certainly no reason to walk on eggshells. He decided to wait.

He accepted her offer of a drink, and as she moved to the whiskey cupboard, he seated himself in one of the armchairs. After pouring a stout shot, she returned and halted behind his chair. She leaned forward, holding the glass in front of him. Her other hand rested lightly on his shoulder.

"Where have you been keeping yourself?"

"Around," he said, taking the glass. "I manage to stay busy."

"You know what they say," she purred. "All work and no play . . ."

"I thought we hashed this out last time."

She leaned closer. Her hands drifted down his chest, and she put her mouth to his ear. Her breath was like warm velvet.

"Foolish man," she whispered. "I told you then it wasn't finished. When I like someone—"

"What the hell's going on here?"

Stevens' voice lashed at them. He slammed the door behind him and strode forward. Sally straightened and took a hasty step back from the chair. She flung an arm at Ryan.

"Blame him!" she declared. "I made him a drink and he grabbed my hands. I was trying to get loose."

Ryan hoisted his glass in a sardonic toast. "Evening, Colonel."

"Well?" Stevens demanded. "Aren't you going to answer the charge?"

"Why bother?" Ryan said, smiling. "You know a fairy tale when you hear one—don't you?"

"Are you telling me she's lying?"

"You be your own judge." Ryan gestured in her direction. "Nobody would ever take that for the look of girlish modesty."

Sally tried to cover her embarrassment with a derisive laugh. Her features only reddened more, and she crossed quickly to Stevens. Her hand gripped his arm.

"Don't believe him, Bob! He got fresh and I just tried—"

Stevens slapped her. The blow was delivered so sharply that her head snapped back. She staggered, blood trickling from her mouth, her eyes round. She looked shocked.

"I should have known," Stevens said hotly. "Once a whore, always a whore!"

"No, honey!" she pleaded. "It's not what you—"

"Go to your room. *Now!* I'll deal with you later."

Sally wavered, slowly turned from him. On the way past she shot Ryan a venomous look. Then, her eyes brimming with tears, she retreated to the bedroom. The door closed with a muted click.

Stevens dropped into a chair. His face was wreathed in a dark scowl and a pulse throbbed in his forehead. There was a moment of oppressive silence as Ryan took a long pull on his drink. Finally, trying for a light touch, he waved his glass.

"Don't fault her too much, Colonel. She just likes to flirt, that's all."

"Indeed?" Stevens snapped. "Am I to understand it's happened before?"

"Would it make any difference if it had?"

"No," Stevens said. "To be frank, I expected it long before this. I knew what she was when I brought her along."

"In that case," Ryan allowed, "you've got no room for complaint. A flirt here and there seems like pretty tame stuff."

"Perhaps," Stevens conceded. "But I didn't call you over here to discuss my personal life. I have an assignment for you."

Ryan permitted himself a smile. "Aren't you afraid the town'll go to hell if I'm away?"

"You'll only be gone two days."

"Whereabouts am I going exactly?"

"Tahlequah," Stevens informed him. "I want you to pay a call on William Ross."

"Oh?" Ryan appeared surprised. "I recollect you told me to steer clear of Ross."

"Necessity dictates otherwise. We're running short of roadbed ties, and I suspect it's Ross' handiwork. He's not above anything."

"So you want me to negotiate a new delivery schedule?"

"I certainly do," Stevens acknowledged. "First, it was the rain, and now it's the damnable Cherokees. We simply can't afford further delay."

Ryan understood his concern. The rain had finally abated, and the track layers were now within a few miles of Big Cabin Creek. Once there, Stevens would move to lure a vestige of the cattle trade away from Abilene. A steady supply of railbed ties and bridge timber was therefore crucial. And it was obtainable only from the Cherokees.

"You mustn't fail me," Stevens went on. "You have to persuade Ross to live up to his agreement. We must have those ties!"

"Easier said than done," Ryan observed. "What makes you think he'll listen to me?"

"Ross is a pragmatic man. He can use you as a pipeline to me. And vice versa. He'll listen because he doesn't want to lose your . . . services."

Only later that night did Ryan appreciate the irony of it. Lying in his bunk listening to Scullin snore, it occured to him that pragmatism was color-blind. A Cherokee was using him no less than a lily-white railroader.

"Your Colonel Stevens is a fool!"

"I hope that doesn't mean I'm here on a fool's errand."

"Don't bandy words with me, Mr. Ryan."

"Never entered my head. I'm not that good with words."

Ryan had arrived less than an hour ago. He'd been ushered into Ross' study, all the while wondering if Elizabeth was home. After observing the formalities, he had relayed the gist of last night's conversation with Stevens. The reaction was scarcely more than he'd expected.

Seated opposite him, William Ross looked swelled with indignation. His copper complexion was noticeably redder, and his mouth clamped in a tight line. He stared at Ryan with a bemused expression.

"Tell me," he said at length. "Why haven't I heard from you?"

"From me?" Ryan said, genuinely puzzled. "Why'd you expect to hear from me?"

"For one thing, I asked you to carry a message to Stevens. For another, it's been well over a month since I made that request. Simple courtesy would have dictated a reply."

"Stevens wasn't interested in your proposal. I figured it was up to him to tell you so."

"Let me be frank," Ross said in an exasperated tone. "When a week or so passed, it was obvious that Stevens wasn't interested. His failure to communicate that decision was hardly unexpected." He paused and slowly shook his head. "I was very disappointed in you, however. I thought we had an understanding."

Ryan suddenly got the message. In subtle terms, he was being told how the game of diplomacy worked. Delivery on the railbed ties had purposely been delayed. The purpose, aside from impeding construction, was to prompt another visit by him to Tahlequah. So Stevens had been right all along. William Ross would go to great lengths to keep a friend in the enemy camp.

"Next time," Ryan finally replied, "I'll make it my business to keep you informed. As you said, it's nothing more than simple courtesy."

Ross nodded. "Good. I think it will work to everyone's advantage."

"Now"—Ryan cocked his head with an inquisitive smile—"about the ties . . ."

"An oversight that's easily corrected. I'll instruct whoever's reponsible to speed the delivery."

Ross hesitated, fingers steepled in a thoughtful pose. "I understand Stevens has his eye on the Texas cattle trade. Tell me how it's going."

Ryan was quicker this time. He understood that he was being asked to enter into a trade. He would secure Ross' cooperation in exchange for information. And he had no doubt that the crafty old Cherokee knew most of the details anyway.

He told Ross almost everything. What he left out was in deference to the man who paid his wages. He thought Robert Stevens would have approved.

Their discussion drew to a close some minutes later. From Ross' manner it was apparent he had satisfied himself regarding the Katy and the cattle trade. While the financial problems of the railroad had not been mentioned, it was unnecessary to state the obvious. No one had to tell Ross that the Katy was actively seeking a new source of funds.

Toward the end Ryan's thoughts turned to another subject entirely. He waited for Ross to broach the matter of the wild terminus town and the saloon shootout. But there was no reference to the Cherokee father and son now buried alongside a white man. Somewhat gingerly, he finally raised the subject himself.

"You're aware," he said, "that two of your people were killed recently."

"I am," Ross said gravely. "The Light Horse Police keep me very well informed."

There was no need to pursue the statement. Ryan took it as confirmation that the railroad was under constant surveillance. He merely nodded and went on.

"Then you know I'm the one who killed them."

"Yes, I do."

Ross' expression was unreadable. The silence deepened as Ryan waited for him to ask questions, demand the particulars. But the Cherokee sat there, silent and immobile, asking nothing. After a moment Ryan felt obligated to resume.

"I want to explain," he said. "How it happened—and why."

Ross held up a hand. "I require no explanation. I've already been advised of the details."

"Would you mind my asking—"

"Yes, I would," Ross cut him off. "It's not important who advised me. Suffice it to say I am aware of how it happened, and why."

Ryan hesitated, staring at him. "I'd like to hear the verdict. Do you blame me or not?"

"I see no reason to render judgment. That's a matter between you and your conscience."

"What if I said my conscience is clear?"

"As I told you," Ross answered, "I require no explanation. However, you may want to have a talk with Elizabeth."

"Elizabeth?"

"Why do you sound surprised? She's fond of you, and she'd grown to trust you—until this happened."

"Until I killed the boy?"

"Yes," Ross said softly. "As her father, I might offer a suggestion. Give her some rational justification for why it was necessary."

"I appreciate the advice. But I'm not sure I understand it. Why are you so concerned?"

"For the simplest of reasons, Mr. Ryan. Elizabeth is my daughter."

The conversation ended on that note. After a handshake, Ryan walked from the study. He knew he'd been judged by the father, and none too harshly. He wasn't all that certain about the daughter.

He went to look for her.

CHAPTER TWELVE

Stable hands were mucking out the stalls. The interior of the building was dim and musty, ripe with the smell of dung. Outside a late afternoon sun tilted into the westerly quadrant.

Ryan waited near the stables. A house servant had informed him that Elizabeth was off riding. Apparently she was something of a horsewoman and went for a ride every afternoon. Upon hearing that, he'd registered no great surprise. She struck him as someone who would enjoy spirited horses.

South of the stables several horses were grazing in a fenced pasture. Ryan stood with his arms folded over the top rail of the fence, watching them. The horses were clearly blooded stock, with sleek lines and admirable conformation. He thought it very much in keeping with the position and prestige of their owner. Among aristocratic Cherokees, there was none who ranked higher than William Ross. He lacked only a scepter to be king.

Thinking back to their conversation, Ryan was somewhat saddened. In his view William Ross was fighting a losing battle. A valiant effort, with noble ideals, but one that was certain to fail. The forces allied against the Civilized Tribes were too strong, too determined. In a very real sense, the white man held all the cards in a game the Indian was still learning to play. Men such as Ross could postpone the inevitable through diplomacy and transitory political alliances. But delay, even for another generation, would not alter the end result. Eventually the Cherokees, and all the other tribes, would be stripped of sovereignty. Their days of independence were numbered.

Still, as he reflected on it, Ryan couldn't help but admire the Cherokee leader. Ross was a farsighted man of intellect and wisdom. Without question, he saw what the future held for the Five Civilized Tribes. Yet he never flagged in his efforts to outfox Washington and the white power structure. Almost alone, he continued to mobilize the Indians and hammer out a spirit of unity among the tribes. Except for his dogged zeal, his refusal to admit defeat, the battle would have been lost long ago. By sheer force of character, he spurred his people to fight for the next generation.

All of which left Ryan with mixed feelings. His sympathy toward the Indians conflicted with his practical nature. Today, for no apparent reason he'd come very close to forming a private alliance with William Ross. Since it was of no benefit to him, common sense dictated that he should avoid such entanglements. Yet he'd walked a narrow line between his loyalty to Stevens and his affinity with Ross. He wondered why he'd done it, and no ready explanation presented itself. He knew it wasn't conscience, and certainly he was no idealist. So that brought him around to perhaps the only reason that made any sense. He found it difficult to admit that he'd done it for a girl.

Pondering on it, he was tempted to laugh. She had been uppermost in his mind since the day they'd met. Ostensibly, every trip he'd made to Tahlequah had been on railroad business. But beneath a surface of pretext, the underlying reason was of a more personal nature. He wanted to see her, and he had capitalized on every opportunity that brought him to the Cherokee capital. However hard to admit, there seemed no getting around it. Otherwise he wouldn't have waited for nearly an hour like some moonstruck schoolboy and worried all the while about the reception he would receive.

Presently Elizabeth appeared over a low rise of ground.

She was riding sidesaddle, and as she approached, Ryan thought she looked more the eastern lady than a young Cherokee. Her clothes were informal, with a short jacket, a pleated skirt, and dark, supple boots. She was bareheaded, her cheeks spanked by the wind.

As she neared the stables, Ryan took a closer look at her mount. A magnificent stallion, the horse was barrel-chested, all sinew and muscle, standing fifteen hands high. His color was blood bay, with black mane and tail, and his hide glistened in the sun like dark blood on polished redwood. She held him to a canter, and he moved with the pride of power, hooves scarcely touching the earth. His nostrils were flared, testing the wind.

Elizabeth reined to a halt before the stables. She glanced at Ryan as he walked forward, and her cheeks seemed to flush even more. Her eyes were curiously impersonal, and she avoided looking directly at him. With casual grace, she dismounted by herself and waited, reins in hand. Ryan tipped his hat, forced himself to smile.

"I admire your taste in horses."

"Thank you," Elizabeth said, not returning his smile. "When did you arrive?"

"A little while ago," Ryan lied. "I had business with your father."

"You're quite the messenger these days."

Her tone stung. There was an edge to her voice just short of sarcasm. Ryan knew he was being rebuffed, and he wasn't sure how to handle it. He tried another smile.

"Truth is, I've been upgraded to negotiator. Stevens sent me down to work out delivery on railroad ties."

"What a shame."

"Beg your pardon?"

"A shame that your construction crews are at work again. We'd hoped the rains would last longer."

"Any more rain and we'd be taking boats, not trains."

"Given the choice, I would much prefer a boat. But then, Cherokees aren't allowed a choice, are they?"

Ryan was saved from a reply. A stable boy hurried outside, and Elizabeth tossed him the reins. The stallion rolled his eyes, prancing sideways, then allowed himself to be led away. An awkward silence was punctured by the thud of his hooves on the stable floor.

"I was thinking—" Ryan stopped and began over. "There's something I'd like to explain to you."

"You owe me no explanation."

"Your father said the same thing. But he wasn't mad at me."

"Nor am I," she said coolly. "I think 'disgust' would be the better term."

"Well, you call it what you want. All I'm trying to do is tell you my side of the story."

"Would it really make a difference?"

"It might," Ryan said earnestly. "You've got nothing to lose by listening."

Elizabeth studied him a moment. "All right," she said. "You can walk me up to the house. I'll listen until we're there."

Ryan fell in beside her. He felt tongue-tied, almost at a loss for words in the face of her anger. But it was a short walk, and he had a lot of explaining to do. He cleared his throat, made a start.

"You blame me for killing the boy, don't you?"

"Should I blame someone else?"

"How about his father?"

She glanced at him, aghast. "You're not serious!"

"Why not?" Ryan countered. "He brought the boy there and he killed a man practically over nothing. The way I look at it, he put the boy in harm's way."

"And that absolves you?"

"No, it doesn't. But it makes it easier to understand what happened."

"What happened requires no understanding. You were simply doing your job, weren't you?"

"Yeah, I was," Ryan said defensively.

"And your job requires you to kill"—her voice dropped, suddenly harsh—"to kill even children."

"Have you asked yourself why?"

"It doesn't matter."

"You're wrong there," Ryan said hotly. "That boy was just about man-size. He had a gun in his hand, and he tried to kill me. He fired first!"

"What did you expect?" she demanded. "He'd just seen you kill his father."

"Who also tried to shoot me!"

"And there was no way to stop him? No way to avoid killing him?"

"None," Ryan said. "He made his play and I had no choice."

"Oh?" Her voice was icy. "Does that mean you chose to kill the boy too?"

"Hell, yes!" Ryan growled. "What was I supposed to do—let him kill me?"

"Why, of course not. That would spoil your record, wouldn't it?"

"What record?"

"Come now, John, don't be modest. I understand you've killed four Cherokees since going to work for the railroad. Or does father and son make it six?"

Ryan gave her a quick, guarded look. "Who told you that?"

"No one you know," she said matter-of-factly. "It's just a rumor I've heard now and again. I hadn't put any faith in it—before."

"But you do now?"

"Yes," she said, staring straight ahead. "I believe every word of it."

"Then I reckon it doesn't matter what I say. You've already got your mind made up."

She stopped abruptly. Her eyes blazing, she turned on him, forcing him to pull up short. Her voice was tinged with scorn.

"You lied to me, John! The first time we met, you told me you would quit the railroad if it meant policing Indians. Do you remember saying that?"

"Sure I remember, and nothing's changed. I'm not policing Indians."

"Oh, but isn't that a fine distinction. You just kill them, is that it?"

"I kill anyone who tries to kill me. And I don't make excuses for it."

Ryan left her standing there. He strode off toward the stables, calling for his horse. She watched after him a moment, murmuring a low, indelicate curse. Then, slowly, her eyes misted with tears.

She turned and fled into the house.

Some three weeks later the bridge was completed over White Oak Creek. Tom Scullin drove the work gangs relentlessly, starting at dawn the next day. By sundown track had been laid south of the bridge onto a broad expanse of prairie.

Waiting there was Elias Boudinot's town site. Almost two square miles had been fenced off with posts and rough-sawn lumber. Under Cherokee law an individual could claim as much land as he was able to fence and improve. Technically, it was designated his homestead, but there was no limitation on the amount of acreage one man could claim. The law, enacted in a simpler time, had been designed for farmers.

As a Cherokee national, Boudinot was entirely within his rights. The stretch of prairie was situated on unoccupied tribal lands, and his claim, though hardly qualifying as a homestead, was valid. Still, if he had not violated the letter of the law, he had cleverly twisted it in spirit. A sign nailed to a tree identified the site as the town of Vinita. Boudinot had named it after a talented white sculptress who was rumored to be his paramour in distant Washington.

By no small coincidence, the Atlantic and Pacific survey line crossed west to east at this exact spot. While the rival railway was still twenty-five miles short of the juncture, Stevens had taken no chances. He pushed Scullin to span White Oak Creek and thereby disrupt his only competitor. Boudinot's massive land grab was the icing on the cake, a shrewd and well-orchestrated move. The Atlantic and Pacific would lose a month or more surveying a route around the town site.

Katy representatives had already fanned out through Texas. They carried the message that recently erected loading pens would cut the trail time to railhead by several days. With a bridge over White Oak Creek, the new town site was now being touted as a trade center. Overland freighters, engaged to haul from end-of-track southward, were standing by for the first run into Texas. There the trade goods would be exchanged for cotton and hides and brought back for transshipment to eastern markets. Vinita was already a bright new dot on the map and hardly a day old.

By the second day the town site had assumed a bustling look of permanence. The sporting crowd deserted their shanties up the line and moved bag and baggage to the new railhead. With them came the drifters and the outlaws, a creaking caravan of overland freighters, and the girls who populated Poonville. A tent town sprang up south of White Oak Creek overnight, and it was larger than anything yet seen. Boudinot, for cash in hand, rented lots previously laid out to accommodate the invasion. By nightfall, Vinita was a white settlement deep in the Cherokee Nation.

The existence of a town site had been common knowledge for almost two weeks. Enclosing two thousand acres with sturdy fence had attracted considerable attention. While the work was under way Boudinot had been closely guarded by a squad of Southern Party supporters. Establishment of a town populated with whites left no doubt that he'd cast his lot with the railroad. Opposing forces on the Cherokee council would view it as the supreme betrayal, and another assassination attempt seemed a virtual certainty. He was guarded day and night.

As dusk fell, Boudinot and his followers approached Stevens' private car. Ryan was already stationed there, summoned earlier by Stevens. His orders were to oversee security while Boudinot took supper with the railroader. The dinner was something of a celebration, marking the Katy's first major railhead in Indian Territory. Stevens was determined that the evening would not be marred by unpleasant incident.

Boudinot's followers were already familiar with Ryan. As the man who had saved Boudinot's life, he was something of a celebrity in the Southern Party. Once Boudinot was safely inside, Ryan began posting the men around the car. He stationed them at intervals of ten feet and assigned men to both the front and back doors. Armed with rifles, they were alert and clearly intent on keeping their leader alive. So far as Ryan was concerned, the greater threat was to railroad workers. Anyone who approached the car in the dark risked being shot to ribbons.

The evening progressed without mishap. Sally Palmer joined Stevens and Boudinot and champagne was served. Stevens proposed a toast and they all drank to continued good fortune. At the dinner table there were more toasts, and the conversation was frequently punctuated by laughter. Boudinot, who was something of an actor, treated Sally with the courtly air normally reserved for a lady. She thrived on the attention and failed to notice Stevens' smile.

Outside Ryan could see them through the windows. As the champagne flowed and their laughter grew louder, he wondered if the celebration was premature. Boudinot, who was under a sentence of death, might never live to enjoy his new prosperity. And for all the toasting, Stevens' problems had only just begun. Hostile Cherokees who were willing to kill to protect their land would stop at nothing to halt the railroad. All things considered, the laughter had a false ring to Ryan.

It occurred to him that there would be no celebration in Tahlequah tonight. Elizabeth would no doubt blame him, at least in part, for the new town site. As for William Ross, there was no question that today's events would provoke some sort of drastic action. In Ryan's view it wasn't a matter of whether or not the tribal leader would retaliate. It was only a matter of time and opportunity.

And where it would hurt Stevens most.

CHAPTER
THIRTEEN

"Good evening, John."

"Evening, Elizabeth."

Ryan removed his hat and stepped past a servant into the vestibule. Elizabeth stood framed in the doorway of the parlor, hands clasped at her waist. There was an awkward pause as the servant disappeared down the hallway. Then, hat in hand, Ryan crossed the vestibule.

"Sorry for the late hour," he said. "But I need to see your father."

"Doesn't everyone," she replied. "Half the tribal council will be here before the night's out."

"I take it you've heard about Vinita?"

"Yes, of course," she said in a normal voice. "Mr. Boudinot's town site could hardly be called a secret."

"How'd your father take it?"

"Aren't you here to ask him yourself?"

"More or less," Ryan admitted. "Word's out the council went into session today. We're hoping nobody decides to act in haste."

"So you're here with another message, is that it?"

"Yeah, I guess you could say that."

She smiled coolly. "How valuable you've become. Colonel Stevens' eyes and ears in the Indian camp."

Ryan silently conceded the point. Not quite two weeks

ago, Stevens and Boudinot had celebrated establishment of the new town site. Since then, the Cherokees had been curiously silent. The track laying went ahead, pushing southward, unmarred by incident or threat. And as yet, no attempt had been made on Elias Boudinot's life.

Then, for no apparent reason, the Cherokee council had been called into session. Earlier in the day, upon hearing the news Stevens had summoned Ryan. Ordered once again to Tahlequah, Ryan had declared it a fool's errand. Still, even as he voiced the objection, he'd known it was a waste of breath. He was being sent not as a peacemaker or with any thought of arranging a truce. He was instead exactly what Elizabeth had termed him: the railroad's eyes and ears. He'd been sent there to gather information.

Now, in the face of her cool anger, he sought another topic of conversation. He wondered what he might say that would restore things between them. At their last meeting she had rebuffed him, severed the relationship. Unless he won her over tonight, he doubted that there would be another chance. Yet for all his resolve, he knew she would not be persuaded easily. She considered him inseparable from the railroad and therefore guilty by association. He saw no simple way around the argument. It was in large measure the truth.

Elizabeth led him into the parlor. Her attitude was polite but distant. She explained that her father was still conferring with council members after spending a day at the Cherokee capital. When, or if, he would be able to see Ryan was open to question. Major David Tappin was expected at any moment.

Once seated, Ryan attempted to steer her onto another subject. He asked about her blood-bay stallion and got a monosyllabic answer. Then, still searching for neutral ground, he inquired as to the source of her father's thoroughbred saddle stock. Her reaction convinced him that it was a futile effort. She stiffened, and her tone was unmistakably crisp.

"You needn't make small talk for my benefit. It won't change anything."

Ryan tried to gauge her mood. "I gather," he said after a moment, "you still hold me responsible for that last shooting."

She averted her eyes. "Why go into it again? We've said all there was to say."

"Maybe so," Ryan said quietly. "But I'd like to think there are other things we could talk about."

"Apart from the railroad, you mean? No, I think not, John. Not anymore."

"Why?" Ryan demanded. "Nothing's any different than the first couple of times I came here."

"I'm different." Her eyes were dark and strangely tormented. "At first I forgot who I was. Who you are."

"And who am I?"

"A *tibo*." Her voice was tinged with sadness. "A white man who works for the railroad."

Ryan gave her a searching look. "Does that make me your enemy? No allowances for anything else?"

Her eyes widened. "Are you so naive? You must know what Stevens and Boudinot intend."

"Nobody's confided in me just yet."

"How convenient! Does that somehow excuse you?"

"Excuse me of what?"

"Working against my father," she said fiercely. "Isn't it obvious that Stevens wants to undermine him—force his resignation?"

"To what purpose?" Ryan pressed her. "Stevens will get his railroad no matter what."

"Perhaps he will," she acknowledged. "But wouldn't it be easier—and quicker—if my father were no longer chief? Or president of the Intertribal Council?"

"You're serious, aren't you? You think Stevens has concocted some elaborate scheme."

"I think he wants Elias Boudinot in—and my father out!"

"Just to speed up the railroad?"

"No!" She spat the word at him. "The railroad is only

a means to an end. The end of the Cherokee Nation! Why won't you see that?''

''And you think Boudinot's the man to get the job done?''

''Why else would he organize a town site? He's forced the issue and ridiculed my father. Forced my father to act!''

Ryan shook his head indulgently. ''Maybe Boudinot just wants to get rich. It's not all that odd a motive.''

''Do you honestly believe that?''

''I think it's as believable as your version. Stevens just doesn't need a conspiracy like that. Not to build a railroad.''

Her voice was barely audible. ''Won't you feel foolish when you finally learn the truth.''

Elizabeth rose and walked from the room. Staring after her, Ryan realized she'd taken with her the last word. She'd spoken a truth, her truth.

And challenged him to prove it false.

William Ross received him in the study. Upon entering, Ryan was struck by the older man's look of exhaustion. He thought Ross appeared to have aged ten years in the past weeks.

There was no warmth in Ross' greeting. He nodded grimly and motioned Ryan to a chair. Without a word he proceeded to stuff his pipe with tobacco. Then, over the flare of a match, he puffed away for a few moments.

''Forgive me,'' he said eventually, ''but I haven't much time. I'm expecting someone.''

''Elizabeth told me.''

''Then perhaps you won't mind being brief. It's been a long day.''

''And a longer night,'' Ryan said pleasantly. ''From the looks of it, you've still got a ways to go.''

Ross ignored the comment. ''What brings you here at such a late hour?''

''I have a message from Stevens.''

''Do you, indeed?''

The words were spoken around quick spurts of smoke. Puffing furiously, Ross ground the pipe stem between his teeth. His eyes were rimmed with fatigue, but his fiery look indicated he was struggling to control his temper. At last, almost wreathed in smoke, he pulled the pipe from his mouth.

"Very well," he said. "What's the message?"

"Stevens got wind that you called the council into session."

"I made no particular secret of it."

"All the same," Ryan went on, "he's worried you might do something hasty. He thinks it would be to everyone's benefit to arrange a meeting."

"A meeting?"

"Just between you and him. The sooner the better. Wherever you say would suit him fine."

"How accommodating!" Ross snorted. "And what does he suggest we discuss at this meeting?"

"He wants to work out a compromise of some sort."

Ross peered at him owlishly. "I once heard the definition of a white man's compromise."

"Oh?" Ryan said. "What's that?"

"A compromise is when both parties to an agreement feel equally buggered."

Ryan was visibly startled. The crude language was somehow at odds with the man. He thought it revealing that the Cherokee leader, who was normally so dignified, had resorted to a gutter phrase, Whether intentional or not, it indicated the degree of Ross' anger.

"The point being," Ross continued, "a compromise is out of the question. Anything Stevens suggests would not be in the best interests of my people."

"No harm in listening," Ryan insisted. "All it could cost you is a little time."

"Offer declined," Ross said firmly. "Although I will give Stevens credit for audacity. To suggest a compromise after conniving on Boudinot's town site . . ." He paused, shook his head. "Well, you must admit, it takes a certain amount of gall."

"No argument there."

"Shall we move on, then?"

"Beg your pardon?"

"To your next question," Ross chided him. "Stevens wouldn't have sent you all this way merely to request a meeting. What else does he want to know?"

"Now that you mention it"—Ryan smiled, clearly embarrassed—"he told me to find out why you ordered the council into session."

Ross gave him a thoughtful stare. "I suppose it's no real secret. I've asked the council to consider measures which might impede construction of the railroad."

"Impede?" Ryan repeated quizzically. "Are you talking about delaying construction or stopping it?"

"The council has its share of hotheads. They advocate stopping the railroad by whatever means necessary."

"And you?"

"I prefer a more businesslike approach."

"Anything you can talk about?"

"Of course," Ross said easily. "By tomorrow it will be common knowledge anyhow. I intend to raise the tax on cattle to a dollar a head."

Ryan inclined his head in a faint nod. "Won't the other tribes tend to follow suit and raise their taxes?"

"I wouldn't be at all surprised."

"Which means the Texans will go right on trailing to Abilene. Why pay a high tariff just to ship your cows with the Katy?"

"If I were a Texan, I would ask myself that very question."

"Stevens won't like it," Ryan noted. "He's counting on the cattle trade as a source of funds."

"Tell him he'll have to look elsewhere."

"You really think that'll put a crimp in his plans?"

"If it doesn't," Ross said, "then I'll think of something else."

"All right," Ryan said, rising to his feet. "I'll deliver the message."

"One other thing, John."

Ross carefully laid his pipe in an ashtray. He folded his

hands on the desktop, staring down as though hesitant to continue. Finally he looked up at Ryan.

"This will be our last visit. I regret to say, you're no longer welcome here."

"Listen, I know Elizabeth—"

"Let me finish," Ross interrupted. "It has nothing to do with Elizabeth. You'll recall I mentioned certain hotheads in the council."

"Yes?"

"Some of them believe I've aided the railroad by my— association with you."

Ryan laughed. "That's pretty farfetched."

"Nonetheless," Ross informed him, "the charge has been made. If I'm to govern effectively, then I've no choice but to put such allegations to rest. I hope you understand."

"Keep the *tibo* at arm's length. Isn't that the gist of it?"

"Yes, it is." Ross smiled ruefully. "A practical man sometimes has to bend before the political wind. I'm genuinely sorry."

Ryan accepted his handshake. Then, aware that there was nothing left to say, he walked to the door. Outside, still somewhat dazed, he proceeded along the hallway. It occurred to him that Elizabeth must have known of her father's decision. And yet in their earlier conversation she'd said nothing. He wondered why.

As he crossed the vestibule, a servant hurried to open the door. Then, abruptly, he stopped short. Major Tappin stepped through the entryway, removing his hat and handing it to the servant. He gave Ryan a jaundiced look.

"We meet again, Mr. Ryan."

"Just passing through, Major."

"Good. I'm pleased to hear it."

Ryan started around him, then turned back. "What's that supposed to mean?"

"I'd think it's obvious. After all, *I* am a peace officer, Mr. Ryan."

"I still don't get your drift."

"Tell me," Tappin said, watching him with undisguised hostility, "killed anyone lately?"

For what seemed a sliver of eternity, their eyes locked. Then, his expression murderous, Ryan took a grip on his temper. Only a fool allowed himself to be baited on ground of another man's choosing. And Tappin was clearly trying to bait him.

He smiled and stepped through the open door.

CHAPTER
FOURTEEN

By the middle of June, end-of-track had progressed to within a few miles of Pryor's Creek. The winding tributary lay fifty miles south of the Kansas border, and halfway to Fort Gibson.

The summer heat cloaked the land like a shroud. Track laying, even in the early morning hours, became a grueling and sometimes maddening business. Swarms of flies and mosquitoes fed on the work gangs with a ravenous appetite for blood. Heat and festering insect bites slowed construction to a torturous pace.

Approaching Pryor's Creek, the survey line had been laid three miles west of the Texas Road. The purpose was to avoid an irregular stretch of hilly terrain, and thereby speed construction. Yet the Irish Brigade was forced to slash their way through dense canebrakes, with the ground underfoot like muddy, jungle sloughs. What had originally seemed a good plan gradually evolved into a nightmare of agonizing labor. Everyone cursed the survey crew and the mosquitoes alike.

With all their other problems, the work gangs gave little thought to the Indians. Hardly a day passed without a party of Cherokee horsemen being spotted on a distant hill. But the riders never lingered, and the nearest village was ten miles to the east, on the banks of the Neosho River. Out of sight was out of mind, and the beleaguered workmen ceased to think of the Indians as a threat. The swampy bottomland and a sorching sun became the enemy.

Still, for all the construction delays Robert Stevens was very much aware of the Cherokees. He convened a war council on a muggy evening, not long after Ryan's meeting with Ross. The section chiefs, led by Tom Scullin, trooped into the private car and took seats. Ryan, who had returned from Tahlequah that afternoon, was the last to arrive. He'd made his report earlier, and he already knew that Stevens was in a foul mood. He stood by the door, separating himself from the others.

Stevens waited until the men were settled. Then, in a carefully measured voice he related the details of Ryan's meeting with William Ross. He paused and allowed the news to percolate a few moments. Finally, when no one spoke up, he went on in a somewhat harsher tone.

"The bastard intends to cripple us financially. A dollar a head would sound like a death knell to the Texans."

Scullin cleared his throat. "You think we'd lose the cattle trade, is that it?"

"Hell, yes!" Stevens said roughly. "The other tribes play monkey see, monkey do with the Cherokees. Before it was over, every cow would be taxed three dollars—maybe more!"

Scullin swapped a look with Otis Gunn. The engineer glumly shook his head, obviously disturbed. His gaze shifted to Stevens.

"Is there any way we could reason with Ross? Maybe he could be persuaded to withdraw this plan."

Stevens gestured toward the rear of the room. "How about it, John? You're the one who spoke with Ross. Will reason work?"

The other men turned in their chairs. Ryan stared back at them and was all too aware that he'd been put on the spot. He was also aware of the answer Stevens expected. Yet he saw nothing to be gained by hedging.

"No," he said levelly. "You could talk yourself blue in

the face, and it wouldn't matter. Ross won't budge.''

Stevens arched one eyebrow. "While you're at it, give the boys the benefit of your thinking. How far would Ross go to stop us?''

Ryan's face was impassive. He wrestled with himself a moment, then shrugged. "I think he'll go the limit. Whatever it takes, that's what he'll do.''

"Thank you, John.''

Stevens took a furled map off a nearby table. Holding it overhead, he stopped before the seated men. His mouth curled in an odd smile as he let the map drop open. In the lamplight was revealed a large-scale rendering of the Cherokee Nation.

"Here's how we deal with William Ross!''

Tracing an inked line on the map, Stevens' smile turned to a smug grin. His finger skirted Tahlequah, then leaped past Fort Gibson to the Arkansas River. His eyes blazed with excitement.

"We're going to bypass Ross and his damned Cherokees! We'll lay track on a beeline to the Creek Nation.''

"God's blood!'' Scullin protested. "Are you sayin' you mean to bypass Fort Gibson?''

The question claimed everyone's attention like a clap of thunder. Fort Gibson, apart from being a key military post, was the only white settlement in the Cherokee Nation. To bypass it seemed unthinkable, perhaps impossible.

Stevens uttered a low, gloating laugh. "We'll leave the Cherokees high and dry. Their one and only railhead will be Boudinot's town site—Vinita!''

"Jesus,'' Scullin muttered. "I'd think the army might take a different view. They'll not appreciate being tossed aside so lightly.''

"I intend to discuss that very thing with General Sherman.''

Stevens grinned and stuck his thumbs in his vest. The men stared at him with a look normally reserved for sword swallowers and magicians. At length Scullin managed to recover his voice.

"And where would you be seein' the General?"

"Fort Gibson," Stevens said. "He arrived yesterday."

"Well now, that is a piece of news. Do you think he'll actually go for your idea?"

"What I intend to propose will be to everyone's benefit, including the Army. I think General Sherman will approve it quite readily."

At the rear of the room, Ryan looked on with a grudging sense of admiration. He thought Stevens had all the moral scruples of a hungry spider. Yet there was no denying the man's cunning and his commitment to a vision. The railroad would be built despite all obstacles. There was simply no stopping it.

Still, the irony of the situation was not lost on Ryan. Bypassing Fort Gibson might well be viewed as a mixed blessing. For William Ross and his supporters were about to see a dream partially realized.

The Katy would make only one stop in the Cherokee Nation.

At dawn Stevens and Ryan departed for Fort Gibson. They traveled by horseback, and their route generally followed the Texas Road. Ryan, as he had before, acted as bodyguard and guide. He rode with his shotgun laid across the saddle.

Stevens was in a talkative mood. He dwelled at length on a plan he'd formulated overnight. At Three Forks, where the major rivers of Indian Territory converged, he would build a sprawling railhead. There, without interference from the Cherokees, he would construct as well a vast complex of shipping pens. All of which placed him even closer to the Texans and their herds of longhorns. The cattle trade would still fall to the Katy, although a bit later than he'd calculated. In so many words he congratulated himself on turning adversity to advantage.

Ryan marked again the voice of an ambitious man. He'd always considered such men to possess an equal mix of arrogance and pride. He understood them as well as their motives. Ryan realized that to a lesser degree he had many of the same traits. He took pride in his work, prided himself on being better at it than most men. And there was a certain arrogance involved when he bet his life that he could out-wit—or outshoot—robbers and killers.

Ryan was disturbed by these similarities. Yet in the end he believed there was an essential difference between himself and Robert Stevens. He was content with the respect of other men and the satisfaction of a job well-done. Stevens was driven to build empires and would never know contentment. His reach would forever exceed his grasp.

They rode into Fort Gibson just before sundown. Several such garrisons, built following the Civil War, were scattered across Indian Territory. Part of a containment strategy, the purpose of these outposts was to hold hostiles such as the Kiowas and Comanches within established boundaries. Gen-erally manned by cavalry with supportive infantry units, the forts were crude wilderness bastions. No one lived well, or comfortably, serving on the frontier.

General of the Army William Tecumseh Sherman had ap-propriated the post commander's office. An aide-de-camp ushered Stevens and Ryan through the door with starchy for-mality. Sherman rose and came around the desk, his hand outstretched. He and Stevens traveled the same circles in Washington and neither of them was a stranger to the White House. Their handshake was cordial, almost fraternal.

Watching them, Ryan's first impression of the General was one of surprise. Sherman was a stocky bulldog of a man, rather short in stature. His face was square and pugnacious, covered by a wiry beard, and there was a rocklike simplicity in his manner. His badly fitting tunic gave him a curiously unmilitary appearance. Yet his piercing eyes and command-ing presence left little doubt as to who or what he was.

The Plains Tribes called him the Great Warrior Sherman and the sobriquet aptly suited the man. Sherman had led the legendary Union march through Georgia, which split the Confederacy and hastened the end of the Civil War. His peacetime command was at first the Division of the Missouri, which embraced the Great Plains. Then he had been appointed General of the Army and ordered to "pacify" the hostile tribes. Blunt and brutally practical, his instructions to his cavalry commanders were typical of the man. "The more Indians we kill this year, the less will have to be killed the next. . . ."

The Bureau of Indian Affairs branded his policies as genocide. Sherman simply labeled the bureaucrats "rosewater dreamers" and went about his business with total indifference to public opinion. Sherman argued that the Army's duty was to protect American citizens and not nomadic savages. The current U.S. President and Sherman's former commander, Ulysses S. Grant, sympathized with the view. Sherman operated with the ruthless tactics of a soldier bent on destroying an enemy army.

Sherman's fame had only recently gone up another notch. A band of Kiowas and Comanches had gone on a bloody rampage through Texas, and Sherman had assumed personal command of their pursuit and capture. The upshot was several dead Indians, and their leaders sentenced to life in prison. Wholly in character, Sherman had urged that the leaders be hanged in the most expeditious manner. Afterward, he'd undertaken a tour of frontier outposts which brought him to Fort Gibson.

Intrigued by the General, Ryan was a rapt observer as the discussion got under way. It occurred to him that Sherman and Stevens were very much birds of a feather. Both men were obsessed by their own visions of the future, and their ambition, by any yardstick, was remarkable. Moreover, they shared a mutual trait that bonded them like brothers. Their contempt for Indians was absolute and immutable.

As the conversation progressed, Ryan sensed that Stevens was employing verbal sleight of hand. The railroader first recounted all his previous difficulties with the Cherokees. Then he elaborated on William Ross' latest ploy to undermine the Katy. From there, he raised the specter of what would happen if the Katy folded and the Five Civilized Tribes prevailed. He underscored the logistical threat to the Army if rails could not be laid through Indian Territory and on into Texas. On that patriotic note, he concluded, awaiting a reaction.

Sherman gave him a hard, wise look. "You've made your case, Bob. Suppose you tell me what it is you want—specifically?"

"For several reasons," Stevens said forcefully, "I want your permission to bypass Fort Gibson."

"Forget several," Sherman growled. "Give me *one* good reason."

Stevens leaned forward, very earnest now. "The Cherokees are the greatest single threat to western settlement. William Ross, by his high-handed manner, sets a bad example for all tribes. And it's an example that breeds resistance and encourages hostility. He has to be stopped!"

"Not a bad argument," Sherman said slowly. "A bit overstated but still fairly believable. So how do I justify bypassing one of my key forts? How does that put the quietus on Ross?"

"It bypasses him!" Stevens said triumphantly. "We leave Ross and his Cherokees to wither on the vine. No railheads, no towns, no money pouring in! The other tribes will see the light soon enough."

Sherman mulled it over a moment. When he finally spoke, his tone was calculating and military. "How would you adjust the survey line? Keep in mind it has to be done with no detriment to the Army. We're still a long way from pacifying the hostiles."

Stevens popped out of his chair. He moved to a large operations map mounted on the wall. With his finger he traced a line from the present end-of-track to a stretch of high ground situated above Three Forks. He rapped the spot with his knuckles.

"There!" he thundered. "On that spot I'll build you a railhead and supply depot bigger than you ever imagined. We'll centralize all military shipments"—his finger skipped westward on the map—"supplying Fort Sill as well as the Texas posts. It will be the hub of military operations!"

Sherman's eyes crinkled with what passed for a smile.

"By jingo!" he said. "That's a sound plan. You've just cut my logistics problem by half."

"Then you'll approve the new survey line?"

"Well"—Sherman hesitated, gave him a conspiratorial look—"one of my commanders won't be too happy. What you're proposing pretty much consigns Fort Gibson to the ash heap."

"And the Cherokee Nation!" Stevens added with vine-gary satisfaction. "William Ross will have no more influence than a toadstool. He'll be silenced!"

"So he will," Sherman agreed. "All right, Bob, get to it. I approve."

Ryan knew he'd just witnessed a turning point in the rail-road's fortunes. His thought was borne out not quite two weeks later. On June 28, with the bridge completed, track was laid over Pryor's Creek. The drive was on to the Creek Nation.

Looking back, Ryan was no less impressed by the meeting with Sherman. Yet even as the rails extended southward, a vestige of doubt still remained. Stevens' words had seemed too optimistic, almost overconfident. Ryan was certain that they hadn't heard the last of William Ross.

Or the Cherokee assassins.

CHAPTER
FIFTEEN

Ryan was bored. To him, idleness was all but intolerable, and there suddenly seemed no need for the services of a special agent. He found himself with time on his hands.

One reason was the relative quiet that had settled over the Cherokees. By imposing a stiffer cattle tax, William Ross had apparently stilled his opposition. The tribal council, after approving the measure, appeared to be awaiting some countermove by the railroad. As yet, of course, no one knew of the decision to bypass Fort Gibson. The Cherokees were sure to retaliate in some fashion when it became public knowledge. But for now neither side seemed in a rush to provoke the other.

Apart from the Cherokees, there was still another reason for the period of calm. The work gangs were now laying track seven days a week. There had been no respite and therefore no opportunity for a tent town to spring up around end-of-track. As a result the sporting crowd hadn't moved forward from Vinita. The absence of whiskey and whores in particular seemed to have put a damper on violence. After dark the railroad camp was quiet as a church, and almost as peaceful. No one had the time, or the energy, to hunt trouble.

For Ryan it was sheer tedium. He tried to stay busy by following a normal routine. Morning and afternoon he scouted ahead of the track-laying crews but found nothing to report. He silently prowled the camp at night but was aware that the effort was largely wasted. With time to spare his thoughts dwelled more and more on Elizabeth and her distant attitude. He brooded on the obstacles separating them and gradually worked himself into a disgruntled state of mind. His temper grew even shorter when he was forced to admit an uncomfortable truth. However hard he tried, he was unable to forget her.

A reprieve of sorts came three days after track had been laid across Pryor's Creek. Stevens sent for him shortly before suppertime. He found a meeting underway at the private car. Otis Gunn, the chief engineer, and George Walker, head of the survey crew, were huddled around a map with Stevens.

Sally Palmer intercepted him as he entered. She was wearing a low-cut gown that was almost an exact match for her china-blue eyes. Unwittingly, she put a hand to her hair, patting a stray curl. It occurred to him that her vanity was curiously inward. She resembled a cat admiring itself in a mirror. She smiled and offered him a drink, and he was aware that he'd arrived sooner than expected. She was attempting to distract him until the meeting ended. He politely declined the drink.

Looking around, Stevens rather abruptly ended the meeting. He rolled up the map and turned from the table with the other two men. Gunn and Walker seated themselves, and Stevens motioned Ryan forward. His manner seemed almost jolly.

"Evening, John," he said, smiling. "Hope I didn't pull you away from supper."

"It'll keep till later."

"Good. Have a seat, join us."

Ryan lowered himself into an armchair. Gunn and Walker bobbed their heads in greeting, all smiles. Some inner voice warned him that things were not as they appeared. The pleasantries and the smiles, particularly on Stevens' part, were overdone. There was a strong scent of snake oil in the air.

"I need your help," Stevens went on. "You're familiar with Colbert's Ferry, aren't you?"

"I've been there," Ryan acknowledged.

"Are you acquainted with Ben Colbert?"

"Only in passing."

"What does that mean?"

"Couple of years ago I was on the trail of a whiskey smuggler. I stopped overnight at Colbert's place."

"Did he know you were a marshal?"

Ryan shook his head. "I never went out of my way to advertise the fact. Indians tend to get closemouthed when they know they're talking to the law."

"So it's true, then?" Stevens asked. "Colbert really is part Chickasaw?"

"No, not part," Ryan said. "He's a full-blood."

The Chickasaw Nation lay at the extreme southwestern boundary of Indian Territory. Ben Colbert was something of a backwoods businessman who operated a ferry across the Red River. Apart from natural fords, it was the only way back and forth between Texas and the Nations. Colbert's name was known all along the frontier.

"Since you've met him," Stevens continued, "let me ask your opinion. Would you consider him a shrewd trader?"

"Hard to say," Ryan allowed. "I only met him the one time."

"Is he an educated Indian?"

"Not to hear him talk."

"Do you think he'd remember you?"

"Probably not. Lots of people pass through there every day."

"I see."

Stevens exchanged a look with Gunn and Walker. Then, still smiling, he glanced back at Ryan.

"I'm sending Otis down to have a talk with Colbert. I'd like you to act as his guide."

"We've had this conversation before."

"I know," Stevens conceded. "But for the most part you'll be traveling outside the Cherokee Nation. There shouldn't be any trouble this time."

"I seem to recall that's what you said last time. And I ended up killing two men."

"Which we all regret," Stevens said with exaggerated gravity. "Suppose I threw in a bonus—say five hundred dollars. Would that change your mind?"

"Why so much," Ryan said skeptically, "if you're not expecting trouble?"

"To insure your discretion. You and Otis will be traveling incognito."

"You'll have to spell that out."

"For the time being, we want Colbert kept in the dark. There's to be no mention of your association with the railroad."

"Why not?"

"Everything will become obvious once you're at Colbert's Ferry. Until then, let's just say it's privileged information."

Stevens paused, nodding to himself with a cryptic smile. Ryan was confused, but he'd long since ceased being surprised by the railroader's convoluted schemes. The man was like a Chinese box, a puzzle within a puzzle.

"Trust me for now," Stevens insisted. "You won't regret it. You have my word."

Ryan shifted his gaze to Otis Gunn. He stared hard at the engineer a moment. "How about it, Otis?" he said at length. "Any chance I'll regret it?"

"Not on my account," Gunn said with a weak smile. "We're going there to talk, nothing more."

Ryan mulled it over awhile. Then, finally, he shrugged. "All right," he said. "I could use a change of scenery anyway."

"Excellent!" Stevens said, grinning. "I knew you wouldn't let me down, John."

Sally Palmer walked forward, joining the men. She caught Ryan's eye for an instant, looked quickly away. There was a trace of amusement hidden in her expression. And that, more than anything else, bothered Ryan.

He wondered if he'd been snookered again.

* * *

The water appeared dark against the washed blue of a plains sky. A massive ferryboat stood docked on the north bank of the river. Above it, dotting the shoreline, were the outbuildings of Colbert's Ferry.

Ryan, with Otis Gunn at his side, rode into the compound about midafternoon. Their trip had consumed four days, traversing the lands of the Creeks, Choctaws, and Chickasaws. The Texas Road, which angled southwestward through the Nations, brought them directly to the ferry landing. On the opposite side the Texas shoreline provided a backdrop for the Red River.

Grimy with trail dust, Ryan and Gunn passed themselves off as butt-sore travelers. They found Ben Colbert on the porch of the main house. He was a grizzled character, with a broad, good-humored face and a shock of white hair. His jaw was stuffed with tobacco and a quart of whiskey rested beside his chair. He informed them that he was now a man of leisure and the overseer of the operation. A gaggle of relatives attended to running the ferry.

Gunn engaged the old man in conversation. With little prompting, Colbert drifted off into a recollection of days past. In 1858, with hardly a nickel to his name, he'd obtained a tribal license to operate a ferry. At the same time he had claimed a Chickasaw head right of several hundred acres. The land included a wide stretch of river frontage and fanned out northward from his homestead.

The venture had prospered from the outset. Wagon trains loaded with heavy freight were ferried back and forth. The Butterfield Stage Line, with coaches operating between Missouri and Texas, used the ferry on a regular basis. Before long a small town appeared on the Texas side directly above the ferry landing. The inhabitants grandly named it Red River City, even though its principal commerce was the sale of rotgut whiskey. And through it all, like a link in a chain, the ferry remained the connecting tie between Texas and Indian Territory.

"Bad times or good," Colbert concluded, "everybody

needs a way across the river. I've done right well for myself over the years."

"You surely have," Gunn beamed. "Tell you the truth, I'm surprised you don't have competition. How come another ferry never got started?"

Colbert squirted a jet of tobacco juice over the edge of the porch. He wiped his mouth and let go a wheezy chuckle. "Only one license ever gonna be granted, and that's mine. I got blood kin on the Chickasaw council."

"Just the same, you have a real moneymaker here. I'd imagine lots of people have tried to buy you out."

"Not so many. Even then, most of 'em tried to steal it. Figgered me for one of them ignorant Injuns."

"Their mistake," Gunn said, his voice bland as butter. "If you'd been offered a fair price—who knows? You might very well have been tempted."

Colbert cocked his head, appraising the other man with a crafty look. "You talk like you got somethin' on your mind. Whyn't you toss 'er out and let's have a look-see?"

Gunn gave him a slow nod. "My partner and I," he said, gesturing at Ryan, "like the looks of your operation. We might just make you an offer to buy it, lock, stock, and barrel."

Colbert shifted his quid to the off cheek. "You talkin' about the land too?"

"I certainly am. We'd want the land, the house—everything."

"You're out of luck, then. A Chickasaw can't sell land to a white man. Only thing for sale is the ferryboat license."

"Not necessarily," Gunn said cautiously. "I've heard there are ways around tribal laws."

"Yeah, there are," Colbert said with a lopsided smile. "If you're willin' to marry yourself a Chickasaw woman."

"If not me," Gunn advised him, "then one of my associates. We can always find a man who's eligible and willing."

Colbert chortled out loud. "You're serious, aren't you? You come here to talk a deal!"

"I'll do more than talk, Mr. Colbert. I'm prepared to put my money where my mouth is."

Colbert turned out to be a shrewd haggler. After an hour or so of hard bargaining, they finally struck a deal. The figure agreed upon included Colbert's land, all the buildings, and the ferry. Only one item in the negotiations remained tentative. Gunn would have to arrange for a bridegroom before the deal could be finalized.

Some while later the conversation ended with a round of handshakes. Gunn and Ryan collected their horses and rode back the way they'd come. A short distance up the road, Ryan finally succumbed to curiosity. He fixed the engineer with a thoughtful stare.

"It's his land you're after and not the ferry, or did I miss something?"

"No, you're right, it's the land. The Katy certainly doesn't need a ferryboat."

"What's so important about his land?"

Gunn laughed heartily. "A small fortune, John. Some might even call it a bonanza."

As they rode, Gunn briefly explained the details. Stevens' goal was to secure large tracts of land on both sides of the river wherever the Katy crossed the Red. The arrangement would be kept secret until all the railroad's plans were completed. To that end three different survey lines would be run to the river. No one would know where the Katy actually intended to cross until it happened.

"I don't get it," Ryan said when he finished. "Why three survey lines?"

"Town sites!" Gunn announced. "We'll run one line up-river to Preston. Another will be downriver, somewhere around Sherman. And the third to Colbert's Ferry."

"Then you'll play one off against the other, Sherman against Preston, is that the idea?"

"On the button," Gunn admitted. "Whoever makes the most land available, that's where we'll cross the Red River. We intend to sell a world of town lots."

Ryan gave him the same disquieting stare. "So your offer

to Colbert wasn't legitimate. You're just hedging your bet?"

"Colbert's Ferry is our ace in the hole. If things fall through elsewhere, we've always got Colbert on tap. Not to mention Red River City."

"What about it?"

"We could buy the whole town dirt cheap—and own both sides of the river!"

"Why not do it, then?"

"We want to create a boomtown atmosphere. And that's easier done where a town already exists. Preston or Sherman, either one would do very nicely."

Ryan shook his head. "Stevens must've lost a lot of sleep figuring that out."

"Never underestimate him, John. He's as shrewd as they come."

"And tricky too."

"I beg your pardon?"

"Nothin'," Ryan said. "Just thinking out loud."

Gunn gave him a funny look. "Well anyway, we're on the verge of something great. And you're part of it, John! Just think of that."

"I am thinking. All the time."

Ryan's thoughts would have surprised Gunn. He felt no triumph in the railroad's progress, only sympathy for the old Chickasaw. One way or another, he told himself, Ben Colbert was out of business. Whether the railroad crossed at Colbert's landing or elsewhere was immaterial. Ferryboats were about to become a thing of the past. Ryan understood that Colbert's only hope was Gunn's ace in the hole: a breakdown in negotiations with all the other towns along the river, which would leave the railroad no choice but to cross at Colbert's Ferry.

Ryan silently cast his own vote for the old Chickasaw.

CHAPTER
SIXTEEN

A searing midday sun beat down on the work gangs. Graders cursed their mules while laborers wrestled railroad ties into place on the roadbed. The men's faces were streaked with a mixture of sweat and choking dust.

Ryan rode past on his horse. The morning, like so many other mornings, had been spent scouting ahead of the construction site. As he'd come to expect, there was nothing out of the ordinary, no sign of trouble. He hadn't seen a Cherokee for the last three days.

The grind of a daily routine was again starting to wear on him. Over a week had passed since his return from Colbert's Ferry. As yet, there was no clue that the railroad was slated to bypass Fort Gibson. Soon enough, however, the tracks would take a sharp turn to the southwest and angle toward Three Forks. Then, without question William Ross and the Cherokees would discover Stevens' plan.

What would happen at that point was anyone's guess. After another tedious morning, Ryan was in no mood to forecast the future. His mind turned instead to the noonday meal as he neared the supply train. He was contemplating a hot cup of coffee when he spotted Sam Irvin. The marshal stood talking with another white man whose strident voice carried up and down the roadbed. Crowded around them were a half dozen Cherokees, listening intently. All along the tracks, railway workers had paused to watch.

Several things went through Ryan's mind. He wondered what brought Irvin to end-of-track. Even more, he questioned why a deputy U.S. Marshal was traveling in the company of six dour-faced Cherokees and a white man who appeared mad with rage. He wasn't at all sure that he wanted to hear the reasons.

Approaching them, Ryan inspected the group closely. The white man was lean and rawboned, with shifty eyes and sleek, glistening hair. He wore mule-eared boots and a slouch hat, and strapped around his hip was a Remington pistol. The Cherokees were armed with an assortment of carbines and vintage muskets and appeared ready to take the warpath at any moment. Their features were taut with barely constrained anger.

Ryan dismounted, hitching his horse to the end of a flatcar. As he started forward, the marshal looked around and saw him. Irvin silenced the white man with a gesture and turned away. He hurried along the roadbed, motioning Ryan to stay back. His expression was a mix of disgust and simmering exasperation. He stopped where Ryan waited beside the flatcar.

"Howdy, John."

"Sam." Ryan nodded, cutting his eyes toward the white man. "Who's your friend?"

"Friend, hell!" Irvin grunted. "He's a shiftless no-account by the name of Bud Wilson."

"And the Cherokees?"

"They're relatives. Or maybe in-laws would be better. He was married to a Cherokee woman."

"What do you mean *was*?" Ryan inquired.

"His wife's dead," Irvin replied. "Got herself killed pretty near a week ago."

"Well," Ryan sighed heavily, "I guess I'm going to hear it anyway. So go ahead and tell me. Who killed her?"

Irvin told the story quickly, without frills. Bud Wilson and a Cherokee man, Frank Proctor, were enemies of long standing. A chance meeting in Tahlequah led to an exchange in results, and Proctor pulled a gun. In the ensuing melee, Wilson's wife was mortally wounded while Wilson himself managed to escape unharmed. Proctor was arrested by the Light Horse Police and charged with murder.

"Sounds reasonable to me," Ryan remarked when he had finished. "What's the problem?"

Irvin looked pained. "Proctor goes to court tomorrow. Word leaked out that the charges will be dropped."

"Any truth to it?"

"Who knows?" Irvin said sourly. "But if he is released, I've got a federal warrant for his arrest."

"On what charge?"

"Attempted murder."

"You're joking!"

"Wish I was," Irvin muttered, lowering his eyes. "He killed a Cherokee woman, and it rightly belongs in a Cherokee court. But if he goes free, then it falls in my jurisdiction. His intent was to murder a white man—and that's a federal crime."

Ryan was silent a moment. "How'd you get tangled up with Wilson and his in-laws?"

"Sorry bastard," Irvin swore. "He's worried Proctor will slip loose and run. He tagged along to make sure I get the job done."

"And brought reinforcements just to make double damn sure. Why was he giving you a hard time when I rode up?"

"Hold your hat," Irvin said wearily. "The sonovabitch wants me to deputize him and that bunch of Cherokees. He says I'll need a posse to get Proctor away from the Light Horse."

"You'd be a fool to deputize them."

"Christ, wouldn't I! But that won't stop them from trailing me into the courtroom tomorrow. I'm liable to have a hell of a lot more than I can handle alone."

Ryan stared at him, eyes narrowed. "I've been waiting for you to get around to it."

"Hell, John," Irvin said lamely. "I can't ride herd on

Wilson's bunch and the Light Horse and still arrest Proctor. I'm only one man.''

"Last time you asked my help, I ended up getting shot at.''

Bud Wilson suddenly took a step toward them. His features were flushed, and his voice went up a couple of octaves in an angry shout. "What d'ya say, Marshal? We're tired of coolin' our heels. Is he gonna lend a hand or not?''

Irvin groaned and rolled his eyes. He looked back over his shoulder. "Keep your shirt on, Wilson. I'll be with you in a minute.''

"Time's awastin','' Wilson said defiantly. "You let my wife's murderer get away and there'll be hell to pay. I guarantee it!''

"So you keep telling me.''

Irvin turned back to Ryan, wagging his head. Wilson and the Cherokees began talking among themselves in low monotones. Watching them, Ryan got an odd sensation about the white man. He looked at the Marshal.

"Lemme ask you something, Sam. You think Wilson's playing with all his marbles?''

"No, I don't,'' Irvin said crossly. "The man's a goddamn half-wit. Why?''

"Half-wits sometimes go off half-cocked. He's liable to start something you'll have to finish.''

"All the more reason I need your help. He'll be in that courtroom tomorrow, no matter what I say. I'd feel easier knowing you've got me covered.''

"Hell, why not?'' Ryan grinned. "I've got nothing better to do.''

"Won't cause you any problem with Colonel Stevens, will it?''

"No problem at all, Sam.''

Ryan felt as confident as he sounded. He'd come to the conclusion that Stevens needed him more than he needed the job. Which tended to switch the leverage in their dealings on to his side. The thought made him smile.

*　　*　　*

Early next morning they rode into Tahlequah. The stores were already open, and the square was crowded with people. Several paused to stare as the armed column rode past.

Marshal Irvin and Ryan, who now wore a badge, were in the lead. Behind them rode Wilson and one of his brothers-in-law. The other family members rode three abreast and two in the rear. All of the Cherokees had their long guns propped against the saddle, muzzles pointed skyward. Their bearing was that of determined men, prepared to fight.

Ryan saw a squad of Light Horse Police up ahead. There were four out front and four in the rear, with a lone civilian sandwiched between. On foot and armed with Spencer lever-action carbines, the Light Horse were escorting the civilian to the courthouse. Ryan figured the man to be Frank Proctor, the accused murderer. He also counted the Light Horse again, puzzled by their number. So many police to guard one man seemed to him a bad sign.

Ryan dismounted before a hitch rack on the street. Looking up, he saw a Light Horse with sergeant's stripes on his sleeves glance in their direction. The sergeant barked a command and hurried the squad and their prisoner up the steps and into the courthouse. A moment later the sergeant and another Light Horse returned, positioning themselves on either side of the door. Behind them, Major David Tappin stepped outside onto the landing. He stood with his hands clasped behind his back.

Irvin mumbled something unintelligible under his breath. He swapped a worried look with Ryan, then moved around the hitch rack. Ryan fell in beside him and they started up the walkway to the courthouse. Bud Wilson and the Cherokees formed a wedge immediately behind them. Passersby on the square watched curiously as the small phalanx of men trooped forward. Irvin halted them at the bottom of the steps. He nodded curtly to Tappin.

"You're blocking my way, Major."

Tappin smiled, a mere baring of his teeth. "We're in Tahlequah, not Fort Smith. What business do you have here today?"

"Frank Proctor," Irvin said. "I understand he's scheduled to appear in court."

"A Cherokee court," Tappin remarked. "On a tribal murder charge. You have no jurisdiction here."

"I do if he's released."

"Why would he be released?"

"Good question," Irvin said flatly. "But if it happens, I've got a federal warrant on him."

"And the charge?"

"Attempted murder." Irvin jerked a thumb over his shoulder. "You know Bud Wilson, don't you?"

Tappin bristled, his eyes dark as slate. "Have you any proof that the shot was meant for Wilson?"

"I only arrest people, Major. Juries decide whether or not there's enough proof."

"The juries in Fort Smith," Tappin said viciously, "always find enough proof when it's an Indian."

"You're entitled to your opinion. All the same, I've got a job to do, and I intend to do it."

"So it appears," Tappin said, indicating the other men. "Quite a show of force, Marshal. Are these your deputies?"

Irvin gave him a dull stare. "Mr. Ryan's been duly sworn. Wilson and the others asked to come along. You might say they're interested parties."

"Too interested," Tappin observed. "How do I know they won't start trouble in the courtroom?"

"It's your courtroom, Major. You're welcome to stop them from going inside."

The Light Horse sergeant stepped away from the door. His face looked as though it had been hewn from rough walnut, with an angular nose and cold, brooding eyes. His thumb was hooked over the hammer of his carbine, finger on the trigger. He stared directly at Wilson.

"Nobody moves," Ryan said with chilling calm. "Major, do yourself a favor. Call the sergeant off."

Tappin gazed down at them a moment. Then he motioned the sergeant to move back beside the door. His eyes finally settled on Ryan.

"You've chosen the wrong side again, Mr. Ryan. It seems to be a habit."

"Some habits are hard to break."

"Are you here under Colonel Stevens' directions?"

"I'm here," Ryan said through clenched teeth, "because the Marshal asked. No other reason."

Tappin's voice was alive with contempt. "Any excuse will do so long as it involves Indians. Is that it?"

"I'm here, and I'm sworn. You make what you want of it."

"One day," Tappin said ominously, "you'll regret this. You have my solemn promise on that, Mr. Ryan."

Tappin wheeled around abruptly and walked into the courthouse. The sergeant and the second Light Horse followed a pace behind. Irvin glanced at Ryan, one eyebrow raised in a questioning look. When Ryan said nothing, the Marshal proceeded up the steps. Ryan and the others trailed him through the door.

They moved along a central corridor inside the courthouse. Halfway down they turned left into the open door of the courtroom. Irvin was in the lead when he suddenly halted, his expression tense. The others crowded in behind him and were jammed together in an aisle between rows of benches. Irvin's tension was contagious, and Ryan went stockstill, his every sense alerted.

An oppressive sense of violence hung over the courtroom. There were no spectators occupying the benches, and the jury box was empty. Frank Proctor, who stood beside his lawyer at the defense table, looked terrified. The prosecutor sat at another table across from them and nervously fanned through a sheaf of papers. The Light Horse Police were spread out between the front row of benches and the defendant. They formed an armed line across the middle of the room.

At the center of the line, Major Tappin was engaged in a one-sided conversation with the Light Horse sergeant. While Tappin talked, the sergeant listened and slowly nodded his head. After a moment Tappin turned, no longer talking, and looked directly at Ryan. The sergeant followed his gaze and both men stared at Ryan. Then the sergeant's eyes became hooded, his face devoid of expression. He nodded once.

Instinct told Ryan he'd been marked for death. He watched as Tappin turned and moved through a door at the rear of the room. Several moments passed, then the door opened and a man attired in a frock coat entered. He walked straight to the judge's bench and stopped in front of a high-backed chair. His gaze shuttled around the courtroom before fixing on Sam Irvin. He glared down at the lawman.

"Marshal Irvin," he intoned, "I order you to remove yourself and those men from my court. If you refuse—"

"*No!*"

Bud Wilson's strangled scream echoed off the walls. He leaped past Irvin, his Remington six-gun extended at arm's length. The pistol roared and Proctor staggered backward into the defense table. He clutched at his throat and blood poured through his fingers. He made an ugly gurgling sound and dropped to the floor. In the next instant gunfire became general throughout the courtroom.

Ryan acted on reflex alone. He saw the Light Horse sergeant's carbine aimed directly at him. Ryan's arm moved like light in a mirror, blurred motion. The Colt appeared in his hand and spat a sheet of flame. The slug impacted beneath the sergeant's breastbone and jerked him sideways. His arms flailed wildly and the carbine slipped from his grasp. He pitched raglike into the front row of benches.

A hail of lead whistled across the room as the Light Horse Police exchanged shots with Wilson and the Cherokees. The ranks of both sides were winnowed as though chopped down by a giant scythe. Three of the Cherokees were hurled backward, splattered with blood. Another dropped, then another, and finally Wilson staggered. He slumped to the floor without a sound.

Only two Light Horse were still standing in the courtroom. The others were sprawled in death or wounded. Sam Irvin and one of the remaining Light Horse fired on each other almost simultaneously. The Light Horse collapsed to his knees and toppled over like a felled tree. Irvin stiffened, a gaping hole blown in his shirtfront, and his eyes went opaque. His knees buckled and he folded at the middle. He fell dead across Wilson's body.

Ryan was vaguely aware that he'd been wounded himself. His shirt was wet and sticky, and there was a faint buzzing in his ears. He turned, drawing a quick bead on the last Light Horse left standing. The man fired, and Ryan felt a burning sensation sear his left arm. He touched the trigger and the Colt bucked in his hand. A whoosh of breath exploded from the Light Horse as he let go of the carbine and clutched his stomach. He took a step sideways, then slowly pitched forward on his face.

There was an instant of tomblike silence. Through a haze of gunsmoke, Ryan sensed all around him the carnage of a bloodbath. He realized for the first time that the judge and the defense attorney were down. A moan caught his attention, and he saw the prosecutor sitting beside the jury box, cradling a shattered arm. It came to him that no one was left on his feet. He was standing alone.

His vision suddenly dimmed. The stench of death mixed with the sweet smell of blood was overpowering. The courtroom blurred before his eyes and the gun dropped from his hand. Slowly, all feeling gone, he folded to the floor. He lay perfectly still.

CHAPTER
SEVENTEEN

The toll from the courtroom shootout was eleven killed and eight critically wounded. Among the list of dead were the judge, the defendant and his attorney, and Bud Wilson. The Cherokees filed a formal protest with Washington, which was studiously ignored. The death of deputy U.S. Marshal Sam Irvin apparently balanced out against five dead Light Horse. No federal warrants were issued on the Cherokee survivors.

Nor were any federal charges preferred against Ryan. He'd been a duly sworn officer of the federal court at the time of the shootout. His actions were in the discharge of duty and therefore both legal and defensible. Because he was white, the Cherokee Nation was unable to prefer charges of any nature. But there was little doubt that he'd been judged and found guilty by certain factions within the tribe. For all practical purposes, he was under a sentence of death.

Grievously wounded, Ryan had barely survived the shoot-out itself. At William Ross' order, he'd been tended for several days by a Cherokee physician. A bullet had been removed from his side, and only after forty-eight hours had the danger of infection been dismissed. The wound in his left arm, which passed clean through, had presented no complications. Three days after the shootout, he had been moved by wagon to end-of-track. There, under the watchful eye of

Tom Scullin, he'd been nursed back to health by the camp's cooks.

On July 20 end-of-track crossed the northern border of the Creek Nation. The Katy was now sixty miles deep in Indian Territory, roughly a third of the way to the Red River. Texas and the Great Southwest no longer seemed a pipe dream.

Robert Stevens and his section chiefs breathed a collective sigh of relief. Behind them lay the land of the Cherokees and nearly five months of bitter strife. Bypassing Fort Gibson would surely provoke some act of reprisal from William Ross. Yet there had been a curious silence out of Tahlequah and the Cherokee council. No one believed it would last indefinitely.

Still, there was a sense of deliverance throughout the camp. The lowliest track layer was aware that a crisis had been averted. While the Creeks were by no means allies, they were notably less antagonistic toward white men. The Creeks were perhaps more fatalistic than the Cherokees. The iron horse was treated somewhat like a natural disaster: regrettable but unavoidable. The tribal council effectively turned a blind eye to the railroad.

The Creek Nation represented a personal haven for John Ryan as the long weeks of his convalescence passed. At first, while confined to his bunk he'd had plenty of time to reflect on the shootout. His principal regret centered around the death of Sam Irvin. He had genuinely liked the lawman, and he felt somehow diminished by the passing of a friend. There was, as well, an idle thought that his presence might have jinxed the entire courtroom affair.

Violence seemed to have followed wherever he went since he first arrived in Indian Territory. Looking back on the men he'd killed—which now included two Light Horse—he began thinking of his job as a sort of death work. He was the lightning rod that drew the Cherokees' fire almost as if he'd been destined to attract violence and death. And he wondered if it had been Irvin's misfortune to share his ill luck.

Lying in his bunk, he had brooded about it for several

days. Whether or not his luck had rubbed off on Irvin would remain an unknown. But there was no question that he'd spent too much time on the killing ground. Nor was it entirely happenstance that the men he'd killed over the past several months were Cherokee. The tribe he admired most seemed somehow slated to be his deadly antagonist.

However much he pondered on the problem, the reason eluded him. There was no explanation for why he and the Cherokees had been brought to a common killing ground. But all his pondering led to a seed of thought that slowly took root. As though drawn to it, he had years ago chosen a line of work that dealt largely with death. Now with new-found clarity, he saw something he'd been blinded to in the past. Despite the best of intentions, death work was too often indiscriminate. The man who performed it was seldom given choices. He killed almost by random lot, for by the nature of his work he killed anyone who tried to kill him.

In that respect, there was still a score to be settled. Ryan knew that the courtroom shootout and the death of the Light Horse sergeant had changed nothing. Major David Tappin had personally marked him for death, and the sentence would not be withdrawn. There was no court of last resort, no appeal. Tappin would simply pick another executioner, and if he failed, then another, until the job was done. To save himself, Ryan would have no option but to respond in kind. He would have to kill Tappin.

Oddly, the thought of killing always brought to mind Elizabeth. He had entertained the notion that she might visit him after the courtroom shootout. While he was under the care of the Cherokee doctor, he'd finally come to his senses. She wouldn't look in on him or inquire about his condition, and she had an excellent reason. Of the eleven dead men, nine were Cherokee, all of them her people. She would assign at least part of the blame to him, and no explanation would alter the judgment. In a sense, the Tahlequah courtroom had been his last bridge. And he'd burned it to a cinder.

The realization gave Ryan some long and restless nights. Still, for all his regrets he was not a man to dwell on the past. By the third week of his recovery, he was able to hobble around on a cane, and he was getting restless. Tom Scullin, returning one night to the bunk car they shared, found him cleaning his guns. The Irishman shook his head with a look of amusement.

"By all the saints! What d'ya think you're about here?"

"Just what it looks like. I'm cleaning a shotgun."

"Are you daft?" Scullin rumbled. "You're not yet mended!"

Ryan ran a swab through the off-hand barrel of the scattergun. He held the open breech to the lamplight and peered down the bore. Satisfied, he began swabbing the other barrel.

"You'd make a hell of a wet nurse, Tom. Only you're not exactly built for it."

Scullin huffed indignantly. "Full of piss and vinegar, aren't you?"

"I've felt worse," Ryan commented. "And you can stop treating me like I'm an invalid. I threw the cane away today."

"Did you now? I suppose you'll tell me next you're ready to start work?"

Ryan smiled. "You must be a mind reader."

"God's teeth!" Scullin rumbled. "We've not had a speck of trouble since you were shot. What's the rush?"

"I figure it's time I earned my keep. Besides, I'm tired of you hovering over me like a mother hen."

"You're an ingrate, John Ryan. And a poor excuse for an Irishman too!"

Ryan inspected the bore against the light. Then he snapped the breech closed and leaned the shotgun in a corner. He finally looked up at Scullin.

"Tomorrow"—he paused, grinning—"I think I'll ride out and scout around. What do you say to that?"

"Jesus, Mary, and Joseph!"

Toward the end of August, the railroad reached Three Forks. The track stopped on the north bank of the Verdigris River, waiting a bridge. But the delay was momentary and lasted only one night.

Scullin and his work gangs forded the stream early next morning. Behind them a caravan of wagons hauled construction supplies to the opposite shore. By noontime the graders had started a roadbed and the track crews were hard at work. Not quite four miles ahead lay the Arkansas River.

From the Verdigris crossing point, the muddy stream curved south to mingle with the Arkansas and the Neosho. The confluence of these three great rivers, along with the stretch of land between the Verdigris and the Arkansas, was the famed Three Forks. A small Creek settlement located where the waters met served as the tribal headquarters. The area had been the commercial hub of Indian Territory scarcely four decades ago.

Keelboats and shallow-draft paddle-wheelers plied upriver to the landing at Three Forks in the 1830's. Vast shipments of baled furs were assembled at Chouteau's Trading Post. Boatloads of the valuable cargo were transported downriver to New Orleans and eventually to the fur market in St. Louis. At the time Sam Houston, who later led Texas to independence, lived in a wilderness area near Three Forks. His log cabin, which he called Wigwam Neosho, was a gathering place for officers stationed at Fort Gibson.

Three Forks had fallen on lean times with the decline of the fur trade. But there was a new explosion of activity with the arrival of the Katy. A terminus, which was quickly dubbed Gibson Station, was located on high ground north of the Verdigris crossing. The station depot was completed, and daily passenger service began operating between Kansas and Indian Territory. Track sidings and a turntable were installed, and shortly afterward loading pens were erected to serve the cattle trade. The first herd of longhorns trailed in from Texas a week later.

The freight of military and civilian goods further intensified the boom. Army detachments hacked a wagon road through the wilderness from Fort Gibson to the terminus. Caravans from Overland Transit, which had obtained the

contract for hauling government supplies, began departing
with quartermaster stores and Indian allotments for tranship
ment throughout the Southwest. Towns in northern Texas
were also quick to take advantage of the new railhead. From
the south long wagon trains bulging with cotton were soon
strung out along the trail between Gibson Station and the
Red River.

A hastily constructed warehouse was packed to over
flowing within days of being built. Mountains of freight
awaiting available wagons, lay stacked in the rail yard and
along the tracks. Almost five hundred tons of materials were
offloaded for transshipment to military posts in Indian Ter
ritory and Texas in a matter of weeks. Swamped by the flood
of supplies, Overland Transit scarcely put a dent in the mas
sive piles at end-of-track. The problem quickly added to the
already herculean task of organizing and policing a wilder
ness settlement.

Spanning the barriers of the Verdigris and Arkansas rivers
was expected to delay railroad construction for several
months. As a result Gibson Station was designated the Katy's
base of operations and main supply depot. Trainloads of con
struction materials were brought down from Pryor's Creek
and dumped beside the mounds of government goods. Fol
lowing close behind was the sporting crowd from Elias Bou
dinot's town site. Gamblers and saloonkeepers, whores and
grifters simply packed up and deserted the Cherokee Nation
en masse.

Gibson Station began to take on a look of permanence
within a fortnight. A tent town of more than fifty structures
sprang to life around the depot. The ladies of Poonville
opened for business, and raucous music blasted from a row
of dance halls and saloons. Texas cowhands and outlaws
along with the usual assortment of cardsharps and footloose
wanderers were thrown together with the roughnecks of
Scullin's Irish Brigade. Added to this volatile mix was a new
element: full-bloods and breeds who were drawn to the
hurdy-gurdy boomtown. The Creeks, unlike the Cherokees,
evidenced a great curiosity about the white man's ways.

Gibson Station was like an elixir to Ryan. By now completely recovered, he needed a stimulant, some new challenge to seize his interest. He quickly laid out rules of conduct for the sporting crowd as he had at previous railheads. Word spread that gunplay and mayhem would not be tolerated by the Katy's special agent. His reputation alone, which had been enhanced greatly by the courtroom shootout, served to dampen the rowdier element's enthusiasm. No one made even a halfhearted attempt to hoorah the town.

The military supply dump was an altogether different matter. The jumble of crates, stuffed with every imaginable type of goods, proved to be a magnet for thieves and looters. At Ryan's suggestion Stevens telegraphed the railroad's main office, ordering armed guards to be hired in Kansas and rushed south. The Fort Gibson commander also detached a platoon to act as sentries. The sight of soldiers patrolling the rail yard quickly had the desired effect. Thieves soon began to give the supply depot a wide berth.

Early in September Ryan got the first real challenge to his authority. Word reached him that Brad Collins, a whiskey smuggler and desperado, had drifted into town. Collins was a half-blood Cherokee outcast, renounced by his own tribe and posted from the Cherokee Nation. A federal warrant was still out on him for shooting a deputy marshal. He traveled with a pack of cutthroats and robbers, vicious breeds who to a man were wanted by the law. To date, none of them had been arrested.

Ryan walked uptown. He carried the shotgun under the crook of his arm, proceeding along the rutted street at a deliberate pace. A knot of men loafing outside one of the saloons quickly took their business indoors. Several tents farther down, he turned in at the Acme Saloon and Gaming Parlor. He moved through the door and stopped.

Brad Collins stood at the bar. He was whipcord lean, light-skinned for a half-breed, with a hard smile and empty eyes. His men were gathered around him and listened attentively when he spoke. Three of them flanked him on one side and two on the other, and their deferential attitude was a message in itself. Even a casual observer could readily spot the gang leader.

Ryan moved to the end of the bar. He laid the scattergun across the countertop and eared back both hammers. The metallic snick brought the saloon to a sudden standstill. Several men along the bar eased to the opposite side of the room. Hands on the bar, the gang members waited for Ryan to make his play. Collins watched him with a frozen smile.

"Hello, Collins," Ryan said, nodding. "Figured we ought to have ourselves a talk."

Collins returned his stare levelly. "You're Ryan, ain't you? The one they call the Indian Killer."

Ryan's look betrayed nothing. "I reckon some people call me that."

"Well, what can I do for you, Indian Killer? You sorta busted up our party."

"I'm here to deliver a warning. Behave yourself and you're welcome at Gibson Station. I'll even overlook the federal warrant on you."

"You shore make it sound hospitable. But lemme ask you—what happens if I get out of line?"

"Don't," Ryan said in a low, dangerous voice. "Otherwise I'll have to kill you."

"Yeah?" Collins snarled. "It'd take more'n you and that shotgun to get the job done."

"Then go ahead and try me."

A leaden silence descended on the saloon. Collins' eyes flicked down at the shotgun and back to Ryan. He kept his hands in plain sight.

"You're bluffin'! No way you'd get us all. Not even with that!"

Ryan lifted the snout of the shotgun. He centered the barrels on Collins' head. "I'm tired of talking. Either we've got a deal or we don't. Which is it?"

Collins swallowed, thinking hard. "You won't try to ride herd on me and the boys?"

"Not unless you cause trouble."

"And you won't take sides with the *tibo* marshals? I got your word on that?"

"You've already heard me say it."

"Awright, then," Collins said, bobbing his head. "You got yourself a deal."

"Don't break it. I won't try to talk you around next time."

"What next time?" Collins laughed. "Here, lemme buy you a drink. Just to prove there ain't no hard feelings."

"No, thanks."

Ryan walked to the door. His head was turned slightly, watching the bar out of the corner of his eye. As he went through the door, the metallic whirr of his shotgun's hammers being lowered sounded through the saloon. He passed from view onto the street outside.

Brad Collins took a long sip of whiskey. His eyes fixed on the middle distance in a thoughtful stare, and his mouth tightened at the corners. He smiled to himself.

CHAPTER EIGHTEEN

William Ross stood at the window in his study. A pipe was clamped in his mouth and tendrils of smoke drifted slowly toward the ceiling. His gaze was abstracted and far away.

Over the past several weeks he had aged visibly. There were dark rings under his eyes and worry lines creased his forehead. His features appeared tight, almost stretched, like those of a man who has experienced a sudden loss of weight. His shoulders were unnaturally stooped and he looked somehow defeated.

Ross had led his people for five years. Not once in all that time had there been serious opposition to his policies. As principal chief, he had ruled the tribal council by sheer force of character. Even Elias Boudinot and the Southern Party had conceded Ross' preeminence among the Cherokees. He had never been challenged in the political forum.

All that had changed with the advent of the railroad. Political opponents such as Boudinot and Stand Watie had denounced him as backward and uninformed. Worse, a schism had developed within the ranks of his own followers. A silent conspiracy which advocated violence and bloodshed had arisen. Assassins once more roamed the land of the Cherokees.

The identity of the leader, or leaders, of the conspiracy was an absolute mystery. Whoever issued the orders was a master of secrecy and thus far an invisible presence. The organization itself indicated a brilliant mind at work behind the wall of silence. Nothing was known about the band of assassins or their objectives, for there had been no public pronouncement. Their intent was made clear only by the names of those they tried to kill.

The assassins appeared to be Ross' allies. Their enemies— the railroad and the Boudinot faction—were his enemies as well. Yet he was opposed, both philosophically and on general principle, to their activities. They advocated a return to the old tribal customs by resorting to violence. Ross thought their methods were a return to the savagery of bygone times. He'd let it be known that such men were to be considered renegades. He would not countenance cold-blooded murder.

Opposing the assassins had done nothing to improve Ross' political position. There was a faction within the tribal council that openly supported violence. Until now, despite their rebellious attitude he'd been able to hold them in check. But events of the past few weeks had forced him into an extremely tenuous situation. When the railroad bypassed Fort Gibson, he'd lost still more influence with council members. The courtroom shootout, though not directly related to the railroad, had further undercut his support. The tribal council, to a man, declared it the work of *tibo* interlopers.

Ross agreed with the allegation in principle. Every problem besetting his people stemmed in one way or another from the railroad. But he'd considered it futile to prefer charges against the railroad's special agent, John Ryan. He had further fanned the flames of discontent by providing medical care for Ryan. A vote of censure in the tribal council had been averted by the narrowest of margins.

Ross saw little reason for optimism as he stared out the window today. His leadership of the Cherokee Nation was still in great jeopardy. One more misstep, and there was every likelihood he would be driven from office. He resolved not to let that happen at any cost. He knew his people would need him even more in the years to come.

There was a knock at the door. Ross squared himself up,

shoulders back and head erect. He turned as Major Tappin entered the study. He nodded briskly in greeting.

"Good afternoon, David."

"Good afternoon, sir."

Ross waved him to a chair. He crossed the room, halting at the edge of his desk as Tappin seated himself. He chose to remain standing.

"What can I do for you? Your message sounded urgent."

"Are you aware," Tappin asked, "that the council plans to meet tomorrow?"

"I am."

"Do you plan to address them?"

"No, I do not."

"May I ask why?"

"Because my presence would serve no useful purpose. I think it's best to let them get mired down in the routine conduct of business."

"Then you haven't heard," Tappin said. "There's talk that you'll face another vote of censure tomorrow."

"On what grounds?" Ross demanded.

"Failure to act in the tribe's best interests. Specifically, your failure to convene an emergency session of the Intertribal Council."

"I wasn't aware an emergency existed."

"Perhaps you should be," Tappin said pointedly. "It's been three weeks since the railroad entered the Creek Nation."

"To date," Ross observed, "I've heard no complaint from the Creeks."

"The Creeks are not at issue. We're discussing your people, what the Cherokee council wants."

"And what is that?"

"Some form of retaliation. At the very least, an act of defiance. We've been made to look the fools."

"On the contrary," Ross informed him. "Our prohibitive cattle tax drove the railroad from Cherokee lands."

Tappin laughed too loudly. "Stevens lost nothing in that bargain. He's shipping trainloads of cows from Three Forks."

"Precisely my point! As a practical matter, there is only one railhead in the Cherokee Nation. And I understand Boudinot's town site is all but deserted."

"Boudinot's another matter entirely. A majority of the council believes he deserves the death sentence. If it's ever put to a vote, he's as good as—"

"No!" Ross announced. "I will not be a party to barbarism."

Tappin studied him with a thoughtful frown. "You would do well not to state that opinion in public. By tribal law, Boudinot is subject to the extreme penalty."

"Times change," Ross said. "Ancient laws sometimes have no place in a modern world."

"I suggest you keep that opinion to yourself as well."

"Your advice was much the same regarding John Ryan. What would have happened if I hadn't voiced my opinion then?"

"He would have been killed," Tappin said harshly. "Or allowed to bleed to death. Which was exactly what he deserved."

Ross looked at him inquisitively. "Could you have let him bleed to death?"

"He killed two of my men!"

"You haven't answered the question."

Tappin was seething inside. He took a grip on his anger, forced himself to appear outwardly calm. "I suppose no man deserves a slow death. But that's neither here nor there. We're talking about the council."

"Yes, so we are."

Ross stuffed his hands in his pockets, moved behind the desk. "You know, of course, that Fort Gibson will eventually be closed down."

"Why do you say that?"

"It's a burdensome expense and serves no useful purpose. Unless, of course, we create an incident to justify its existence."

"An incident involving the railroad?"

"Precisely," Ross affirmed. "By biding our time, we end

up with no military posts and only one railhead. We can then devote our energies to the critical engagement—the fight for Cherokee independence.''

''Well . . .'' Tappin said doubtfully, ''I'm not sure the council would be persuaded. You're talking long-range, and they tend to be very shortsighted.''

''Then we'll give them a short-term solution. Suppose an incident were to occur in the Creek Nation. Would that suffice?''

''What sort of incident?''

''You know the Creeks as well as anyone here does. What would you suggest?''

Tappin considered a moment. ''I received a report that Ryan had some trouble with Brad Collins and his gang. Perhaps I can arrange an incident through Collins.''

''No harm must come to John Ryan! You would have to make that clear to Collins.''

''I think he'll listen to reason.''

''Have I your assurance on that point?''

''Leave it to me,'' Tappin said, grinning. ''Outlaws can always use friends in high places.''

After Tappin had gone, Ross slumped wearily into his chair. He scrubbed his face with his palms but was unable to erase his dour expression. For all practical purposes, he'd just struck a bargain with the devil. And for little more than momentary political gain.

He knew he'd sold himself cheap.

The rose was dark magenta in color. Elizabeth clipped it with shears, careful to avoid the thorns. She held the flower to her nose and breathed deeply.

The aroma was faint, barely detectable. She lowered the rose and looked around the garden with a melancholy expression. At the height of the summer, the flower garden was a riotous explosion of colors and hues. But now it was early September and only a few of the rosebushes were still in bloom. Windswept petals, already dry and faded, littered the earth.

Elizabeth dreaded the passing of summer. A short autumn inevitably led to a long, dreary winter. The rain and sleet brought with it a dank, bone-chilling cold that sapped her spirits. An occasional snow, particularly at Christmastime, relieved the monotony. But the seemingly endless months of dismal weather left her dispirited and out of sorts. Her vivacity returned only with the arrival of a new spring.

Her mood today was only partly caused by summer's end. Even the dying roses were a reflection rather than the source of her low spirits. Hard as it was to admit, she was lost in a morass of conflicting emotions. One minute she prided herself on having driven John Ryan away. In the next, she ached for the sight of him.

The courtroom gun battle had provided her with an almost painful emotional confusion. She'd rushed to Tahlequah upon hearing that Ryan had been wounded. There, heedless of public reaction, she had spent the night at Ryan's bedside. Elizabeth surprised herself with the strength of her concern for him but felt strangely glad that he couldn't see her clutching his hand and very close to tears. Although the operation had gone well, he'd been heavily sedated with laudanum and therefore unaware of her presence. When the crisis ended the next morning, she had undergone another shift in mood. She departed before he'd regained consciousness.

She had been revolted by the aftermath of the shootout. The final count of eleven dead and many others wounded left her sick at heart. She rejoiced that Ryan had survived, and would recover in time. Yet she couldn't ignore the fact that he'd again taken sides and killed two more Cherokees. Once again she found herself torn between loathing and a compulsion to be with him. In the end, unable to live with half measures, her conscience had prevailed. She restrained herself from seeing him again.

For all her restraint, she never tried to deceive herself. She was concerned for his welfare and vitally interested in his recovery. Through her father she was able to gather bits and pieces of information. She heard that Ryan was up and around and walking with a cane. A short time later she learned that he was practically fully recuperated. While the news relieved her anxiety, it also left her saddened. She knew he would soon resume his work with the railroad. For all her fear and worry, nothing had changed.

There was one small consolation. The railroad, and Ryan, were now in the Creek Nation. She thought it unlikely that he would be thrown into another confrontation with Cherokees. The Creeks were somewhat less rigid in their attitude toward whites, so it seemed to her a remote possibility that Ryan would kill anyone else. She wanted to believe that he resorted to a gun only when provoked.

Yet she was not altogether sanguine. She couldn't help being depressed by the growing distance between herself and Ryan. The deeper tracks were laid into the Creek Nation, the more isolated she felt. With each passing day, Ryan was farther away, moving inexorably southward. She knew he would be gone forever once he crossed the Red River. All that might have been between them would then become a bittersweet dream.

Her reverie was suddenly broken by the sound of her name. She turned and saw her father on the veranda. He moved down the steps, then proceeded along a path to the flower garden. She waited, still holding the rose.

"Well, well," Ross said, halting beside her. "The last rose of summer, hmm?"

"Don't tease," she said seriously. "You know the thought of winter depresses me."

"Winter?" Ross asked. "Nothing else?"

"Why do you say that?"

Ross took a moment to light his pipe. He snuffed the match and ground it underfoot. Finally he looked up.

"Major Tappin was just here."

"Oh?" she replied without interest. "What new calamity did he have to report?"

"You shouldn't be so hard on him. Tappin is a very capable administrator."

"I'm sorry, Father. I just don't like the man. He's too . . ."

"Unsociable?"

"Worse than that. He's always impressed me as being very insensitive. I know it sounds silly, but somehow he . . . Well, he frightens me."

Ross smiled, puffing on his pipe. "I suppose Tappin frightens many people. But then, policemen are seldom loved. It's part and parcel of the job."

"Perhaps you're right," she said with a shrug. "What brought him here today?"

"Among other things, he had a bit of news about John Ryan. I thought you might be interested."

"Maybe I am," she said indifferently, "and maybe I'm not. What is it?"

Ross was aware that she'd begun plucking petals off the rose. He suppressed a chuckle, forcing himself not to look at her hands. "According to Tappin's information, Mr. Ryan is back on the job. In fact, he recently had words with Brad Collins."

Her eyes widened. "The outlaw? *That* Brad Collins?"

"Don't worry," Ross reassured her. "As such things go, it was rather inconsequential. Ryan simply warned Collins to behave himself."

"Why would I worry?" she murmured uneasily. "Apparently he's happy doing what he does best."

Ross could see the hurt deep in her eyes. He gently touched her arm, saying nothing more. At length she nodded, then smiled a little. As he turned to leave, she found her voice.

"Father."

"Yes?"

"Is he still at Three Forks?"

"So far as I know. Why do you ask?"

"No reason."

Ross wisely let it drop. As he walked toward the house, Elizabeth glanced down at her hands. She saw that the rose was completely bare of petals. Nothing remained but the stem and sharp thorns. Her mouth softened in a wan smile.

Winter seemed distant, and yet so near. She suddenly felt cold.

CHAPTER
NINETEEN

"I want your personal guarantee."

"No soap, Colonel."

"You refuse?"

Ryan's jawline tightened. "I'm telling you there's no way to guarantee any man's safety. The best we can do is whittle down the odds."

"Odds?" Stevens repeated. "Are you saying something's bound to happen?"

"The sporting crowd's a rough bunch. None of them has any particular love for politicians. That goes double for the Indians."

"You refer to Collins and his gang of half-breeds."

"Not altogether," Ryan corrected him. "Any Indian— Creek, Cherokee, Choctaw—they've all got a bone to pick. A Washington bigwig makes a pretty inviting target."

"Target!" Stevens said incredulously. "Good God, you sound like he's certain to get shot!"

"You want my best advice, Colonel? Wire Secretary Cox and make some excuse. Tell him you've had to postpone the ceremony."

"Absolutely not! Cox is one of our most influential supporters. And we need all the clout we can get with Congress. I just won't risk offending him!"

"Then I suggest you ask the Army for some help. Surround him with soldiers and maybe nothing will happen. It's your best bet.''

Stevens shook his head adamantly. "Everyone would think we're incapable of safeguarding our own railhead. We can't afford that kind of publicity."

Ryan spread his hands. "Can you afford to have someone take a shot at the Secretary of the Interior?"

There was a prolonged silence. Stevens seemed to stare at him and past him at the same time. For a moment Ryan thought he intended to ignore the question. At last Stevens appeared to rouse himself. His voice was edged, almost raspy.

"Put out the word," he ordered. "We *will not* tolerate troublemakers. And that's final!''

"When you say *we*, you're actually talking about *me*, aren't you?"

"John, your job is to maintain peace and order. I expect you to do no less."

"It's just about even money," Ryan warned. "You go through with this and somebody's liable to get himself killed.''

"Make sure it's not Secretary Cox."

"I'll do my damnedest, Colonel."

Ryan told himself it was a hell of a way to run a railroad. Later that night, lying awake in his bunk, it seemed even more asinine. He thought it likely that his damnedest might be too little and too late. Lots of people in Indian Territory would consider it an honor to kill the Secretary of the Interior. Some of them would willingly sacrifice themselves for that honor.

The occasion for the Secretary's visit was the completion of the Verdigris River bridge. The trestles were in place and engineers estimated the river would be spanned by the middle of September. Across the muddy stream, four miles of track had been laid to the next barrier, the Arkansas River. Scullin and his work gangs were idle while awaiting construction of both bridges. Stevens saw the slack time as a golden opportunity, capable of garnering wide publicity in the eastern press. He planned to stage a celebration around the Verdigris River crossing.

To mark the event, a ribbon-cutting ceremony would be held on September 18. Secretary of the Interior Harold Cox had been invited to officially open the bridge and afterward deliver a speech. An astute bureaucrat, Cox jumped at the chance to make an appearance in Indian Territory. The attendant publicity would benefit everyone involved, himself included. As an added sweetener, Stevens laid on a special train to transport Cox and his retinue westward. The event promised to make front-page news.

Ryan viewed the ceremony, at best, as a calculated risk. Harold Cox, as Secretary of the Interior, was directly responsible for the Bureau of Indian Affairs. No friend of the red man, the Bureau was largely a tool of robber barons and railroad czars. To a great extent, the Katy was traversing Indian Territory under the auspices of the Bureau. Moreover, should the Five Civilized Tribes lose their independence, it was the Bureau that would bring it about. So Harold Cox was vilified by the Indians as the most visible symbol of *tibo* greed. His appearance in the territory would serve as a goad to those who felt victimized.

Ryan believed it was entirely possible that someone would attempt to kill the Secretary. He'd gone to Stevens voicing his concern for Cox's safety. The upshot was that he'd been appointed to play guardian angel. Just before going to sleep, he reminded himself never again to volunteer an opinion. By doing so, he'd gone from the frying pan to the fire.

He already felt singed around the edges.

The special train arrived on schedule. The ribbon-cutting ceremony was set for high noon at the north end of the Verdigris River bridge. To add to the festivities, all the railroad workers had been awarded a day off.

Harold Cox detrained at Gibson Station like Caesar triumphant. He was a short, rotund man, completely bald, with watery eyes and a bogus smile. He wore a cutaway coat, striped pants, and a shiny top hat. His retinue consisted of several bureaucratic flunkeys and his own personal press contingent. A newspaperman from Washington and a journalist for *Harper's* magazine trailed him like hounds on a fresh scent. Following close behind was a photographer with camera and powder box.

Their arrival created an immediate sensation. A crowd of almost five hundred people gathered around the depot. Tom Scullin and his Irish Brigade, cheering lustily, were positioned in the front rank. Behind them was the sporting crowd, gamblers and whores tricked out in all their finery. On the fringe of the assemblage were an assortment of Creeks and Cherokees who were drawn by the spectacle. A brass band, drafted piecemeal from the dance halls, thumped a sprightly tune. Bunting and streamers decorating the stationhouse lent an exuberant, carnival air to the scene.

The festive atmosphere continued on the walk to the bridge. The band led the way and was followed by the dignitaries and their party. The procession resembled a circus parade. Ryan maintained a position close beside Stevens and Secretary Cox. Spread out around them were armed railway agents who normally performed guard duty at the warehouse. Wary of the crowd, Ryan constantly scanned the sea of faces. His unease was heightened by the fact that Cox was built like a bale of cotton. He thought the Secretary made an inviting, and almost unmissable, target.

Stevens delivered a short and somewhat flowery introduction at the bridge. Then Secretary Cox posed with Stevens for the photographer. Ryan thought the Secretary looked like a trained bear. Cox and Stevens' handshake, as well as the ribbon cutting, was immortalized with several explosive flashes of the powder pan. When Cox actually cut the ribbon, the Irish Brigade, led by Scullin's bull-like roar, broke out in a fresh round of cheers. As planned, the special train then chugged onto the bridge, halting halfway across. The last car groaned to a stop where the ribbon drooped on the tracks.

Secretary Cox mounted the rear platform. With Stevens beside him, he launched into a speech commending the railroad. His reedy voice was punctuated by a powder flash, which caused him to pause and hold an artificial pose for the camera. Oblivious to the crowd's laughter, he then resumed with an ornate tribute to Colonel Robert Stevens. He hailed the railroader as "a giant of a man, leading the vanguard in America's march to progress."

"*Bullshit!*"

A voice from the crowd cut the bureaucrat short. Cox halted, sputtering and red-faced, suddenly dumbstruck. Ryan, who was positioned on the car steps, searched the crowd. Toward the rear he spotted Brad Collins and the gang of half-bloods. The outlaw's eyes were lighted by a cold tinsel glitter, and he seemed to be staring straight at Ryan. His mouth curled in a ferocious grin.

"Goddamn *tibos!*" he shouted. "You're robbing us blind, stealing our land!"

The Indians standing nearby muttered agreement. Scullin and the Irish Brigade, as well as the sporting crowd, turned angrily toward the voice. Then off to one side there was a flash of sunlight on metal. Out of the corner of his eye, Ryan saw a man raise a cocked pistol. He had only a moment to identify the man as a breed and wonder why he was separated from the Collins gang. In the next instant the pistol roared and Harold Cox's top hat went spinning into the air.

Stevens grabbed Cox and threw him down on the platform. Drawing as he turned, Ryan leveled his Colt, sighting over the barrel. He feathered the trigger, holding dead on the man's chest. The Colt leaped and the half-breed seemed to suck in a great lungful of air. A starburst of blood spread across his shirtfront and he went down like a stone.

Wheeling around, Ryan once more searched the crowd. Off in the distance, he saw Collins and the gang of breeds hightailing it toward town. The Irish Brigade, led by Scullin, had formed a protective circle around the car. The armed railway guards clambered aboard the rear platform amid shouts and panicked confusion. As Ryan sighted on Collins, one of them jostled his arm and spoiled his aim. He slowly lowered the Colt, all too aware that the gang was racing for their horses. For the moment there was nothing to be done.

Ryan holstered his pistol. He heard Stevens consoling Harold Cox, who was blubbering in a high-pitched, hysterical voice. Then, turning on the steps, he looked down at the dead half-breed. It occurred to him that someone had, after all, risked suicide in an attempt to commit murder. But the man had not acted alone or on his own initiative.

He'd been sacrificed by Brad Collins. A stalking horse used to kill and then be killed.

The crowd slowly dispersed. Their festive mood was gone, replaced by sober amazement. What they had witnessed left them in a total quandary. No one could figure the dead man's motive.

Ryan ordered the body removed. With Secretary Cox safely inside the car, the special agent then turned his attention to security. Another assassination attempt seemed to him highly unlikely. Yet, given the number of Indians in town, he saw no reason to take chances. He quickly stationed the railway guards around the train.

A short while later he entered the rear door of the private car. He found Stevens and Cox seated opposite one another. Cox was slumped in an armchair, a brandy glass clutched in one hand. His face was pasty and beads of perspiration glistened on his forehead. His hand trembled as he drained the last of the brandy.

"Madness," he said in a shaky voice. "Why would anyone want to kill me?"

Stevens nodded sympathetically. "Who can say, Mr. Secretary? All Indians are deranged savages anyway."

Cox looked at him blankly. "The man was Indian?"

"A half-blood," Stevens said. "But a dead one, now. You've no reason to concern yourself further."

"I—" Cox faltered, passed a hand over his eyes. "I don't feel so well."

"Perfectly understandable. Why not lie down for a while? We can talk later."

Stevens assisted him to the bedroom. There was a murmured conversation, and then, closing the door, Stevens returned to the parlor. He angrily bit off the end of a cigar and lit up. Inhaling deeply, he gave Ryan a sideways look.

"You were right. I should have called it off."

"We got lucky," Ryan said. "All the same, if I were you I wouldn't push it."

"What are you suggesting?"

"Get him out of here muy pronto. Our luck might not hold next time."

"You think someone else might try?"

"I'd just as soon not find out."

Stevens' expression was grim. "It all happened so fast. Who was the gunman?"

"One of Collins' gang."

"Well, that's a hell of a note! Why weren't you watching him?"

"You seem to forget," Ryan said evenly. "Collins had everybody distracted, including me. The way he rigged it damn near worked too. His man got a little nervy and rushed the shot."

"Why would Collins try to kill Cox? It makes no sense."

"I've been thinking along those lines myself."

Stevens was thoughtful a moment. "Perhaps it was revenge of sorts. After all, you did put him on warning, and in open public."

"I tend to doubt it. He could have killed me easy enough out there. But the whole thing, start to finish, was aimed at Cox."

"And?" Stevens said, puzzled. "What are you saying?"

Ryan moved to the window. He stared down, looking past the bridge timbers to the muddy river below. Then, as though talking to himself, he spoke in a slow, pensive tone.

"It's got the smell of a put-up job. Collins is small-time. He runs whiskey and robs people. Why would he turn assassin all of a sudden?"

Stevens looked surprised. "Are you suggesting that someone paid him to do it?"

"Tell you what I think," Ryan said, turning from the window. "Collins never dreamed that up on his own. Unless

I'm way off, somebody put the idea in his head.''

"Yes, but who?"

"We keep asking ourselves the same question, don't we?"

"Christ," Stevens muttered. "You think whoever tried to kill Boudinot is behind this too?"

"Anything's possible. Like I said, Collins is no assassin."

"Perhaps not. But we don't know who put him up to it. At the moment he's our only lead."

"I wouldn't argue that."

"Well, then . . ." Stevens hesitated, puffed a cloud of smoke. "How soon can you get on his trail?"

"Why borrow trouble? Half-breed or not, Collins is still an Indian. We'd have to start a war to smoke him out."

"You intend to do nothing?"

"No," Ryan said in a flinty voice. "If he shows up here, I'll kill him. Otherwise, it's a job for federal marshals or the Army."

"I don't care for that," Stevens grumbled. "It looks like we're trying to pass the buck."

"Seems to me it's out of our jurisdiction. The Secretary of the Interior works for the government, not the railroad."

Stevens' mouth hardened. "Perhaps I haven't made myself clear. We have to take care of our own dirty laundry. I want you to find Collins."

"No can do, Colonel."

"What?"

"Before I got to Collins, I'd have to fight my way through half the Creek Nation. I want him as much as you do, maybe more, but I'm tired of killing Indians."

"What the hell does that have to do with anything?"

"It says all I've got to say."

"Are you refusing a direct order?" Stevens demanded. "Because if you are, don't think you can't be replaced!"

Ryan smiled. "It's your railroad, Colonel."

Stevens seemed on the verge of saying something more. Then, as though to halt the words, he stuffed the cigar in his mouth. He made a brusque, dismissive gesture with his hand and turned away.

Outside the car Ryan stood grinning to himself. What he'd only suspected before was now a hard fact. Stevens needed him more than Ryan needed the job.

He went down the steps whistling a lively tune.

CHAPTER
TWENTY

The weather was unseasonably warm. A forenoon sun reflected off the Verdigris in ripples of orange and gold. The tent town of Gibson Station appeared almost lifeless in the late morning hour.

Weather dominated conversation in the railroad camp. Even though the days were balmy, the temperature dropped sharply at night. There was a hint of frost in the air during the darkness hours; potbellied stoves in the bunkhouse cars were being stoked shortly after dusk. No one expected the warm days to last much longer.

Robert Stevens' forecast was especially pessimistic. He viewed the weather as a capricious and sometimes menacing adversary. The chilly nights left him convinced that winter would arrive early. Drizzling rain, followed in the harshest months by snowfall, would severely hamper railroad construction. He was determined to make the most of what promised to be a short autumn.

Delay on the Arkansas River bridge was particularly worrisome. To span the river required an immense structure at least 840 feet in length. It was by far the largest bridge yet attempted by Katy engineers. The latticework of trestles and support beams gave it the look of a gigantic spider's web. By the very nature of its complexity, it was a slow and tedious project. With maddening regularity, the estimated completion date was revised time and time again.

Stevens had been temporarily distracted from his worries by the Verdigris River bridge opening. Following the attempted assassination and Secretary Cox's hasty departure, there was a lull before things returned to normal. By the third day, however, Stevens' attention focused once more on the Arkansas River crossing. Track laying through the Creek Nation had been brought to a standstill until the barrier was surmounted.

Tom Scullin was summoned to the private car. There Stevens informed him that the Irish Brigade was being pressed into service. Scullin and his work gangs, idle now for almost a week, were to report to Otis Gunn. The chief engineer would assign them jobs alongside his bridge-building crew and thereby speed the completion date. Scullin readily agreed and expressed the opinion that his Irish Brigade would show Gunn a thing or two about spanning a river. At Stevens' insistence he further agreed to place himself at Gunn's command. No rivalry, Stevens told him, would be tolerated over leadership of the project.

The first construction train was loaded by late morning. There were two flatcars, one stacked with supplies and rough-hewn timbers, and the other carrying fifty men. Scullin placed one of his foremen in charge, ordering him to report with the work gang to Otis Gunn. As for himself, Scullin planned to supervise loading of the second train, then bring it forward to the river crossing. The first train pulled out of the rail yard shortly after eleven o'clock. A caboose that had been converted into a kitchen car was coupled on at the last minute.

On impulse, Ryan swung aboard the caboose. He generally visited the construction site once a day, covering the four miles by horseback. He decided to make the trip by train today for no particular reason. The shantytown was of no immediate concern since it seldom came alive before dark. He'd be back by then, as one of the supply trains always returned before nightfall.

A brakeman boarded from the opposite side as the train was switched onto the main track. Ryan looked around, nodding to him, then once again turned his attention forward. His senses suddenly alerted when the locomotive picked up speed and rolled onto the Verdigris River bridge. A loud creaking noise like trees swaying in the wind sounded over the rumble of the locomotive's driving wheels. An instant later there was an earsplitting *crack* from somewhere beneath the bridge.

Ryan saw the center span of the bridge buckle. Beams and splintered timbers flew like matchsticks as supporting trestles collapsed underneath the weight of the locomotive. In an eerie sort of slow motion, the two-hundred-foot-long center span simply vanished. Too late, the engineer cut the throttle and slammed on the brakes. The locomotive screeched forward, showering sparks along the rails, and teetered on the edge of the chasm. Slowly, hissing steam and smoke, it nosed over the last upright trestle.

As it hurtled downward, the locomotive jerked the entire train forward. Ryan felt the sudden acceleration in speed even as he saw the tender and the first flatcar disappear. Directly ahead, men were leaping off the second flatcar, arms and legs akimbo as they slammed into vertical beams on both sides of the bridge. One man missed completely, sailing through the opening between beams, and plummeted to the riverbed fifty feet below. A dozen or more of the work gang rode the flatcar over the shattered roadway.

Ryan jumped, landing hard on his shoulder beside the bridge rails. He rolled, stopping himself against a beam, and looked up as the caboose toppled over the edge. He saw the brakeman on the rear platform, paralyzed with terror, unable to move. The man's eyes were bugged, his mouth frozen in a silent oval, as he vanished from sight. The sound of rending steel filled the morning as one car after another crashed into the water. A moment later the firebox in the locomotive exploded with a thunderous roar.

The blast struck Ryan with cyclonic force. A towering fireball leaped skyward, shooting through the chasm of the

center span. The heat singed Ryan's eyebrows and pocked
his shirt with tiny, smoking holes. For an instant it was as
though the air had been sucked from the earth, and he
couldn't get his breath. Then, with an effort of will, he levered himself to his feet. His breathing returned with a ragged
gasp, and he stumbled away from the heat. His eyeballs felt
seared, but his vision, oddly enough, had never been more
acute.

He saw Tom Scullin running toward the bridge.

The riverbed resembled a funeral pyre. Twisted steel and
burned timbers were fused in a mound of smoky rubble. The
locomotive, at the very bottom of the debris, looked like an
incinerated dinosaur.

Scullin directed teams of men searching through the
wreckage. On the riverbank the bodies of the engineer and
the fireman, charred beyond recognition, were covered with
blankets. Nearby lay the body of the brakeman, broken and
torn as though trampled to death. Eighteen of the work gang
had been found, and miraculously, none of them were dead.
All the men were seriously injured and many had not yet
regained consciousness. Three of them clung to life merely
by a thread.

Overseeing the operation, Stevens moved back and forth
between the injured and the rescuers. His features were sallow and his eyes glowed with a feverish look. He paused to
watch several whores and dance hall girls tending the injured
with bandages and kindness. His mouth went dry as a man
with a compound fracture moaned in agony. It occurred to
him that more men would die unless they received medical
attention. Turning away in disgust, he tried not to think of
the truth. The nearest hospital was in Topeka, Kansas.

As Stevens stared toward the rescue operation, he happened to spot Ryan. He'd noticed Ryan earlier, standing knee
deep in the river, looking up at the bridge. But now, to his
amazement he saw Ryan some ten feet above the water,
wedged in among the trestles. As he watched, Ryan inched
along a crossbeam and stopped underneath the yawning gap

of the center span. It seemed to him that Ryan was inspecting one of the first trestles to have collapsed.

After a time Ryan began making his way down the understructure. Stevens walked along the shoreline and waited for him near the north end of the bridge. Ryan splashed through the water, skirting the last masonry piling, and waded ashore. His eyebrows were gone, replaced by two ugly red streaks. He appeared otherwise uninjured as he halted in front of Stevens. The look in his eyes was flat and cold, somehow chilling.

"What's wrong?" Stevens asked.

"The bridge gave way awful damn fast. Too fast, for my money. So I had a look around."

"Yes, go on."

"It wasn't an accident."

"Sabotage!" Stevens said hoarsely. "Are you certain?"

Ryan stared at him. "No doubt about it. Somebody cut halfway through the trestles and the support beams. I figure it took at least two men with a crosscut saw."

"My God! Someone did that—killed all these men. Why?"

"No mystery about that. You've made yourself some powerful enemies, Colonel."

"The Cherokees," Stevens grated. "William Ross finally got his revenge. That scheming bastard!"

Ryan looked skeptical. "Why should he wait until we're in the Creek Nation? He could've started a war a long time ago."

"Because everything else failed! I outfoxed him at every turn, made him look the fool. Now he's evened the score, and very cleverly too! Suspicion will just naturally fall on the Creeks."

"Maybe," Ryan said slowly. "Seems like a mighty big coincidence, though. Three days after an attempted assassination and a bridge suddenly collapses. Good timing, wouldn't you say?"

Stevens' brow furrowed questioningly. "You think Brad Collins did this—was ordered to do it?"

"Yeah, I sure do," Ryan said flatly. "One thing failed, so they tried another. I'd say the same man's behind both."

"And you don't think that man is William Ross?"

"It's not Ross' game. He's tough, but he doesn't kill people. He'd never deal with scum like Collins."

Stevens averted his eyes, thoughtful a moment. Finally he let out a deep breath. "We've no proof either way, so it's a moot point. For the moment, however, I hope you're right. I need a favor from Ross."

"What sort of favor?"

Stevens gestured to the injured workers. "Some of those men will die unless they get medical attention. The nearest doctor is in Tahlequah, but he won't come without Ross' approval. I want you to arrange it."

"I'll do my damnedest," Ryan said. "No guarantees, but I'll try."

"Good," Stevens said, nodding. "In the meantime I'll lay on a train for Topeka. With or without the doctor, we have to get those men to a hospital."

Ryan consulted his pocket watch. "It's going on twelve now. I ought to make it back here by dark."

"Tell Ross I'll do anything he asks. Just so he sends the doctor."

"Sounds like an invitation to write his own ticket. How far should I go?"

"Anything within reason, short of closing down the railroad," Stevens said. "I have an obligation to these men, and I'll stick by them."

"I'll deliver the message."

Ryan turned to leave. Stevens caught his arm, stopping him. "One other thing, John. After today Brad Collins has to pay the piper. I want him dead."

"I want the man who pulls Collins' strings. Once I've got him—"

"Yes?"

"Then," Ryan said, walking away, "I reckon I'll kill Collins."

*   *   *

A midafternoon sun streamed through the study window. William Ross sat behind his desk, fingers steepled, in thought. Across from him Ryan was seated in a wing-back chair, waiting. The older man finally lowered his hands to the desktop.

"You couldn't be mistaken?"

"No," Ryan said with conviction. "Somebody used a crosscut saw to weaken the bridge."

"Even so," Rose inquired, "how can you be so positive about Collins? From what I gather, the sabotage was done at night. No one actually saw Collins."

Ryan gave him an odd look. "Why all the interest in Collins?"

"It seems out of character for him. I understood Collins was just a garden-variety bandit."

"So did I," Ryan said, "till he tried to assassinate the Secretary of the Interior."

Ross' expression was bland, unreadable. Yet on the inside he was boiling with anger. He'd already spoken to David Tappin about the assassination attempt, but Tappin had shrugged it off, saying Collins had acted on his own initiative. Now, after hearing about the bridge, Ross was even more troubled. He made a mental note to question Tappin thoroughly, and soon.

"Unfortunate," he said softly. "Good men, red and white, dying for no reason."

"More will die," Ryan added, "unless you send the doctor. For once you've got Stevens over a barrel."

"He actually said he'll grant anything I ask?"

"Well, almost anything. He won't shut down the railroad."

"Perhaps there's hope for Stevens yet. At least he appears to have feelings for his own men."

"I don't mean to press," Ryan said, "but time's short. What's your price for the doctor?"

"Nothing," Ross informed him. "I don't trade in men's lives. I'll give you a note to Dr. Porter."

Ryan was visibly impressed by the gesture. But he

thought the lesson in humanity would be lost on Robert Stevens. He watched as the older man hastily penned a short note. Finished, Ross folded the sheet of paper and pushed it across the desk.

"There is a price," he said quietly. "I understand that today was an emergency. However, you will oblige me by not coming here again."

"Some things don't change, do they?"

"We are who we are, Mr. Ryan. If I weren't accountable to the tribal council, things might be different."

Ryan tucked the note in his jacket pocket. He rose, nodded acceptance of the condition, and walked from the study. He proceeded along the hallway to the vestibule and abruptly stopped. Elizabeth was standing beside the central staircase.

"Hello, John."

"Afternoon, Elizabeth." He moved forward, trying for an offhand manner. "You're not waiting for me, are you?"

"As a matter of fact"—she paused, her eyes sad—"I wanted to tell you how sorry I am. It's just terrible . . . all those men."

"How'd you hear about it?"

"Moccasin telegraph," she said, smiling. "The Creeks and the Cherokees keep each other very well informed."

"So your father knew all along. He just let me talk to hear my version, is that it?"

"Why, is there more than one version?"

"Not so far as I'm concerned."

"Your eyebrows!" she said, suddenly staring at him. "Were you hurt in the accident?"

She would learn soon enough that it was no accident. Ryan saw no reason to correct her. "Nothing serious," he said. "I got off luckier than most."

"I . . ." She faltered, groping for words. "I'm glad you're all right. I really am."

"Would it have made any difference?"

"Yes, John. Whatever you may think, it would have made a great difference—to me."

Ryan searched her eyes. What he saw there sparked a faint

hope. "Elizabeth, let me ask you something. Your father says I'm not welcome here, regardless of the reason. How do you feel?"

For a moment it seemed as though she would reach out to him. Then, her voice almost inaudible, she lowered her eyes. "I never contradict my father."

A moment of stark silence passed between them. Ryan waited, willing her to look up at him. But she kept her eyes fixed on the floor, saying nothing. He walked out without another word.

CHAPTER
TWENTY-ONE

The death toll mounted. By morning three more men had succumbed to their massive injuries. Of the remaining survivors, four were in critical condition.

Shortly before sunrise, the hospital train pulled out of Gibson Station. Dr. Frank Porter, who had worked through the night, agreed to accompany the injured to Topeka. The men of the Irish Brigade treated him with respect and deference and appeared unmindful of the fact that he was a Cherokee. Several of their comrades were alive only as a result of his efforts.

The bridge collapse was a monumental setback for Robert Stevens. The loss of a locomotive, not to mention a score of seasoned workers, was catastrophe enough. But the greater reverse was the bridge itself. To rebuild it before winter arrived became an imperative of the first order. All railroad construction was stymied until the Verdigris was once again spanned.

Under Otis Gunn's supervision, Scullin took charge of the project. Gunn meanwhile hopped back and forth between the Arkansas River bridge and the Verdigris. Within the week, with both crews working fourteen-hour days, there was modest reason for optimism. The Arkansas crossing was nearing completion, and the Verdigris bridge was progressing faster than anyone had dared anticipate. Gunn estimated an overall completion date of late October.

On October 1 Stevens sent for Ryan. Entering the private car, Ryan noted that the railroader was in an agitated state. A cigar stuck in his mouth, Stevens trailed a cloud of smoke as he paced the floor. Sally Palmer sat quietly in one of the armchairs and watched him with an apprehensive look. She glanced at Ryan and rolled her eyes in mock fright. Then, without waiting to be asked, she retired to the bedroom.

Stevens motioned Ryan to a chair. He continued pacing, all the while puffing his cigar as if it might go out. He put Ryan in mind of a mad bull hooking at cobwebs, frustrated and angry. Finally he halted at the window and turned to Ryan.

"It's showdown time!" he said, waving his cigar. "I've just found out who sabotaged the bridge."

"You have?"

"I have, indeed! It was that mealymouthed back-stabber, Andrew Peirce."

"Who?"

"Andrew Peirce!" Stevens growled. "Head of the A&P. Here, read this."

He handed Ryan a telegraph form. It was a wire from the station agent at Vinita. The message briefly related that the Atlantic and Pacific Railroad was within a few miles of the Katy right-of-way. All indications were that the A&P would intersect the Katy roadbed some three miles north of Vinita. On that spot, the station agent advised, A&P crews were constructing what appeared to be a depot.

Ryan recalled that the Katy charter granted a north-south right-of-way through Indian Territory. The A&P grant, as stipulated by Congress, was for an east-west right-of-way. It was further stipulated that the two lines were to intersect somewhere in the Cherokee Nation. Within the past month word had leaked that the A&P was about to gain control of the Missouri Pacific Railroad. The move was a direct challenge to Robert Stevens and the Katy.

As Ryan was aware, the Missouri Pacific was a main ar-

tery into St. Louis and points eastward. Should the A&P gain
control of that line, it would represent a coup of major pro
portions. In effect, Stevens' working arrangement with the
Missouri Pacific would be voided; the end result would be
to block the Katy from direct access to eastern markets. The
A&P, at that point, would then command all trade with the
Southwest.

"Sounds like trouble," Ryan said, looking up from the
telegram. "But what's all this got to do with the bridge?"

"Everything!" Stevens snorted. "Andrew Peirce is a
blackhearted scoundrel. He makes the Cherokees look like
Good Samaritans."

"And you think he's behind the sabotage?"

"Who else has a better reason? We'll end up a month
behind schedule because of that bridge. By the time we get
moving again, he'll have track laid halfway across Indian
Territory. Jesus Christ, just think of it."

Ryan pondered a moment. "Would Peirce kill all those
men just to get a jump on you?"

"*Would he?*" Stevens parroted. "He'd cut his own
mother's throat! The man is morally bankrupt."

"But would he kill?" Ryan insisted. "Have you ever
known him to resort to violence, calculated or otherwise?"

"Well . . ." Stevens hesitated, munching his cigar. "No
I suppose not. But that doesn't mean a goddamn thing. We're
playing for table stakes here! Murder wouldn't stop him."

"Maybe not," Ryan allowed. "All the same, I'd still tap
Brad Collins for the honors. It's more in his line of work."

"Whether it is or isn't doesn't matter. The fact remains
that Peirce and his railroad are on our doorstep. I want you
to leave for Vinita on the next train."

"What's in Vinita?"

"The A&P!" Stevens thundered. "Or at least they're
only three miles away. You go up there and nose around
See what they're up to."

"What makes you think they're up to anything?"

"Because I know Andrew Peirce! The man's middle

name is 'devious.' So don't argue with me about it. Just get on up there and keep me informed."

Ryan boarded a freight train that afternoon. His horse was stalled in a boxcar, along with his camping gear. As the train rolled out of Gibson Station, his attitude toward the trip darkened. He figured it for a wild-goose chase.

Vinita looked like a ghost town. Apart from the stationhouse, the community consisted of three frame structures. The buildings were slapdash affairs, crudely constructed, and appeared to be deserted. There was no one in sight.

Ryan dumped his gear on the ground after unloading his horse. Asa Johnson, the station agent, wandered over as the train got under way. Johnson was a cadaverous man, all knobs and joints, with a loose-gaited stride. He gave the impression that life held no surprises, aside from a sudden attack of constipation. He halted, nodding as though it were an effort.

"You'd be Ryan," he said. "The Colonel wired me you was on your way."

Ryan began saddling his horse. "Looks sort of lonesome around here."

"Yep," Johnson said laconically. "Nobody but yours truly."

"Who belongs to those houses?"

"Boudinot owns 'em," Johnson said. "Empty now, though. Have been since everybody pulled up stakes for Gibson Station."

"That a fact?" Ryan tied off the latigo and began strapping his saddlebags into place. "When's the last time you saw Boudinot?"

"Hell!" Johnson cackled. "Been so long I plumb forgot. He lit out with everybody else."

"What's new with the A&P?"

"I dunno much more'n I telegraphed the Colonel. Only got wind of 'em late yesterday."

"You said they're about three miles north of here?"

"Yeah, 'bout that."

Ryan stepped into the saddle. "Much obliged, Asa. Enjoyed our little chat."

"You ridin' up there for a look-see?"

"That's why I'm here."

"Take some free advice," Johnson said. "Don't try to ask questions. Them boys ain't too friendly."

"Gave you a hard time, did they?"

"Told me to haul ass and don't look back. Bastards meant business too!"

"I'll keep it in mind."

Ryan reined the gelding around. As he rode off he pulled the shotgun from the saddle boot and laid it across his lap. The station agent impressed him as a man who spoke between the lines and left a great deal unsaid. He decided to take the warning the way it was meant.

A short time later Ryan halted the gelding in a stand of trees. He had followed the railroad tracks two miles or so and then turned off into the woods. His approach had been unobserved, and he was now concealed by the treeline. What he saw convinced him that it was no wild-goose chase.

To his immediate front a passenger depot was situated within twenty feet of the Katy tracks. Nearby a crew of carpenters were hammering together what appeared to be a freight warehouse. The location of the buildings left no doubt that the A&P tracks would cross east to west at that point.

Far in the distance a dust cloud smudged the skyline. With the sun at his back, Ryan was able to make out the figures of men and animals. The dust cloud was raised by graders who were carving a roadbed from virgin soil. Behind them work gangs were methodically laying track on a line almost due west. Smoke from the engine of a construction train was dimly visible even farther away. The distance to the graders appeared to be something more than two miles.

The sound of voices suddenly broke the silence. Startled, Ryan peered through the woods and saw a work gang beyond the treeline. They were pulling fence posts from a wagon and planting them on a north to south line. Looking closer, he spotted another crew working east to west on a perpendicular line. By rough estimate he judged that the fence, when joined on four sides, would enclose at least a thousand acres.

The meaning of what he saw was all too clear. Within a few days, three at most, the A&P track would intersect the Katy right-of-way. The purpose of the fencing operation was clearly to establish land for a new town site. Once in place, with the track crossing on the map, the A&P's town site would totally overshadow Vinita. It was apparent that Andrew Peirce meant to steal a march on the Katy.

Yet however clear the intent, there was a riddle attached. The A&P, being owned by white men, could not organize a town site on Indian land. Only a Cherokee, exercising tribal head right, could claim such a vast homestead. So the conclusion was inescapable. A Cherokee was in league with the A&P.

Ryan thought it an ironic joke. Stevens, with great cleverness, had seduced Elias Boudinot. And now, borrowing the tactic whole, Andrew Peirce had bought himself a Cherokee. All that remained was to turn up the name of the newest Judas.

Ryan reined about and rode back through the woods.

Ryan camped late that night outside Tahlequah. After hobbling his horse, he built a small fire for warmth. His supper was cold vittles from his saddlebags and creek water. The meal finished, he crawled into his bedroll and went to sleep.

He broke camp and rode out before sunrise. He skirted Tahlequah, avoiding roads and people. His course was generally southeast, traveling cross-country through woodlands and rolling hills. He was some five miles south of the Cherokee capital by full light. He halted in a grove of trees overlooking William Ross' home.

Around ten o'clock he saw Elizabeth walk to the stables. A few minutes later she rode out on the blood-bay stallion. He marked her general direction, and then, sticking to the woods, he followed on a parallel course. His appearance bothered him, for she'd never seen him unshaven and grubby from a night on the trail. He wondered how she would react.

He intercepted her on a stretch of open ground a mile from the stables. Her hair was upswept and she wore a pale doeskin jacket over her riding habit. The sight of her quickened his pulse, and he tried to smile. She looked him over like he was a bearded highwayman, unwanted company. She held her stallion to a prancing walk.

"Morning," Ryan said. "Mind if I join you?"

She stared straight ahead. "You seem intent on ignoring my father's wishes."

"No choice. Leastways not if I want to see you."

"Then I suggest you consider my wishes in the matter." She turned her head just far enough to look at him. "I don't want to see you, John. I thought you understood."

"Oh, I hear you," Ryan said with a wry grin. "I just don't believe you."

"Well!" she sniffed. "Aren't you the vain one. I believe you overestimate yourself, Mr. Ryan."

"Suppose we save that discussion for another day. I'm not here on a personal call—it's business."

"Now you do presume! Your business affairs are the least of my interests."

"Your father wouldn't agree."

"Then speak with him."

"After last time," Ryan commented, "I doubt I'd get past the front door."

"In that case," she said haughtily, "why should I bother listening to you?"

"Because it involves your people. The Cherokees."

"How ominous. Are you trying to frighten me?"

"Maybe I am," Ryan admitted. "Unless you help me, it'll go bad for everyone."

"What do you mean, go bad?"

"A railroad war," Ryan told her. "A battle royal between Stevens and the Atlantic and Pacific—with the Cherokees caught in the middle."

She reined to a halt. The stallion acted skittish and cast Ryan's gelding an evil eye. Ryan kept his distance, waiting while she considered his statement. Finally, as though somehow resigned, she agreed to listen.

Ryan quickly explained the problem, expressing no uncertainty about the A&P's intentions.

"In a nutshell," he concluded, "Stevens won't roll over and play dead. He'll start a shooting war to stop Peirce."

"And if he did?" she asked. "It would be a white man's war. How does that involve my people?"

"Boudinot rigged a land deal with the Katy. Now some other Cherokee has sold his soul to the A&P. Town sites mean big money. So it won't stay a white man's war for long."

"All right," she conceded, "you have a point. What do you want of me?"

"A name," Ryan said. "Whoever threw in with the A&P has to be convinced he made a bad deal. I need his name."

"So you can persuade him to deal with the Katy, is that it?"

Ryan spread his hands. "Sounds better than people shooting at one another."

She seemed to look through him. At length she smiled with a touch of mockery. "Well, why not? All we're talking about is which railroad controls the town site. Isn't that so?"

When Ryan nodded, she went on. "I've heard rumors, nothing definite. Apparently there are members of the tribal council who will go to any lengths to destroy Stevens and the Katy. They've made their peace with Elias Boudinot."

"Boudinot?" Ryan repeated. "What's he got to do with it?"

"From what I hear, his allegiance no longer belongs to Stevens. He abandoned the old town site, and he's now filed claim on a new plot of land—for the A&P."

"Well, I'll be . . ." Ryan's voiced trailed off. He shook his head with amazement. "Boudinot's even trickier than I thought. He sold himself to the highest bidder."

"So it would appear," she said. "Of course, he had support this time. It seems there are other Cherokees willing to sell their birthright."

"Any names?" Ryan asked. "You said they're members of the council."

"The only name mentioned was Boudinot's. I assume the others don't want their names tarred with the same brush."

"Probably not."

Ryan paused and his expression underwent a change. His features softened under the dirt and beard, and his eyes were warmer. "Look, we've made a pretty good start today, haven't we? Don't you think we could—"

"No!" she interrupted. "You said you wanted to talk business, and we have. Don't read anything personal into it."

"Who are you trying to convince—me or yourself?"

"Good-bye, John. Let's make this the last time."

She wheeled the stallion sharply about. Ryan sat there motionless as a statue and watched as she rode away. His eyes registered nothing.

CHAPTER
TWENTY-TWO

Ryan stood in the dark shelterbelt of the woods. An owl hooted somewhere and farther away a dog barked. He slowly scanned the yard around Stand Watie's home. Finding nothing, his eyes moved to the front of the house. He spotted a guard on the porch.

Earlier, he'd struck out cross-country again after talking with Elizabeth. Traveling almost due south, he had sighted Webbers Falls late that afternoon. He'd skirted the village, still avoiding people and roads, wary of being seen. By sundown he had secreted himself in the woods behind Stand Watie's farmhouse.

So far as Ryan knew, Elias Boudinot was there now. Boudinot, when not off politicking in Washington, stayed with his uncle. The trick would be to get past the guard and inside without raising an alarm. Surprise was vital to what Ryan had in mind.

The moon went behind a cloud. He stepped from the trees as darkness momentarily cloaked the land. His nerves were strung wire tight and his hearing seemed painfully acute. He catfooted to the side of the porch. There he waited until the guard turned toward the opposite side of the house. Timing his move closely, he stepped onto the porch with the Colt raised. He thunked the guard over the head and caught him before he fell. A minute's work left the man bound with his own belt.

Ryan eased through the front door. He gently closed it behind him, hesitating in the darkened hallway. The layout was familiar from his previous visit, and he proceeded to the lighted parlor entrance. A quick look located Boudinot seated at a small desk, writing a letter. There was no sign of Stand Watie.

Ryan lingered a moment longer in the hall. His interrogation of Boudinot would not take long, perhaps ten minutes at the most. He felt confident that all questions would be answered to his satisfaction. Yet he wanted no surprises, and it seemed risky to begin until he knew the whereabouts of Boudinot's uncle. He also wondered about women and children in the house.

A door at the rear of the parlor opened. Stand Watie entered, wearing a floppy nightshirt out over his pants. His hair was mussed and he padded barefoot to the fireplace. He yawned, stood with his back to the flames, and idly watched his kinsman. Finally his voice intruded on the scratch of pen on paper.

"I'm going to bed."

"Good night," Boudinot said without looking up. "Sleep well."

"Don't stay up all night."

"I just want to finish this letter to Vinnie."

"Humph!" Watie snorted. "Bad enough you named a town after her. You don't have to act like a lovesick puppy."

"We've been through that before."

"Well, I still think it's damn foolishness. You've got no business chasing after a white woman!"

"Precisely the point," Boudinot remarked. "It's my business, no one else's."

"She'll never marry you. You know that, don't you?"

"Whether she does or doesn't alters nothing. She provides an entrée into the proper Washington circles. I'm satisfied with the arrangement."

"Still say it's damn fool nonsense!"

Boudinot smiled, dipping his pen in the inkwell. He resumed writing with an amused glance at his uncle. Watie muttered something, then turned from the fireplace.

"Hold it right there."

Ryan stepped into the room. His voice was low, but the words were a whipcrack command. The pistol was extended at waist level, covering Watie. He wagged the barrel in Boudinot's direction.

"Over by your uncle."

Boudinot rose, dropping his pen. He crossed to the fireplace, halting beside Watie. His features congealed in a scowl.

"What's the meaning of this?"

Ryan ignored him, glancing at Watie. "Where are the women and children?"

"In bed," Watie said sullenly. "What happened to the man I had posted outside?"

"Nothing much. He'll wake up with a lump on his head."

Watie glowered at him a moment. Then his eyes went dark and vengeful. "You've got more trouble than you bargained for. I'll see to that personally."

Ryan smiled without warmth. "I'll remember you warned me. Tonight's not your night, though. I'm here to talk with your nephew."

"About what?" Boudinot demanded.

"The A&P," Ryan said. "I understand you've made a deal with Andrew Peirce."

"Who told you that?"

"Do you deny it?"

"No," Boudinot's voice was guarded. "It wouldn't have remained secret long anyway."

Ryan regarded him with contempt. "Stevens will be disappointed in you."

"I had no choice!" Boudinot said with a sudden glare. "My life was threatened. I had to go along."

"Way I hear it, you didn't lose anything. You've still got a town site."

"No, that's not true. I only have a share—a small share—in this one."

"Who are your partners?"

"That's none of your business."

"I just made it my business. Suppose you tell me the whole story."

"And if I refuse?"

Ryan cocked the pistol. "You know what the Cherokees call me?"

"The Indian Killer," Boudinot said weakly.

"Don't make me prove it."

Boudinot stood immobilized, as though frozen in place. Ryan looked to him like the image of death itself. He wondered if Stevens had sent the man here to kill him. A moment slipped past, then he sighed and hung his head.

"What do you want to know?"

"Who's behind it?" Ryan asked. "And don't tell me it's a bunch of council members. It has to be someone with authority."

Boudinot's eyes fell before his gaze. "It was Tappin."

"Tappin?" Ryan said, astonished. "Tappin threatened your life?"

"I swear it's true!"

"And Tappin is your partner?"

"No," Boudinot said in a shaky voice. "Several council members are involved. Tappin wanted it that way so it would appear more legitimate to the tribe. He took nothing for himself."

"Why?" Ryan pressed him. "What's he got to gain?"

"Tappin wants to destroy Stevens and the Katy. He feels the A&P is the lesser of two evils."

"What about William Ross?"

Ryan was alert to the slightest reaction. He watched the other man's eyes, looking for anything hidden or uneasy. Boudinot met his gaze steadily.

"I never met directly with Ross. But, of course, that means nothing in itself."

"Why not?"

Boudinot shrugged. "Tappin is a loyal bootlicker. He wouldn't visit the outhouse without Ross' permission."

Ryan wasn't all that sure he agreed with the assessment. Yet his purpose was to glean information, rather than start a debate. He went on to a more relevant point.

"Think back," he urged. "Did Tappin ever say Ross was involved in the A&P deal?"

"No, he never actually said it. But he certainly implied as much. Why do you ask?"

"I like to know who my enemies are."

Watie grunted aloud. "You've made one here tonight. No man forces his way into my home without paying the price."

Ryan fixed him with a harsh stare. "Do yourself a big favor. Stay out of my way."

Boudinot silenced his kinsman with a gesture. "Forget what he said, Ryan. We're in no position to be threatening people."

"Glad to forget it," Ryan said, his eyes impersonal. "Just don't get crosswise of me, or I'm liable to remember."

Boudinot and Watie looked at him without speaking. Still covering them, he backed through the entryway and into the hall. A moment later the front door closed.

Gibson Station was still going strong. Midnight had come and gone, but the street was crowded with men. Drunken laughter mixed with discordant strains of music echoed from the dives and saloons.

Ryan forded the river south of town. He bypassed the construction camp and rode directly to the livestock pens. Then, after turning the horse into an empty stall, he fetched water and an armload of hay. He thought the roan had earned his keep.

Approaching the rail yard, he noted that the lights were out in Stevens' private car. He mounted the steps and rapped on the door. Several seconds passed before a lamp was lighted. Attired in a nightshirt and dressing robe, Stevens made his way through the car. His eyes were gummy with sleep and a whiskery stubble covered his jawline. When he opened the door, he looked both irritated and surprised.

"Ryan!" he said in a phlegmy voice. "Where the devil have you been?"

"Here and there," Ryan replied. "I just now rode in."

"Why didn't you telegraph me? I wired the station agent at Vinita and he said you'd disappeared."

"Figured you'd better hear this in person."

"Hear what?" Stevens said, motioning him through the door. "Have you turned up something?"

"It's a long story."

Ryan took it step by step. He first related what he'd seen at the A&P construction site. Then he explained why he had called on Elizabeth Ross and what he'd learned. He ended with a recounting of his unannounced visit to Stand Watie's farmhouse. He stuck to the facts, voicing no conclusions.

As he talked, all the color drained from Stevens' face. The railroader seemed turned to stone, his mouth set in a grim line. At one point he bolted from his chair and began pacing the floor with jerky strides. Finally he pulled himself together and once more sat down. When he spoke, there was an undercurrent of rage in his voice.

"Goddamn Boudinot!" he said hotly. "After all I've done for him, and he stabs me in the back. The miserable bastard!"

Ryan nodded. "That pretty well pegs him."

A vein pulsed in Stevens' forehead. "You were right about him being a turncoat. He betrayed his own people easily enough—so why not me?"

"Probably easier with you than it was with the Cherokees. After all, you're a *tibo*."

"Well, as someone once said, hindsight makes the most ignorant of men wise. I won't make the same mistake twice."

"I don't follow you."

"No more side deals with Indians," Stevens declared. "We'll finish building the railroad and get the hell out of the Nations. Whoever called these people civilized had a strange sense of humor."

"Speaking of that," Ryan added, "Major Tappin has had himself a horse laugh at our expense. One way or another, we ought to have the last laugh."

"Tell me," Stevens asked, his eyes grave. "Do you think Ross authorized the A&P deal? Or was it solely Tappin's handiwork?"

"Hard to say," Ryan remarked. "I know Ross has lost some of his influence over the tribal council. But whether Tappin would pull this on his own is another question."

"And in the end," Stevens said in a disgusted tone, "it probably doesn't matter. We've been forced into a fight with the A&P, and it's dog eat dog. We have to take counter-measures."

Ryan looked at him. "What'd you have in mind?"

"Go get Tom Scullin. Roust him out and tell him I said chop, chop! We need to hold a war council."

Ten minutes later Ryan returned with Scullin. The Irishman was half dressed and looked grumpy as a soretailed bear. But his mood underwent an abrupt turnaround when Stevens began talking. Stevens' eyes were fierce and his voice was clipped.

"Tom, I want the Irish Brigade ready to roll by dawn!"

"*Dawn?*"

"You heard me!" Stevens said. "Every man jack of them, bright-eyed and bushy-tailed."

Scullin gave him a sharp, sidelong look. "And where might we be rollin' to?"

"Vinita!" Stevens announced. "Or to be more precise, three miles north of Vinita. I intend to raid the A&P terminal."

"You *what*?"

"A guerrilla raid!" Stevens rasped. "We'll rout their work gangs! Close down their operation!"

Scullin's eyes took on a bright, madcap gleam. "You're serious, are you? You plan to hit them head-on?"

"I do indeed! I want the depot and the warehouse torn down. When you're through with that, pull up all their fence posts—"

"*All* of them?"

"—and build a bonfire to light up the Cherokee Nation. I want the bastards put on warning. We will not tolerate interference!"

Scullin turned to Ryan. "What d'you think, John? Are we within our rights?"

"It's not legal," Ryan ventured, "but possession is nine-tenths of the law. Who's to stop us?"

"Andrew Peirce," Scullin said, glancing at Stevens. "You know him yourself, Colonel. The man's a terrible dirty fighter. He'll not take it lyin' down."

"Let him come!" Stevens said vindictively. "We'll rout him *and* his railroad. No quarter asked and none given!"

"So it's war, then?"

"Yes, goddammit! How many times do I have to say it? A war to the finish!"

"Aye," Scullin said with a harsh bark of laughter. "And we'll be the ones to finish it."

The Irishman turned toward the door. He smote Ryan across the shoulder, grinning broadly. "C'mon, Johnny. We'll give 'em a shellacking they'll never forget!"

"Tom, I wouldn't miss it for all the tea in China."

Scullin roared a great belly laugh.

CHAPTER TWENTY-THREE

The operation was conducted like a military campaign. Throughout the remainder of the night, Scullin attended to logistical matters. His manner was that of a general preparing to occupy a foreign country.

Arms were the first consideration. By company edict railroad workers were not allowed to possess personal firearms. In Scullin's bunk car were several rifles and pistols, which were rotated on a nightly basis among the railway guards. Wary of starting a shooting war, he decided to keep these weapons under lock and key.

Scullin was a seasoned campaigner. He'd fought in railroad wars back east, and he knew that fists were not the weapon of choice. Men determined to inflict injury and rout their opponents selected weapons suitable to the task. Accordingly, he ordered several crates of replacement parts brought up from the warehouse. Every member of the Irish Brigade was then armed with a stout pickax handle.

Stevens appointed himself commander-in-chief. He was neither a physical man nor a warrior. To him violence was merely another business tool to be used with judicious application. His preference was to outmaneuver an opponent, wits over force. Mayhem, while not necessarily repugnant, simply wasn't his strong suit. He wisely left the fighting to Scullin and the Irish Brigade.

Scullin accepted the responsibility with a certain brutish glee. He was a blooded scrapper himself and was confident that his men would make a good showing of themselves. Any true son of Erin fancied pugilism over diplomacy, and all of Scullin's men still spoke with a brogue. He had no doubt that they would carry the day.

Ryan was appointed second in command. The men respected him, and they were by now fully convinced of his fighting ability. Apart from being coolheaded, he was chosen as well for his experience in outwitting wanted men. Scullin knew the battle with the A&P would be decided as much on stratagem as on brute force. He thought Ryan would advise him well.

The construction train was revamped for battle. All flatcars and boxcars were shunted into the rail yard. What remained were the bunk cars, which would serve as troop carriers, and a well-stocked kitchen car. Stripped to essentials, the train was capable of highball speed and quick maneuver. It would carry more than two hundred men and sufficient victuals to feed them for three days. Coupled to the rear was the private car of Robert Stevens.

The Irish Brigade worked through the night. Hours were consumed in the rail yard, breaking down the train and then re-forming it into a sleek war wagon. Scullin constantly exhorted the men to move things along. No one resented his badgering, for they were all caught up in the contagion of an impending fight. Like all good troop commanders, he also knew that an army travels on its stomach. An hour before dawn the men were fed a hot breakfast.

At first light the train got under way. The girls of Poonville turned out to cheer them on with fluttering hankies and ribald hurrahs. Pickax handles thrust overhead, the Irish Brigade responded with a bellowing roar.

Asa Johnson felt the tracks vibrate. He checked the depot clock, noting that it was a few minutes past nine. No train was scheduled through Vinita until late morning.

Walking outside, Johnson peered down the tracks. He saw

the smoke, then the engine, and finally he heard the clickety-clack of steel on steel. He idly wondered why the engineer wasn't sounding the whistle, but his curiosity turned to amazement as the train pulled into the station. He saw it was an entire trainload of Micks. Scullin and his Irish buffoons.

And all of them waving ax handles!

The private car was speedily uncoupled. At Scullin's insistence, Stevens was to establish a command post in the depot. There, with access to the telegraph, he could open lines of communication with Gibson Station. Otis Gunn and his bridge builders could be rushed north if reinforcements were needed.

Stevens, looking properly military, took over Vinita station. Asa Johnson was pressed into service and ordered to clear the telegraph line southward. By half past nine, with the private car shunted onto a siding, the command post was in operation. Stevens stood on the depot platform as the train chuffed away, gathering speed. He waved even though no one waved back.

Some ten minutes later the train topped a small rise. Ahead lay the A&P depot, and nearby the freight warehouse. At the cardinal points of the compass, work crews were putting the finishing touches on a post-and-rail fence. To the east, obscured by a haze of dust, the track-laying gangs were perhaps a mile away. Not more than thirty men were still working around the depot itself.

Surprise, which was critical to Scullin's plan, appeared to be complete. Hanging from the engine cab, he scanned the depot and shot Ryan a wide grin. His primary objective was to occupy the terminal before significant resistance could be mounted. By the look of things, no one expected an aggressive move, much less an invasion from the Katy. For the moment he had superiority in numbers and a jump on the A&P's main force. He meant to press the advantage without delay.

The engineer throttled down, quickly set the brakes. Groaning and squealing, the train eased to a stop directly in front of the depot. Scullin hopped onto the platform with

Ryan at his heels. Behind them the Irish Brigade poured out of the bunk cars like a horde of blue-eyed Mongols. With leaders appointed earlier and the Brigade already split into four companies, the men moved out smartly. In less than a minute, the depot and warehouse were completely surrounded.

The stationhouse door banged open. Lon Kellett, foreman of the depot operation, stalked out onto the platform. He was a tough ox of a man with scarcely any neck, his head fixed directly on his shoulders. He knew Tom Scullin on sight, though they had never before tangled. He looked decidedly unimpressed today.

"What the hell's the idea, Scullin?"

"Why, it's simple enough," Scullin said pleasantly. "You're trespassing on private property. I'll have to ask you to clear out."

"Trespassin'!" Kellett rumbled. "You've got rocks in your head. This here's A&P property!"

"No, Lon, *you're* mistaken. You've built your depot on Katy right-of-way. I want you out—now."

Kellett glared at him, baffled. "That just ain't possible! We can't be on your right-of-way!"

"You are," Scullin said with finality. "And I'll not argue the matter further. So be a good lad and vacate the premises."

"Like shit!" Kellett growled. "The graders are gonna be here after noontime. They're all set to put in the crossing."

"Not today," Scullin informed him. "Until things are put right, there'll be no crossing. Tell Mr. Peirce to stay clear of our tracks."

"Stick it up your ass! I ain't going nowhere."

"That's your last word on it?"

"Goddamn right!"

Scullin hit him. The blow caught Kellett flush between the eyes, staggered him backward, and he dropped to one knee. Uncommonly agile for his size, Scullin shifted and took a quick step forward. He lashed out, exploding two splintering punches on the other man's jaw. Kellett went down like a wet sack of oats. He was out cold.

Grinning wickedly, Scullin dusted his hands and glanced around at Ryan. "Some men just won't listen to reason. And wouldn't you know, I gave him the straight of it. He is on our right-of-way!"

"No doubt about it," Ryan said, smiling. "You were entirely justified, Tom."

"Oh, indeed I was! Can you imagine the man's gall? Tellin' *me* to stick it! Blood of Christ!"

The A&P work crew was herded up to the depot. Three wagons were brought around, with mules already harnessed, and Lon Kellett was loaded aboard. He regained his senses just as the wagons took off across the prairie, headed toward the distant track-laying operation. Wobbling to his knees, he rose and shook his fist in the air. Scullin laughed uproariously, waving good-bye with his hat.

The Irish Brigade went to work with a cheerful vengeance. One company began dismantling the depot while another assaulted the warehouse. With wagons and teams the two remaining companies set out to destroy the fence. Ryan thought they looked like overgrown boys pulling an outlandish prank. It all seemed so good-natured and playful, some sort of jest.

Then his gaze shifted to the A&P end-of-track. He wondered how Andrew Peirce would enjoy being made the butt of the joke. He knew the answer wouldn't be long in coming.

There was now a gigantic bonfire where the station once stood. Already the wreckage of the depot and the warehouse had been consumed, reduced to ashes over the afternoon and early evening. Fence posts were being fed a wagonload at a time into the roaring blaze. Sparks showered the air and great tongues of flame leaped skyward.

Scullin and Ryan stood near the tracks. They were amused by the men's antics, watching quietly as another load of posts fueled the fire. The beefy track-layers whooped and shouted, not unlike Indian braves engaged in a war dance. Their exuberant cries filled the still night air.

Scullin had ordered the bonfire rekindled after the men had been fed a hot supper. Several lookouts were posted atop the train and told to keep a watchful eye on the A&P camp. But Scullin's confidence seemed to ebb as the night wore on. He'd waited all afternoon for Andrew Peirce to retaliate. He had felt certain the roaring bonfire would provoke the other side. Yet now he'd begun to have his doubts.

"Hell of a note," he said gruffly, holding his pocket watch to the light. "Going on midnight and still no sign of them. Where are they?"

Ryan was silent a moment. "Maybe Peirce doesn't like the odds. It's possible he's got something else in mind."

"Such as?"

"Well, for one thing, there's the law. He might've sent to Fort Smith for a marshal."

"What would that accomplish?"

"If nothing else, it'd be a standoff. They were trespassing, but we destroyed their property. The law would order us to move out of their way—let them lay track."

"Oh, we'll not stop them from laying track. Peirce has a federal grant and nothing to be done about that."

Ryan looked at him. "Then why not pull back to Gibson Station? You've wrecked their depot and warehouse. What's left?"

"Nothing," Scullin said. "Unless Peirce still has some notion of organizing a town site. If he does, then we'll sit here till doomsday."

"How will you know whether he does or not?"

Scullin smiled. "If he wants a town site, then he knows he'll have to drive us off. It's a case of might makes right. To hell with the law!"

"What about Boudinot? From a legal standpoint, the land belongs to him and his new cronies."

"The Colonel will hold Boudinot to the original deal. Assuming, of course, that nobody kills him in the meantime. How do you feel on that score—will they try?"

"Hard to say," Ryan allowed. "We still don't know who they are."

"You're talking about the assassins?"

Ryan nodded. "Boudinot crawled in bed with Tappin, and that might help him some. We'll just have to wait and see."

"Jesus," Scullin grunted. "It makes you wish for the good old days. Building a railroad used to be a damnsight easier."

Ryan chuckled. "Some folks call it progress, Tom."

Scullin's reply was cut short. One of the lookouts whistled and caught their attention. Standing on top of the nearest bunk car, the man rapidly motioned eastward. They crossed the tracks and halted in front of the locomotive. Their eyes were drawn to movement far out on the prairie.

Moonlight bathed the landscape in a pale glow. The distant movement slowly became distinct human forms. Looking closer, Scullin and Ryan were able to make out a large body of men. As the gap narrowed and the figures became more distinguishable, their number appeared to be something over two hundred. They were carrying pickax handles and lengths of chain and approaching at a determined stride.

Scullin laughed and spat on his hands. "Well now, it appears we've got ourselves a donnybrook!"

"In spades," Ryan added. "Where do we meet them?"

"Where else? On our own right-of-way!"

The Irish Brigade was mustered in a matter of minutes. With Scullin and Ryan in the lead, they took up position on the east side of the tracks. After the long wait, the prospect of a skulldusting contest seemed to raise the men's spirits even higher. They began shouting catcalls, slapping their pickax handles into open palms. Behind them the bonfire cast a shimmering light across the tracks.

Lon Kellett was in the vanguard of the A&P track layers. He carried a three-foot length of logging chain and his eyes glinted with cold ferocity. The men around him closed ranks. They advanced in a burly wedge, weapons gripped tightly. As they approached, the catcalls died off and the Irish Brigade fell silent. There seemed no reason to talk, nothing left to negotiate. Whatever was to be settled would be settled by force.

Leaping out front, Kellett snarled a murderous oath and swung the logging chain overhead. Scullin went to meet him, ducking aside to let the chain whistle past. He clouted Kellett square in the knee with the pickax handle, and there was a loud crack. As Kellett screamed and toppled sideways, the A&P tracklayers surged forward. A roar went up along the tracks, and the Irish Brigade jumped into the fray. The earth seemed to quaver under the impact as the two sides collided head-on.

Ryan waded in to join Scullin at the forefront. Together, almost shoulder to shoulder, they clubbed and hammered in a blurred flurry. The men of both sides battered their way into the center of the action like ancient warriors, hurling themselves at one another with savage abandon. The struggle quickly became a contest of brute strength, a barbarous melee of ax handles and swinging chains. Over the grunts and curses came the dull whump of blows, and louder still the strangled cries of those struck down.

The battleground soon turned wet and slick with blood. The mushy thump of wood on flesh and the crunch of shattering bone beat a steady tattoo in the otherwise still night. Men fell in increasing numbers, trampled and crushed underfoot, reduced to bleating, terrified animals. Yet the struggle raged on, never slackening as the strongest ones hacked their way toward each other. Neither side wavered, and no man backed off.

The momentum of the battle slowly shifted as foot by foot the A&P tracklayers were forced to give ground. The Irish Brigade smelled victory and their ax handles flailed faster. Kellett's men broke ranks and scattered before the attack. Once the retreat began, a sense of panic swept through the A&P forces. Those in the rear quietly deserted their comrades, fleeing across the prairie. The few who still fought on were quickly hammered into the ground.

The battle ended with abrupt suddenness. Breathing hard, Ryan stepped back from a man he'd just clubbed on the head. The special agent lurched, wobbling unsteadily, pinwheels of light flashing before his eyes. Blood oozed down over his cheekbone and an ugly cut split his lower lip. His hat was gone and one side of his jacket was ripped across the shoulder. He dimly remembered the blows, the punishment he'd absorbed. But he had lost count of the men who had fallen before his ax handle.

Ryan became slowly aware of his surroundings. He was some thirty yards beyond the railroad tracks, with no recollection of how he'd gotten there. The moonlit earth was littered with fallen men, many of them severely injured and moaning pitifully. Others lay sprawled where they'd been struck down, unconscious and bleeding, perhaps dead. Those still standing were the men of the Irish Brigade. Their breathing was ragged, frosty spurts in the chill night air, and most of them had already cast aside their ax handles. They looked curiously unlike victors.

Ryan turned, then suddenly stopped. He saw Scullin a few yards away, bent down on one knee. The Irishman was matted with blood, his scalp laid open along the hairline. He seemed dazed, blinking his eyes as he surveyed the carnage. After a moment, as though he sensed Ryan's stare, he looked around. Their eyes met, and Scullin seemed to gather himself. His mouth twitched in a game smile.

"We whipped 'em, Johnny. Whipped 'em good!"

CHAPTER
TWENTY-FOUR

The light of day was sobering. All the exhilaration of the fight seemed to have evaporated overnight. There was little talk in the Katy camp, and a somber mood prevailed. No one crowed victory or slandered the vanquished.

As the sun rose higher, men paused to look at the battle-ground. Sometime during the night a string of torchlit wagons from the A&P camp had collected their injured. One of the bunk cars had been converted into a hospital and quickly filled with the Irish Brigade's casualties. Before the moon waned, all those struck down had been removed.

To Ryan's amazement, no one had been killed. He'd worked late into the night helping tend some of the fallen men. Broken arms and legs were the most common injury. Several men, their heads split open and their features horribly mangled, were in serious condition. None would die, but weeks, perhaps months would pass before they were once again whole. The price of victory had been extreme.

Ryan considered himself lucky. Compared to some in the Irish Brigade, he'd come through almost unscathed. Fleeting images of the night before were still with him, and he found himself in a dark, introspective mood. Violence was part and parcel of his work; over the years he'd killed more men than he cared to admit, but some aspect of last night's struggle left him reflective, and vaguely troubled. While the Civil War raged, he had taken part in many of the bloodiest battles. He'd seen death in every known form, from grapeshot to entrails spilled by a cavalryman's sword. Later, as a marshal he had killed swiftly and without regret. But now, for some reason he was unable to identify, he felt demeaned by what he'd done last night. He didn't understand it, and more to the point, he didn't understand himself. He wondered if a man might somehow become tired of violence and bloodshed the way he might become surfeited with rich food. The question nagged at him and that bothered him all the more.

Stevens walked into camp late that morning. Advised of the battle's outcome, he had hiked the three miles from Vinita. His attitude was triumphant, and he lavished high praise on Scullin as well as Ryan. But then, as he marched around congratulating the Irish Brigade on their victory, a strange thing happened. The men avoided his eyes, nodding wordlessly, their manner distant. Unspoken, though felt by everyone, was the thought that Stevens, like his rival, Andrew Peirce, had sat out the fight in safety. He was therefore not one of them, and the men resented his Johnny-come-lately camaraderie. Stevens was obviously wounded by the men's coldness and withdrew in confusion and embarrassment. He looked like a general who had arrived late and missed the parade.

Around one o'clock the train departed for Gibson Station. There was a brief stop in Vinita, where Stevens' private car was hooked on to the rear. Scullin and Ryan both declined an invitation to join the railroader for the balance of the trip. Instead, they rode in the hospital car, assisting those who had volunteered to look after the injured. Scullin, whose head was wrapped in a bloody bandage, seemed particularly sensitive to the needs of the hurt men. He acted very much like someone with a guilty conscience.

Ryan became absorbed in watching Scullin. He wondered if the Irishman was having second thoughts similar to his own. The idea intrigued Ryan for Tom Scullin was no stranger to bloodshed. Nor was he known for putting the welfare of his men before the dictates of the railroad. He tended to see the world in bold black and white even more than Ryan, and the demands of the job took precedence over all else. Still, he looked troubled today and ministered to the wounded men as though he'd smote them down himself.

Some miles down the road, Ryan moved to the open door for a breath of air. He was lost in his own thoughts when he became aware that Scullin had joined him. The Irishman filled a pipe from his tobacco pouch and cupped his hands into the wind to shield a match. He puffed smoke, saying nothing, and seemed content to share the silence. After a while he gave Ryan a sidelong glance. Then he nodded back into the hospital car.

"I've been thinkin'," he said in a muted voice. "All these boys crippled and hurt—it's a hell of a price."

"During the war," Ryan remarked, "I heard it called the aftereffects of battle. Once the fighting's over, you get to wondering whether it was worth it—who really won."

"God help me," Scullin said half to himself. "Last night I did my damnedest to kill somebody. And a blessed wonder I didn't too! I had a taste for blood."

"Nothing unusual in that. It happens to lots of men in the heat of a fight."

"Do you think so, John?"

"I know it for a fact. I've seen it too many times to doubt it."

"Well, I don't mind tellin' you, it's new to me. I've busted heads, fought rough and tumble all my life. But I've never killed a man—never wanted to—till last night."

"It's the way of things," Ryan said quietly. "One day you do it and the next day you wish you hadn't. I reckon you just got lucky."

Scullin puffed thoughtfully on his pipe. He'd heard a rueful note in Ryan's voice, and he was suddenly tempted to ask a question that he had always avoided. He hesitated even now, fearful the younger man would take offense. But the compulsion to ask, regardless of the consequences, was too great. After last night he had to know.

"We've known each other how long, John? Eight months or thereabouts?"

"Close enough," Ryan said. "What makes you ask?"

"Because I'm about to trade on friendship. I want to ask you a personal question."

"Go ahead."

"Well . . ." Scullin paused, then rushed on. "So I'll quit wonderin', I'd be obliged if you'll tell me. What's it like to kill a man?"

Ryan wasn't offended. Had it been anyone else, he would have responded curtly. But he'd shared a bunk car and a great many confidences with Tom Scullin. And he'd never forgotten the Irishman's genuine concern following the courtroom shootout. He decided to answer the question.

"The first time," he said evenly, "you get a little queasy at your stomach. It's like you've suddenly learned what death means—it's not pretty."

"And the next time?" Scullin asked softly.

"Unless you're a mad-dog killer, it never gets easier. You're able to do it without a whole lot of thought while it's happening. But afterward you always wish there'd been another way."

Scullin searched his eyes. "And the man you've killed, what do you feel for him?"

"Anger," Ryan said simply. "You wonder why the damn fool forced your hand. You want to jerk him up and box his ears good for making you do it."

"Are you bothered by it later?"

"Your conscience isn't bothered. You're sorry and you wish it'd turned out different. But what you think about mostly is whether you did it quickly and cleanly. Your biggest regret is if you didn't and he suffered."

"So it's not all that cold-blooded, is it?"

"No," Ryan told him. "It's damn personal. Just as personal as you'll ever get with another man."

Scullin considered a moment. "When it's happenin', are you ever afraid, Johnny? Do you think about the other man killin' you?"

Ryan nodded, as though it was a question he'd already asked himself. "You don't think about anything. You trust your instincts and you get the job done the best way possible. When you start thinking, you're almost certain to get yourself killed."

Scullin realized his pipe had gone cold. He stared out the door, watching the countryside rush past. He thought he had never heard anything sadder than what he'd just been told. And he was sorrier for John Ryan than any man he'd ever known. After a time, he looked around.

"Thank you, John," he said genuinely. "You've done me a service. I'll go out of my way to avoid that first time."

"You could do worse, Tom. A hell of a lot worse."

Neither of them spoke again. They stood there, warmed by the sun, while the train rattled southward. An hour or so later they crossed into the Creek Nation.

Gibson Station celebrated their return. Stevens magnanimously gave the men of the Irish Brigade a bonus and awarded them two days off. Those of them who were able to walk beat a path first to the saloons and then to Poonville. The girls welcomed them like a conquering army.

Early the next morning Ryan rode out of camp. After a restless night, he'd decided to resolve the mystery of Elias Boudinot. There were unanswered questions in his mind, and he knew he'd heard only one side of the story. He told no one where he was going, for he considered it a personal matter. Outside town he turned his horse northeast, toward Tahlequah.

Autumn was slowly settling over the land. Frosty nights and cool days were gradually chilling the wooded terrain. Trees already gave promise of leaves turned umber and gold and fiery red. Yet Ryan saw nothing of the burgeoning splendor, for his mind was preoccupied with other matters. As he rode he tried to organize his thoughts, phrase the questions that needed to be asked. He decided on the direct approach, rather than cat and mouse. He'd had his fill of diplomacy.

An hour before noontime he sighted William Ross' home.

When he stepped out of the saddle, the stable boy took his horse with a great show of reluctance. At the door one of the house servants admitted him as though he was unwelcome. Some twenty minutes passed while he cooled his heels in the vestibule. At last, without apology, he was shown into the study. By then Ryan himself was not inclined to be tactful.

Ross received him with austere civility. He looked openly displeased. There was no offer of a chair, even though the older man was seated behind his desk. Nor was there any pretense of welcome, or a handshake.

"I can only assume," he said formally, "that you've chosen to ignore my wishes. I thought I made myself clear the last time you were here."

Ryan halted in front of the desk, hat in hand. "You did, but there's no way around it. I need a question answered, and you're the man to ask."

"Indeed?" Ross replied. "Why should I answer anything put to me by Colonel Stevens' emissary?"

"I'm not here for Stevens or the railroad. I'm here to satisfy myself about something."

"And what might that be?"

"Elias Boudinot."

Ryan let the name drop, then waited. There was no flicker of reaction on Ross' features. He merely sat there unsmiling, returning Ryan's stare. At length he made a noncommittal gesture.

"Very well—ask your question."

"I braced Boudinot," Ryan said. "According to him, Tappin rigged the A&P land deal. The new town site was a put-up job, start to finish."

"Go on," Ross said faintly.

"Tappin threatened Boudinot to make him cooperate. Scared him so bad that he agreed to betray Stevens and throw in with the A&P."

"You still haven't asked a question."

"Tappin's your man." Ryan paused, looking him straight

in the eye. "I want to know if he was following your orders."

"Is that what Boudinot told you?"

"Yeah, more or less. He said Tappin doesn't hop unless you say 'frog.'"

Ross appeared bitterly amused. "Whether I gave the order or not seems somewhat academic. What does it matter to you?"

"Let's just say it matters. Are you going to answer me or not?"

Ross grew silent, staring at a shaft of sunlight filtering through the window. His expression was abstracted, a long pause of inner deliberation. Finally he glanced up, motioned to Ryan.

"Please sit down, John."

Ryan took a chair. He was keenly aware of the abrupt change in Ross' manner. The tension between them seemed to melt away.

"When I was younger," Ross said in an avuncular voice, "I thought a strong leader could impose his will on an entire people. In time I learned that it's sometimes necessary to turn a blind eye and exercise pragmatism."

"So you knew," Ryan ventured, "but you didn't actually issue the order. You just let Tappin go ahead with it."

Ross inclined his head. "I had little choice in the matter. Had I attempted to stop him, I would have been accused of taking sides with Stevens. Any hint of that would destroy my influence with the tribal council."

"Weren't you worried about what Stevens would do? You must've known he wouldn't let the A&P get away with it."

"I'm not responsible for what Stevens does or doesn't do."

"Yeah, but you're responsible for what Tappin does."

"In a sense, I condoned it with my silence. So, yes, you're right."

"And that got a lot of good men hurt the other night. Some of them could've been killed."

Ross looked at him squarely. "A number of my people *have been* killed."

"There's a difference," Ryan said with studied calm. "They went looking for a fight and found it. You forced Stevens' hand—and got a bunch of men crippled—by doing nothing. You could've pulled in the reins on Tappin."

"I regret very much that those men were injured. But why should I create dissension within the council merely to stop Tappin? After all, any squabble between Stevens and the A&P can only benefit my people."

"Like it or not," Ryan pointed out, "the railroad's here to stay. All you've done is make yourself—and the Cherokees—some more enemies in Washington. You ought to start mending your fences instead."

Ross raised a questioning eyebrow. "Why are you so concerned with the Cherokees' welfare?"

Ryan didn't answer the question directly. "Stevens won't quit till he whips the A&P. He aims to make the Katy the dominant line in the Nations, and he will. You'd better learn to live with it."

"Would you suggest I run up the white flag today or wait awhile?"

"What I'd suggest," Ryan urged, "is that you face the facts, accept reality. Otherwise you'll just make it tougher on your people."

Ross regarded him thoughtfully for a moment, then shook his head. "You still haven't explained your sudden concern for the Cherokees."

"Nothing sudden about it. I'm just tired of killing people, that's all. I want it to stop."

Ryan stood, ending the conversation. When he walked from the room, Ross looked rather confounded. He thought the younger man's outburst was highly revealing. It seemed to him on the order of a confession or a plea for absolution. Or perhaps both.

The realization triggered something deeper and more personal. He sensed he'd misjudged John Ryan.

*   *   *

Elizabeth was waiting in the hallway. After being informed of Ryan's arrival, she had hurried downstairs. The door to the study was ajar, and while she hadn't meant to eavesdrop, she couldn't help herself. Some quick-felt hope had compelled her to listen.

Her sudden appearance startled Ryan. He seemed embarrassed, uncertain as to how much she'd overheard. Falling in beside him, she quickly dispelled any doubt. She smiled as they walked toward the vestibule.

"I heard everything," she said happily. "And I don't apologize for eavesdropping. I'm so very proud of you, John."

"For what?"

"For your . . ." She hesitated, choosing her words. "For your change of heart. You'll never regret breaking with the railroad."

"Hold on!" Ryan said, halting in midstride. "You jumped to the wrong conclusion. I'm still on the Katy payroll."

"But I thought—"

"All I said was, I'm tired of the killing. I want it stopped, but quitting my job wouldn't accomplish anything. I can do more to end it by staying right where I am."

"Can you?" Her voice dropped. "Or will it just go on until someone kills you?"

Ryan looked down, studied the floor. "What do you want of me, Elizabeth?"

"Too much, it seems," she said coolly. "So I'll just repay you for the advice you gave Father."

"You don't have to repay anything."

She smiled wanly. "Perhaps it will help end the killing. In any case, you should beware of David Tappin. He doesn't like talk of compromise."

"I knew that a long time ago."

"And he will never accept reality—or the railroad."

"If you're trying to tell me he's vindictive, I already got the message. He showed that with the A&P."

"There's more," she went on quickly. "I believe he's

trying to force my father's resignation. He has visions of himself as chief of the Cherokee Nation.''

Ryan looked surprised. "How does your father feel about that?''

"He thinks I'm foolish," she admitted. "He won't listen, or discuss it."

"Well, if it means anything, I believe you. Tappin strikes me as being too shifty for his own good."

"John"—she touched his arm—"won't you reconsider . . . about the railroad?''

"Sorry, but I'm no quitter. I couldn't walk away when the fight's half done.''

They parted on that note. When he went through the door, her breath caught in her throat. She folded her arms around her waist, clasping herself as if she were cold. There was a look of anguish in her eyes.

She felt a strange sense of loss.

CHAPTER
TWENTY-FIVE

The Verdigris River bridge once more took shape. Working marathon hours, Otis Gunn and his men swarmed over the demolished two-hundred-foot span. The resurrected structure was a visible testament to their efforts.

Support timbers were in place and work had begun on the superstructure as early as mid-October. Gunn estimated the center span could be opened to traffic toward the end of the month. Four miles south of Gibson Station, work was progressing as well on the Arkansas River bridge. The projected completion date was early December.

Robert Stevens fretted at the delays. Always the visionary, his mind leaped ahead of ongoing construction. He pored over maps of the Choctaw and Chickasaw nations, planning depot stops and rail yards, estimating freight traffic. Yet, however preoccupied, his eyes would involuntarily skip down the map to the Red River. And Texas.

Negotiations were under way for the first terminus in the Lone Star State. Stevens had written off the Colbert's Ferry idea, principally because it would involve the Chickasaw Nation in his affairs. After his problems with the Cherokees, he was no longer fascinated with the notion of a town site in Indian Territory. Instead, his attention had turned downriver to the Texas shoreline. He focused on the town of Sherman.

An existing community, it offered certain advantages.

Foremost was the possibility of a bond issue, which represented payment by the town for the privilege of being selected a railroad terminus. But the town fathers of Sherman, who impressed Stevens as a bunch of skinflints, were resisting the proposal. While they wanted the railroad, they felt a bond issue was a legalized form of extortion. Their obduracy led him to yet another idea.

Stevens conceived a grand vision. A few miles north of Sherman was a stretch of prairie occupied by small ranchers and hardscrabble farmers. The land was literally dirt cheap and could be purchased secretly through land agents. All of which raised the possibility of an enormous financial coup. It was within his grasp to *create* an entire town.

Unknown to anyone at Gibson Station, Stevens had sent a confidential emissary to Texas. Henry Denison was a trusted aide, charged with overseeing the Katy's interests in Kansas. His mission in Texas was to contract for the purchase of several hundred acres north of Sherman. One section that immediately bordered the Red River was particularly suitable. The terrain was relatively flat and adequately watered, perfect for a town site.

Everything depended now on Henry Denison's progress. If he was able to put together a block of land, the surveyors would be sent south to plan a town site. As an added inducement, Stevens had promised him that the new town would be named Denison. Once the contracts were signed, a land company would be organized to sell town lots. The arrival of the railroad would instantly transform raw farmland into a veritable pot of gold.

Stevens was absorbed by the idea. While the project was a year away from completion, he already imagined it as a full-blown reality. Part of the lure was the fortune he himself would pocket through the land company. But the greater enticement was to put his mark on the map, create a town from whole cloth. There was the added attraction of watching the Sherman skinflints go apoplectic over having lost the railroad. He thought of it as icing on the cake.

Still, for all his stargazing, Stevens was in a wretched

mood. The present was depressingly bleak, however bright the future looked. Completion of the Arkansas River bridge was six weeks away, and track laying through the Creek Nation was stalled until the broad stream could be spanned. To compound the delay, twenty-three men from the Irish Brigade were still confined to the hospital car. Some of them would be hobbling on crutches for months to come and drawing full pay the entire time.

The drain on the Katy treasury was enormous and maddening. But expenses weren't restricted to the track-laying operation being bogged down or to so many of the Irish Brigade on the invalid list. Within the last two weeks independent freighters hauling up the Texas Road had begun avoiding Gibson Station. The long cavalcades of wagons were swinging north upon reaching the Fort Gibson cutoff and trailing on to Vinita. There the goods were shipped eastward on the A&P line.

The sheer audacity of this situation left Stevens in a fierce rage. Andrew Peirce, only four days after the moonlit battle, had reoccupied the original site. He correctly reasoned that the Katy, with so many injured men, would shy away from another confrontation. On the strength of his deal with Boudinot, he'd also obtained a federal court injunction barring the Katy from further interference. In short order, a track crossing was put through and the depot, as well as the warehouse, was rebuilt. To rub salt in the wound, the new station was named Vinita.

Stevens' hands were tied. He had staked everything on a show of force by routing the A&P construction crew, and he'd lost. All the planning, the savage battle and the injured men, not to mention the cost of the operation, had come to nothing. He'd been betrayed by Boudinot and undermined still again by the Cherokees. But the deeper humiliation had little to do with the Indians' treachery or the fact that a battle had been fought to no advantage. What stung him most was that he'd been outmaneuvered by his rival, Andrew Peirce.

There was a practical aspect to be considered apart from injured pride. Several freighters had been questioned as to their reason for bypassing Gibson Station. Their response was chilling in its implications. Agents for the A&P were offering large rebates to anyone who would take their wagons all the way to Vinita from northern Texas. The A&P made it profitable for teamsters to haul the longer distance. Fully nine out of ten wagons coming up the Texas Road were now shipping with the A&P.

Andrew Peirce's intent was patently obvious. He meant nothing less than the financial ruin of Stevens and the Katy line. Whether it was revenge or merely underhanded business practice, the blow was timed perfectly. With the onset of winter and the trailing season at an end, revenue from the Texas cattle trade had fallen off sharply. Army contracts, however profitable, would never generate sufficient income to keep the Katy solvent. The loss of business from independent freighters represented a critical blow.

Problems seemed to beget problems. Over the past week guerrilla warfare had broken out along the Katy line. Sections of track were ripped from the roadbed at isolated spots throughout the Cherokee Nation. The ties were then piled into mounds and set afire. Rail traffic out of Gibson Station ground to a halt until work gangs could repair the damage. While the Cherokees were the logical suspects, no one had yet been caught in the act. There was no way to patrol a hundred miles of track, and the saboteurs had struck only at night. Putting a halt to the raids seemed almost impossible at this point.

Stevens' dour mood was understandable. Loss of sleep left him cranky and irritable, and the prospect of financial ruin put a steely edge on his anger. The morning's news from north Texas, relayed by letter from Henry Denison, was the proverbial last straw. He sent for John Ryan.

Stevens wasted no time on preliminaries. He went straight to the point, his voice hot with rage. "I've just had word that Peirce has upped the stakes. As of today, it's a cutthroat game!"

"What's he done now?"

"The dirty bastard!" Stevens ranted. "His agents in

Texas are offering an even trickier deal. Anyone who ships freight with us from Gibson Station and transfers to the A&P at Vinita will get a fatter rebate than before!''

"It's clever," Ryan acknowledged. "We make chicken-feed running back and forth between Vinita, and he winds up with the business."

"Precisely!" Stevens said acidly. "In effect, he's turned Vinita into a strangler's knot. We're cut off from routing through traffic to St. Louis."

"What's the difference? Unless we put a stop to the sabotage, we're snookered anyway. We'll never get a train out of the Cherokee Nation."

"That's another thing!" Stevens bridled. "I'm told that the A&P agents in Texas have been doing a bit of bragging. They said Peirce is working hand in glove with some unnamed Cherokee to stir up the tribe. Would you care to guess who the Cherokee is?"

"Probably Boudinot," Ryan said. "And he's likely operating under Tappin's protection. That would account for why we haven't caught anybody. Who's going to spill the beans on another Cherokee?"

Stevens grimaced. "We're talking about conspiracy! A criminal act of the worse sort, and I want it stopped."

"You can't send *me* back to Tahlequah. I've just about played out my string with Ross."

A wintry smile lighted Stevens' eyes. "Forget Ross and Boudinot and everyone else. I want you to pay a call on Andrew Peirce."

Ryan stared at him. "You're not talking about any rough stuff, are you?"

"On the contrary," Stevens reassured him. "I merely want you to deliver a message."

"What sort of message?"

"Tell him two can play the same game. I demand—*demand!*—that he cease all of his underhanded schemes. Otherwise it's tit for tat from now on."

"You're saying you would sabotage his tracks, maybe blow his bridges—is that it?"

"Exactly!"

Ryan studied him a moment, finally nodded. "I'll deliver your message. But don't count on me if push comes to shove. I'm not a hit-and-run night rider—not for you or anyone else."

"Don't worry," Stevens said, smiling. "I can always import outside help. All I want from you is one thing—make a believer out of Peirce."

"I'll do my damnedest, Colonel."

Later, reflecting on it, Stevens decided he'd taken the right step. Andrew Peirce was a buccaneer and a scoundrel, the type of man who responded only to force. So it was fitting, Stevens told himself, to send a man who was something of a natural force.

He thought Ryan's "damnedest" would do very nicely.

The sky was like dull granite. Heavy clouds rolled in from the north and a sharp wind rattled branches on the trees. A flock of crows took wing from the woods, cawing raucously as they wheeled away.

Ryan scanned the overcast sky. It was too early for snow, and he'd forgotten to bring along a rain slicker. Later yesterday, after talking with Stevens, he had saddled the roan and ridden out of Gibson Station. The night had been spent on the trail, and now, in the early afternoon, he was within a few miles of the A&P camp. He followed the tracks northward, holding the roan to a walk.

Earlier when he'd passed a section of rebuilt track, it occurred to him that he wasn't surprised by the sabotage. For several months now, he'd been expecting some form of reprisal from the Cherokees. Nor was he surprised that Elias Boudinot had been made the straw man, the apparent leader of the night riders. The true leaders of a conspiracy were seldom willing to reveal themselves publicly. Major David Tappin was no exception; he would, at all costs, try to avoid the limelight of a conspiracy. Tribal politics dictated that he at least appear above reproach.

There was, as well, the matter of William Ross. While

Ryan doubted that Ross was directly involved in the conspiracy, he recalled Elizabeth's concern for her father. Her
comment about Tappin and his ambition to take over as tribal
chief seemed all the more relevant. The sabotage, though
directed at the Katy, might easily have a hidden purpose.
Open rebellion by the Cherokees could be turned inward,
brought to the floor of the tribal council and used as a means
of forcing Ross to resign his office. And thereby open the
door for David Tappin.

The prospect troubled Ryan. He admired Ross, believed
him to be an honorable man. So it was in the interest of
everyone involved to expose the conspiracy. Yet curiously
enough, he felt no great urge to catch the night riders. They
were merely dupes, sacrificial pawns in a larger game, even
less important than Boudinot. There was, moreover, a personal reason for not attempting to trap them. To avoid capture, they would almost certainly fight. And he simply didn't
want to kill any more Cherokees. Or anyone else, for that
matter. White or red, he was weary of killing men.

The thought gave Ryan a moment of sardonic reflection.
In the Cherokee Nation, he was already something of a leg-
end. They called him the Indian Killer, and spoke it with the
harsh inflection of a curse. The burden of the name weighed
heavily on him as he rode into the A & P camp. He reminded
himself that he was there to deliver a message and nothing
more. He wouldn't be goaded into a fight, or another killing.

The area around the depot was crawling with men. To
Ryan's great relief, none of them seemed to recognize him.
He was nonetheless on edge, for these were the very men
who had taken part in the midnight battle. West of the new
track crossing, he saw a construction train, and farther away,
the track-laying gangs. He spotted a private railway car
shunted on to a siding. Ryan noted wryly that Peirce's private
car was almost identical to Stevens'. He reined his horse
toward the siding.

On the rear platform of the car, he knocked loudly. A
voice ordered him to enter and he stepped through the door.
The interior layout was more businesslike than Stevens' car.

A section had been partitioned off and furnished as an office. Seated at a wide mahogany desk was a man who appeared to be in his early fifties. He was heavily built, with a sweeping mustache and a square, thick-jowled face. Behind wire-rimmed spectacles his eyes were gray and chill, stern as a church deacon's. He motioned Ryan forward.

"What is it?"

"Are you Andrew Peirce?"

"I am," Peirce said impatiently.

"I've got a message for you, Mr. Peirce—from Robert Stevens."

Peirce looked surprised, then suddenly irritated. "Who the hell are you?"

"The name's Ryan." Halting at the desk, Ryan held his gaze. "I work for the Colonel."

"John Ryan?" Peirce asked. "Stevens' hired gun?"

"I'm not here to swap insults, Mr. Peirce. Let's just stick to business."

"Well, Ryan, you have some nerve coming here. Every man in this camp would give his eyeteeth for a crack at you."

A smile appeared at the corner of Ryan's mouth. "I reckon they've already had that and more. I don't especially care for a rematch."

"No doubt," Peirce said with a short, emphatic nod. "Although my boys tell me you and Tom Scullin gave a good account of yourselves."

"We got about as much as we gave."

Peirce took off his glasses, wiped them with a handkerchief. "So Bob Stevens sent you with a message? Knowing him, I'd wager it's some half-assed threat."

"No, sir," Ryan said evenly. "It's more on the order of a declaration of war."

"What's that?" Peirce looked as though his ears were plugged. "What did you say?"

"I'll give it to you in Stevens' own words. He said two can play at the same game. If you don't back off, he plans to let you have tit for tat."

"What does that mean exactly?"

"Word's out," Ryan said, "that you've riled up the Cherokees. Our tracks are being torn up faster than we can rebuild them. The Colonel wants you to have a talk with Boudinot—or Tappin—and put a stop to it."

Peirce shook his head in mock wonder. "Are you accusing me of sabotaging the Katy?"

Ryan ignored the question. "There's more," he said. "Stevens wants you to lift the freight rebates, starting today. If you don't, then the fat's in the fire."

"Tell him to go straight to hell! I'll run my business any way I see fit."

"Sorry to hear you say that, Mr. Peirce. Whatever else he is, the Colonel's a man of his word. He'll make you pay a dear price."

"Will he?" Peirce demanded. "And what form would this tit for tat take?"

"Hit and run," Ryan answered in a low voice. "Your tracks would be torn up and burned. Your bridges would be blown and your rolling stock derailed. Stevens would go whole hog and then some."

Peirce's eyes were angry, commanding. "If he wants war, then by God he can have it! I'll destroy him, run him out of the Nations!"

Ryan regarded him with great calmness. "Yeah, you could do that. But while you were about it, he'd take you down with him. When the dust settled, you'd both be out of business."

Peirce sat quietly for a moment with his eyes narrowed thoughtfully. After a moment he looked around. "How would you like a job, Mr. Ryan?"

"Thanks all the same," Ryan said. "I've got a job."

"A pity," Peirce observed. "I could use a man with quick wits. I'd be willing to double your salary."

"No sale, Mr. Peirce. What should I tell the Colonel?"

Peirce glowered back at him with an owlish frown. "Tell your boss he's the sorriest excuse for a railroader that I've ever met. And then tell him''—he paused, waved his hand disdainfully—''he's got himself a deal.''

Ryan nodded, moving to the door without another word. Outside the car he went down the steps and walked directly to his horse. After climbing into the saddle, he turned the roan away from Vinita. As he rode off, he wondered what sort of reception Peirce would get in Tahlequah.

Major David Tappin had his own ax to grind. And in some ways it had nothing to do with the railroad.

CHAPTER
TWENTY-SIX

On November 7 the Verdigris River bridge was once more opened to traffic. The first construction train, loaded with bridge timbers, crossed the river late that morning. Crowded onto one of the flatcars were Scullin and a contingent of the Irish Brigade.

Stevens observed the operation from a window inside his private car. The weather was dismal, with low-hanging clouds and whirling snow flurries. While the interior of the car was toasty warm, it did nothing to improve his mood. He munched an unlit cigar, watching the train disappear across the bridge. The sight gave him only fleeting comfort.

For every problem resolved there seemed to be a dozen more awaiting his attention. With the bridge open and four miles of track completed to the Arkansas River, it was now possible to move vast amounts of supplies forward. He'd considered doing just that and then ferrying the materials to the south shore of the Arkansas. It would have required a herculean effort by the Irish Brigade, loading and offloading every shipment at least four times. But the alternative was to wait another month while the Arkansas River bridge was being completed.

Frustrated by delay, Stevens had ordered the plan implemented. Scullin could once again start laying track, and thirty days gained would put end-of-track deep in the Creek Nation. Yet as though fated, the plan began to unravel. A week of cold, drizzling rain turned the canebrakes south of the Arkansas into a waterlogged swamp. On the heels of the rain, there was freezing sleet and then several days of intermittent snowfall. The plan was scotched, awaiting a hard freeze to make the canebrakes passable. Scullin and the Irish Brigade were assigned instead to resume work with the bridge builders.

So far as Stevens could see there was only one bright spot in the whole affair. Ryan's talk with Andrew Peirce had produced immediate and highly profitable results. All freight rebates were rescinded, thereby removing any incentive to ship with the A&P through Vinita. Wagon trains from northern Texas again began arriving at Gibson Station, their freight consigned for shipment with the Katy. The sudden jump in revenue averted what might have been a financial debacle. The railway line was restored to solvency just in the nick of time.

Of no less consequence was the abrupt disappearance of the night riders. The message delivered by Ryan apparently had a profound effect. While the details were unknown, it could be surmised that Peirce had in some way blackmailed Major David Tappin. Sabotage of the Katy tracks had ceased virtually overnight, and there had been no further encounters with the Cherokees. What that portended for the future was a matter of conjecture. But for the moment the Katy was enjoying a time of peace and prosperity.

Stevens took mordant satisfaction in the victory. He reveled in the fact that he'd had the last laugh on Andrew Peirce. Though he hadn't destroyed the A&P, he had upset Peirce's time schedule beyond repair. The Katy would be the first to cross the Red River and roll onward into the Southwest. For that, Stevens owed a large vote of thanks to John Ryan. Few men could have brought Peirce to see the light so quickly and with such clarity. The outcome spoke reams about Ryan's persuasive talents.

What form that persuasion had taken was still something of a mystery. To Stevens' questions, Ryan had replied in only the vaguest terms. Thereafter, Stevens became increasingly concerned, for he noticed an unaccountable change in Ryan's attitude. A quiet man by nature, Ryan had now become withdrawn and almost taciturn. He spoke only when he was spoken to, and even with Scullin, who was his closest friend, he seemed strangely distant. His manner was somehow neutral, as though he'd lost interest in what went on around him.

Stevens lit his cigar and stared out the window. His reverie was suddenly broken as he saw Ryan emerge from the bunk car. Wearing a woolly mackinaw, Ryan walked off toward the stock pens, carrying his shotgun. Stevens watched until the solitary figure disappeared into the snow flurries. He knew Ryan would saddle the roan gelding and ride off on a morning scout of the bridge site. What he didn't know was why Ryan had withdrawn into a shell.

Not knowing troubled him. He valued Ryan, and while they'd had their differences, they had always managed to work together. He puffed on his cigar, vaguely uneasy.

Ryan propped his shotgun against a fence post. The gelding trotted over, whinnying in recognition, and stood waiting. One of the mules in the next pen over brayed and that set off a chorus from the other mules. With track laying at a halt, none of them had been out of their pens in almost two months.

Ryan started toward the harness shed to collect his saddle. He suddenly stopped, watching as a number of horsemen materialized like ghostly apparitions out of the snow flurries. A cold sense of foreboding swept over him as he recognized the lead rider, Major David Tappin. Behind, ranked two by two, rode six Light Horse Police. He moved swiftly to the fence and picked up his shotgun. Hefting it, he hooked a thumb over the near-side hammer.

Tappin reined to a halt. He sat there a moment, the Light Horse drawn up behind him, their mounts snorting frosty puffs of air. His expression was one of veiled mockery, amused contempt. At length he lifted his chin, indicating the shotgun.

"Are you expecting trouble, Mr. Ryan?"

"Never know," Ryan said woodenly. "There's lots of it around these days."

"Oh?" Tappin replied. "I understood your problems were all solved."

Ryan looked him directly in the eye. "Things have been pretty quiet the last couple of weeks. You and Peirce must've had a heart-to-heart talk."

Tappin studied him with a kind of clinical detachment. "I assume you're referring to Andrew Peirce, president of the A&P. To the best of my knowledge, we've never met."

"How about that!" Ryan said with a touch of disbelief. "And here I thought you two were bosom buddies."

"I repeat"—Tappin paused to underscore the words—"we've never met."

"I suppose a go-between works just as well. Course, Boudinot must get tired of hotfootin' it back and forth between Vinita and Tahlequah. Or do you meet him out on a dark road somewhere?"

"Who I meet, and where, are none of your concern, Mr. Ryan."

"Another time maybe," Ryan said, letting it drop. "What brings you to Gibson Station, Major?"

"Brad Collins."

"What about him?"

"I believe you have a payroll shipment coming through tomorrow afternoon. I understand it's usually aboard the express car, locked in a strongbox—and all cash."

Ryan frowned. "How'd you know that?"

"I hear things," Tappin answered genially. "Collins got drunk and bragged to the wrong people. He and his gang plan to rob the payroll train."

"That a fact?" Ryan said without expression. "Why would you ride all the way down here to save the Katy's payroll?"

"Just following orders," Tappin said with an odd smile.

"When I informed Chief Ross, he asked me to alert you personally. He feels that the Cherokee Nation cannot condone robbery—even by a half-breed outcast."

Ryan considered a moment. "Any idea where the holdup might take place?"

"Pryor's Creek," Tappin said. "Collins intends to block the bridge."

"And you figured I might want to prepare a reception for him?"

"No," Tappin said firmly. "Your payroll means nothing to me one way or the other. I'm here at Chief Ross' request."

"You'll be sure to thank him for me, won't you?"

Tappin ignored the wry tone. "As a gesture of good faith, he's also offering assistance. I was ordered to bring along a squad of Light Horse and place them at your command."

Ryan hesitated, doubly vigilant now. "Why would the Light Horse serve under me? I killed a couple of their friends at the courthouse."

"These men," Tappin said, gesturing to the stolid-faced horsemen, "will obey without question. Their orders are to place themselves at your disposal."

"I have my own guards."

"Hardly enough," Tappin noted. "Collins has that many or more in his gang. Besides, if you refuse, it will be a direct affront to Chief Ross. As I said, these men represent a token of his good faith."

"Tell you what; I'll leave it up to Colonel Stevens. You and your men just wait here."

Ryan moved around the riders, eyeing them as he went past. The Light Horse sat like bronzed statues, staring straight ahead. He walked toward the rail yard.

"I don't like it!" Stevens grunted, shaking his head. "Why should Ross want to save our bacon?"

Ryan stood with the shotgun in the crook of his arm. His mackinaw was wet with melting snow and a puddle had formed around his boots. He nodded imperceptibly, his mouth set in a narrow line.

"It's Tappin I'm worried about. I don't trust him as far as I could spit."

"Do you believe Ross actually sent him here?"

"Yeah," Ryan said slowly. "Tappin wouldn't have come otherwise. His story's too easy to check out."

Stevens' eyes squinted in concentration. "So that brings us back to Ross. What's he after?"

"Maybe it's on the up-and-up. I'd like to think Ross would side with us over Collins."

"You'd like to," Stevens asked, "but the question is, do you?"

Ryan rubbed his jaw, considering. "I've always figured Ross for an honorable man. So I'd have to say he's given us the straight goods."

"Then we've no choice, do we? We either accept his help or risk offending him. And who knows where that would lead?"

"All right," Ryan said. "I'll tell Tappin we're agreeable."

"Just make damn sure you take our men along! We can't trust that payroll to a bunch of redskins."

"Don't worry, Colonel. It's as good as done."

Outside, the wind had dropped off and heavy snowflakes were falling in a thick, white curtain. Ryan began formulating a plan as he walked back to the stock pens.

A freight train pulled out of Gibson Station early next morning. Aboard the caboose were Ryan and five railway guards, as well as the squad of Light Horse. Tappin had returned to Tahlequah the previous afternoon.

Shortly before noon the northbound freight stopped at Boudinot's original town site. Asa Johnson, the station master, exhibited only mild curiosity as Ryan and his peculiar alliance trooped into the depot. For the next two hours, with hardly a word spoken they warmed themselves around a pot-bellied stove. Johnson played the attentive host and kept the coffeepot perking.

The southbound train arrived only a few minutes behind

schedule. Coupled to the rear of the engine and tender were
the express car and two passenger coaches. Earlier, from
Gibson Station Ryan had wired ahead to Kansas, ordering
that no passengers be allowed to board the train. He now
split his force of eleven men into separate teams. The railway
guards were placed inside the first passenger coach, and the
Light Horse were seated in the rear coach to be less visible.
His position was with the regular express messenger, locked
in the express car.

Ryan's orders to the men were precise and clear. All of
them understood that there was to be no gunplay unless the
outlaws opened fire first. Even then, any of the robbers who
could be captured rather than killed were to be taken prisoner. He particularly wanted Brad Collins taken alive, and
he'd repeatedly stressed that point. Only in the last extreme
was the gang leader to be fired on. His purpose, which he
kept to himself, had to do with the Verdigris River bridge
and other acts of sabotage. He wanted the opportunity to
question Collins.

Pryor's Creek was roughly twenty miles south of the depot. An hour or so later, as the train rounded a slight bend,
the engineer suddenly throttled down and set the brake.
While it had stopped snowing, the roadbed and the surrounding countryside were blanketed with white. A short distance
downtrack the bridge had been sealed off with a barricade
of fallen trees. The engine lost speed rapidly and jarred the
men in the cars behind. Only a few yards short of the bridge,
the train rolled to a halt.

On the east side of the tracks, several men emerged on
foot from a thick stand of woods. They were spaced far apart,
their guns drawn, and appeared to be well organized. One
man hopped onto the steps of the engine, covering the engineer and the fireman. Another hurried toward the end of
the train, blocking any exit from the last passenger coach.
Still another halted at the steps between the passenger
coaches, and a fourth took a similar position between the
lead coach and the express car. Brad Collins and the sixth
gang member walked directly to the express car, stopping in

front of the door. Collins hammered on it with the butt of his pistol.

"Open up in there! If you don't, we're gonna start killin' your friends. The engineer goes first!"

The door slammed open. Ryan stood to one side, the shotgun pointed downward, both hammers cocked. The express messenger was opposite him, also partially concealed, his pistol extended through the open door. Collins and his partner appeared stunned, frozen in a moment of indecision. Ryan wagged the muzzle of his shotgun.

"Drop your guns or you're dead."

Collins obeyed, his eyes glued to the scattergun. The other man hastily followed suit, tossing his revolver into the snow. Without being told, they both raised their hands overhead. Ryan motioned them back a step, then took a quick peek out the door. He saw the remaining gang members moving cautiously toward the express car, their guns leveled. He looked back at Collins.

"Tell your boys to call it quits. I've got men back—"

At the rear of the train, the Light Horse Police poured out of the last passenger coach. As though on command, they shouldered their carbines and delivered a withering volley into the robbers. The four gang members at the rear were cut down from behind, shot in the back. Collins and the man at his side were knocked sprawling under the impact of the heavy slugs. They went down, arms and legs flailing, flattened alongside the snowy roadbed. The only robber to escape was the man on the steps of the locomotive. A bullet whizzed past his head, and he leaped, rolling down the embankment. He darted into the woods before the Light Horse could unleash another volley.

Ryan jumped through the open door. He landed on his feet and turned, planting himself solidly. Facing the rear of the train, he shouldered the shotgun and took dead aim at the Light Horse. Bunched together, they hesitated uncertainly and slowly lowered their carbines. At that instant the railway guards tumbled from the lead coach, looking from Ryan to the Light Horse. Ryan rapped out a command.

"Disarm the bastards! Keep 'em covered!"

Whirling around, Ryan hurried down the embankment. Collins lay on his side, the snow underneath him stained a bright cherry red. When Ryan knelt down, rolling him over, the outlaw appeared dead. His eyes were closed and the upper part of his coat was matted with blood. Then he wheezed, coughing raggedly, and his eyes fluttered open. A trickle of blood leaked out of his mouth as he focused on Ryan.

"Funny, ain't it?" he said shallowly. "Shot down by the goddamn Light Horse."

"Tough luck, Collins," Ryan said, bending closer. "I told them not to fire unless you started it."

"How'd they get here?"

"Major Tappin sent them along. He warned me about the holdup."

"Warned you!" Collins feebly grabbed the front of his mackinaw. "Tappin told you I was gonna rob the train?"

Ryan nodded, watching him closely. "How else would I have found out?"

Collins gasped, fighting for breath. "Son of a bitch double-crossed me . . . murdered me. . . ."

"Why would he do that, Collins?"

"I dunno," Collins whispered, barely audible. "I wouldn't never have talked. Not about the bridge or tearin' up tracks or nothin' . . . he wanted . . . done. . . ."

A reddish froth bubbled over his lips and his voice trailed off. His mouth opened in a low death rattle, then he trembled and lay still. His eyes rolled back in his head.

Ryan stared down at the outlaw a moment. As if a veil had been lifted, everything was suddenly clear. Only one man could link Tappin to the bridge collapse and the track sabotage. But to put the Light Horse on Collins' trail or kill him outright would have been too obvious. The better plan was to arrange a bogus loan of the Light Horse, with orders to shoot on sight. And credit the railroad with Brad Collins' death!

Hefting the shotgun, Ryan climbed to his feet. He considered questioning the Light Horse, then discarded the idea.

Threats wouldn't work and no amount of interrogation would make them betray Tappin. With a sense of resignation, he ordered the railway guards to turn them loose. It was a thirty-mile walk to Tahlequah, and snow all the way. The thought gave him some satisfaction, but it ended nothing. Ryan made himself a solemn promise.

David Tappin would be brought to accounting—for murder.

CHAPTER
TWENTY-SEVEN

The train pulled into Gibson Station late that afternoon. Ryan hopped off the rear passenger coach as the engineer decreased speed in the rail car. He walked toward Stevens' private car.

All the way from Pryor's Creek, he had maintained a thoughtful silence. The railway guards who had loaded the outlaws' bodies onto the express car were equally pensive. Seated by himself, he'd stared out the window, considering his next move. The decision he had finally made seemed the only one possible under the circumstances. He felt comfortable with himself for the first time in a long while.

Stevens' manservant answered his knock. Inside the car Ryan found Stevens and Sally Palmer seated in lounge chairs. The girl, who was sipping a rye and water, looked at him inquisitively. Her expression was neutral, as though his safe return prompted only mild curiosity. Stevens bounded out of his chair with a laugh, hurrying forward. His eyes were ablaze with excitement.

"I knew it!" he said, grinning. "You pulled it off, didn't you?"

"The payroll's safe," Ryan informed him. "And there are six dead men in the express car. One of them is Brad Collins."

"What'd I tell you?" Stevens whooped, glancing back at

the girl. "Didn't I tell you Ryan wouldn't let me down?"

"That's what you told me," she said indifferently.

"Only one trouble," Ryan interjected. "It was the Light Horse that got him, not me."

"What?" Stevens said, looking baffled. "The Light Horse got Collins?"

Ryan quickly recounted the day's events. He ended with the gang leader's dying words about Tappin's involvement in the conspiracy. When he finished, there was a moment of stunned silence.

"I'll be damned," Stevens finally muttered. "It was an execution! Tappin rigged the whole thing just to get Collins!"

Ryan nodded. "Collins was the only witness against him. Nobody else could tie him to the bridge collapse."

"And the murder of six of our men—six *white* men!"

"Not much doubt about it. He couldn't risk a federal murder warrant or a trial in Fort Smith. He knew he'd wind up getting hung."

"So he suckered us into helping him! A payroll robbery makes Collins' death look legitimate."

"Except for one thing," Ryan noted. "He never figured on Collins living long enough to talk."

"Wait a minute," Stevens said anxiously. "Will that hold up in court?"

"It should," Ryan allowed. "I think it'd be treated the same as a deathbed confession. Especially where it concerns murder."

"Then we've got him! And don't forget, it's premeditated murder. He *ordered* the trestles on that bridge to be cut through."

"We don't have him until we get him to Fort Smith. But I'll see to that myself, first thing tomorrow."

"Why not send for federal marshals?"

"It's personal." Ryan's voice was hard and determined. "I aim to settle Tappin's account myself."

Stevens agreed. "I understand completely. You handle it however you see fit."

"One other thing."

"Yes?"

"As of today, I'm off the payroll. I quit."

"You . . ." Stevens faltered, gave him a dumbfounded stare. "You're resigning?"

"That's about the size of it."

"But you can't! We're only halfway through the Nations. I still need your help!"

"Not anymore," Ryan said. "Tappin was behind all your trouble, start to finish. I'll tend to him tomorrow."

"Even so, you're leaving me in the lurch. Why not delay awhile and think it over?"

"Nothing to think over. Besides, you'll replace me easy enough. You pay too good for the job to go begging."

Stevens fixed him with a skeptical look. "There's more to it, isn't there? You're just using Tappin as an excuse."

"Why push it any farther? I've already quit."

"No!" Stevens said sharply. "I want to hear your reason. I insist on it!"

"All right," Ryan said without expression. "I don't like you and I don't much care for the way you do business. Guess I finally got a bellyful."

Stevens waved his hand as though dusting away the insult. "Why do we have to like each other? What's that got to do with your job?"

Ryan's mouth lifted in a tight grin. "You're one of a kind, Colonel. It's been an education knowing you."

"Now, hold on!" Stevens said as he turned away. "At least give me a chance—"

Ryan went through the door without looking back. As he started down the steps, Sally Palmer rushed out onto the rear platform. Her china-blue eyes were dancing, and her face was wreathed in a big smile. She stuck out her hand.

"Before you go, I just wanted to shake your hand."

"Yeah?" Ryan said, taking her hand. "Why's that?"

"You told him off good, and he was overdue. I suppose it makes up a little for the way you've treated me."

"Nothing personal," Ryan assured her. "Another time, another place, we might've got together."

"I tend to doubt it. But I'll make believe you're telling me the truth."

"Look, if things are so bad, why not pack a bag? I'll see to it you get on the next train out."

She laughed, shook her head. "I'd just end up in another parlor house. And believe it or not, Stevens beats that!"

"Maybe so." Ryan smiled. "Take care of yourself, Sally."

A short while later Ryan found Tom Scullin. The big Irishman was overseeing loading of a train for the Arkansas River bridge site. He whooped when he saw Ryan.

"By the Jesus! You're back and all in one piece!"

"Just passing through, Tom."

"Passin' through?" Scullin repeated. "You talk like a man on his way to somewheres."

"I guess I am, at that. I just quit the railroad."

"You *what*?"

Ryan explained the reasons behind his decision. He went on to elaborate regarding sabotage of the Verdigris River bridge and David Tappin's involvement. Cursing savagely, Scullin's features mottled with rage. The murdered men were members of the Irish Brigade, and he swore revenge. Ryan firmly declined his offer of assistance.

"Leave it to me, Tom. It's a job for one man, and it's the kind of work I know best. I'll see to it that Tappin gets his neck stretched."

"God's blood!" Scullin said, frowning. "How do you hope to pull it off by yourself?"

"I don't," Ryan said calmly. "William Ross will deliver him into my hands."

"You're mad!"

Scullin's arguments were wasted. He saw that Ryan simply would not be dissuaded. He wished the younger man Godspeed and good hunting. They shook hands with the warmth of two strong men who had shared a dangerous time and emerged friends.

An hour later Ryan rode out of town on the roan gelding. His direction was northeast.

The sky was dark as indigo. Ryan tied his horse behind the stables and paused only long enough to loosen the cinch. Then, skirting the corral, he walked toward the house.

A chill wind knifed out of the northwest. The snow had crusted over and his footsteps sounded crunchy as he circled the house. On the front driveway he spotted a shaft of light from a side room. Cautiously, he made his way to the tall windows outside the study. He saw Ross seated at the desk, bathed in the glow of lamplight.

The Cherokee leader was alone, hunched over a sheaf of papers. Visibly startled, he jumped when Ryan rapped on the window. Then, peering closer, he rose and moved across the room. His features were set in a scowl as he raised the window and stepped aside. Ryan boosted himself over the sill and onto the floor.

"Your gall amazes me," Ross said, closing the window. "Unannounced and uninvited, in the dead of night."

"Sorry about the hour," Ryan replied. "But it won't wait till morning. I have to talk to you now."

"About what?"

"David Tappin."

Once more Ryan recounted the details of the aborted train robbery. He stressed Brad Collins' last words, which implicated Tappin in the murder of six railroad workers. Then, after mentioning that he'd quit the Katy, he went to the reason for his late night visit.

"I intend to arrest Tappin," he said in a low voice. "I'll need your help to do it without bloodshed."

Ross appeared at a loss for words. He walked to his desk and stood there a moment. Then without turning he finally spoke.

"I have a confession to make," he said. "I suspected that Tappin was behind the assassination attempts and all the rest. But there was no proof and I chose to take the easy way out. It seemed politically expedient."

"What's past is past," Ryan said quietly. "All I'm interested in now is getting Tappin to Fort Smith. He's got a date with the hangman."

Ross turned from the desk. He studied Ryan with a thoughtful frown. "You're no longer a marshal," he said. "In fact, you're no longer a special agent for the railroad. You have no authority to make an arrest."

Ryan's eyes narrowed. "What's your point?"

"You could never arrest Tappin without a fight. In the end you would have to kill him."

"Are you saying you won't help?"

"No," Ross said crisply. "I'm offering you an alternative."

"Such as?"

"Bring Tappin to trial for murder in a Cherokee court."

"I don't follow you."

"Brad Collins," Ross said in a musing tone, "was both an outlaw and an outcast. But he and his gang were nonetheless members of the Cherokee tribe. And Tappin ordered them shot down in cold blood."

Ryan regarded him with an odd, steadfast look. "You're joking! Charge Tappin with Collins' murder? It'll never stick."

"On the contrary," Ross assured him earnestly. "I have the authority to make it stick. I'll see him tried, convicted, and executed."

"Without witnesses?"

"We have your testimony as to Collins' dying words. That establishes a motive."

"It's not enough for conviction."

Ross pursed his lips, nodded solemnly. "Could you identify the Light Horse who shot Collins and the other gang members?"

"What if I could?" Ryan persisted. "They're not about to testify that they acted on Tappin's orders."

"Oh, I think they will. In exchange for immunity, they'll gladly betray Tappin. In fact, I can guarantee you their testimony."

"Maybe so," Ryan said with no inward conviction. "But you can't guarantee that a Cherokee jury will deliver a verdict of guilty. Not against the head of the Light Horse Police for killing outlaws."

"Then you've lost nothing," Ross countered. "You can always prosecute Tappin on the federal charge. Or kill him yourself."

There was a long moment of deliberation. Then, finally, Ryan conceded the point. "All right, we'll try it your way."

"Good," Ross said equably. "Now while I attend to things here, I suggest you return to Fort Smith. Otherwise Tappin will most certainly make an attempt on your life."

"How soon can you bring him to trial?"

Ross smiled. "Far sooner than in a white man's court. Don't worry, I'll send for you in plenty of time."

"Well . . ." Ryan hesitated, staring at the older man. "Before I leave, I'd like to see Elizabeth. Any objection?"

"None whatever. I'll wake her and ask her to come down. Just wait here."

Ross walked from the room. Ryan took off his hat and mackinaw and slumped into one of the armchairs. He suddenly felt worn out.

Elizabeth joined him several minutes later. Her hair was pinned atop her head and she wore a cambric housecoat over her nightgown. There was an awkward moment before they got themselves seated opposite one another. Then Ryan began talking.

Her father had briefly explained the situation. She was dismayed, though hardly shocked, by the charge lodged against Tappin. Her reaction to Ryan's break with the railroad was a mix of hope and appreciation. But now, attentive to his every word, she listened without comment or interruption. She let him talk himself out.

"So that's it," he said at length. "I've quit the railroad for good."

"I know it wasn't easy, John. I'm proud of you, and very happy. Happier than you could ever imagine."

"Then maybe you'll understand what I've been leading up to. I want you to come with me."

Surprise washed over her face. "Come with you?"

"I know it's a little sudden. We've never exactly talked about it, but I . . ." He paused, groping for words. "Well, I just figured you felt the same way."

Her voice was hushed. "Are you talking about marriage?"

Ryan nodded soberly. "We could find a preacher in Fort Smith."

"I couldn't," she murmured. "I'll never fit into the white world. Even if they accepted me, I could never accept them."

Ryan slowly shook his head. "Doesn't that make you as prejudiced as them?"

"Yes," she said softly. "What they've done to our people—what they are still doing—breeds prejudice. I'm ashamed of it and wish it were different, but it's not."

"So what's the answer?"

She looked at him and tried to smile. "You could stay here."

"Never work," Ryan said darkly. "I've killed too many Cherokees. Their kin would be honor bound to come after me."

"And there would be more killing."

"Neither one of us wants that—do we?"

"No," she whispered, desperation in her voice.

Ryan took a deep breath and let it out heavily. "How about farther west? Maybe somewhere in California or Oregon. It's a long ways from the Nations."

"I . . ." Her eyes were shining moistly. "Will you give me some time? Let me think about it . . . please?"

"I reckon I owe you that."

"Thank you, John."

"Maybe . . ." Ryan began, then stopped with a sudden grin. "Well, maybe you could give me an answer when I come back for Tappin's trial. Think so?"

"I'll try."

Ryan stood, extending his hands, and took a step forward.

Her mouth quivered and she fought to control the tears. She rose from her chair and rushed into his arms. He embraced her and she buried her face against his chest, holding him with fierce possession. Her voice was husky, almost inaudible.

"Don't say anything. Just hold me."

CHAPTER
TWENTY-EIGHT

Justice in the Cherokee Nation moved swiftly. Major David Tappin was arrested and brought to trial within a week. He pleaded not guilty to five counts of murder.

There were grave repercussions throughout the Cherokee Nation. Supporters of David Tappin, including several influential members of the Union Party, were enraged. The murder charges were labeled a plot of the railroad and Robert Stevens, designed to neutralize the Katy's most resolute opponent. A movement arose to bring the matter to the floor of the tribal council. Some men spoke of armed rebellion.

The Southern Party wisely made no attempt to capitalize on the situation. Shunned because of their alignment with the railroad, the party leaders cautioned their followers to take a nonpartisan stance. Elias Boudinot, fearing new reprisals, went on a long trip to Washington and points east. Stand Watie surrounded himself with loyal guards, and seldom went outside after dark. No one sympathized publicly with the railroad.

Robert Stevens took equally prudent measures. He hired a former Texas Ranger as the Katy's new special agent. Additional railway guards were also hired. Every train crossing the Cherokee Nation bristled with armed men. Work on the Arkansas River bridge went forward without incident, with completion set for early December. No great resistance was expected from either the Choctaws or the Chickasaws. Stevens' target date for crossing the Red River was revised to late 1872.

William Ross moved decisively to quell his opposition. His first step was to appoint a Union Party loyalist as head of the Light Horse Police. Assured that order would be maintained, he then called all his political markers with members of the tribal council. Pressure was applied on the followers of David Tappin, and any thought of a fight on the council floor quickly went by the boards. Those who had spoken of armed rebellion retreated to a position of tactful silence. A sense of calm and political coexistence once more settled over the Cherokee Nation.

On November 16 David Tappin was brought to trial. A jury was impaneled by late morning and the prosecution began its case after the noon recess. One by one the six Light Horse Police who had taken part in the aborted train holdup were called to the stand. They testified that Tappin had ordered them to kill Brad Collins and his gang. Further, Tappin had instructed them that no prisoners were to be taken, even though some might attempt to surrender. Collins and his men, as ordered, had been shot down while their hands were in the air.

The prosecutor was granted wide latitude by the judge. Over defense objections, he was allowed to pose questions not directly related to the case. The six Light Horse were asked whether they believed William Ross had any foreknowledge of Tappin's orders. To a man, they related how Tappin had insinuated that Chief Ross had been gulled into authorizing the mission. They further testified that Tappin had spoken openly about his plan to hoodwink the railroad. The onus for the killings was to be laid at the doorstep of John Ryan and the Katy.

Spectators and jurors alike were aware that politics had entered the courtroom. The central issue was to establish the guilt or innocence of David Tappin, but a secondary purpose of the testimony was to remove any stigma from William Ross. The principal chief of the Cherokee Nation was shown to be a victim of his misguided trust. It was Major Tappin, deceiving both his tribal superior and the railroad, who had orchestrated the murder of Brad Collins. The responsibility, and the blame, stopped there.

John Ryan took the witness stand last. He'd ridden into town that morning after being summoned by messenger from Fort Smith. A squad of Light Horse, sworn to protect him with their lives, surrounded him the moment he'd dismounted in front of the courthouse. His testimony represented the pivotal point of the prosecution's case. Under oath, he recounted the attempted holdup, the killings, and Brad Collins' dying words. Tappin's motive, which was to silence Collins about the Verdigris River bridge, was established beyond doubt. The prosecutor allowed Ryan to put on record that six railway workers had died in the bridge collapse.

Counsel for the defense unleashed a vitriolic personal attack on Ryan on cross-examination. He secured an admission that Ryan and Major Tappin were bitter enemies. He next established that Ryan had killed no less than nine Cherokees while employed by the railroad. He tried to create the illusion that Ryan and his railway guards had killed the Collins gang. His contention was that the railroad sought to throw the blame on Tappin and thereby rid itself of the Katy's most outspoken opponent in the Cherokee Nation. The jurors looked unpersuaded by the argument.

The prosecution rested its case shortly before three o'clock. After a brief recess, defense counsel called Major David Tappin to the stand. In his own defense Tappin rebutted the testimony of the six Light Horse, as well as that of John Ryan. He termed the trial a travesty, the work of perjuring tribesmen and *tibo* railroaders. He swore his innocence, depicting himself as a Cherokee patriot and a man of honor. The prosecutor on cross-examination was unable to rattle Tappin. Looking composed and confident, the defendant parried every question with sardonic brilliance.

After closing arguments, the judge instructed the jury. By Cherokee law, he told them, the defendant was required to prove nothing. The burden of proof fell on the prosecution, and even the slightest doubt was sufficient to forestall conviction. When the jurors withdrew for deliberations, an uneasy tension settled over the courtroom. Some of the spectators stepped out for a smoke, only to be called back inside before ten minutes had elapsed. The jury filed back into the box with an air of grave solemnity. Their verdict, read aloud by the foreman, was unanimous: guilty on all counts.

The judge pronounced sentence immediately. Ordered to rise, Tappin was informed that Cherokee law exacted the death penalty for a capital crime. The date of execution was set for November 18, at the hour of dawn. The judge hammered his gavel and adjourned the proceedings. It was 4:32 on the courtroom clock.

The appellate process in the Cherokee Nation was no less efficient. Early the following morning, the Supreme Court heard an eloquent appeal, delivered by David Tappin's lawyer. Pleading insufficient proof as well as mitigating circumstances, defense counsel requested that the sentence be reversed. The court promptly upheld the conviction and declined to stay the execution. The appellate hearing took only slightly more than an hour.

Dawn tore a gray line across the horizon on the morning of November 18. It was bitter cold, with a metallic sky and gusty winds. Light flurries carpeted the ground with a fresh layer of snow.

The wagons halted in a wooded clearing outside Tahlequah. David Tappin rode in the lead wagon, his hands manacled and shackles locked around his ankles. Escorting him were four grim-faced Light Horse armed with Spencer carbines. In the second wagon, similarly armed, was a squad of six Light Horse. Their new commander, Joseph Starr, rode beside the wagon, mounted on a dun gelding.

A short distance to the rear was the carriage of William Ross. Acting as outriders, a squad of Light Horse rode with their carbines laid across the saddle. The carriage drew to a stop behind the wagons and the mounted Light Horse fanned out along the road. The carriage door opened and William Ross, wearing a somber greatcoat, stepped down. Ryan followed directly behind, bundled in the woolly mackinaw. The two men waited at the edge of the clearing.

Tappin was assisted from the lead wagon by his escort. The leg shackles were taken off and he was marched to the far end of the clearing. The treeline formed an irregular oval, with densely wooded terrain on three sides. One of the Light Horse removed Tappin's hat and his outer coat, which had been draped over his shoulders. Underneath he wore a dark suit, with a matching vest and a four-in-hand tie. He looked, as always, impeccably groomed.

Execution in the Cherokee Nation was performed by firing squad. With Tappin in place, the six Light Horse in the second wagon moved forward. They were accompanied by Joseph Starr, who formed them on line some twenty paces from the condemned man. Starr then walked purposefully to Tappin, who studiously ignored him. From his pocket Starr took out a piece of white cloth cut in the shape of a circle and exactly three inches in diameter. He pinned the white circle onto Tappin's suit jacket, directly over the heart.

No one had spoken a word during the preparations, but now, taking a step backward, Starr pulled a sheet of paper from his pocket. He unfolded it and began to read the death warrant in a loud, clear voice. The crisp air punctuated every word with a puff of frost. Tappin betrayed no emotion as he heard himself sentenced to execution. He stood there, seemingly impervious to the cold, his manacled hands drawn tightly together. He appeared vaguely bored by the proceedings.

Starr finished reading and returned the paper to his pocket. He looked at Tappin. "Do you wish to say anything?"

"Yes," Tappin answered in a resolute voice. "I am a *Tsalagi* and I will die well. Let no one say otherwise when I am dead."

"Anything else?"

Tappin seemed to consider a moment. Then, as though it

wasn't worth the effort, he shook his head. Starr pulled a large black kerchief from his coat pocket. He started forward.

"No blindfold," Tappin said flatly. "I prefer to see the men who kill me."

Starr nodded, replacing the kerchief in his pocket. He turned and walked away, followed by Tappin's four-man escort. Upon reaching the firing squad, he halted and took a position off to one side. The escort continued on to the edge of the clearing.

David Tappin stood alone. His features were immobile under the dappled light of oncoming dawn. Squaring his shoulders, he stared past the firing squad. His gaze settled on William Ross, and an ashen smile touched the corner of his mouth. After a moment his eyes shifted almost involuntarily to Ryan. His expression altered into a cold look of hate.

"Ready!"

At Starr's command the firing squad shouldered their carbines. Tappin's eyes snapped around as though compelled to watch. He stared straight into the muzzles.

"Aim!"

The firing squad seemed frozen in place, staring impassively across their sights. Everyone but the condemned man held his breath.

"Fire!"

All six carbines cracked in unison. The white cloth circle imploded, vanishing in a ragged starburst of blood. Tappin wilted under the impact of the slugs, literally blown off his feet. He hit the ground on his back and one leg jerked in an afterspasm of death. His eyes were open and stared at nothing.

A powdery silt of snow, shaken off the trees by the muzzle blast, dusted the clearing. The firing squad slowly lowered their rifles and there was a long moment of silence. Finally, as the others watched quietly, Joseph Starr walked to the fallen man. He went down on one knee, inspecting the body closely. Satisfied, he climbed to his feet and turned, nodding to William Ross. His voice was firm and clear.

"Sentence has been carried out according to warrant. David Tappin is dead."

Ross gave no sign of acknowledgment. He wheeled sharply about and walked to the carriage. Ryan was only a pace behind, following him through the door. The driver lightly popped the reins and the matched set of grays took off down the road. The mounted Light Horse, formed in a column of twos, brought up the rear.

Some while passed before Ross seemed to recover himself. When he spoke, his tone was curiously muted. "A nasty business and well finished. At least he died with dignity."

Ryan nodded. "Tappin was never short on grit."

"Indeed he wasn't." Ross hesitated, then turned to Ryan. "Tell me, what are your plans now?"

"I reckon that depends on Elizabeth."

For appearance's sake, Ryan had spent the last two nights with Dr. Frank Porter. It seemed the wiser choice, since he was a witness in the case and Ross was technically an officer of the state. His plan was to call on Elizabeth sometime later in the day.

"May I speak frankly?" Ross asked.

"Don't see why not."

"Elizabeth and I discussed your idea about moving west."

Ryan waited, his expression stoic.

"Her place is here," Ross went on. "As she told you, she could never be happy in the white world. But more importantly, she could never be happy away from her people. Before anything else, she is a Cherokee."

"Yeah, I know," Ryan said, looking down at his hands. "I guess I was just kidding myself."

Ross studied him intently for a moment. "Do you think the Cherokees can win the fight to retain independence?"

"No," Ryan said without hesitation.

"Why not?"

"Because you're up against the United States government. Add that to crooked politicians and men like Stevens and it's a lost cause. You'll win a few battles, but you won't win the war."

"How long do you think we could stave them off?"

"All depends," Ryan said. "You could take a lesson from Boudinot, though. Whatever battles you win will be won in Washington—not here in the Territory."

"Fork-tongued diplomacy," Ross said with a smile. "Is that the idea?"

"Sometimes you've got no choice but to play by the other fellow's rules."

"Suppose it would postpone the inevitable for another twenty years, perhaps a generation. Would you say the end justifies the means?"

"If I were you," Ryan said honestly, "I'd go at it no holds barred. The longer the fight lasts, the longer you keep your independence."

"I couldn't agree more. In fact, after our experience with the railroad, I've decided to revise our tactics completely. Washington will soon be overrun with red delegations."

Ryan laughed out loud. "That ought to be a sight to see."

"Would you care to join me in the fight?"

"Join you!" Ryan said, visibly startled.

Ross gave him a wise look. "You've had experience with bureaucrats and crooked politicians and men like Robert Stevens. I also have faith in your sympathy with the Cherokee cause. I'd say you're well qualified for the job."

"Wouldn't work," Ryan observed. "Too many Cherokees want a piece of my hide. It'd just start another round of killing."

"I think not," Ross said confidently. "You'll recall that I have a certain influence within the Cherokee Nation. No one would seriously consider antagonizing my son-in-law."

Ryan stared at him. With an easy laugh, Ross patted his arm. "Put your worries aside, John. Once you've joined us, the past will soon be forgotten. Cherokees love no man quite so much as the one who rallies to their cause."

"Level with me," Ryan said pointedly. "Elizabeth put you up to this, didn't she?"

"Well, after all, John, she is her father's daughter."

William Ross chuckled with robust good humor. His words were all the affirmation Ryan needed. Father and daughter had extended the greatest gift of all. It was what he himself wanted most—a new life and a fresh start. A chance to dwell among the Cherokees.

A short while later the carriage rolled to a stop before the house. As Ryan stepped out of the coach, the front door opened. Elizabeth hurried across the veranda, then halted at the top of the steps. Her eyes went past him and something unspoken passed between father and daughter. Her face suddenly radiated joy and she rushed to meet Ryan. Her voice was warm and inviting.

"Welcome home, John."

Ryan gathered her into his arms. Some smoldering instinct told him that he was where he belonged, where he would stay. The killing, all his days of wandering were in the past.

His death work was done.

DEATH SHOT

McCluskie's knees buckled and he was suddenly gripped with the urgency of killing Anderson . . . He heard the gunfire and the terrified shrieks of dance-hall girls, sensed the crowd scattering. But it was all somehow distant, even a little unreal. Blinded, falling swiftly into darkness, he willed his hand to move. To finish what he had come here to do.

Another bullet smacked him in the ribs, but like a dead snake, operating on nerves alone, his hand reacted and came up with the Colt. That he couldn't see Anderson bothered him not at all. In his mind's eye he remembered exactly where the Texan was standing, and even as he pressed the trigger, he knew the shot had struck home . . .

"MATT BRAUN IS ONE OF THE BEST!"
—Don Coldsmith, author of the Spanish Bit series

"HE TELLS IT STRAIGHT—AND HE
TELLS IT WELL."
—Jory Sherman, author of *Grass Kingdom*

Look for MATT BRAUN's

EL PASO

and

THE WILD ONES

Also available in a special two-in-one edition for $6.99

. . . and don't miss the author's
other classic Western adventures

Available from St. Martin's Paperbacks

KINCH RILEY

(Previously published as *Kinch*)

MATT BRAUN

St. Martin's Paperbacks

All characters in this book are fictitious. Any resemblance to actual per-
sons, living or dead, is purely coincidental.

Kinch Riley was previously published under the title *Kinch*.

KINCH RILEY

Copyright © 1975 by Matthew Braun.

ISBN: 0-312-94853-0
EAN: 9780312-94853-5

Printed in the United States of America

Ace edition / May 1978
St. Martin's Paperbacks edition / June 2000

St. Martin's Paperbacks are published by St. Martin's Press, 175 Fifth
Avenue, New York, NY 10010.

10 9 8 7 6 5 4 3 2 1

For
JTA
A Kindred Spirit
Who Was Always There

This is an epitaph for Kinch Riley.

Essentially it is a true story, gleaned from musty newspaper archives and the chronicles of men who were there. The place is Newton, Kansas, during the summer of 1871. On a sweltering August night a gunfight occurred which came to be known as "Newton's General Massacre." According to the *Topeka Daily Commonwealth*, six men died in the space of ninety seconds. Three more were wounded, one of whom was later killed under curious circumstances. Witnesses to the slaughter credited a young boy, known only as Riley, with having accounted for most of the dead.

Kinch Riley is the story of what led to that fateful night in Newton. More significantly, perhaps, it is a reasonably accurate account of how a bond of loyalty came to exist between a lawman and a consumptive youth of seventeen. Certain liberties have been taken with names and events, but *Kinch Riley* nonetheless explores one of the Old West's most enduring mysteries. While supporting details are available regarding events leading to the shootout, little is known of the boy named Riley.

After killing five men he simply vanished from the pages of history.

The enigma of Kinch Riley has confounded Western scholars for better than a hundred years. Though the story which follows is fiction based on facts, it provides one solution to a seemingly unfathomable riddle. Perhaps the only solution.

At last, it lays a ghost to rest.

KINCH
RILEY

ONE

McCluskie swung down off the caboose and stood for a moment surveying the depot. It was painted a dingy green, the same as all Santa Fe depots. Not unlike a hundred others he had seen, it had all the warmth of a freshly scrubbed privy. The only notable difference being that it was newer and bigger. Rails had been laid into Newton less than a week past, and the town had been designated division point. Otherwise, so far as McCluskie could see, there was nothing remarkable about the place. Just another fleabag cowtown that would serve as home base till the end of track shifted west a couple of hundred miles.

Hefting his war-bag, he walked to the end of the platform and paused for a look at Newton. The corners of his mouth quirked and he grunted with surprise. It wasn't Abilene, but it was damn sure more than he had expected. Especially out in the middle of nowhere, with the rails hardly a week old.

Newton was laid out much on the order of all cowtowns. Main Street spraddled the tracks, with the red-light district on the southside and most of the business establishments on the north. Side streets, none of which were more than a block long, branched off of the dusty main thoroughfare. Nearly every building had the high false-front that had become the trademark of Kansas railheads, and the structures looked as if they had been slapped together with spit and poster glue. What amazed McCluskie was not that Newton existed, but that it had sprung from the earth's bowels with such dizzying speed.

He dropped the war-bag at his feet and started rolling a smoke. The paper and tobacco took shape in his hands without thought, almost a mechanical ritual born of habit. Searching his vest, he found a sulphurhead and flicked it to life with his thumbnail. Touching flame to cigarette, he took a long draw and let his eyes wander along the street. His inspection was brief, for a well-chucked rock would have hit the town limits in any direction. But little escaped his gaze, and except for the hodge-podge of buildings, there wasn't much to stir his interest.

Whatever Newton had to offer wouldn't be all that different. He'd seen the elephant too many times to expect otherwise. Cards and shady ladies and railhead saloons were the same wherever a man hung his hat. Such things didn't change, they just shifted operations whenever the end of track changed. Most times it seemed they had even hauled along the same batch of customers.

McCluskie stuck the cigarette in his mouth, again hefted the war-bag, and started down the platform steps. Somewhere behind him he heard his name called and turned to find Newt Hansberry, the station master, bearing down on him. He didn't care much for Hansberry and had purposely avoided the depot for just that reason. But then, he was sort of stand-offish about people in general, so it wasn't as if he had anything personal against the man.

"Mike, you ol' scutter!" Hansberry rushed up and commenced pumping his hand like he was trying to raise water. "Where the hell did you spring from?"

"Just pulled in on the cowtown express." McCluskie retrieved his hand and wiped it along the side of his pants.

The station master shot a puzzled glance at the cattle cars, then barfed up an oily chuckle. "Cowtown express! That's rich, Mike. Wait'll I try that on the boys." The laughter slacked off and his brow puckered in an owlish frown. "Say, what's a big mucka-muck like you doing in Newton, anyway? The head office didn't tell me you was comin' out here."

McCluskie's look was wooden, revealing nothing. "Why, Newt, you know how the brass are. They're so busy shufflin' people and trains they don't tell no-body nothin'."

"Yeh, but they don't send the top bull to end of track just for exercise." Hansberry cocked one eye-brow in a crafty smirk. "C'mon, Mike, 'fess up. They sent you out here on some kinda job, didn't they? Something hush-hush."

"Sorry to disappoint you, Newt. They just wanted me to have a looksee. Sorta make sure the division has got all the kinks ironed out. Y'know what I mean?"

Hansberry blinked and nodded, swallowing his next question. What with him being station master,

that last part had struck a little close to home. "Sure,
Mike. I get your drift. But don't worry, I run a tight
operation. Always have."

"Never thought you didn't." McCluskie let it drop
there and jerked his thumb back toward the main part
of town. "What's the low-down on this dump? Anything happened I ought to know about?"

"Well I ain't seen Jesse James around town if
that's what you mean. Course, I don't guess the likes
of him would go in for robbin' cattle cars anyways."

"Not likely. That wasn't what I was drivin' at,
though. Anybody tried to set himself up as the king-
fish yet?"

"Hell, ain't nobody had time. They been too busy
gettin' this place built. 'Sides, Newton's not rightly a
town anyway. Wichita's the county seat and this here
is just a township. Won't never be nothin' else, neither. Leastways till somebody proves it's on the map
to stay."

"So I heard."

The station master gave him a guarded look. "Yeh,
I guess you would've. Don't s'pose there's much that
gets past you boys at the head office."

McCluskie let the question slip past. "What about
law? They got anybody ridin' herd on the trailhands?"

"Oh, sure. Some of the sportin' crowd and a few
of the storekeepers got themselves appointed to the
town board and they pestered Wichita into sendin' a
deputy up here permanent. Good thing they did, too.
Otherwise them Texans would've hoorawed this place
clean down to the ground."

"This lawdog, he anybody I know?"

"Sorta doubt it. Name's Tonk Hazeltine. Some

folks says he's a breed, but he don't look like no Injun I ever saw. Queer kind o' bird, though. Acts like he just drunk some green rotgut and didn't care much for the taste."

"Don't think I ever heard of him. How's he handle himself? Been keepin' the drovers in line?"

"Yeh, what there is of 'em. Y'know the stockyards have only been built a couple of weeks. We're just now startin' to steal a few herds away from Abilene."

"They'll come, don't worry yourself about that. Before the summer's out we'll have the K&P stewin' in their own juice."

"I 'spect you're right. Leastways I ain't never known the Sante Fe to make no foolish bets."

McCluskie merely nodded, his eyes again drifting to the street. "Understand Belle Siddons is in town."

"Sure is. Got herself a house down on Third Street. I seem to recollect you and her was sorta thick in Abilene."

"You oughtn't to listen so good, Newt." McCluskie flicked his cigarette stub onto the tracks and started down the platform steps. When he reached the bottom, he stopped and looked back. "What's the best hotel in town?"

"Why, I guess that'd be the Newton House. Fanciest digs this side of Kansas City. Just turn north across the tracks and keep goin'. You can't miss it."

McCluskie turned south and headed down the street, walking toward a ramshackle affair that proclaimed itself the National Hotel.

Hansberry watched after him, cursing softly under his breath. There was something about McCluskie that rubbed a man the wrong way. Even if he was head of security for the line. But it wasn't the kind of thing a fellow could put into words. Not out loud anyway.

McCluskie had a certain Gaelic charm about him, with a square jaw and a humorous mouth that was about half covered with a brushy mustache. Yet he was also something of a lone wolf, and damn few men had ever gotten close enough to say they really knew him well. Not that he threw his weight around, or for that matter, even raised his voice. He didn't have to. Most folks just figured he preferred his own company, and they let it go at that.

Part of it, perhaps, had to do with his size. He was a tall man—over six feet—and compactly built. Sledge-shouldered and lean through the hips, he had the look of a prizefighter. Which he might have been at some time in the past. Little was known about him before he showed up in Abilene back in '69. There, working for the Kansas & Pacific, he had killed one man with his fists and a couple more with a gun. After that nobody felt the urge to ask questions.

Yet, as he thought on it, Hansberry was struck by something else entirely. The queer way the Irishman had of looking at a man. Not just cold and unfeeling, but the practiced eyes of a man who stayed alive by making quick estimates. It was sort of unsettling.

The station master watched McCluskie disappear through the door of the hotel, then turned away, muttering to himself. Somehow the day didn't seem so bright any more, but a quick glance at the sky merely confirmed his misgivings. There wasn't a cloud in sight.

* * *

McCluskie came down the hall from his room and entered the lobby. He had shaved, changed to a fresh shirt, and brushed the dust from his suit. His face glowed with a ruddy, weathered vitality, and he was whistling a tuneless ditty to himself. Except for his size and bearing, and the bulge on his right hip, he might have been a spiffy drummer out to sweet-talk the local merchants. As he approached the desk, the room clerk brightened and gave him a flaccid smile.

"Yessir, Mr. McCluskie. What can we do for you? Hope that room met with your satisfaction. We don't often get folks like yourself in here. Railroad men, I mean. Mostly the rougher crowd. Y'know, trailhands and muleskinners and the like."

McCluskie simply ignored the chatter. He took out the makings and started building a smoke. "Need some directions. Belle Siddons' house on Third Street."

The clerk's smile widened into a sly, dirty grin. "You sure know how to pick 'em, Mr. McCluskie. Belle's got the best sportin' house in town. Oughta warn you, though, it's awful expensive."

McCluskie nailed him with a flat, dull stare. "Something tickle your funny bone?"

The man blinked a couple of times and looked a little closer. What he saw was a face that sobered anyone with the savvy to read it. His grin dissolved into a waxen smile.

"No offense, Mr. McCluskie. Just tryin' to be friendly. Service of the house."

"Forget it. What about the directions?"

"Sure thing. Belle's house is just this side of Hide

Park. Big yellow house right on the corner of Third. You won't have no trouble recognizing it."

"What's Hide Park?"

"Why, the—uh—y'know. The sportin' district. The parlor houses are on Third and down below that are the dancehalls and the cribs. That's why they call it Hide Park. Nothin' but bare skin and lots of it."

McCluskie just stared at him for a moment, then turned and walked from the hotel.

Striding down South Main, the Irishman found it about as he had expected. Within the first block there was a grocery, two hotels, a mercantile, and a hardware store. Then for the next couple of blocks both sides of the street were lined with saloons and gambling dens. Evidently everything below that was Hide Park.

The more he saw, the better he liked it. Plainly the townspeople had been at some pains to lay it out properly. Newton straddled the Chisholm Trail and was sixty-five miles south of Abilene. Which meant that its future as a cowtown was pretty well assured. At least for a couple of seasons, anyway. Once track was laid into Wichita, some twenty miles farther south, Newton's bubble would burst like a dead toad in a hot sun. But that was for him to know and them to find out. There was nothing to be gained in letting it get around that the Santa Fe had a finger in the pie. Right now it was enough to wean the Texans away from Abilene. The next step would come in its own good time.

Late afternoon shadows splayed over the town, and already the street was crowded with Texans. Watching them as he strolled along, McCluskie marveled again at the cowhands' childlike antics. Somehow they never seemed to change. After two months on the trail, eating dust and beans and working themselves to a frazzle, they couldn't wait to scatter their money to the winds. Painted women, watered-down whiskey, and rigged card games. That was about their speed. Almost as if they had some perverse craving to be flimflammed out of the dollar a day they earned wet-nursing longhorns. It just went to prove what most sensible folks already knew. Texans, give or take a handful, weren't much brighter than the cows they drove to railhead.

Still, a man had to give the devil his due. Without the Texans and their longhorns, the Santa Fe would be hard pushed to pull off the scheme that brought him to Newton. The thought triggered another, and he reminded himself to have a look at North Main before dark. Might even be well to introduce himself to some of the town fathers. Let them know he was around if they needed a hand with anything. Texans or otherwise. Never hurt to have a foot in the door with the uptown crowd. Especially the ones who fancied themselves as politicians.

Nearing Third, he spotted the yellow house on the northeast corner and angled across the street. Inspecting it closer, he decided the room clerk had been right after all. Upside the drab buildings surrounding it, the yellow house stuck out like a diamond in an ash heap.

McCluskie went through the door without bothering to knock and found himself in a small vestibule. The layout was as familiar as an old shoe and he proceeded immediately to the parlor. There he came on a black maid, humming softly to herself as she set things in order for the evening rush. She straightened up and gave him a toothy smile.

"Mistah, you're gonna hafta come back. I knows you got the misery jest from lookin' at you, but we ain't open till aftah suppahtime."

That was something he had always admired about Belle. She taught the help how to diddle a man and make him like it. Even maids.

"Tell Miss Belle she's got a gentleman caller."

Apparently that was a new one on the black woman. Her sloe eyes batted furiously for a moment, then she hitched around and scurried from the room. As she went through a door to the back part of the house, she muttered something unintelligible. From the little he could make out, it was a fairly one-sided conversation.

Left to himself, McCluskie examined the parlor with a critical eye. It was nothing less than he would have expected of Belle Siddons. She had a reputation for running an elegant house. Not at all like the two-bit cribs and dollar-a-dance palaces down the street. Plainly, from the looks of the parlor, she hadn't lost her touch. Grunting, he silently gave the room his stamp of approval.

"Well as I live and breathe! If it's not the big Mick himself."

Turning, he saw Belle standing in the doorway, smiling that same soft smile he remembered so well. Outwardly she seemed to have changed not at all, though it was something over a year since he had last seen her.

She wasn't a small woman, yet there was a delicacy to her that somehow belied the shapely hips and full bust. Her hair was the color of a raven's wing, glinted through with specks of rust when the light struck it just right, and her eyes had always reminded him of an emerald stickpin he once saw on a riverboat gambler. But it was her face that stopped most men. Not hard or worn, like what a fellow who frequented sporting houses would expect to find on a madam. It was an easy face to look at, pleasurable. Maybe something short of beautiful, but with a devilish witchery that made a man sit up and do tricks just so he could watch it smile.

"Belle, you look nifty as ever." McCluskie was hard put to keep from licking his mustache. "Appears life's been treatin' you with style."

"I can't complain." She walked toward him, airily waving her hand around the parlor. "What's the verdict? Think it'll pass muster?"

McCluskie caught a whiff of jasmine scent as she stopped before him, and for a moment he couldn't get his tongue untracked. "The house? Why, sure. Even classier than the place you had in Abilene."

"Yes, good old Abilene. Every now and then I think back on it and have myself a real laugh." A curious light flickered in her eyes. Somehow it put him in mind of a tiny flame bouncing off of alabaster. "But that's water under the bridge. Tell me about yourself, Mike. What have you been doing since the good old days?"

The way she was looking at him made him uncomfortable as hell. Almost as if he should be scuffling his toe in the dirt and apologizing for some fool thing he'd done.

"Nothin' much. Just pickin' up a dollar here and a dollar there."

"I do declare, a modest Irishman. Never thought I'd live to see the day."

"Well, you know me, Belle. I never was one to toot my own horn."

"Don't be bashful, honey. You're among friends. Why, everybody in Kansas has heard about Mike McCluskie. Some folks say the Santa Fe would fall apart without him to fend off those big, bad train robbers."

The conversation wasn't going quite the way McCluskie had expected. In fact, it seemed to be all uphill, with him pulling the load. He decided to try another tack.

"I just got in this afternoon. Thought I'd come down and invite you out for a bite to eat after you close up tonight."

"Then we could go up to your room for a drink and talk about old times."

McCluskie grinned. "Well, something like that had crossed my mind."

Fire flashed in Belle's eyes, and it was no longer a tiny flame. "Listen you thick-headed Mick, forget the sweet talk and trot yourself out of here. You left me high and dry in Abilene, and once burned is twice beware. So just scoot!"

"Aw, hell, Belle. It wasn't like—"

"Don't 'aw, Belle' me, you big baboon! Waltz on down the street and find yourself another sucker. They're a dime a dozen and standing in line."

Singed around the ears and smoking hot, he headed for the vestibule. "Well, don't say I never asked you.

If you change your mind I'm stayin' at the National."

"Don't hold your breath," she fired back. "And don't let the door hit you in the keester on the way out!"

McCluskie didn't. But he came near jarring it off the hinges when it slammed shut behind him.

TWO

McCluskie stalked back up Main Street like a mad bull hooking at cobwebs. With each step his temper flared higher and his mood turned darker. There was just no rhyme nor reason to Belle's attitude. There'd never been any understanding between them, and she sure as hell hadn't had any claim on him. She'd known that from the outset when they started keeping company back in Abilene. It was simply an arrangement. Pleasant enough, and something they had both seemed to need at the time. But nothing more. Just two people having a few laughs and enjoying one another whenever the mood struck them.

That was the trouble with women. They could never accept a little monkey business for what it was. Somehow it always came out larded with mush and lickety-split got itself embroidered into a four letter word. L-O-V-E. Even crib girls weren't immune to the disease. Countless times he'd seen blowsy tarts go sweet on a certain man and just eat their hearts out when they couldn't have him all to themselves. While all the time they were plying their trade regular as clockwork.

It surpassed all understanding. Goddamn if it didn't!

Yet, when it got down to brass tacks, that wasn't what had him boiling. Lots of females had got that goofy look after he'd flushed the birds out of their nest. That was something a fellow learned to live with, for it seemed to be the universal affliction of anything that wore skirts. What had his goat—and the mere thought of it set him off in a rage—was that he'd never before been dusted off by a woman.

And a madam to boot!

The gall of the woman, and her not even Irish. If her name was Adair or Murphy or O'Toole, just maybe he could have swallowed it. Understood, anyway. But for the likes of Belle Siddons to think that she had something special! Something he wanted badly enough to let her put a ring through his nose.

Great crucified Christ! It defied belief.

The hell of it was, he'd never given her any reason to think that way. Not the slightest inkling. He'd always been aboveboard, a square shooter from start to finish. Maybe he hadn't discouraged her. Or put the quietus on her syrupy talk. But that was no reason for her to give him frostbite now. Merely because he'd pulled up stakes in Abilene without inviting her along. There just wasn't room for a woman in his line of work. Not a regular woman anyway. Belle had been around long enough to know that. Leastways if she hadn't then she must have had her head stuck in the sand.

Yet she had still kicked his butt out the door!

McCluskie was barreling along under a full head of steam when the doors of the Red Front Saloon suddenly burst open and he collided head on with a half dozen Texans. One look told him that they were pretty well ossified, and mad as he was, he started to let it pass. Just at the moment he figured he had all the troubles he could say grace over. Besides which, there was nothing to be gained in swapping insults with a bunch of trailhands. Shouldering them aside, he plowed through and headed up the street.

"Jes a goddamn minute, friend! Who'ya think yer shovin' around?"

The big talker knew he had made a mistake when the pilgrim in the bowler hat wheeled about and started back. McCluskie was obviously no friend. The Texan wasn't so drunk that he couldn't recognize a grizzly bear when he saw one, and he had the sinking sensation that he was on the verge of becoming somebody's supper. Out of sheer reflex he made a grab for his gun, but he never had a chance.

McCluskie's fist caught him flush on the jaw and he went down like a sack of mud. The suddenness of it was a little too much for the other cowhands. They just stood there slack-jawed and bewildered, gawking at their poleaxed comrade as if he had been struck by lightning.

The Irishman rubbed his knuckles and glowered down on them. "Anybody care to be next?"

Apparently it wasn't a thought that merited deep consideration. Even at five to one the Texans weren't wild about the odds. Not after the way their partner had nearly got his head torn off. They just shook their heads, exchanging sheepish glances, and let it slide.

McCluskie spun on his heel and walked off, just the least bit irked with himself. He shouldn't have let a loudmouth drunk set him off that way. Anger was something to be conserved, held back, so that a man could choose his own time and place to let fly. Otherwise he'd get snookered into fighting on somebody else's terms, which was a damn fine way to wind up with a busted skull.

Still, he wasn't fooling himself on where the score stood. It was Belle that had set him off. Not the Texans. If anything, the cowhand was just an innocent bystander. And any time a woman got a man to acting like a buzz saw it was time to pull back and check the bets.

Satisfied with his estimate of the whole affair, he struck off in search of the big nabobs uptown. It was high time he quit horsing around and got down to business. Which didn't include yellow cathouses or dagger-tongued madams.

Some twenty minutes later McCluskie wandered into the Lone Star Saloon just north of the tracks. After a stop at the depot, and a brief conversation with Hansberry, he came away with an interesting piece of information. Bob Spivey, owner of the Lone Star and Newton's guiding light, was chairman of the town board. All things considered, it seemed a good place to start.

The barkeep was an amiable sort by the name of Mulhaney, who had a weakness for fellow Irishmen. Before McCluskie had time to polish off his first drink Bob Spivey had been summoned from the back room. Mulhaney positively glowed that his countryman was decked out like a Philadelphia lawyer, and made the introductions as if he were presenting a long lost cousin from the old sod. After filling their glasses, still beaming from ear to ear, the barkeep drifted off to let them get better acquainted.

Spivey hoisted his glass in salute and downed the shot in one neat gulp. Plainly he liked his own whiskey. "Welcome to Newton, Mr. McCluskie. Pardon me for sayin' it, but I can't help admirin' that suit you're wearin'. Real nice duds. Just between you and me and the gatepost, we haven't had many visitors with any real class as yet. Hope you'll decide to stay with us for a while."

"Might take you up on that." McCluskie smiled and tapped the brim of his bowler. "Don't pay any mind to this, though. It's my travelin' outfit. Once I change into workin' clothes you couldn't pick me out in a crowd."

"Is that a fact?" Spivey refilled their glasses, glancing sideways as he set the bottle on the bar. "If you don't mind my askin', what line of work are you in?"

The question was breach of etiquette in a cowtown, and both men knew it. But Spivey was playing the role of a well-meaning, if somewhat curious, host. His face bore the look of a plaster saint, all innocence.

McCluskie didn't bat an eye. "I'm with the railroad. The Santa Fe."

"Well now, that is news." Spivey's grin suddenly turned spare, inquiring. "Would I be out of line in askin' what brings you to our fair metropolis?"

"Nope, not at all. Understand you folks are gettin' ready to open a bank."

"That a fact. The Cattlemen's Exchange. You

might have noticed it directly across the street. But I don't see the connection, just exactly."

"The money shipment will be comin' in on tomorrow evening's train. I sort of look after things like that for the Santa Fe."

"I see." The saloonkeeper's gaze drifted off a moment, then snapped back. "Say, wait a minute. McCluskie? Aren't you the fellow that used to ride shotgun for the K&P up in Abilene?"

"Yeah, I did a turn or two along the Smoky Hill."

"Then you're the one that killed the Quinton brothers when they tried to hold up that express car."

"Guess you got me pegged, all right. Course, that was about a hundred lifetimes ago."

"Well I'll be dipped. Mike McCluskie." Spivey's mouth widened in a toothsome grin. "Hell, I feel safer about our money already. I'm just guessin', but I'd speculate the Santa Fe sent you out here to see that things come off without a hitch."

"That's close enough, I guess." McCluskie paused, knuckling back his mustache, and decided on the spur of the moment that it was time to test the water. "Newt Hansberry tells me you're the he-wolf on the town board. Thought we might have a little talk about this lawman of yours. I'm sort of curious as to how much help he'll be if push comes to shove."

"You mean if somebody tries to rob the train?" When the Irishman nodded, Spivey gave him a concerned look. "That sounds like you know something we don't."

"Wouldn't say that exactly. But when you're talkin' about that much money it never hurts to hedge your bet."

"Then you know the amount being shipped?" McCluskie just stared at him, saying nothing. "Listen, if there's anything in the wind, I'd like to hear about it. Just between you and me, I own a piece of that bank, and all this talk of train robbers don't do my nerves much good."

"Mr. Spivey, I knew you were in on the bank deal before I came out here. Otherwise I wouldn't even be talkin' to you. But so far as I've been able to find out, there's nobody plannin' a stick up. Like I said, I just wanted the lowdown on this deputy of yours. In case I had to call on him."

"Well there's not a whole lot I can tell you. He's from Wichita, y'see. The county sent him up here after a bunch of us pitched in and raised a kitty to pay his salary. Way we figured it, the town needed some sort of John Law to keep the Texans in line. So far Hazeltine's done the job. Leastways we haven't had no killin's."

"Has anybody braced him yet?"

"Can't say as they have. He don't believe in postin' a gun ordinance. Says it can't be enforced without a lot of killin'. So far nobody's tried him on for size, if that's what you mean."

"Something like that."

"Guess I can't help you there. All we know is that he's supposed to be some kind o' tough nut. The sheriff says he's a real stemwinder. Evidently made himself a reputation somewheres down in the Nations. Tell you the truth, though, you sort of lost me. What's Hazeltine got to do with a Santa Fe money shipment? I always heard you boys weren't exactly slouches at lookin' after your own business."

"We generally manage." McCluskie's look revealed nothing. "But it don't hurt to take a peek at your hole card, just in case you have to play it. Might be an ace and it might be a joker. Pays to know what you're holdin'."

Spivey fell silent, sipping at his whiskey. He was a short man, tending to bald with the years, and he perspired a lot. Mainly from the bulge around his beltline, which was the result of indulging himself with good food and plentiful liquor. But what he lacked in size and muscle he made up for with an agile, inquiring mind. In the past he had been able to stay a step ahead of bigger men simply by outwitting them, and it was this ferret-like shrewdness which had given him some degree of influence in the affairs of Newton. Right now that inquisitive nature was focused on the Irishman. Something about McCluskie's sudden appearance and his guileless manner just didn't jell. Granted, the money shipment warranted the presence of someone of McCluskie's caliber, but there was something here that didn't meet the eye. Puzzling over it, he decided to try a shot in the dark.

"Say, I just remembered something I wanted to ask you about. You being a railroad man and all." Spivey's expression was bland but watchful, searching for any telltale sign. "What's the word at Santa Fe about this new outfit down in Wichita? Way I heard it, a couple of sharp operators name of Meade and Grieffenstein are tryin' to promote themselves a railroad."

McCluskie didn't even blink. "Beats me. There's so many small-timers around a man's hard put to keep 'em sorted out. Why, they been up here tryin' to dump some stock?"

"Naw, they're smarter'n that." The saloonkeeper hadn't detected anything suspicious, but he wasn't willing to let it drop so easily. "They're tryin' to float a bond issue by organizin' a referendum vote. Course, they got the courthouse crowd in their hip pockets, but that don't go for all of Sedgwick County. Up here, we mean to fight 'em right down to the wire."

"That so? Any special reason?"

"Reason? Why, hell yes! You mean to say you don't know where they intend to build this railroad?"

"Don't recollect hearin' one way or the other."

"That curious, for a fact, since they mean to run a line between Wichita and here. Offhand I'd think the Santa Fe wouldn't let a piece of news like that slip past 'em. Naturally, you can see that if the bond issue ever went through, Newton'd be dead as a doornail. Leastways where the cattle trade is concerned."

Whatever reaction this sparked in the Irishman, Spivey missed it completely. His little game came to an abrupt end as the door burst open and a man stomped in as if he was looking for a dog to kick. The cast of his eye said that it didn't make much difference which dog. Just any that happened to be handy would do nicely.

McCluskie caught the glint of a badge and his interest perked up. The man striding toward them was tall and slim, and there was something glacial about his face. Almost as if it had been shrunk and frozen and nailed down tight, so that nothing moved but his eyes. Nature hadn't let him off that lightly, though. His teeth were stained and square as cubes, not unlike a row of old dice, and his eyes gave off a peculiar glassy sparkle. Queer as it seemed, he looked like a stuffed eagle that had had a couple of marbles wedged into his eye sockets.

Plainly, this was Tonk Hazeltine. Newton's principal claim to law and order.

The deputy marched up to Spivey and gave him a hard as nails scowl. "You heard about it?"

"About what?" Spivey sounded like a befuddled parrot.

"Don't nobody in this town keep their ears open 'cept me?" Hazeltine's curt tone was underscored by a kind of smothered wrath. "Some jasper just cold-cocked a drover down at the Red Front and the lid like t' blew off. I hadda hell of a time talkin' them boys out o' startin' a war. Got it in their heads they was gonna tree the whole shebang 'til they found this bird and hauled his ashes."

"Well, Tonk, that don't sound like a major calamity to me. I mean, it was just a fight, wasn't it?"

"Fight, hell! The way them boys tell the story, it was closer to murder. This feller stiffed him with one punch and come near cripplin' him for life. Why, the boy only woke up a minute ago. He's still stumblin' around like a blind dog in a slaughterhouse."

"Then why don't you just arrest this rowdy for disturbin' the peace? Seems to me that'd be the simplest way 'round the whole thing."

"Can't find him, that's why. Searched all over town and ain't seen hide nor hair of him. Them boys said he was about seven feet tall, with a big bushy mustache, and sportin' one of them hats like the drummers—"

Something clicked in Hazeltine's head and his eyes glistened like soapy agates. Since storming into the saloon he hadn't paused for wind, and in a sudden rush of awareness, he finally swiveled around for a look at the Irishman.

McCluskie grinned. "Deputy, it appears you've got your man."

"Well I'll be go to hell." Hazeltine's jaw snapped shut in a grim line. "Mister, you're under—"

Spivey broke in hurriedly. "Now hold on a minute, Tonk. This here's Mike McCluskie. Chief security agent for the Santa Fe. You can't go arrestin' him for clobberin' some damn trailhand."

"Who says I can't? 'Sides, I already told you, it weren't no fistfight. It was a massacre. Why, he's likely addled that boy permanent."

Spivey groaned and shot the Irishman an imploring look. "What about it, McCluskie? You must've had some reason to hit that drover."

"Best reason I know of. He tried pullin' a gun on me."

"The hell you say!" Hazeltine's lip curled back over his yellow teeth. "That whole bunch is ready to swear you jumped that boy before he even had time to get unlimbered."

"What you're sayin' is that one of them let the cat out of the bag about him makin' a grab for his gun."

"Is that right, Tonk?" Spivey demanded.

"What if it is? He just reached. Never even cleared leather."

The saloonkeeper let out a long sigh. "What d'ya say we just forget it? Seems pretty clear that Mr.

McCluskie was provoked and I got an idea the judge would see it the same way."

Hazeltine glowered back at him for a moment, then turned his gaze on the Irishman. "Mister, you'd better watch that stuff in my town. Next time it won't go so easy. Railroad or no railroad."

McCluskie regarded him with impassive curiosity. "Heard you made quite a name for yourself down in the Nations."

"What's that to you?"

"Nothin'. Just funny, that's all. Way I heard it, the tribes don't allow a white man to wear a badge down there."

Hazeltine tried staring him down and found that he couldn't. At last, face mottled with anger, he brushed past and stalked out of the saloon. McCluskie watched him through the door, then grunted, looking back at Spivey.

"Just offhand I'd say that's the queerest lookin' breed I ever saw."

"Breed? Why hell, McCluskie, he's got no more Injun blood in him than you do."

"Think not?" McCluskie idly toyed with his glass, joining a chain of wet little rings on the bar.

"Well, maybe you're right. Course, that being the case, I'd give a bunch to know which side he was ridin' with when he made that name for himself."

"What d'ya mean, which side?"

"Why, there's only two sides, Mr. Spivey. Always has been. And one of 'em don't wear badges."

The saloonkeeper started to say something, but couldn't quite manage to get it out. McCluskie filled their glasses again and lifted his own in salute.

"Here's mud in your eye."

THREE

The sun was an orange ball of fire, settling slowly earthward, when McCluskie came out of the cafe. He paused for a moment, working at his teeth with a toothpick, and speculated on the evening ahead. The train wasn't due in for a couple of hours, which left him with time on his hands and damn few ways to spend it. Wine, women, or cards. That's about what it boiled down to in a whistlestop like Newton. Texans had little use for much else, and the vultures who preyed on them were old hands at keeping the entertainment raw and uncomplicated.

Mulling it over, he decided that women were out. Leastways for tonight, anyway. He still hadn't simmered down from yesterday's donnybrook with Belle, and it bothered him more than he cared to admit. Oddly enough, her raking him over the coals that way had made him want her all the more. There was something about a woman with spirit that made the game a little spicier, and there was no denying that Belle could be a regular spitfire when the notion struck her.

Trouble was, she could get awful damned possessive in the bargain. Which sort of threw cold water on the whole deal.

Still the idea of stopping off at one of the other houses left a sour taste in his mouth. Maybe tomorrow, or the next day, after he'd got Belle off his mind. It wasn't like he had to have a woman, anyhow. There were lots of things a man needed worse, although at the moment nothing occurred to him that just exactly fitted the ticket.

Grunting, he snapped the toothpick in half and flipped it into the street. Hell, it was too damned hot to start messing around anyway. That was one thing a man could always count on. Kansas in July. Hotter'n Hades, and not enough shade to cool a midget.

They ought to give it back to the Indians.

With women crossed off his list, that left only cards and whiskey. McCluskie hauled out the makings and started building a smoke. Dusk wasn't far off, and what with the money shipment set to arrive, he didn't rightly have time to get himself snarled up in a poker game. A man needed to be loose and easy when he gambled, with nothing on his mind but the fickle lady. Otherwise some slick operator would punch his ticket and hand him his head on a platter.

Besides, Santa Fe trains had been known to come in on time. Not often, and certainly with nothing that would tempt a man to set his watch by their regularity. But every now and then an engineer somehow managed to limp into a station at the appointed hour. In a way, it was sort of like bucking the roulette wheel. Pick a number and make your bet. There was a winner every time and no such thing as a sure-fire cinch. Which went double for the Santa Fe. The odds went out the window where their train schedules were concerned.

By process of elimination, McCluskie had pretty well whittled down his alternatives. Women and cards would have to wait, and in Newton that made for slim pickings. Whiskey seemed to be the only thing left, and the way things were shaping up, a pair of wet tonsils sounded better all the time. Little gargle water might just do wonders for his mood.

Flicking a match, he lit his cigarette and headed toward the tracks. He could just as easily have crossed the street and had a drink at the Lone Star. But tonight he didn't feel like matching wits with Spivey. It was a dull pastime anyhow. The saloonkeeper was sharp as a tack in his own way, but he was about as subtle as a sledgehammer. Thought he was going to outfox the big dumb Mick, and all he did was wind up getting himself sandbagged. If it wasn't so pitiful, it might have been funny. Besides, Spivey would likely turn up at the depot later anyway, so there was no sense wasting good drinking time playing cat and mouse.

South of the tracks was more McCluskie's style at any rate. Everybody down there was crooked as a dog's hind leg and nobody tried to pretend otherwise. In a queer sort of way, it was perhaps the purest form of honesty.

Crossing the tracks, it occurred to the Irishman that he tended to think of them as birds of prey. Most were just vultures. Hovering around, waiting to pick the bones after the trailhands had been shorn of their illusions and their pocketbooks. In this class could be lumped together the soiled doves and dancehall operators and saloonkeepers. Of course, there were the turkey buzzards, too. Like Rowdy Joe Lowe and his wife, Crazy Kate. They were the real carrion eaters, the bottom of the heap. What they wouldn't do for a nickel hadn't yet been invented.

Looking at it the other way round, though, the sporting crowd had its own brand of nobility. At the top were the hawks, and a mere handful of crafty old owls. This group, small in number and worlds apart from the grungy bone-pickers, was comprised strictly of highrollers, bunco artists, thimble riggers, and slippery fingered gamblers. Not a tinhorn among them. The elite of whatever underworld they chose to frequent.

Already McCluskie had heard that the highrollers were flocking to Newton like a gathering of royalty. Dandy John Gallagher. Jim Moon. Pony Reid. Names to be reckoned with wherever men talked of faro, three-card monte, chuck-a-luck, or poker. Beside them the likes of Ben Thompson and Bill Hickok and Phil Coe were small potatoes. Amateurs. Chickenfeed sparrows trying to fly high in the company of hawks.

Passing Hoff's Grocery, he noted that the southside was already humming. Cow ponies lined the hitch rails, standing hipshot and drowsy in the dusky heat. Their owners, either three sheets to the wind or fast on their way, were in evidence everywhere along the street. After nearly two years in Abilene, McCluskie could just about slot Texans into the right pigeonhole simply by observing their actions.

The newcomers, fresh off the trail, made a beeline for some place like the Blue Front Clothing Store, splurging a hefty chunk of their pay on fancy duds. Those who had had a bath and sprinkled themselves with toilet water could be found in one of three places. Getting their ears unwaxed down in Hide Park. Swilling snakehead whiskey at two-bits a throw. Or testing their none-too-nimble wits against the slick-fingered cardsharps. The ones who gave lessons in instant poverty.

Lastly, there was the motley crew who were flat on their rumps. Broke, busted, and hungover. Most times they could be spotted cadging drinks, or loafing around Hamil's Hardware eyeballing Sam Colt's latest equalizer. Some of these were reduced to selling their saddles in order to get home, which in a Texan's scheme of things was only slightly less heinous than herding sheep.

McCluskie had to laugh everytime he thought about it. Whichever way a man looked at it, cowhands were a queer breed. They had the brass of a billygoat, but the Good Lord had somehow put their behinds where their brains were supposed to be. Heaven for them didn't have nothing to do with the Hereafter. It was fast women and a jug of rotgut. In just that order.

Shouldering past a bunch of drunks crowding the boardwalk, he pushed through the doors of the Gold Room Saloon. The Texans paid him no mind this time. He was garbed in a linsey shirt, mule-ear boots, and a slouch hat. Along with the Colt Navy strapped high on his hip, the outfit made him one of the crowd. Taller than most, beefier through the shoulders perhaps, but to all appearances just another sporting man out to see the elephant. Which was exactly how he liked it. Having worked his way up from a track layer, he always felt more at ease among men who sweated for a living. Even Texans.

Apparently the Gold Room was one of Newton's better watering holes. Unlike most of the dives, it wasn't jammed to the rafters with caterwauling trailhands. Then he saw the reason. Standing at the bar was Dandy John Gallagher. High priest of the gambling fraternity.

Plainly he had stumbled upon the lair of the highrollers. Where sparrows and pigeons alike were separated from their pokes with style and consummate skill.

Walking forward, he stopped at Gallagher's elbow, who was in the midst of lecturing another man on the merits of some strange new game called Red Dog.

"Mister, I'm lookin' fer a tinhorn name o' Gallagher. The one they run out o' Abilene fer dealin' seconds."

The gambler went stiff as a board, shoulders squared, and slowly turned around. The look in his eye would have melted a cannonball. Then, quite suddenly, the tight-lipped scowl exploded into an infectious grin.

"Mike! You sorry devil. Put'er there!"

McCluskie clasped his hand in a hard grip. "Been a long time, Johnny."

"Too long, by God." Gallagher gave a final shake, then jerked a thumb at his companion. "Why, not ten minutes ago I was saying to Trick here—hey, you two haven't met. Mike McCluskie, say hello to Trick Brown."

The two men hardly had time to exchange nods before Gallagher was off again. "Anyways, I was say-

ing to Trick that there just aren't enough real gambling men around these days. No competition. But,
hell's bells, now that you're here, I might just change
my tune."

"Johnny, you're out of my league. No contest."

"Don't grease me, boy. I've seen you play. Remember?"

"Hell, I ought to. The lessons cost me enough."

"Judas Priest! You could churn that stuff and make
apple butter. C'mon now, Mike, what do you say?
Let's get a real headknocker going. Table stakes.
Straight stud. Just like the old days."

"Well, I guess I might try you on for size. Just for
old time's sake, you understand. But it'll have to be
later tonight. I've got an errand to tend to first."

The gambler punched him on the shoulder. "Something young and full of ginger, I'll lay odds. Never
change, do you?"

McCluskie laughed easily. "You've got a lot of
room to talk. I didn't feel any calluses on your hand.
Bet you're still coatin' them with glycerin morning,
noon, and night, aren't you?"

"Christ A'mighty, Irish! They're tools of the trade.
Wouldn't want me to disgrace the profession, would
you?"

McCluskie was distracted by someone waving
from a faro layout at the back of the room. He looked
closer and saw that it was Pony Reid. "Listen, I'm
gonna have a quick drink and say hello to Pony. I'll
catch up with you somewhere around midnight. Just
don't let anybody peel your roll till I get back."

"Fat chance. Take care you don't get waylaid yourself. Remember, Irish, a poker game is elixir for the

soul. You keep that in mind, you hear?"

McCluskie was still laughing as he strode toward Pony Reid. Gallagher and Brown watched after him a moment, then turned back to their drinks. Brown sipped at his liquor for a minute, apparently lost in thought, and finally glanced over at his friend.

"Johnny, did I get the drift right? The way you talked that hayseed is some kind of bearcat with a deck of cards."

"He's more than that, Trick. In a straight game he could hold his own with anyone you want to name."

"Yeah? Well I'll bet I've got a few moves that'll leave him cross-eyed. Maybe I ought to sit in on that game myself. We might just clean his plow faster'n scat."

Gallagher seemed vastly amused by the idea. "Trick, you're new to the circuit, so I'm going to give you some free advice. Don't ever try to slick Mike McCluskie. He'll kill you quicker than anthrax juice. Looks are deceiving, my boy, and if you're going to live long in this trade, you'd better learn to size a man up. What you just saw wasn't a hayseed. It's a Bengal tiger crossed with an Irish wolfhound."

The gambler's pale, milky eyes drifted again toward the back of the room. "Besides, he could probably outdeal you with his thumbs chopped off."

McCluskie left the Gold Room an hour or so later. His humor was restored and his mood was considerably lighter. While he'd meant to have only one drink, he found it difficult to quit the genial company. There was a camaraderie among professional gamblers that had always intrigued him, and strangely enough, he felt drawn to it in a way he had never fully fathomed. Not that he was blinded to their flaws. They had feet of clay just like everyone else, and the brotherhood they shared was dictated more by circumstances than any need of fellowship. Essentially they were loners, preying on the unwary and the gullible with no more scruples than an alleycat. Within the fraternity there were petty squabbles and jealousies, and an incessant bickering as to who held title to King of the Hill. The same as would be found among any group of men who lived by their wits and felt themselves superior to the great unwashed herd.

Yet there was a solidarity among gamblers that was rare in men of any stripe. They saw themselves as a small band of gallants pitted against the whole world. Though each of them was concerned with feathering his own nest, they could close ranks in an instant when it suited their purpose. Such as combining forces to trim a well-heeled sucker, or standing together when confronted by an indignant mob of righteous townspeople. More than that, they seemed to genuinely enjoy each other's company, much as a breed apart prefers its own kind, and their good-natured banter was seldom extended to outsiders. Except for a select few who were somehow allowed to join the inner circle.

McCluskie was one of those. A fellow lone wolf. The fact that he played shrewd poker, and on occasion had sent even the best of them back to the well, was only incidental. They accepted him mainly because, when it got right down to the nub, he shared their outlook on life. The Irishman didn't give a damn for

the entire human race, and within a congregation of
cynics that made him a kindred spirit.

The offshoot of this mutual affinity was that
McCluskie could meet them head-on across a gaming
table without fear of being greased. With a morality
peculiar to the breed, they never cheated friends. Unless, of course, it tickled their fancy. For just as they
were addicted to gambling, so were they congenital
scamps. With them the practical joke was a universal
pastime, engineered and executed with such flair that
it frequently approached an art form. Like the time
Pony Reid had palmed a cold deck into the game and
dealt each of the players four aces. The betting sky-
rocketed like a roman candle, and when it was over
every man at the table had raised clean down to his
stickpin and pocket watch. The showdown had been
nothing short of spectacular, and the look on the players' faces was a classic study in slack-jawed stupe-
faction. Even years afterward, it was generally
conceded that Pony Reid had taken the brass ring for
sheer gall. To cold deck a gathering of one's own
confederates was considered the ultimate in technical
virtuosity.

McCluskie had prompted Reid to retell the yarn
again tonight, when they were on their fourth drink.
Now, walking up Main toward the train station, he
was still chuckling to himself. Taken as a whole,
gamblers were a cutthroat bunch. Born thieves with
no more conscience than a hungry spider. But they
were likeable rogues, practicing their own brand of
honor, and in a curious way, a notch above those who
used the law to whitewash their sleazy schemes.
Leastways it had always been his observation that not

all of a town's rascals came from the wrong side of the tracks.

Mounting the steps to the depot platform, Mc-Cluskie's amiable mood did a bellyflop. Standing there, like a double dose of ice water, was Newt Hansberry and his assistant flunky, Ringbone Smith.

"Evenin', Mike."

"Evenin', Newt."

"Howdy do, Mr. McCluskie."

McCluskie just nodded to Smith. They had met earlier in the day and Smith impressed him as a near miss of some sort. A gangling lout whose name was derived from his habit of wearing a hollowed-out marrow bone on his pinky finger. Seeing them together, the Irishman felt his good cheer begin to curdle. A long-nosed busybody and a dimdot who had been shortchanged when the marbles were passed out.

It was a match made in heaven.

Hansberry hawked and spat a wad of phlegm at the tracks. "Gettin' on time for that train of yours. Oughta be seein' it any minute now."

McCluskie eyed him narrowly. "Had any word from up the line?"

"Nope, nary a peep. Seems like ever'body's got lockjaw where that train of yours is concerned."

"Newt, I'm not interested one way or the other especially, but what makes you think that it's *my* train?"

"Well, it ain't like it's a regular run, now is it! I mean, hell's fire and little fishes. I didn't even know the dangblasted thing was comin' in till you told me this mornin'."

"The Santa Fe moves in mysterious ways, Newt. Not that it performs many wonders."

"Humph!" Hansberry snorted and screwed his face up in a walleyed look of righteous indignation. "Y'know, I am the station master around here. Seems like some people has a way of forgettin' that."

"You're thinkin' the brass should've informed you official-like. Instead of leavin' it to me."

"That'd do for openers. Contrary to what some folks think, I ain't the head mop jockey around here. I run this place with a pretty tight hand, and seems to me I oughta know what's what and whyfor."

"Guess it all depends on how you look at it. Some things are for the doing and not the talking. What you don't know can't hurt you. Specially if you keep your trap shut."

McCluskie saw Spivey and Tonk Hazeltine approaching with a stranger. Leaving Hansberry to fry in his own fat, the Irishman walked off to meet the greeting committee. The safest bet in town was that they would have been on hand to oversee the money shipment.

Ringbone Smith whistled softly through his teeth, spraying his chin with spit. "Lordy mercy, Mr. H. That feller must've been brung up on sour milk to get so downright techy."

Hansberry just grunted, and ground his jaws in quiet fury. Sometimes he wished he were back on the farm slopping hogs. Lately he'd come to think that pigs were downright civil alongside some people he knew.

FOUR

~~~~~

McCluskie stopped short of the three men and waited. Leaning back against a freight cart, he started rolling a smoke. Out of the corner of his eye he saw them mount the steps, and for some reason he was reminded of an old homily that Irishmen were fond of quoting.

"The fat and the lean are never what they seem."

Spivey and the stranger were both on the stout side. The charitable word would have been portly, but McCluskie wasn't feeling charitable. They looked like a couple of blubberguts that had just put a boardinghouse out of business. One thing was for sure. Matched up against one another, the pair of them would make a hell of a race at a pie-eating contest.

Trailing behind them, Hazeltine seemed like a starved dog herding a couple of hogs. He was what Texans called a long drink of water, only more so. Standing sideways in a bright sun, his shadow wouldn't have covered a gatepost. The brace of Remingtons cross-cinched over his hips seemed likely to drag him under if he ever stepped in a mud puddle.

McCluskie stuck the cigarette in his mouth and lit
it, purposely letting them come to him. It was an old
trick, but effective. Forcing the other man to make
the first move, especially with talk and shaking hands.
Somehow it put them on the defensive, just the least
bit off balance. Considering the unlikely trio bearing
down on him, it was a dodge well suited to the moment.

Spivey commenced grinning the minute he cleared
the steps. "Mike, where the hell you been all day?
Thought sure you'd drop by for a drink."

McCluskie exhaled a small cloud of smoke.
"Couldn't squeeze it in. Had some business that
needed tendin'."

"No doubt. No doubt." Spivey fairly oozed good
cheer. "Well don't make yourself a stranger, you
hear?" Suddenly his jowls dimpled in a rubbery smile.
"Say, I almost forgot you two don't know each other.
This here's Judge Randolph Muse, our local magis-
trate. Randy, shake hands with Mike McCluskie."

The Irishman waited, letting the older man extend
his hand. Only then did he take it, nodding slightly.
"Judge. Pleased to meet you."

Randolph Muse was no fledgling. He knew the
gambit well, had used it on other men most of his
life. Still, he'd let himself get sucked in. His ears
burned, and despite a stiff upper lip, he felt like a
bumbling ass. Perhaps Spivey was right, after all. This
ham-fisted Mick would bear watching.

"The pleasure's all mine, Mr. McCluskie. Bob has
been telling me about you. According to him, you're

about the toughest thing to come down the pike since Wild Bill himself."

"That's layin' it on pretty thick, Judge. From what I hear, Hickok's got Abilene treed about the same way he did Hays City. Just offhand, I don't think I'd want to try twistin' a knot in his tail."

Tonk Hazeltine snorted through his nose. "Hell! Hickok ain't so much. Just got himself a reputation, that's all. There's lots of men that could dust him off 'fore he ever had time to get started."

Spivey and Muse looked embarrassed. McCluskie blew the ashes off his cigarette and studied the coal without expression. It was obvious to everyone that the lawman's raspy statement was sheer braggadocio. A penny-ante gunslick tooting his own bugle. With all the finesse of a lead mallet.

The saloonkeeper cleared his throat and nimbly changed the subject. "Mike, what time's this train suppose to be in, anyway? Near as I recollect, all you ever said was somewhere after suppertime."

McCluskie smiled and cocked one eye eastward along the tracks. "With the Santa Fe it's sorta a case of you pays your money and you takes your chances. I didn't give you an exact time because my crystal ball is busted."

"You mean to say nobody's got any idea of when it'll be in?"

"Your guess is as good as mine, I reckon. Best I can tell you is that we'll know it's here when we see it."

The judge grumped something that sounded faintly like a belch. "That's a hell of a way to run a railroad, if you don't mind my saying so."

McCluskie eyed him closer in the flickering light from the depot lantern. Clear to see, Newton's judicial wizard was a crusty old vinegaroon. Yet his character didn't exactly fit any of the handy little pigeonholes McCluskie normally used to catalogue people. There was something of a charlatan about him. Not just the precise way he spoke, or the high-falutin clothes he wore, but a secretion of some sort. A smell. The kind the Irishman had winded all too often not to recognize it when he was face to face with the live goods. All the same, he exuded a dash of dignity that lacked even the slightest trace of hokum. It was the real article. Which made for a pretty queer mixture, one that didn't lend itself to any lightning calculations. Plainly, Randolph Muse wasn't a man to be underestimated. Especially if he was tied in with Spivey somehow.

"Your Honor, I couldn't agree with you more. Course, I'm just hired help, you understand. The Santa Fe don't pay me to solve their riddles, frankly, I've never paid it much mind one way or the other. 'Fraid you'll have to take it up with the brass if you want the real lowdown."

Spivey leaped in before the judge could reply. "Now don't get off on the wrong track, Mike. Randy didn't mean nothin' personal. It's just that we've both got a lot at stake in this deal. He's one of the investors in our little bank, and it's only natural he'd be skittish about this train being late and all. Hell, to tell you the truth, I'm sorta jumpy myself. What with everyone in town knowin' we're supposed to open for business tomorrow, it kind o' puts us behind the eightball."

"I wouldn't worry too much, gents." McCluskie

took a drag off his cigarette and flipped the stub into the darkness. "The Santa Fe might be slow as molasses, but they're not in the habit of losin' strongboxes. Besides, till the money gets here, it's the railroad's lookout, not yours."

"That's all very well, Mr. McCluskie," Judge Muse remarked. "But it isn't the Santa Fe who must face the townspeople tomorrow morning if those bank doors don't open."

"Like I said, Judge. There's no need gettin' a case of the sweats. Not yet, anyway."

Spivey frowned like a constipated owl. "That's not offering us much encouragement, Mike. Just to be blunt about it, I never did understand why you're bringin' the money in at night, anyhow. Randy and me talked it over, and the way we see it, that's about the worst time you could've picked."

"It's called security. Which means doing things the way folks don't expect. Specially train robbers. So far I haven't lost any strongboxes playin' my hunches. Don't expect to lose this one either."

"Good God, man!" the judge yelped. "Are you standing there telling us that you shipped one hundred thousand dollars on a hunch?"

"Get a hunch, bet a bunch." The Irishman grinned, thoroughly amused that he'd given the two lardguts a case of the fidgets. "What you fellows can't seem to get straight is that it's out of my hands. Leastways till the train gets here."

"Judas Priest!" Spivey groaned. "That's what we're talkin' about. Where the hell is the train?"

"Somewhere between here and there, most likely. Tell you what. Why don't you and the judge go get

yourselves a drink? Little whiskey never hurt anybody's nerves. When the train gets in, I'll bring your
money over with a red ribbon on it."

"Don't you fret yourself none, Mr. Spivey." Tonk
Hazeltine came on fast, trying to regain lost ground.
"I'll stick right here and make sure ever'thing goes
accordin' to snuff." He gave the holstered Remington-
tons a flat-handed slap. "Long as we got these backin'
the play there ain't gonna be no miscues on this end."

The other men stared at him as if he had just
sprouted measles. McCluskie's earlier suspicions had
now been confirmed in spades. As a peace officer
Tonk Hazeltine was long on luck and short on savvy.
The man's attitude was that of flint in search of stone.
Abrasive and needlessly pugnacious. Anybody who
went around with that big chip on his shoulder was
running scared. It was the act of a tinhorn trying to
convince everybody he was sudden death from Bitter
Creek. Inside, his guts probably quivered like jelly on
a cold platter.

"Deputy, it strikes me you've pulled up a chair in
the wrong game." McCluskie's voice was smooth as
butter. "If I need help you'll hear me yell plenty loud.
Otherwise I guess I'll just play the cards out my own
way."

Hazeltine went red as ox blood, and the scorn he
read in the Irishman's gaze pushed him over the edge.
"Mister, you might be somethin' on a stick with your
fists, but you ain't messin' around with no cowhand.
I'll go wherever I goddamn please and do whatever
suits me. Now if that notion ain't to your likin',
whyn't you try reachin' for that peashooter on your
hip."

McCluskie smiled and eased away from the freight cart. "Girls first, Tonk. You start the dance and we'll see who ends up suckin' wind."

The goad was deliberate, calculated. An insult that left a man only two outs. Fish or cut bait.

But whatever the lawman saw in McCluskie's face sent a shiver through his innards. Just for a moment he met and held the flinty gaze, then his eyes shifted away. He had a sudden premonition that the Irishman would kill him where he stood if he so much as twitched his finger.

"Another time, mebbe. When we ain't got all this money to keep watch on." Hazeltine's eyes seemed to look everywhere but at the three men. "Guess I'll mosey down and see if Newt's got any word over the wire. Wouldn't surprise me if he knows more about that train than the whole bunch of us."

The deputy walked off as if he hadn't a care in the world. But his knees somehow seemed out of joint, and when he tugged at the brim of his hat, there was a slight tremor to his hand. Spivey and Muse stared after him in pop-eyed befuddlement. They had seen it, but they couldn't quite believe it. Tonk Hazeltine with his tail between his legs. It shook them right down to the quick.

Randolph Muse was the first to recover his wits. "Mr. McCluskie, if I wasn't standing here, I'd swear on a stack of Bibles that such a thing could never happen."

"Me too," Spivey agreed. "Beats anything I ever heard tell of. Why, I would've bet every nickel I own there wasn't nothin' that could make Hazeltine eat dirt."

McCluskie started building another smoke. "Yeah, it's queer awright. The way a man'll lose his starch when his bluff gets called. Interestin' though." He licked the paper and twisted one end of the cigarette. "Seein' which way it'll fall, I mean."

The older men digested that in silence and remained quiet for what seemed a long while. McCluskie's statement, perhaps more than his actions, left them momentarily nonplused. They had seen their share of hardcases since coming west. Cowtowns acted as a lodestone for the rougher element, and the sight of two men carving one another up with knives or blasting away with guns wasn't any great novelty. But they had never come across anyone exactly like the Irishman. The way he'd goaded Hazeltine was somehow inhuman, cold and calculated with a degree of fatalism that bordered on lunacy. Like a man who teases a rattler just to see if he can leap aside faster than the snake can strike. They had heard about men like that. The kind who had ice water in their veins, and through some quirk of nature, took sport in pitting themselves against danger.

McCluskie was the first one they had ever met, though, and it was a sobering experience.

Presently Judge Muse came out of his funk and remembered his purpose in being there. He tried to keep his voice casual, offhand. "Bob tells me you're chief of security for the Santa Fe."

"One handle's as good as another, I guess." McCluskie glanced at him, alerted somehow that new cards had just been dealt. "The railroad's got a habit of pastin' labels on people."

"Now that's passing strange, for a fact." Muse

stared off into the night, reflective, like a dog worrying over a bone.

The Irishman refused the bait. Leaning back against the freight cart, he puffed on his cigarette and said nothing.

After a moment, failing to get a rise out of McCluskie, the judge shook his head and grunted. The act was a good one. He looked for all the world like a man faced with a bothersome little riddle. One that stubbornly resisted a reasonable solution.

"Puzzles always intrigue me, Mr. McCluskie. Just a personal idiosyncrasy, I suppose. But something Bob said struck me as very curious. He told me that neither you nor the Santa Fe had heard about the Wichita & Southwestern."

"You mean this two-bit railroad somebody's tryin' to promote?"

"That's the one. To be more precise, the men behind it are a certain James Meade and William Grieffenstein. Reputedly, they have connections back east."

"You sort of lost me on the turn, Judge. What's a shoestring outfit like that got to do with me or the Santa Fe?"

"Well it does seem strange. That a line as large as the Santa Fe would remain in the dark on an issue this vital. Don't you agree?"

"Beats me. Course, in a way, you're talkin' to the wrong man. The Santa Fe don't tell me all its secrets, y'know. There's lots of things the brass keeps to themselves. Most likely they don't think it's as vital as you do. Assumin' they even know."

"That seems highly improbable. A line between

here and Wichita would provide some pretty stiff competition. Unless, of course, the Santa Fe bought it out."

McCluskie held back hard on a smile. The old reprobate had finally sunk the gaff. He felt Muse's bright eyes boring into him, waiting for him to squirm. It was downright pathetic. Especially from a man he'd sized up to be a slick article.

"Judge, much as I hate to admit it, all that high finance is over my head. Just offhand, though, I'd say the Santa Fe has got all the fish it can fry. What with the deadline on pushin' rails west, they're stretched pretty thin. Don't seem likely they'd start worryin' about some fleaflicker operation out of Wichita."

Spivey came to life with a sputtered oath. "By damn, there's nothin' silly about it to us! It's just like I told you, Mike. If they ever get that bond issue through, Newton's gonna dry up and blow away."

The Irishman pursed his lips and looked thoughtful. "Well, it's sort of out of my bailiwick, but if I can lend a hand some way, you give a yell. I don't guess the Santa Fe would object to me helpin' you folks out. Not with this being division point and all."

Judge Muse batted his eyes a couple of times on that and started to say something. But as his mouth opened the lonesome wail of a train whistle floated in out of the darkness. The three men looked eastward, and through the night they spotted the distant glow of an engine's headlamp. The light grew brighter as they watched, and the distinct clack of steel wheels meshing with spiked track drifted in on a light breeze. Then the train loomed up out of the darkness, passing between Hoff's Grocery and Horner's Store. A groaning squeal racketed back off the buildings as the engineer throttled down and set the brakes. Like some soot-encrusted dragon, the engine rolled past the station house and ground to a halt, belching steam and smoke and fiery sparks in a final burst of power.

Spivey and the judge stood transfixed, staring at the slat-ribbed cars in aggrieved bewilderment. It was a cattle train.

McCluskie left them open-mouthed and gawking, and walked off toward the caboose. Tonk Hazeltine, trailed by the station master and Ringbone Smith, followed along. Judge Muse and Spivey exchanged baffled frowns and joined the parade. None of them had even the vaguest notion of what was afoot, but they were determined to see the Irishman play out his string.

Climbing aboard at the forward steps, McCluskie rapped on the caboose door. There was a muffled inquiry from within and he barked a single word in response.

"McCluskie!"

The door edged open and the barrels of a sawed-off shotgun centered on his chest. Somewhere behind the cannon a disembodied voice rumbled to life.

"Everything all right out there, Mike?"

"Right as rain, Spike. Open up."

The door swung back and Spike Nugent ducked through the opening. The shotgun looked like a broomstick in his meaty paws, and the onlookers fully expected him to bound down off the train and start walking on his knuckles. He was what every young gorilla aspired to and seldom attained. Even Mc-

Cluskie seemed dwarfed by the sheer bulk of the man.

"Any trouble?" McCluskie asked.

"Quiet as a church," the burly guard observed. "Me and Jack played pinochle the whole way."

"Good. You boys get the strongbox out and we'll waltz it over to the bank. Sooner we get their receipt for it, the sooner I can get back to my poker game."

Nugent's laugh sounded like dynamite in a mountain tunnel. He turned back into the caboose and McCluskie scrambled down the steps to the station platform.

Spivey was fairly dancing with excitement. "By God, Mike, I got to hand it to you. That was slicker'n bear grease. Nobody in his right mind would've thought of lookin' in a caboose for a hundred thousand simoleons."

"That was sort of the idea," McCluskie commented.

Tonk Hazeltine stepped out from the little crowd and hitched up his crossed gunbelts. "Now that you got it here, I'll just ride herd 'tween here and the bank to make sure nobody gets any funny ideas."

McCluskie gave him a corrosive look, then shrugged. "Tag along if you want, but remember what I said. This is railroad business. You get in the way and you'll get beefed. Same as anyone else."

The lawman's reply was cut short when Spike Nugent and another man stepped through the door of the caboose. They each had a shotgun in one hand and grasped the handles of an oversized strongbox in the other. McCluskie started toward them but out of the corner of his eye he caught movement. Wheeling, he saw a shadowy figure drop from one of the forward cattle cars and take off running.

Hazeltine's arm came up with a cocked Remington, centered on the fleeing man. The impact of McCluskie's fist against his jaw gave off a mushy splat, and the deputy collapsed like a punctured accordion.

"Spike! Get that box back in the car!"

The Irishman took off in a dead sprint as the two guards lumbered back aboard the caboose. Ahead, the dim shape of a man was still visible in the flickering light from the depot lanterns. But there was something peculiar about him even in the shadowed darkness. Instead of running, he seemed to be bounding headlong in a queer, staggering lurch. Almost as if momentum alone kept him from falling. McCluskie dug harder and put on a final burst of speed.

He overtook the man just back of the engine. When he grabbed, a piece of shirt came away in his hand, and the man stumbled to a halt. McCluskie saw him turn, sensed the cocked fist, and the looping roundhouse blow. Slipping beneath the punch, the Irishman belted him in the gut and then nailed him with a left hook square on the chin. The man hit the cinders with a dusty thud and lay still.

McCluskie stooped over, gathered a handful of shirt, and began dragging the limp form toward the front of the engine. Oddly, the man didn't seem to weigh any more than a bag of wet feathers. Clearing the cowcatcher, McCluskie heaved and dumped the body in the glare of the headlamp. Then his jaws clicked shut in a wordless curse.

It was nothing but a kid. A scarecrow kid.

FIVE

꧁ ꧂

McCluskie sat in a chair across the room, elbows on his knees, staring vacantly at a glass of whiskey in his hands. Every now and then he would glance up, watching the doctor for a moment, and afterward go back to studying his glass. The whiskey seemed forgotten, just something to keep his hands occupied. Whatever it was that might have distracted his mind didn't come in a bottle. Not this night, anyway.

Gass Boyd, Newton's resident sawbones, hovered around the bed like a rumpled butterfly. Though unkempt in appearance, he had a kindly bedside manner; the townspeople had found him to be a competent healer, if not a miracle worker. Since arriving in Newton, something less than a month past, most of his patients had been the victims of gunshot wounds or knifings. The youngster he worked over now had a far greater problem.

Boyd painstakingly bound the boy's ribcage in a tight harness, easing a roll of bandage under his back and around again. The youth's face was ashen, almost chalky, and a bruise the color of rotten plums covered his chin. But that wasn't what concerned the doctor. Even as he worked, he listened, and what he heard was far from encouraging. The boy's breathing was labored, more a hoarse wheezing, and a telltale pinkish froth bubbled at the corners of his mouth. Boyd had seen the symptoms plenty of times after the war, back in Alabama. It was the great ravager. Slow and insidious, without the swift mercy of a rifled slug or a steely knife.

Finished with the bandaging, Gass Boyd once again took out his stethoscope and placed it on the youngster's chest. He listened intently, moving the instrument from spot to spot, wanting desperately to be wrong. But he heard nothing that changed his diagnosis.

Then he grunted sourly to himself. At this stage it ceased being diagnosis. It became, instead, prognosis.

Folding the stethoscope, he placed it in his bag, snapped the catch shut, and stood. Just for a moment he studied the boy, seeing him for the first time as more than a body with sundry ailments and bruises. Hardly more than eighteen. If that. Haggard, hollow-cheeked, gaunt. A face of starved innocence. One of God's miscalculations. Or perhaps the immortal bard had been right after all. Maybe the gods did make wanton sport of men.

Boyd heard rustling behind him and turned to find the Irishman out of his chair on his feet. Their eyes locked and the doctor had a fleeting moment of wonder about this strange man. Beat a boy half to death and then turn a town upside down to save his life. It was a paradox. Classic in its overtones. From a clinical standpoint, perhaps one of the more interesting phenomena in man's erratic tomfoolery.

The doctor set aside such thoughts and came back to the business at hand. "Mr. McCluskie, the boy has a couple of broken ribs and a badly bruised chin. Fortunately your blow didn't catch him in the nose or he might've looked like a bull-dog the rest of his life."

"Then he'll be all right?"

"I didn't say that."

McCluskie's mouth tightened. "What're you gettin' at, Doc?"

"The boy has consumption of the lungs. Rather advanced case, I'd say."

"Consumption?" McCluskie's glance flicked to the bed and back again. "You sure?"

Gass Boyd sighed wearily. "Take my word for it, Mr. McCluskie. The boy has consumption. He's not long for this world."

The Irishman stared at him for what seemed a long while. When he finally spoke his voice had changed somehow. Gentler, perhaps. Not so hard.

"How long?"

Dr. Boyd shrugged. "It's difficult to say. Six months. A year, perhaps. I wouldn't even hazard a guess beyond that."

"Guess? Hell, Doc, I'm not askin' for guesses. He's just a kid. Don't it strike you that somebody punched his ticket a little bit early?"

"Mr. McCluskie, it's an unfortunate fact of life that God plays dirty pool. All too often the good die young. I've never found any satisfactory answer to that, and I doubt that anyone ever will."

"What you're sayin' is that you've given up on him. Written him off."

Far from being offended, the physician found himself fascinated. McCluskie was a strange and complex man, and the irony of the situation was inescapable. Within a matter of minutes he had run the gauntlet of emotions. From hangdog guilt to concern to outraged indignation. Right now he was gripped by a sense of frustrated helplessness, and the only response he knew was to lash out in anger. It was as if this big hulk of a man had unwittingly revealed a part of himself. The part that was raw and vulnerable and rarely saw the light of day.

"I've hardly written him off, Mr. McCluskie. Matter of fact, I'll look in at least twice a day until we have him back on his feet. He's underfed and weak as a kitten, and we have to get his strength built up. Unless things take a drastic turn for the better, I'd judge he won't set foot out of that bed for at least two weeks."

Boyd tactfully avoided any mention of the beating the youngster had taken. There was no need. The punishment absorbed by the frail body was apparent and spoke for itself. McCluskie could scarcely bear to look at the bed, and the loathing he felt for himself showed in his eyes. Watching him, it occurred to the doctor that victims weren't always the ones swathed in bandages. The Irishman's shame at having thrashed a sickly boy would endure far longer than a broken rib or a bruised chin.

McCluskie still hadn't said anything, as if his anger had been blunted by the doctor's unruffled manner. After a moment Boyd gathered his bag and nodded toward the boy. "I've given him a dose of laudanum, so he should rest easy through the night. I'll come by first thing in the morning and see how he's doing."

"Thanks, Doc. I'm—" The Irishman faltered, having difficulty with the words. "Sorry I talked out of turn."

"Completely understandable. No apologies necessary." Boyd smiled, clamped his hat on his head, and crossed the room. But at the door he turned and looked back. "There is one thing, though. If you don't mind my asking. What prompted you to bring the boy here to your room? Instead of over to my office."

McCluskie blinked, taken off guard by a question he hadn't as yet asked himself. "Why, I can't rightly say." He took a swipe at his mustache and shrugged, fumbling with a thought which resisted words. "Just seemed like the thing to do, I guess."

The doctor studied him a moment with a quizzical look. Then he smiled. "Yes. I can see that it would."

Nodding, he opened the door and stepped into the hall.

The Irishman stared at the door for a long while, overcome with a queer sense of unease. The question hung there, still unanswered, and tried to sort it out in his head.

Why had he brought the kid to his room?

Everything else was clear as a bell. The commotion at the depot. Everybody running and shouting and yelling bloody murder at the top of their lungs. Hansberry bleating some asinine nonsense about train robbers, and the little crowd scattering like a bunch of quail. Then later, Spivey and the judge raking him over the coals for coldcocking Tonk Hazeltine. And later still, somebody carting the deputy off like a side of beef. Somewhere in all the fussing and moaning he'd even managed to get the strongbox over to the bank. That part he remembered clearly. But there was just a big blank spot where the kid was concerned. For the life of him, he couldn't recall when or how he'd gotten the kid to his room.

Or why.

Returning to his chair, he sat down and tried to muddle it through. But it was hard sledding, and all uphill. Distantly, as through a cloudy glass, he got an impression of sending Jack off to fetch the doctor. Then something else. Something to do with Spike.

That must have been when he was carrying the kid across Main toward the hotel.

But it still didn't answer the question. The one Doc Boyd had started rattling around in his head. The one that even now didn't make any sense.

Why the hotel? Why *his* room?

McCluskie reached for the whiskey glass and his eyes automatically went to the bed. Jesus! The kid was nothing but a bag of bones. Didn't hardly put a dent in the mattress. Just laid there wheezing and spewing those little bubbles. Like he was—

The rap at the door startled McCluskie clean out of his chair. He crossed the room in two strides and threw open the door. Just for a moment nothing registered. Then those green eyes nailed him and everything came into focus all of a sudden.

It was Belle.

"Well don't just stand there, you big lummox. Let me in."

Wordlessly he stepped aside, his head reeling. He

couldn't have been more surprised if she had materialized out of a puff of smoke.

Belle sailed into the room and whirled on him. "I almost didn't come, you know. Not until Spike told me—"

"Spike?"

"—about the kid."

She stopped and gave him a funny look. "Are you drunk, or what? You did send Spike to get me, didn't you?"

"Yeah, I guess so."

"You guess so?" One eyebrow lifted and she inspected him with closer scrutiny. "Mike, are you all right? You look sort of green around the gills."

Suddenly it all came back to him in a rush. As if somebody had wiped the window clean and he could see it again. The way it had been in those last moments when he walked away from the depot with the kid in his arms.

"Sure I sent Spike. The kid was bad hurt and I didn't know what kind of sawbones they had in this jerkwater burg. You've patched up more men than most of these quacks anyway, so I didn't figure it would hurt nothin' for you to have a looksee."

She gave him that queer look again, still a little leery. "Well, as long as I'm here I might as well inspect the damages." She turned toward the bed. "Where's Doc Boyd? Didn't he show?"

"Yeah, he just left a little while ago."

"What was the verdict? Castor oil and mustard plaster?"

McCluskie had no chance to answer. Belle stopped short of the bed and uttered a sharp gasp. In the pale cider glow of the lamp the boy looked like he had been embalmed. Her eyes riveted on the bandages and the bruised chin and the froth at the corners of his mouth. Her back went stiff as a poker and she mumbled something very unladylike under her breath. Suddenly galvanized, she wheeled around, and green-fire shot out of her eyes in a smoky sizzle.

"You miserable excuse for a man! Is that how you earn your keep? Beating up kids for the Santa Fe?"

"Belle, it's not like it looks. The kid swung on me—"

"Swung on you! My God, Mike, that boy doesn't have enough strength to kill a fly."

"I know that now." He flushed and went on lamely. "But it was dark out there and I couldn't tell. I just knew he was swingin' on me."

"So you let him have the old McCluskie thunder-bolt." Her stare was riddled through with scorn. "You must feel real proud of yourself. Why aren't you down at the saloon telling the boys all about your big fight?"

McCluskie's shoulders sagged imperceptibly, and he had trouble meeting her gaze. They stood like that for a moment, frozen in silence. Then, quite without warning, Belle felt her anger start to ebb. Something had just become apparent to her. The big Irishman was ashamed. Really ashamed! This was none of his slick dodges. Those cute little tricks he'd always used to get around her temper. He was genuinely shamed by what he had done. Which rocked her back on her heels.

So far as she knew, Mike McCluskie had never apologized to anybody for anything in his entire life.

Much less hung his head and looked mortified to boot.

Curiously, the question she'd been saving for later no longer needed to be asked. She knew why the kid was here. In this room. Laid out in Mike's bed.

But the knowing left her in something of a quandary. One question had been answered yet others were popping through her head like a string of firecrackers. Questions she had never before even considered about the Irishman.

Suddenly it came to her that perhaps she wasn't as good a judge of men as she had thought. Maybe she'd been running a sporting house too long. Saw things not as they were but distorted and flawed, like a cracked mirror.

She took a closer look at Mike McCluskie.

What she saw was different from what she had seen before. Or perhaps different wasn't the right word. Maybe it was just all there, finally complete. Like a jigsaw puzzle that had at last had the missing parts fitted into place.

She decided to withhold judgment for the moment. "What did Doc have to say about the kid?"

"Couple of busted ribs and a sore jaw."

Belle darted a skeptical glance back toward the bed. "That's all?"

"No, not just exactly." McCluskie swallowed hard. "Doc says he's got lung fever. Consumption."

She just stared at him, unblinking. After a while she managed to talk around the lump in her throat. "He's sure?"

"Sure enough. Said the kid had a year at the outside. Leastways if you're partial to bettin' longshots."

She turned and stepped nearer the bed. Her eyes

went over the frail, emaciated boy, missing nothing. Hair the color of cornsilk, dirty and ragged, but bleached out by the sun. A sensitive face, with wide-set eyes and a straight nose, and the jawbone squared off in a resolute line. Large bony hands with fingers that were curiously slim and tapering. Like those of a piano player. Or a cardsharp. Or a surgeon.

Or any one of a hundred things this kid would never live to become.

Belle jumped, scared out of her wits, as the pale blue eyes popped open. They reminded her of carpenter's chalk, only with a glaze of fresh ice over the top. But the boy didn't see her. His face mottled in dark reddish splotches, and he started sucking for wind in a hoarse, dry rattle. Belle didn't think, she simply reacted.

"He's choking, Mike! Sit him up."

McCluskie reached the bed in one stride, slipping his arms beneath the youngster, and lifted him to a sitting position. Belle wrenched the boy's mouth open, prying his tongue out, and began gently massaging his Adam's apple. Suddenly the boy heaved, his guts pumping, and went into a coughing spasm that shook the entire bed. Globs of sputum and scarlet-tinged mucus shot out of his mouth and nose, and for a moment they thought he was vomiting his life away right in their arms. Then the coughing slacked off, gradually subsiding, and a spark of color came back to his face. The film slowly faded from his eyes and he slumped back, exhausted. The attack had run its course, but he was still laboring for each breath.

Belle plumped up both pillows and wedged them

in behind him. McCluskie eased him back, so that he rested against the pillows in a half-sitting position. Feeling somewhat drained themselves, they just stood there watching him, uncertain what to do next.

Suddenly the boy's lids fluttered and they found themselves staring into the blue eyes again. Only this time they were clear, if not fully alert. The youngster's lips moved in a weak whisper. "Am I back in the hospital?"

McCluskie exchanged puzzled glances with Belle, then shook his head. "You're in a hotel room, kid. We brought you here from the train depot."

The boy closed his eyes and for a minute they thought he was asleep. Then he was looking at them again. Focusing at last on the Irishman. "You the one that clobbered me?"

McCluskie nodded sheepishly. "Thought you was somebody else."

The kid's mouth parted in a sallow grin. "You got a good punch."

McCluskie smiled. The button had plenty of sand, even flat on his back. "What's your name, bucko? Got any family we could get word to?"

"Just me. Nobody else."

"Yeah, but what's your name?"

"Kinch." The boy's eyelids went heavy, drooping, and slowly closed. "Kinch Riley."

The words came in a soft whisper as the laudanum again took hold. Breathing somewhat easier, he drifted off into a deep sleep.

They watched him for a long while, saying nothing. Oddly enough, though they hadn't touched since Belle entered the room, they felt a closeness unlike anything in the past. Almost as if the boy, in some curious way, had bridged a gap in time and space.

At last McCluskie grunted, and his voice was a shade huskier than usual. "Belle, something damned queer happened to me tonight. I've been in brawls, knife fights, shootouts—and afterward I always remembered every minute of it. Every little detail. But tonight—after I slugged the kid—it's all fuzzy. Just comes back to me in bits and snatches. That's one for the books, isn't it?"

She put her arm around his waist and laid her head on his shoulder. "Mister, would you buy a girl a drink?"

The Irishman pulled her close, warmed by her nearness and the scent from her hair. But his eyes were still on the kid.

Then it struck him. The name.

Riley.

Sweet Jesus on the Cross! No wonder he was a gutsy little scrapper.

The kid was Irish.

SIX

McCluskie rode past the stockyards, letting the sorrel mare set her own pace. Now that they were headed back to the livery stable she was full of ginger, apparently cured of her tendency to balk and fight the reins. Several times throughout the day he'd seriously considered the possibility that he had rented a mule disguised as a horse. Along toward midday he started wishing for a pair of the roweled spurs favored by Texans, and would have gladly sunk them to the haft in the mare's flanks. Even coming back from Wichita the hammerhead had acted just like a woman. Wanted her own way and pitched a regular fit when she didn't get it.

The Irishman had ridden out of Newton early that morning on the pretext of inspecting the track crew west of town. While he could have hitched a ride on a switch-engine, he let it drop at the hotel and again at the stables that he felt like a hard day in the saddle. Just to work out the kinks and melt off a bit of the lard from city living. The truth was, he had an absolute loathing for horses. Having served under Sherman during the late war, his rump had stayed galled the better part of three years. Upon being mustered out he had sworn off horses as a mode of transportation for the remainder of his life.

Still, renting a horse was the only practical dodge he could think of for a flying trip to Wichita. It had to be done in one day so as not to arouse the suspicions of Spivey and his cronies. Heading west, he had crossed Sand Creek, passed the stockyard, and kept on a couple of miles farther before turning back southeast. Except for the iron-jawed mare, the twenty miles to Wichita had proved uneventful. There he had quickly hunted down Meade and Grieffenstein, and managed to gain entrance to their offices under an assumed name.

The promoters had been elated when he revealed his identity and the purpose of his call. Although deeply enmeshed in a financial conspiracy with the Santa Fe, they had been kept virtually in the dark by the brass. They knew only that someone would be sent to Newton, and that when the time seemed ripe, they would be contacted.

Some six months past the Santa Fe had entered into an agreement with the partnership of Meade and Grieffenstein. They were to organize a railroad between Wichita and Newton, and float a county bond issue for its construction. Once it was operating, the Santa Fe would buy them out at a tidy profit. The pact was struck and now the vote on the bond issue was less than a month away. The partners had the political muscle to control the southern townships, Wichita in particular, but the upper part of Sedgwick

County still had them worried. Unless the referendum carried, the Wichita & Southwestern railroad would simply evaporate in a puff of dust, and McCluskie's message brought with it a measure of reassurance.

His orders were to establish himself in Newton working undercover as long as practical, and to influence the vote of the northern townships to whatever degree possible. Wherever divisive tactics would work, he was to drive a wedge between the town leaders, splitting them on the bond issue. The sporting crowd, with whom he enjoyed a certain reputation, was to be cultivated on the sly. Hopefully, their ballots could be controlled in a block and provide the swing vote in Newton itself. Further than that, he was instructed to give the promoters any help they might request. But within certain limits. Money and muscle were not included in the bargain.

Retracing his steps across the buff Kansas prairie, McCluskie had hit the tracks a few miles west of the stockyards and turned the mare toward Newton. So far as anyone would know, he had spent the day in the Santa Fe camp, performing some errand for the head office brass. Which was stretching the truth only in terms of time and place. The errand had been real enough, if not precisely as reported.

Now, entering the outskirts of town, he was reminded again of the Wichita promoters. They were a shifty pair, well versed in the rules of the game, and the Irishman had come away with the impression that they still had a few dazzlers left to be played. After years of rubbing elbows with grifters and bunco artists, he had an instinct for such things. Meade and

Grieffenstein were about to sound the death knell on lively little Newton.

Thinking about it as he passed the depot, Mc-Cluskie grunted with disgust. All of the skulduggery and underhanded shenanigans left him with a sour taste in his mouth. While he could play the game well enough, it went against the grain. Yet, when it got down to brass tacks, his assignment in Newton was hardly a new role. In a moment of sardonic reflection, it occurred to him that his life had been little more than a lie since the day he headed west.

After the war he had returned to New York, colder and leaner, a man brutalized by the bloodbath that had ended at Appomattox. But he quickly discovered that not all of the casualties had taken place on the battlefield. Only months before, while he rode in the vanguard of Sherman's march to the sea, his wife and small son had been killed in a street riot. Somehow, in those last frenetic days of the war, the army had failed to notify him of their deaths. The homecoming he had dreamed of and longed for during the fighting became instead a ghoulish nightmare. In a single instant, standing dumbstruck before his landlady in Hell's Kitchen, he became both a widower and a bereaved father. Kathleen and Brian, the boy he had never seen, simply ceased to exist.

The blow shook him to the very core of his being. On a hundred killing grounds, from Bull Run to Savannah, he had seen men slaughtered. Grown cold and callous to the sight of death. Accounted for a faceless legion of Johnny Rebs himself. Killing them grimly and efficiently, unmoved toward the end by the bloody handiwork of his saber. Thoroughly accustomed to watching men fall before his gun, screaming and splattered with gore like squealing pigs in a charnel house. But the death of his wife and son left him something less than a man. Cold as a stone, and with scarcely more feeling.

Informed that the riot had occurred at a political rally, he investigated further and unearthed a chilling fact. Kathleen and the boy had been innocent bystanders, in the wrong place at the wrong time. Caught up in a brawl deliberately staged by the ward boss of an opposing faction. It was simply another Irish donnybrook, political rivals battling for control of the ward, except that this time it had claimed the lives of three men. And a woman who happened by with her small son.

That very night McCluskie sought out the ward boss and beat him to death with his fists. Afterward, certain to be charged with murder, he vanished from Hell's Kitchen and boarded the first train headed west.

The years since had been rewarding after a fashion, for he was not a man to brood over things dead and gone. But the ache, though diminished with time, was still there. For Kathleen, and for the son he had never seen. It was a part of himself that he kept hidden, and seldom saw the light of day. Yet as he passed the depot and reined the mare across the tracks, he was struck by a curious thought.

He wondered if his boy would have been anything like Kinch.

Somehow he hoped so, and just exactly why didn't seem to matter. It was enough that he might have had a son like the kid. A scrapper who never quit. Never backed off. A boy to make a man proud.

Dismounting in front of the livery stable, McCluskie led the mare inside as the sun settled to earth in a fiery splash of gold. Seth Mabry, the proprietor, looked up from shoeing a horse in the dingy smithy set back against the far wall. When he saw that it was the Irishman, he dropped his rasp and hurried forward, wiping his hands on the heavy leather apron covering his chest and belly.

"Well, Mr. McCluskie. You made a day of it. I was just startin' to wonder if you was gonna get back in time for supper."

"Make it a practice never to miss a meal," McCluskie replied handing over the reins. "Little habit I picked up right after I got weaned."

Mabry's stomach jounced with a fat man's hearty mirth. "Good way to be, Mr. McCluskie. Never was one to pass up a feed myself. Course, there's them that stays partial to milk even when they're full growed. If y'know what I mean."

"Been there myself, Mr. Mabry. Nothin' suits better than going back to the well when your throat gets dry."

"Now ain't that a fact!" The blacksmith squashed a horsefly buzzing about the hairy bristles of his arm. "Say, I didn't even think to ask. Hope Sally gave you that workout you was lookin' for. She's got a lot of sass when she gets to feelin' her oats."

McCluskie snorted and shot the mare a dark look. "Sass don't hardly fit the ticket. She's got a jaw like a cast-iron stove. 'Stead of a quirt you ought to give people a bung starter when you rent her out."

"Just like a woman, ain't it, Mr. McCluskie? Never seen one yet that wasn't bound and determined to make a monkey of a man. Part of bein' female, I guess. Now, you take my wife—"

"Thanks all the same, but I'll pass. Hell, I had enough trouble just handlin' your horse."

The blacksmith was still laughing when McCluskie went through the door and turned down Main Street. Striding along the boardwalk, he almost collided with Randolph Muse in front of the Cattlemen's Exchange. The judge came tearing out of the bank as if his pants were on fire, and McCluskie had to haul up short to keep from bowling him over. It occurred to the Irishman that Muse never seemed to walk. His normal gait was sort of a hitching lope, like a centipede racing back to its hideout.

"Afternoon, Mr. McCluskie." The judge squinted against the sun, grinning, and his store-bought teeth gave off a waxy sheen. "Looks like you had a hard day's ride somewhere."

McCluskie swatted his shirt, raising a small cloud of dust. "Yeah, rode out to have a looksee at the track gang west of town."

"Everything proceeding smoothly, I trust."

"Right on schedule, Judge. Laying 'em down regular as clockwork."

"Good! Good!" They walked on a few paces together and Muse rolled his eyes around in a sidewise glance. "Don't suppose you heard any word about our competition? That Wichita bunch, I mean."

"Can't say as I did, your honor. Most likely they're keepin' their secrets to themselves."

"Well keep your ear to the ground, my boy. Ear to the ground! We need all the information we can get on those rascals."

"I'll do that very thing, Judge. Fellow never knows where he'll turn up an interestin' little tidbit."

"Precisely. Couldn't have said it better myself." Muse took to the street and angled off toward the Lone Star. "I'd ask you to join me in a drink, but I've got a matter of business to discuss with Bob. Say, how is that lad of yours doing? Up and around, is he?"

"Gettin' friskier every day. I figure he'll be ready to try his legs just any time now."

"Excellent. Bring him around to see me. Sounds like a boy with real grit."

Muse turned away with a wave of his hand, kicking up little spurts of dust as he churned along. The Irishman chuckled softly to himself, struck again by the wonder of wee men obsessed with themselves and their wee plans. Passing Horner's Store, he stepped off the boardwalk and headed toward the tracks.

Newt Hansberry waved from the depot platform, but McCluskie merely returned the wave and kept going. This was one time he simply couldn't be bothered with the gossipy station master, or the Santa Fe for that matter. He'd earned his pay for the day and had a sore butt to prove it. The whole lot of them could swing by their thumbs for one night. It was high time he cut the wolf loose and had himself a little fling. Maybe even resurrect that card game with Dandy John and the boys.

The thought came and went with no real conviction. Tonight he'd be doing the same thing he had done every night for the last week. Sitting up with the kid. Just jawboning and swapping yarns till it was bedtime and he could sneak off for a quick one over at the Gold Room.

Not that he begrudged the kid those evenings. Truth was, he sort of enjoyed it. The button had more spunk than a three-legged bulldog, and oddly enough, he'd never felt so proud of anybody in his life. Judge Muse had called it grit, but that didn't hardly fit the ticket. The kid had enough sand in his craw to put them all in the shade. With a little to spare.

Doc Boyd had declared it nothing short of remarkable. The way the kid had perked up and started regaining his strength. Almost as if he had pulled himself up by his own bootstraps. Somehow refused to knuckle under. The sawbones had put a fancy handle on it—the instinct to survive—but McCluskie knew better. It was just plain old Irish moxie, with a streak of stubbornness thrown in on the side. The Gaelic in a man didn't let go without a fight, and Kinch Riley had been standing at the head of the line when they passed out spunk.

Already the color had returned to his face, and he'd lost that skin and bones look. Mostly due to Belle stuffing him full of soup and broth and great pitchers of fresh milk. Every day his spirits improved a notch or two, and he had even started talking about getting out of bed. Doc Boyd had put the quietus on that fast enough, leastways for the time being. But one thing was plain as hell. That kid wouldn't let himself be bound to a bed much longer. Not unless they strapped him down and hid his boots.

Thinking about it, McCluskie had to give most of the credit to Belle. She spent the better part of each day with the kid, returning to her house only when it was time for the evening rush to start. Along with hot food and fresh milk she also dispensed a peck of good cheer. Her sense of humor was sort of on the raw side, but she had a way of joshing the kid that made him light up like a polished apple. Maybe it was just Belle's maternal instinct showing through, but whatever it was, it worked. The kid lapped it up as fast as she could dish it out, and it was her gentle nudging that had finally started him talking.

At first, he had been reluctant to say much about himself. Just his name and the fact that he had no kin. But day by day Belle had wormed her way into his confidence, and when he finally let go it turned out to be a real tearjerker. Even Belle had got that misty look around the eyes, and a couple of times had to interrupt so she could blow her nose.

The kid made it short and sweet, just the bare bones. His folks were from Chicago and had been killed in a fire shortly after he turned seventeen. Afterward, working in the stockyards, he had heard about the Kansas cowtowns and decided to come west. His coughing spells got worse, though, riding the rods. He didn't think much about it at first, because he'd had similar attacks off and on over the past couple of years. But train smoke evidently didn't set well with his lungs and in Kansas City he ended up in a charity ward. The doctors there were a friendly bunch, but they hadn't pulled any punches. They told him what he was up against, and just about what he could expect. Once he was back on his feet, he'd skipped out before anybody got ideas about putting him in a home somewhere. He figured he might as well see the elephant while he had time and he started west again. Things got a little hazy after that, except for being chased and the one haymaker he'd thrown in the Newton rail yard. The next thing he knew, he woke up in Mike's bed.

Later, the Irishman talked it over with Belle and they decided that it was a little more than the luck of the draw. The kid's cards were being dealt from a cold deck, and it was going to be a rough hand to play out alone. McCluskie had surprised himself by volunteering to look after the kid. Just till he got his pins back under him.

Belle wasn't the least bit surprised, though. Not any more. She had laughed and said that it merely confirmed her suspicions. Beneath his stony composure he was all whipped cream and vanilla frosting. In other words, Irish to the core, and a born sucker when it came to siding with an underdog. Then she'd taken him up to her room and come very near to ruining him. When he finally crawled out of her place next morning, he'd felt limp as a dishrag. But good. Restored somehow. Better than he had felt in more than a year.

Now, crossing the hotel lobby, McCluskie had to chuckle to himself as he thought back on it. That was one thing about Belle. Any tricks her girls knew, she knew better, and she could just about cripple a man when her spring came unwound.

Whistling tunelessly, he walked down the short hallway and entered his room. Or what had once been his room. It was the kid's now. He merely kept his clothes there and paid the rent. For the past week he'd been staying at Belle's, and getting himself worn to a frazzle in the process.

The kid was propped up in bed riffling a deck of cards on his lap. When McCluskie came through the door, he looked around and broke out in a wide smile.

"Mike! We was just about to send the cavalry out lookin' for you."

"Evenin', sport." The Irishman sailed his hat in the general direction of a coat rack and walked to the washstand. "Who's we?"

"Why, Belle and me. She just left a minute ago." Kinch laughed and shook his head. "She's a pistol, ain't she? Said she couldn't wait no longer or them cowhands'd be bustin' down the doors."

McCluskie glanced up at him in the mirror. "Belle said that?"

"Yeah, sure. Why?"

"Nothin'." He peeled his shirt and tossed it on a chair. "Guess she figures you're a shade older'n you look."

The boy reared back and scowled indignantly. "Well hell, Mike, I'm pushin' eighteen, y'know. Betcha when you was my age you'd been around plenty."

"Kid, when I was your age I was a hundred years old." McCluskie poured water in a washbowl and began his nightly birdbath. "But that don't cut no ice one way or the other. Now, c'mon, own up to it. You've never had a woman in your life, have you?"

Kinch went red as beet juice and fumbled around for a snappy comeback. "Well I come close a couple of times, don't you worry yourself about that. I'm not as green as I look."

"Hey, cool down. I wasn't rubbin' your nose in it. Just meant there's a few gaps in your education, that's all. Soon's you get the lead back in your pencil we'll have to arrange some lessons down at Belle's."

It took a moment for the meaning to register, and then the youngster burst out in a whooping belly laugh. Suddenly his face drained of color and the laugh turned to a racking cough. The attack was fairly short, and his sputum was no longer flecked with blood, but the pain was clearly evident in his face. Still, he tended to accept it with a stoicism beyond his years. Though hardly an old friend, pain was a familiar companion these days, and lying around on his backsides had given him plenty of time to think it out. There wasn't much to be gained in feeling sorry for himself—and moaning about it wouldn't change anything—so he might as well make the best of what time he had. Besides, what with one thing and another, he'd come out smelling like a rose anyway. It wasn't just everybody that got themselves hooked up with a slick article like the Irishman. Not by a damnsight, it wasn't.

As his cough slacked off, the boy glanced up and saw McCluskie watching him intently. He forced a smile and went back to shuffling the cards. "Y'know, Belle says that with my hands I wouldn't have no trouble at all learnin' how to make these pasteboards sit up and talk."

McCluskie finished splashing and started toweling himself dry. "Seems like Belle's just chock full of ideas for you."

"She's some talker, awright. Smart, too." Kinch cut the deck and began dealing dummy hands of stud on the bed. "But she's right about one thing. I ain't gonna be tied to this bed forever, and I gotta get myself lined up with some kind of work. It's real white of you, footin' all the bills like this, but I'm used to payin' my own freight."

McCluskie stifled the temptation to smile. Sometimes the kid was so damned serious it was all he could do to keep a straight face. Sat there chewing his lip and frowning, like a little old man puzzling over some problem that had confounded the world's scholars. For a button, he was a prize package. In spades.

"Well now, I'll tell you, sport—I've been giving that some thought myself. The Santa Fe has got me wore down to a stump pullin' their chestnuts out of the fire. Just never seems to be no end to it. Truth is, I've been thinkin' of hirin' myself an assistant, and I got an idea you might just fit the ticket. Course, the wages wouldn't be much to start, but it'd get you by."

"Cripes, I ain't worried about that, Mike. Long as I got three squares and a bed, I figure I'm livin' high on the hog."

"You mull it over some. No hurry. When you get back on your feet if you still like the idea, we'll give it a whirl."

McCluskie pulled a fresh shirt out of the bureau and started putting it on. The boy was watching his every move with renewed interest, and a quizzical look came over his face all of a sudden.

"Say, Mike, I ain't never got around to it, but there's something I been meanin' to ask you. How'd you get that scar on your belly?"

The Irishman glanced down at the jagged weal running from his ribs to his beltline, then went on buttoning the shirt. "Some hardcase came at me with a knife one night in Abilene."

"God A'mighty! What happened to him?"

"Nothin' special. Just a regular ten-dollar funeral."

Kinch's eyes went round as saucers and he sat there staring, the deck of cards forgotten.

With his shirt tucked in, McCluskie deliberated a moment and then gave the boy a questioning look. "Listen, bud, if you and me start workin' together, I want you to quit using that word *ain't* so much. It's not the word that bothers me, you understand, but it reminds me of somebody that rubs my fur the wrong way. Likely you'll meet him first time we're over at the depot."

The youngster ducked his head. "Sure, Mike. Anything you say. Won't be no trouble at all."

McCluskie grinned. "Tell you what. I'll go get us a supper tray, and after we eat, maybe I'll show you how to make them cards sit up and say *bow wow.*"

Kinch's face lit up and he got busy shuffling the cards. But as the Irishman went through the door he sobered with a sudden thought and gave a loud yell.

"Tell 'em to hold the milk! Belle's got me swimmin' in the stuff."

SEVEN

The day was bright as brass, a regular Kansas scorcher. Lazy clouds hung suspended against the blue muslin of the sky, and the sun hammered down with the fury of an open forge. The air was still, without a hint of breeze, and across the prairie shimmering heat waves drifted soft as woodsmoke. Already the morning was a small slice of hell, and by noon the blazing fireball overhead would wilt anything that moved.

But it was the kind of day McCluskie liked. Clear and windless, and hot enough to keep a man's joints oiled with sweat. Perfect for burning powder, and testing himself against his keenest rival.

The one that dwelled within himself.

The Irishman came each morning to the rolling plains north of town. There, in a dry wash fissured through the earth's bowels, he played a game. The object was to beat his shadow on the gully wall. To draw and fire the Colt Navy a split second faster than his darkened image. Yet that was only part of the game. For while his shadow was allowed to miss, he granted himself no such edge.

Each slug must strike the target—a kill shot—or the game was lost.

McCluskie had been playing this game for three years, since the spring of '68 when he came west with the K&P. Not unlike most things he did, it was calculated and performed with solemn deliberation. Broiling his guts out with a track gang, laying rails across the parched Kansas plains, he had decided to make something better of himself than a common laborer. Watching and waiting, he studied the matter for a time, and concluded that the job of railway guard would be the first step. That required a certain aptitude with a gun, and with no one to school him, he taught himself. He invented the game and began practicing in his off time. Through trial and error he perfected the rudiments of what would later become rigid discipline, and shortly thereafter, his newly acquired skill came to the attention of company officials.

Later, after he had killed three men, people stopped joshing him about the game. They had seen the results, and the greatest skeptic among them became a devout believer.

McCluskie, along with Hickok and Hardin and a handful more, was a man to be cultivated. Befriended or won over somehow. Failing that, it was best to simply stay clear of him.

Even now, the Irishman still practiced the game religiously. Since killing the Quinton brothers, when they attempted to rob a K&P express car the summer of '69, there had been no occasion to draw the Colt

in anger. His name was known, and anyone deadly
enough to match his skill had better sense than to try.
But this in no way diverted him from the game. The
world was full of men too dumb, or too hotheaded,
to back down, and in his trade, the risk of coming up
against these hardcases was always there. With spar-
tan discipline, he practiced faithfully, seven days a
week. It was a demanding craft, one that allowed no
margin for error. A man's first mistake might well be
his last, and the prize for second place wasn't a gold
watch.

McCluskie had never begrudged the time demanded by the game. Curiously, he'd always thought
of it as an investment. Money in the bank. Better to
have it and not need it than to need it and not have
it. Which in his line of work made a pretty fair maxim
all the way round.

So he practiced and improved and waited.

The past week had been a little different, though.
Generally he played the game solitaire, but lately he'd
started bringing Kinch along. The boy was recuperated, at least as much as he ever would be, and Doc
Boyd had agreed that fresh air and sunshine were cu-
ratives in their own right. McCluskie enjoyed the
company, and the kid seemed fascinated by the game,
so the mornings had become a special time for them
both.

There was only one thing that bothered the Irishman. Puzzled him in a way he couldn't quite fathom.
The kid had been watching him for days now and
never once had he asked to fire the pistol. Hadn't even
asked to touch it, or evidenced the slightest curiosity
in how it worked. Apparently his only interest was in

the game itself, trying to judge who was the fastest. Man or shadow.

All of which seemed a bit queer to McCluskie. Most boys would have given their eyeteeth to sit in on these sessions. More to the point, though, they would have broken out in a case of the blue swivets waiting to get their hands on the gun. To see how good they could do. To learn. To feel the Colt buck and jump and spit lead. That's what he would have expected from any kid old enough to wear long pants.

But Kinch just hung back, watchful as a hawk, plainly satisfied to remain nothing more than a spectator.

McCluskie couldn't figure it, but as yet he hadn't pushed it either. There were lots of reasons that could make the kid shy off. None of them worthwhile from a man's standpoint, and some of them too repulsive even to consider. But he left it alone, saying nothing. The kid would come around in his own time, and if he didn't, there would be plenty of chances to find out why.

This was the fifth morning Kinch had tagged along, and by now the boy was accustomed to the ritual. Squatting down against one side of the gully, he observed silently as McCluskie set about the game. The first step was a target, and for this they had brought along a gunnysack stuffed with empty tin cans. The tins were of assorted sizes, mostly pints and quarts. McCluskie had wedged a plank between the walls of the gully about chest high, and on this he arranged five tins at spaced intervals. Then he stepped off ten paces and turned, facing the target. From his pocket he withdrew a double eagle and placed it in his left hand. Ready now, he stood loose and easy, arms hanging naturally at his sides. The only tenseness was in his eyes, and to the watching boy, it seemed that every fiber of his being was concentrated on the five cans.

Like most Westerners, McCluskie carried the Colt high on his hip, with the butt of the gun resting just below waistline. There were those who used tied-down triggers, low-slung holsters, even swivel affairs that allowed a man to twist the gun upward and fire while it was still in the holster. But experience, and three years of watching self-styled badmen commit suicide, had convinced him that such devices were strictly the work of amateurs. Flash-in-the-pan brag-garts who thought an edge in speed could overcome a shortness in guts. The place for a gun was where it rode comfortable, easy to reach sitting or standing, and where it came natural to the hand when a man made his move.

The Irishman's left hand opened and the double eagle tumbled out. There was a space of only a split second before it hit the rocky floor of the wash. The metallic ring was the signal, and with it McCluskie's right arm moved. To the naked eye it was merely a blurred motion, but the Colt suddenly appeared in his hand and exploded flame.

The center can leaped off the plank and spun away.

Alternating his shots left to right, McCluskie sent the remaining tins bouncing down the gully. From first shot to last, the whole thing had consumed no more than a half-dozen heartbeats. Working with de-liberate speed, McCluskie pulled out powder and ball, and began reloading.

Kinch was no less fascinated than the first time he had seen it happen. There was something magic about it, like a man pulling a rabbit out of a hat. One minute McCluskie was just standing there, and in the blink of an eye the gun was in his hand and whanging tin cans all over the place. It was hard to believe, except that he'd seen it repeated five mornings in a row.

Grinning, he picked up a rock and chunked it at one of the tins. "Better watch it, Mike. The shadow almost caught you that time."

McCluskie grunted, smiling. "Un-huh. Toad's got six toes, too. You keep a sharp lookout, though, sport. Can't let the bogeyman get too close or I'll have to take up cards for a livin'."

The Irishman directed his attention to the cans once more, and for the next half-hour blasted his way through what had become by now a ritualized drill. First, he increased the distance to twenty paces and began walking toward a fresh row of cans. Suddenly he halted in midstride, dropped into a crouch and started firing. Five tins again winged skyward.

Next, he stood with his back to the plank and held his arms in unusually awkward positions. Overhead, out to the side, scratching his nose. The way it might happen if he were taken by surprise. On signal from the coin, he would wheel around and open fire. Again and again he practiced these movements, spinning to the right on one exchange and to the left on another, each time changing the order in which he potted the cans.

Finally, he walked off down the gully a good fifty yards and halted. Turning sideways, he assumed the classic duelist's stance. Thumbing off each shot with precise care, using the sights for the first time, he started on the left and ticked off the cans in sequence. He missed on the last shot.

Kinch felt like the inside of his skull was being donged by the clapper in a church bell. The morning's barrage had left him all but deaf, and reverberations from the staccato bark of the pistol still rang in his ears. But the noise had little to do with the reason for shaking his head. By exact count, the Irishman had fired fifty shots.

He had missed only once. The last can.

While the boy was visibly impressed, McCluskie himself was muttering curses as he walked forward. Granted, it was the best score he'd racked up this week. But it wasn't good enough. Not in this game. The missed shot might have been the very one to put him in a box with a bunch of daisies in his hand. Concentration! That's where he had slipped up. Plain and simple.

Lack of concentration.

The Irishman squatted down beside the boy and began disassembling his pistol. This was something else that fascinated the youngster, the almost reverent care McCluskie lavished on the weapon. Kinch knew that later he would scrub out the black powder residue with soap and hot water. But for now he made do with swabbing a lightly oiled cloth through the barrel and the cylinder chambers.

McCluskie glanced up and smiled at the kid's solemn expression. "Well, bud, we didn't win the war but we scared the hell out of 'em. Still can't figure how I missed that last shot."

"It's important to you, ain't"—he grinned and made a face—"I mean, isn't it?"

McCluskie acted as though he hadn't noted the slip. "Damn right it's important. Not just because it's part of my job, either. Y'know, you're not back in Chicago any more. Out here a man has got to look out for himself."

"Yeah, but they got law in Newton. I mean, it's not like you was off in the mountains somewheres with a bunch of wild animals."

McCluskie snorted and peered down the barrel of the Colt. "Lemme tell you something, sport. The tough things in this life are sort of like takin' a leak. You've got to stand on your own two feet and nobody else can do it for you. That goes double in a place where everybody and his dog carries a gun. The law might arrest your murderer—maybe even hang him— but that's not likely to do you a whole lot of good. Dead's dead, and that's all she wrote."

Kinch picked up a pebble, studying it a moment, then shot it across the gully like a marble. "Belle says you've killed three men."

"Judas Priest, there's nothin' that woman won't talk about, is there?"

The boy gave him a sideways glance, then looked away again. Something was eating at him and it was a while before he could find the right words. "Is it hard to kill a man, Mike?"

"Well, I don't know." The Irishman paused and pulled reflectively at his ear. "Most times you don't think about it when it's happenin'. It's like fightin' off bees. You just do what needs doing to keep from gettin' stung."

"Yeah, but afterward don't you think about it? Maybe wish you hadn't done it?"

"Like feelin' sorry, you mean?"

Kinch nodded, watching him intently.

"What you're talkin' about is all that stuff in the Good Book. Thou shalt not this and that. The way I look at it, guilt is for them that needs it."

"I don't get you."

"Well, it's like this. Some folks are just miserable inside unless they've got something to feel guilty about. Sort of like it'd been bred into 'em, the same as horns on a cow. They're not really happy unless they're sad. All choked up with guilt. Y'see what I mean?"

The boy mulled it over a minute, frowning thoughtfully. "You're sayin' that if they kill a man to keep from gettin' killed, they still feel guilty. Like it was wrong doing it even to save themselves."

"That's about the size of it, I guess."

"But shouldn't you feel sorry, even a little bit? Somehow it don't seem the same as slaughterin' a pig or knockin' a steer in the head."

"Sport, it's not ghosts that haunt our lives. It's people. The live ones are who you've got to worry about. Don't waste your time on the dead. Where they are, it won't make a particle of difference."

Kinch again looked away, troubled by something he couldn't quite come to grips with. The game McCluskie played was fun to watch, the same way there was something grimly fascinating about watching a snake rear back and shake its rattles. But all week something had bothered him about the gun. Not anything he could exactly put his finger on, just a worrisome thought that wouldn't go away. Now he knew what it was.

The game had only one purpose. And it wasn't to perforate tin cans.

Since his little siege in the charity ward back in Kansas City, Kinch had had plenty of time to think. Mostly about death, and especially his own. In some queer sort of way it was as if he and Death had become close acquaintances, without a secret between them. Yet in the closeness came a curious turnabout. It wasn't that death frightened him so much as that life had suddenly become very precious. Each day was somehow special, a thing to be treasured, and every breath his lungs took seemed sweeter than the one before. Death in itself was sort of shrouded, a misty bunch of nothing that even the preachers couldn't explain too well. But the loss of life was very real, something he could understand all on his own. When the candle was snuffed out, everything he was or might have been just stopped. Double ought zero.

The thought of killing someone wasn't just repugnant. It was scary in a way that resisted words. Like killing another man would somehow kill a part of himself. Almost as if the time he had left would be whittled down in the act of stealing from another what he himself prized the most.

Then again, maybe it was like the Irishman said. Life couldn't be all that precious if a man wouldn't fight to save it. Only something of little value was tossed aside lightly, and that didn't include the privilege to go on breathing.

Kinch glanced at the big man out of the corner of his eye. Since the loss of his family a year past he

had been drifting aimlessly, with no real goal in mind
except to taste life before his time ran out. McCluskie
was the first person to show any interest in him, to
take the time and trouble to talk with him. Strangely
enough, these talks somehow put him in mind of quiet
evenings back in Chicago. When he and his father
would sit on the tenement stoop and discuss all manner of things. But that was before the fire. And the
screaming and smoke and charred stench of death.

He shuddered inside, remembering again how it
had been. Then he took hold of himself and wiped
the thought from his mind. There was nothing to be
gained in living in the past. Just bitter memories and
grief and a void that ached to be filled. Here and now,
with the Irishman, he had the start of something new.
A friendship certainly, otherwise McCluskie would
never have taken him in and cared for him and given
him a job. But over and above that there was something more. A closeness shared, unlike anything he'd
ever known for another man. Except maybe for his
father, and even that was somehow different.

Despite McCluskie's brusque manner and gamy
joshing he felt drawn to the man. Not that McCluskie
treated him as full grown. Nor was it just exactly a
father to son kind of thing. Instead, it was something
in between, a partnership of sorts, and perhaps that
was what made it different. One of a kind. A rare
thing, and exciting.

Puzzling over it, Kinch decided on the spur of the
moment that he could have picked worse spots than
Newton to pile off the train. Lots worse. Truth to tell,
getting clobbered by the Irishman might well have
been an unusual stroke of luck. They made a pretty

good team, and it came to him all of a sudden that he had found something he didn't want to lose. Something damned special. And he wasn't about to rock the boat.

Whichever way the Irishman led, he meant to follow.

McCluskie finished assembling the Colt and started loading it. Seating a ball, he rammed it down and looked over at the kid. "Y'know, there's nothin' stoppin' you from tryin' your hand with this thing. Wouldn't be no trouble at all to show you how it's done. Matter of fact, what with you being my assistant, it might be a good idea. Never yet hurt a man to know one end of a gun from the other."

Kinch uncoiled slowly and got to his feet. "I'll give 'er a try. So long as we stick to shootin' at cans."

"Meanin' you're not ready to try your luck with something that shoots back."

The boy grinned. "I'd just as soon not."

"Bud, I hope it never comes to that. What I said a while ago about guilt and all—I meant that. But it's not much fun killin' a man. Just between us, I could do without it myself."

McCluskie devoted the next hour to demonstrating the rudiments of what he had learned through nearly three years of trial and error. Instructing someone in the use of a gun seemed awkward at first, but he found Kinch an eager pupil. Things he had never before put into words made even more sense when he heard himself explaining it, and the boy's sudden interest gratified him in a way he would never have suspected. Nor did he fully understand it. He was just damned pleased.

Concentration and balance and deliberation. According to the Irishman, these were the sum and substance of firing a pistol accurately. Distractions of whatever variety—movement, sound, even gunfire—must be blocked out of a man's mind. Every nerve in his body must be focused with an iron grip on the target. Almost as if he were blinded to anything except the spot he wanted to hit. Without this intensity of concentration, he would more likely than not throw the shot off. Since the first shot was the one that counted, to waste it was a hazardous proposition at best.

Balance had to do with a man's stance and his aiming of the gun. McCluskie demonstrated by dropping into a crouch, feet slightly apart, and leveling the gun to a point that his arm was about equidistant between waist and shoulder. Each man soon determined the position most natural to himself, but the crouch was essential. It not only made him a smaller target, but more importantly, it centered the gun on his opponent's vitals. The chest and belly. At that point a man forgot the sights and aimed by instinct. Much the same as pointing his finger. With his body squarely directed into the target, and the gun jabbed out as an extension of his finger, he had only to bring his arm level and the slug would strike pretty much dead center every time.

McCluskie paused, mulling over the next part, and tried to frame his words to capture the precise meaning of a single thought.

"Forget about speed. That'll get a man planted quicker'n anything. It's not how fast you shoot or how many shots you get off. What counts is that you hit what you're shootin' at. With the first shot. If you can't learn to do that, then you've got no business carryin' a gun."

Kinch gave him a skeptical look. "You sound like one of them preachers that says 'do as I say, not as I do.' Cripes, I've been sittin' here for a whole week watchin' you whip that thing out like it had grease on it."

"That's because you've been watchin'," McCluskie growled, "instead of payin' attention. You've got fast mixed up with sudden. There's difference, and not understandin' that is what gets a man a one way ticket to the Pearly Gates."

The Irishman leveled his pistol at arm's length. "Right there's where you hesitate before you pull the trigger. But it's only a little hesitation, a fragment of a second. Nothin' a man could count even when he's doing it. Just a split-hair delay to catch the barrel out of the corner of your eye and make sure it's lined up on the target. Then you pull the trigger."

The Colt roared and a can spun off the plank.

"Learn that before you learn anything else. It's the difference between the quick and the dead. Deliberation. Sudden instead of fast. Whatever you want to call it. Just slow down enough so that your first shot counts. Otherwise you might not get a second."

McCluskie positioned the boy only five paces from the plank to start. They worked for a while on stance and gaining a feel for pointing the gun. Then he had the kid hold the Colt down at his side and concentrate on a single can. The label on it showed a bright golden peach.

"Whenever you're ready."

Kinch whipped the gun up and blasted off four shots in a chain-lightning barrage.

The can hadn't moved.

"No goddamnit, you're not listenin'. I said hesitate. Take your time. Hell, any dimdot can stand there and just pull the trigger. Now load up and try it again. Only slow down, for Chrissakes."

The next half-hour was excruciating for both teacher and pupil. The boy fired and loaded four cylinders—twenty shots—before he hit the juicy-looking peach. All the while McCluskie was storming and yelling advice and growing more exasperated with each pull of the trigger. Oddly enough, he seemed madder than if he himself had run out the string of misses.

But something had clicked on that last shot, the hit. Understanding came so sudden that Kinch felt as if his ears had come unplugged. The delay had been there. Right under his fingertips, like a sliver of smoke. He had felt it, sensed that it was waiting on him. Known even before he feathered the trigger that the can would jump.

He reloaded, blocking out McCluskie and the heat and the ringing in his ears. Then he crouched, leveling his arm, and the gun began to buck. Spaced shots, neither slow nor fast, with a mere trickle of time between each report.

Three cans out of five leaped from the plank.

The Irishman just stood there a moment, staring at the punctured tins. Then his mouth creased in a slow smile.

"Well I'll be a sonovabitch. You rung the gong."

EIGHT

McCluskie had given the matter of Kinch's birthday considerable thought. The kid was turning eighteen, which was sort of a milestone in a youngster's life. The day he ceased being a boy and set about the business of becoming a man.

Not that a youngster couldn't have fought Indians or rustled cattle or killed himself a couple of men by that time. There were many who had, and lots more who fell shy by only the slimmest of margins. Wes Hardin, who had treed Abilene just last month, was scarcely eighteen himself. Yet, according to newspaper claims, he had even run a sandy on Wild Bill Hickok.

Life west of Kansas City forced a boy to grow up in a hurry. All too often, though, it killed him off before he ever really got started.

Personally, the Irishman had never set much store with this thing of birthdays. The idea of a boy becoming a man just because he'd chalked up a certain number of years seemed a little absurd. That pretty much assumed a kid couldn't cut the mustard, and McCluskie knew different. He had joined the Union army at the advanced age of nineteen, and nobody had ever been called upon to hold his hand. From the opening gun he had pulled his own weight, and when the Rebs finally called it quits, he'd felt like the old man of his outfit.

The killing ground did that. Seared the childish notions out of a boy's head and made him look at things in a different light. Like a man.

McCluskie had learned that lesson the hard way. First hand. When he came west after the war, he was a man stripped of illusions. Life fought dirty in the clinches, so he had discovered, and it didn't pay to give the other fellow an even break. Just as he felt no remorse over the men he had killed in the war, so it was that he felt nothing for the ward boss in Hell's Kitchen, or the three hardcases he had planted in Abilene. There were some people just bound and determined to get themselves killed. The fact that he was the instrument of their abrupt and somewhat unceremonious demise was their lookout, not his. Not by a damnsight. Yet, in some queer way that he'd never really fathomed, he took neither pleasure nor pride in killing. It was like he had told the kid.

It's not much fun killin' a man.

Still, it was one thing to feel a twinge of regret and something else entirely to turn the other cheek. A man tended to his own business and tried not to step on the other fellow's toes. But he also fought his own fights, and anyone who came looking for trouble deserved whatever he got. Whether it was a busted nose or a rough pine box. That's the way the game was played, and while he hadn't made the rules, he wasn't about to break them either. Only dimdots and faint-hearts came west expecting to get a fair shake from the next man, and more often than not, they were the ones who ended up on an undertaker's slab.

Understandably then, McCluskie didn't believe in mollycoddling. The sooner kids learned to wipe their own noses, the better off for all concerned. Curiously enough, though, he had been at some pains to make an event of Kinch's birthday.

The excuses he gave himself were pretty lame. Generally he didn't allow feeling to stand in the way of common sense. He saw himself as a realist in a hard and uncompromising world. A man who met life on its own terms and handed out more licks than he took. Underneath his flinty composure, it grated the wrong way to admit there was still a soft spot he hadn't whipped into line. But he'd never been a man to fool himself, either. It all boiled down to one inescapable fact.

There wouldn't be any more birthdays for the kid. Eighteen was where the string ran out.

Oddly enough, the Irishman was having a hard time dealing with that. It confused him, this feeling he had for the kid. Part of it had to do with a small boy killed in a street brawl, the one he'd never seen. And he understood that. Accepted it as natural that a man would dredge up old feelings, musty and long buried, and allow a skinny, underfed kid to touch his soft spot. Even a man who made his living with a gun wasn't without a spark of emotion. No matter how many times he'd killed. Or told himself there was nothing on earth that could get under his skin and make him breathe life into thoughts dead and gone. That part held no riddle for him, and he had come to grips with it in his own way.

What bothered him, and left him more than a little bemused, was the extent of his feeling. Somehow the kid had penetrated his soft spot far deeper than he'd suspected at the outset. Little by little, over the course of their weeks together, the youngster had burrowed clean into the core. Like a worm that slowly bores a passage in hard-packed earth. Now the Irishman found himself face to face with something he couldn't quite handle. It was Hell's Kitchen all over again. Only this time he was there. Forced to stand helplessly by, as if his hands were tied, and watch it happen. Almost as though life had felt cheated the first time, and out of spite had summoned him back to observe, at last, the death of a boy.

In some diabolic fashion, the death of his own son.

That evening, when he got to the hotel, Kinch had himself all decked out in a new set of duds. The Irishman had forewarned him that this was the night. After nearly three weeks of taking it easy and soaking up sunshine, it was high time he got his feet wet.

Tonight they were out to see the elephant.

Kinch had splurged like a cowhand fresh off the trail. The wages McCluskie paid weren't princely by any yardstick, but the best at the Blue Front Clothing Store had been none too good. Candy-striped shirt, slouch hat, boots freshly blacked, and a peacock blue kerchief knotted around his neck. He was clean scrubbed and reeked of rose water, and his hair looked like it had been plastered down with a trowel.

McCluskie whistled and gave him the full once

over. "Well now, just looky here. Got yourself all tricked out like it was Sunday-go-to-meetin'."

The boy preened and darted a quick look at himself in the mirror. "Just followin' orders. You said bright-eyed and bushy-tailed."

Damned if I didn't. Sort of took me at my word, too, didn't you?"

"Guess I did, at that. Put a dent about the size of a freight engine in my pocketbook."

The Irishman suddenly remembered the package he'd brought along and thrust it out. "Here. What with it being your birthday and all, I figured you was due a bonus."

"Aw, hell, Mike. You didn't have to buy me nothin'."

The sparkle in the kid's eyes belied his words, and it was all he could do to keep from ripping the package open. Setting it on the dresser, he forced himself to slowly untie the cord and peel back the wrapping paper. Then he removed the box top and his jaw popped open in astonishment.

"Hoooly Moses!"

Inside was a Colt Navy with a gunbelt and holster.

Kinch just stood there, mesmerized by the walnut grips and blued steel and the smell of new leather. After a while McCluskie chuckled and gave him a nudge. "Go ahead, try it on. It's not new, you understand, but she shoots as good as mine. I tried'er out this afternoon."

The boy pulled the rig out of the box as if it were dipped in gold and buckled it around his hips. It fitted perfectly, and he knew without asking that McCluskie had had it special made. There wasn't a store-bought gunbelt the near side of Kingdom Come that wouldn't have swallowed his skinny rump.

The Irishman took his shoulders and positioned him in front of the mirror. "Take a gander at yourself, bud. Don't hardly look like the same fellow, does it?"

Kinch just stared at the reflection in the mirror, dumfounded somehow by the stranger who stared back.

McCluskie grinned. "Much more and you'll bore a hole clean through that lookin' glass. C'mon, say something."

The kid's arm moved and they were both staring down the large black hole of the Colt's snout. The youthful face in the mirror laughed, eyes shining brightly. "D'ya see it?"

"See it?" McCluskie's grin broadened. "That's a damnfool question. What was it I taught you, anyway?"

That the hand's faster than the eye."

"Well you've got your proof right there in that mirror. The fellow you're lookin' at didn't even see it. He's still blinkin'."

While it was a slight exaggeration, McCluskie's comment wasn't far wide of the mark. The truth was, he hadn't seen the kid draw. Nor did it surprise him. Not after the last couple of days in the gully north of town.

The swiftness with which the kid learned was nothing short of incredible. In two weeks he had mastered what some men never absorbed in a lifetime. Part of it was the will to learn, and some of it was McCluskie's dogged insistence on practice. But most of it was simply the boy's hands. Slim and tapered, hardened from work, but with a strength and quickness that was all but unimaginable. What those hands knew couldn't be taught. It was there all along, waiting merely to be trained. Reaction and speed was a gift. Something a man was born with. The rest was purely a matter of practice.

Kinch wasn't as good as he would be. Or as yet anywhere close to McCluskie. But he was fast. Even too fast, perhaps. The best score he'd racked up so far was three out of five cans. While he was fairly consistent, and improving every day, he still hadn't overcome a tendency to rush. Quite plainly, despite the Irishman's constant scolding, he had been bitten by the speed bug.

Still, this obsession with speed wasn't what troubled McCluskie the most. That would pass soon enough. As the kid got better, and gained confidence in himself, he would see that sudden beat fast everytime. The worrisome thing was Kinch's attitude. He still looked on the whole deal as one big game. Just a lark. A sporting event of some sort where the only casualties were a bunch of tin cans.

McCluskie wasn't completely unaware of what lay behind the kid's lighthearted manner. Perhaps any man, faced with the prospect of his own death, would have reacted the same way. Yet it was hard to accept, for it overlooked a salient detail. Places like Newton often pitted a man against something besides tin cans. Something that could shoot back.

Thinking about it now, as Kinch preened in front of the mirror, he wondered if he had done the right thing. Maybe giving the kid a gun wouldn't change anything. That remained to be seen. But one thing

was for damn sure. It had put a spark in his eye that
wasn't there before, and for the moment, that in itself
was enough.

When they left the hotel dusk had already fallen,
and the southside was a regular beehive of activity.
Trailhands thronged the boardwalk, drifting from dive
to dive with the rowdy exuberance of schoolboys
playing hooky. Along the street rinky-dink pianos tin-
kled in witless harmony, and over the laughing and
shouting and drunken Rebel yells, it all came together
in a calliope of strident gibberish. Every night was
Saturday night in Newton, and so long as the Texans'
money held out, they flung themselves headlong into
a frenetic swirl of cheap whiskey and fast women.

McCluskie angled across the street toward the
Gold Room. That seemed like as good a place to start
as any, but by no means would it be their last stop.
Before introducing the kid to Belle's girls he figured
to hit at least three or four dives. Somehow he just
couldn't picture the youngster waltzing into a whore-
house stone-cold sober. Better to float his kidneys
first, and then let the ladies instruct him in the ancient
and noble sport of dip the wick.

They came through the door with Kinch hard on
his heels and headed for the bar. Every couple of steps
the youngster took a hitch at his gunbelt, as if checking to make sure it was still there. The pistol felt
strange and somehow reassuring on his hip, and the
temptation to touch it was too much to resist. Had it
been a wart between his eyes he wouldn't have been
any less conscious of its existence.

Pony Reid greeted them at the bar. "Evenin', Mike.

Kinch. You boys are gettin' an early start, aren't you?"

"Pony, we're out to see the elephant." McCluskie clapped the kid across the shoulders. "Not that you'd remember back that far, but Kinch just turned the corner on eighteen. He's ready to cut the wolf loose and let him howl."

By now everyone in town knew the story on the Irishman's young assistant. They had become all but inseparable, and it required only a moment's observation to see that the kid idolized McCluskie. In the manner of rough-natured men, the sporting crowd had adopted Kinch as one of their own.

"Hell's bells, that calls for a drink!" Reid signaled the barkeep. "Set 'em up for my friends here. Celebration like this has to get started off proper."

The bartender poured out three shots and Reid hoisted his glass. "Kinch, here's mud in your eye. Happy days."

The gambler and McCluskie downed their whiskey neat. Kinch hesitated only a moment and followed suit. When the liquor hit bottom it bounced dangerously, exploding in a series of molten eruptions. His eyes watered furiously and he felt sure smoke would belch out of his ears at any moment. But somehow he managed to hold it down, and after a couple of quick breaths, he gave the older men a weak smile.

"Mighty good drinkin' whiskey. Next one's on me."

"The hell you say!" The Irishman slapped a double eagle on the bar and winked sideways at Pony Reid. "Treat's on me. The rest of the night. Barkeep! Set 'em up again."

Kinch had the sinking sensation that another round might just paralyze him, but he merely grinned and bellied up closer to the bar. This was the first time the Irishman had allowed him anything stronger than a warm beer, and he wasn't about to back off now.

Then, as he lifted the glass again, his nose twitched. Cripes! No wonder they called it coffin varnish. That's what it smelled like. Only worse.

They came through the door of Belle's house arm in arm. Kinch was listing slightly, but still navigating under his own power. This, along with his clear eye and steady speech, had the Irishman a little puzzled. After a whirlwind tour of three saloons in the past two hours he'd fully expected to have the youngster ossified and walking on air. But it hadn't worked out that way.

Apparently the kid had a greater tolerance for whiskey than he'd suspected. That or a hollow leg.

Halting in the entranceway to the parlor, they surveyed the room with a look of amused dignity. McCluskie swept off his hat and made a game try at what passed for a bow.

"Ladies, we bring you greetings." Straightening, he gestured toward the boy, who was propped up against the doorjamb. "This here is Mr. Kinch Riley, sportin' man supreme."

Everything in the room came to a stop. Belle, along with three cowhands and five girls, stared back at them as if man and boy had suddenly sprung whole from a crack in the floor. Kinch pulled his hat off and grinned like a cat with a mouthful of feathers. But he had a little trouble duplicating McCluskie's bow. All at once his joints seemed limber as goose grease and he couldn't quite manage to peel himself off the door-jamb.

Belle crossed the room and planted herself directly in their path. She looked them both up and down, shaking her head ruefully. Then she sniffed, as if one of them had broken wind, and her gaze settled on the Irishman.

"Just proud as punch, aren't you? Finally managed to get him drunk."

"Drunk?" McCluskie tucked his chin down and gave her an owlish frown. "Who?"

"Him!" Belle's finger stabbed out and Kinch jerked back, banging his head against the door frame.

McCluskie's frown changed to a sly smirk, as if he had just heard a lie so preposterous it defied belief. "Goddamn, Belle, he's sober as a judge. You better get yourself some specs."

"You really are thick, aren't you?" Her words came clipped and sharp, like spitting grease. "You big baboon, you're so drunk he looks sober. And him sick, too. Just wait till Doc Boyd gets wind of this."

"Cough syrup," Kinch muttered.

They both blinked and gave him a peculiar look. Belle shrugged, not sure she had heard right, and after a moment McCluskie bent closer. "How's that, bud?"

"Cough syrup."

"Yeah, what about it?"

"Tastes just like cough syrup."

"You mean the whiskey?"

"Just like what they gimme at the hospital."

"What them doctors gave you back in Kansas City?"

"Only better. Lots better."

McCluskie sifted it over a minute and all of a sudden the kid made perfect sense. Canting his head back, he gave Belle a crafty look. "Thick, huh? Case you hadn't noticed, he's not coughin'. Matter of fact, he hasn't since we started drinkin'. What d'ya think of that?"

"Oh, pshaw!" she informed him. "That's no excuse to take a boy out and get him drunk."

"Belle, you're startin' to sound like a mother hen. Besides which, we didn't need an excuse. This is his birthday. Or maybe you forgot."

"I didn't forget and you know it very well. But he was supposed to get his birthday present here, not soaking up rotgut in some dingy saloon."

"Well Jesus H. Christ! Whyn't you quit makin' so much noise, then, and do somethin' about it? Hell, he's been standin' here five minutes and you haven't even introduced him to the girls."

Belle started to say something, but thought better of it. She pried Kinch off the doorjamb and waltzed him out to the middle of the parlor. The girls had watched the entire flurry with mild wonder, and now, as she graced them with a dazzling smile, they sensed that something unusual was brewing.

"Girls, you've all heard me talk about Kinch. Well, tonight is his birthday and he's come to spend it with us. Whatever he wants is on the house, so whoever gets picked, make sure he has a good time."

Nothing about her smile changed, but something in her eyes did. "Understand?"

The girls got the message. They dropped the three cowhands like so many hot rocks and came swarming over the kid. A henna-haired redhead reached him first, and wedged herself up next to his chest like a mustard plaster. Close behind came a blond with soft, jiggly breasts the size of gourds. She latched onto his other arm and started running her hand through his hair. Another blond and a mousey brunette charged into the melee, and before he had time to take a deep breath, Kinch was up to his ears in squealing females.

"Sweetie, do you like Lulu?" purred the redhead.

Kinch cast a trapped look back over his shoulder at the Irishman. But he got no sympathy there. McCluskie and Belle were going at it hammer and tongs. Evidently their little spat had only just started.

The blond stuck her melons under his nose and whispered a blast of hot air into his ear. "Ditch these others, honeybunch. Let Francie give you a trip around the world."

The boy felt as though he were drowning in a sea of arms and bosoms and clawing hands. Every time he struggled to the surface they dragged him under to the floor. Suddenly he pitched forward, spun completely around, and broke clear. Dazed and still somewhat numb from the whiskey he'd absorbed, he lurched away and almost plowed over the fifth girl. Drawing back, he swayed dangerously and tried to bring her into focus.

She was smaller than the others, just a little sprite of a girl. Her hair was black as tarpitch, and she had large almond eyes that stared out wistfully from a kewpie-doll face. Just at that moment he thought she was the most beautiful creature he'd ever seen. More importantly, if it came down to it, he thought he could whip her in a fair fight. The others he wasn't too sure about.

"Hi." Her mouth dimpled in a smile. "I'm Sugartit."

That threw him off stride and for an instant he couldn't get his jaws working. Then he felt the pack closing in behind him and he grabbed her hand.

"Let's go!"

Kinch didn't know where they were going, but right about then his choices seemed pretty limited. He reeled forward, head spinning crazily, aware of nothing but the girl before him.

Sugartit clutched his hand and took off toward the rear of the parlor. The thing he always remembered most afterward was her laugh as they went through the door.

It was like the patter of rain on a warm spring night.

NINE

⊸⊷⊷∿⊶⊶⊷

Kinch was having a hard time looking at the girl. But toning his shirt, he kept sneaking peeks at her out of the corner of his eye. If she noticed, she didn't say anything, but he found nothing unusual in that. Anybody with a name like hers was probably used to being stared at. Maybe even liked it.

Watching her dress gave him a strange sensation down around his bellybutton. It was almost as if he could see straight through her clothes. The way she'd been in bed, soft and naked and cuddly warm. All of which was in his mind's eye, of course. He kept telling himself that as his hands fumbled with the shirt buttons. But it made the image in his head no less real.

What he saw wasn't so much the girl as the sum of her parts. Brief flashes that came and went, like lightning bugs in a dark room. Her impish smile and those big, waifish eyes. The delicate buttercup of her breasts. The gentle swell of her hips. And most of all, somehow flickering brighter than the rest, the soft black muff between her legs. That came strong and clear, sharply in focus.

It was something he would never forget. The warmth and pulsating throb and pleasure so sweet it became almost pain.

What he felt just then was so distinct and real that his mind turned inward, living it over again. Suddenly something touched him and a shiver rippled along his spine. He blinked, awareness returning in fits and starts, much as a dream fades into wakefulness. Then, all in a rush, he saw Sugartit standing before him. She was buttoning his shirt, her mouth dimpled with that small enigmatic smile.

His hands were motionless, frozen somehow to his shirtfront, just where they were before his mind wandered off. All at once he felt green as grass, clumsy and very foolish, and he quickly lowered his hands.

Sugartit finished the buttoning and began tucking his shirt into the waistband of his trousers. He just stood there watching her, gripped by a sensation so acute he couldn't put a name to it. Goosebumps popped out on his skin and a static charge brought tingly little prickles to every nerve in his body. Curiously, he was overcome by a feeling of utter helplessness. As if this mere slip of a girl, through some witchery he failed to comprehend, had cast a spell and turned him into a bumbling jackass incapable of the simplest thought.

The girl ran her arms around his waist and pressed herself close to his chest. He could feel the taut little nipples of her breasts through his shirt, and his mouth suddenly went thick and pasty. Mechanically, like some wooden Indian come to life, he put his arms around her. He felt light in the head, queer somehow, as if he were standing off in a corner watching it happen to someone else.

"There's sure not much of you." Sugartit ran her fingers over his ribs like a piano player testing chords. "You're just all bone and gristle, aren't you?"

Kinch swallowed a wad of paste. "I guess."

"Well, don't worry about it, lover." Her head arched back and the almond eyes seemed to soak him up in great gulps. "Maybe you got shortchanged on muscle, but you're all bearcat where it counts."

Suddenly he felt about eight feet tall. "You ain't exactly tame yourself."

She laughed softly and snuggled closer. "Did you like it?"

"Better'n a duck likes water." Curiously, his tongue had come unglued and he felt slick as a street-corner pitchman. "What about you?"

"Silly, of course I did. Couldn't you tell?" She gave him a tight little squeeze. "I've had it lots of ways, but never like that. Not even once."

The scent of her hair was like perfume and for an instant he couldn't get his breath. "You're joshin' me."

Sugartit put her arms around his neck and pulled his head down. Her lips came over his mouth, soft and warm, and her pink little tongue started doing tricks. Then her hips moved, undulating and hungry, and a jolt of lightning hit him just below the belt buckle. She pulled back and searched his face with a devilish smile.

"Still think I'm joshing?"

Kinch bent and lifted her in his arms. She was

surprisingly light, and it pleased him that he could heft her so easily. As he carried her toward the bed, Sugartit laughed that soft laugh again and began nibbling on his ear.

When they entered the parlor some time later everything was back to normal. Belle and the Irishman were wedged into a settee like a couple of lovebirds, and from the looks they were giving one another, it was clear that a truce of some sort had been negotiated. The girls had themselves a fresh batch of Texans, and they were paired off around the room making sweet talk. Everybody knew that this was what made Belle's prices so stiff, all the sugar and spice that came beforehand. But the cowhands didn't seem to mind in the least. They were lapping it up as fast as the girls could dish it out.

So far as the kid could see, it was business as usual.

McCluskie spotted him first and gave Belle the high sign with a jerk of his head. She looked around and then they both stood up, waiting for Sugartit and Kinch to cross the room. Belle whispered something and the Irishman smiled, but oddly enough, they had the look of expectant parents. Almost as if they were awaiting news of a blessed event.

"Bud, I'd just about given you up for lost," McCluskie grinned and tried to make it sound offhand. "Enjoy yourself, did you?"

Kinch flushed despite himself. "Yeah, sure. Best birthday I ever had."

The girl giggled and Belle eyed her speculatively.

"Sugartit, I hope you showed our young friend a good time."

"Why, Belle, I just put the frosting on his cake. I taught him the French twist, and the half-and-half, and—"

"Whoa, Nellie!" McCluskie threw up his hand. "All that racy talk is liable to give an old man like me dangerous notions. C'mon, sport. Let's go get ourselves a drink. After a workout like that I've got an idea you need fortifyin'." He dropped an arm over the kid's shoulders and headed for the door. "Belle, I'll see you later. And if I don't, you'll know ol' hollow-leg here had put me under the table."

"Mike McCluskie, you remember what I said! Don't you dare get that boy drunk again. I'll hear about it if you do."

McCluskie laughed and kept on walking. The boy darted a look over his shoulder as he was being hustled into the hallway, and Sugartit gave him a bright smile.

"Come back soon, lover. Don't forget, you hear?"

Kinch's disembodied voice floated back through the parlor entrance. "I will. First thing tomorrow."

Then the door slammed and Belle shot the girl a funny look. Sugartit sighed and dimpled her cheeks in a pensive little frown, wondering if he really meant it.

Outside, McCluskie headed the boy uptown and they walked along at a steady clip for a few paces. After a while the Irishman grunted and shook his head.

"Let that be a lesson to you, bud. Don't ever let women get started runnin' their gums. Once they build up a head of steam, there's no stoppin' them. I got us out of there just in time."

Kinch gave him a quizzical glance. "I don't get you. What's wrong with talkin'?"

"Talkin'? Hell, there wouldn't be no talkin' to it. Just listenin'. They'd sit there and rehash the whole night, and feed it back to you blow by blow. Time they got through you'd come away thinkin' you'd lived it twice."

"Yeah, I guess I see what you mean."

They walked along in silence for a few steps, but McCluskie's curiosity finally got the better of him. Not unlike the temptation to peep through a knothole, there was a question he just couldn't resist.

"What'd you think of Sugartit?"

"She's nifty, Mike. Cuter'n a button, too."

Something in the kid's voice sounded peculiar. Just a little off key. "Well, I didn't mean her, exactly. I was talkin' about what she did for you. How'd you like that?"

Kinch didn't say anything for a moment, but an odd look came over his eyes. "It was like a big juicy toothache that don't hurt no more. All of a sudden *whammo!* And then it's fixed."

"Yeah?" McCluskie detected something more than mere excitement. "Tell me about it."

"Well, I don't know. It was like colored lights whirlin' around inside your head. Y'know, the way a skyrocket does. There's a big explosion and then for a while you can't see nothin' but streaks and colors and bright flashes. Cripes, she was somethin', Mike."

"I'm startin' to get a hunch you were drunker'n I thought."

"No I wasn't, neither. After the first time I was sober as all get out."

"First time!"

The boy grinned sheepishly. "Yeah. Y'see, we was gettin' dressed and then she started rubbin' around on me and—"

"I get the picture. What you're sayin' is that you liked it more'n you thought."

"I liked her. There's somethin' about her, Mike. She's not like the others. Not even a little bit."

The Irishman slammed to a halt and faced him. "Say, you're not gettin' sweet on that girl, are you?"

"I might be." Kinch stuck out his chin and stared right back. "What's wrong with that?"

McCluskie had seen lots of men go dippy over whores. In a cowtown there was always a scarcity of women, and sometimes a man settled for what he could get. But the kid deserved better than that. The only thing special about Sugartit was that she had probably laid half the cowhands in Texas. And her hardly older than the kid, for Chrissakes!

"What's wrong is that she's a whore. Has been since Belle stole her away from a dancehall back in Abilene. That was close to three years ago. You got any idea how many men she's screwed in—"

"Mike, I ain't gonna listen to that. Don't you go badmouthin' her, y'hear me!"

The boy was bristled up like a banty rooster and McCluskie had to clamp down hard to keep from laughing. "Don't get your dander up, bud. I was just tryin' to show you what's what."

"Well, lay off of her. I told you, she's not like the others."

"Awright, just for the sake of argument, let's say she's not. But what do you think she's doin' back there right now?"

"What kind of crack is that?"

"You think about it for a minute. She's not workin' in a sporting house for her health, y'know. There's cowhands walkin' in there regular as clockwork, and before the night's over she'll have humped her share."

Kinch glared at him for a long time, then he shrugged and looked away. "Nobody's perfect. She was probably starvin' and plenty hard up when Belle took her in."

"That's right, she was."

"Same as me, the night you caught me down at the depot."

"Not just exactly. That's what I'm tryin' to get through your head. Call her whatever you want: Soiled Dove. Fallen Sparrow. The handle you put on her won't change nothin'. The plain fact of the matter is, she's a whore."

"Well, holy jumpin' Jesus, that ain't no crime, is it? Cripes, if I was a girl and got stuck in a cowtown, I might've wound up a whore myself."

"All I'm sayin' is that you shouldn't get calf eyes over your first piece of tail. There's lots of women around. Some of 'em better'n Sugartit, maybe. You ought to shop around a little before you let yourself get all bogged down."

"I don't see you makin' the rounds. Seems to me you stick pretty close to Belle."

The kid halfway had a point. McCluskie grunted and turned back uptown. They clomped along without saying much, each lost in his own thoughts. At last, somewhat baffled by the youngster's doggedness, the Irishman decided to try another tack.

"Y'know, it's funny how things work out between a man and a woman. Now you take Belle and me, for instance. Once I get her in bed she's tame as any tabbycat you ever saw. But the rest of the time she's got a temper that'd melt lead. Hell, I don't need to tell you. Not after some of the tantrums you've seen her pitch."

Kinch gave him a suspicious look. "What's that got to do with me and Sugartit?"

"That's what I was workin' around to. You see, it's like this: When a man's puttin' the goods to a woman, she's putty in his hands. There's not a promise on earth she wouldn't make while he's got his shaft ticklin' her funnybone. But out of bed it's a different story. Then she knows he's got his mind on the next time, and that gives her the whiphand. She'll make him sweat and do all kinds of damnfool things before she lets him climb in the saddle again."

"I still don't see what that's got to do with anything."

"You're not listenin', bud. What I'm sayin' is that women calculate things. Plan it all out. A man's brains are between his legs, and that's where he does most of his thinkin'. A woman thinks with her head, leastways when you haven't got her on her back, and she generally winds up gettin' what she wants."

"What you're sayin' is that women know how to wind a man around their little finger."

"That's exactly what I'm sayin'. Just remember, a man rules in bed, but the rest of the time it's the woman that calls the tune. They'll make you dance

whatever jig they want just for the honor of pumpin'
on 'em every now and then."

"And you think that's what Sugartit has got
planned for me?"

"She's female, and I'm just tellin' you that's the
way they work."

Kinch screwed up his face in a stubborn frown.
"Mike, that's the biggest crock I ever heard. Maybe
I'm wet behind the ears, but I'm not stupid. Sugartit
is different, and nothin' you say is gonna budge me
one iota."

It suddenly dawned on McCluskie that he was up
against a stone wall. Not only that, but he was trying
to play God in the bargain. Here was a kid who'd be
lucky if he lived out the winter, and the last thing he
needed was a bunch of second-hand advice—especially from somebody who hadn't made any great
shakes of his own life. If the kid wanted a playmate
till his string ran out, then by damn that's what he
would have. Sugartit was handy and seemed willing,
so it was just a matter of working it out with Belle.
The button wouldn't even have to know.

McCluskie threw his arm over the boy's shoulders.
"Sport, I learned a long time ago not to argue with a
man when he's got his mind set. Besides, maybe you
know something I don't. Hell, give it a whirl. You
and Sugartit might hit it off in style. Just remember
what I said, though. Keep your dauber up and she'll
treat you like Jesus H. himself."

The kid grinned and started to reply, but all at once
his throat constricted and he began coughing. It
wasn't a particularly severe spasm but it was the
worst of the night. Watching him gasp for air, the

Irishman was again reminded of his promise to himself. This kid was going to have whatever he wanted. Served up any way he liked.

"Goddamn, I knew it!" McCluskie growled. "You sobered up and now you're back to coughin'. C'mon, bud, what you need is a drink. Let's find ourselves a waterin' hole."

They crossed the street and entered Gregory's Saloon. This was a Texan hangout and a place McCluskie normally wouldn't have frequented, but just then he wasn't feeling choosy. Whiskey was whiskey, and the kid needed a dose in the worst way.

The dive was packed shoulder to shoulder with trailhands, and reeked of sweat, cow manure, and stale smoke. McCluskie bulled his way through the crowd and wedged out a place for them at the bar. Some of the men he shoved aside muttered angrily, and a curious buzz swept back over the room as others turned to look at the choking, red-faced kid.

The bartender sauntered over, absently munching a toothpick. "What'll you have?"

"The good stuff," McCluskie informed him. "With the live snake in it."

That didn't draw any laughs but it produced a bottle. The Irishman poured and got a shot down Kinch without any lost motion. Apparently even snakehead whiskey was not without medicinal qualities. It had no sooner hit bottom than the kid stopped coughing and commenced to look like himself again. McCluskie poured a second round just for good measure.

"Say, Irish, when'd ya start collectin' strays?"

Several of the men close by chuckled, and McCluskie turned to find Bill Bailey standing a few feet behind him. They had crossed paths back in Abilene and shared a mutual dislike for one another. Bailey was a big man, heavier than McCluskie, with a seamed, windburned face the color of plug tobacco. His legs bowed out like a couple of barrel staves, and it was no secret that he had once been a top hand for Shanghai Pierce. According to rumor, he had a checkered past and couldn't return to Texas—something about a shootout over a card game that had left a reward dodger hanging over his head. But he was a great favorite with the trailhands, and through one device or another, managed to leave them laughing as he separated them from their pay.

McCluskie gave him a brittle stare. "Bailey, I only allow my friends to call me Irish. That lets you out."

"Hell, don't get your nose out of joint." Bailey jerked a thumb at Kinch. "I was just curious about your pardner. Looks a mite sickly to be runnin' with you."

"Don't let his looks fool you." McCluskie turned his head slightly and winked at the kid. "For a skinny fellow he's sorta sudden."

Bailey cocked one eyebrow and inspected the boy closer. "Yeh, that popgun he's wearin' looks real, sure enough. Course, I've seen more'n one pilgrim shoot his toes off tryin' to play badman. What about it, squirt, you lost any toes lately?"

McCluskie leaned back against the bar and studied the ceiling. The kid glanced at him and got no reaction whatever. Then it came to him, what was happening here, and a smile ticked at the corner of his mouth.

The Irishman had slyly brought the game full circle.

Kinch turned his attention back to the Texan. "Mister, that's a bad habit you've got, callin' people names. Some folks might not take kindly to it."

Bailey's eyes narrowed and he darted a puzzled look at the Irishman. "Listen, sonny, my beef's with your friend here. Just button your lip and I'll act like I didn't hear you."

All at once the kid knew what McCluskie had been talking about every day out in the gully: the difference between a tin can and a man. It brought a warm little glow down in the pit of his belly.

"What's the matter, lardgut? Lost your nerve?"

"Boy, I'm warnin' you, don't rile me. You're out of your class."

It was just like McCluskie had said! A four-flusher always toots his horn the loudest. He smiled and edged clear of the bar.

"Try me."

Bailey's hand twitched and streaked toward the butt of his gun. Then he froze dead still. The kid was standing there with a Colt Navy pointed straight at his gut. What the Texan took to be his last thought was one of sheer wonder. He hadn't even seen the kid move.

McCluskie waited a couple of seconds, then looked over at the boy. "You figure on shootin' him?"

Kinch shook his head. "Nope, He's not worth it."

McCluskie shrugged and headed toward the door. The boy backed away, keeping Bailey covered, and only after he was outside did he holster the Colt. The Irishman was already striding up the street, and as

Kinch came alongside he grunted sourly.

"That was a damnfool play. A gun's like what you've got between your legs. If you're not going to use it, then keep it in your pants. Saves a whole lot of trouble later on."

TEN

The five men were seated around a table in the Lone Star. They were alone, for sunrise was scarcely an hour past, and none of the saloon help had yet arrived. Spivey and Judge Muse, flanked by Tonk Hazeltine, occupied one side of the table. Seated across from them were McCluskie and Bill Bailey.

Not unlike dogs warily eying one another, the Texan and McCluskie had their chairs hitched around sideways to the table. They had exchanged curt nods when the meeting began, and afterward seated themselves so they could keep each other in sight. This guarded maneuvering was hardly lost on the others, yet none of them displayed any real surprise. The story of Bailey's humiliation at the hands of the kid was by now common knowledge. It had created a sensation on both sides of the tracks, and except for the upcoming bond issue, the townspeople had talked of little else for the last week.

Word had spread that Bailey meant to even the score, and hardly anyone doubted he would try. Unless McCluskie got to him first, which seemed highly likely. Still, betting was about evenly split, and speculation was widespread as to the outcome if it ever came to a showdown.

When the men first sat down, Spivey had attempted to ease the tension with some idle chitchat. But it quickly became apparent that his efforts were largely wasted. While Muse joined in, the others simply stared back at him like a flock of molting owls. Hazeltine and Bailey shared a bitter dislike for the Irishman, who in turn, looked through them as if they didn't exist. Spivey finally gave it up as hopeless and at last got down to business.

"Gents, I called this meetin' so we could get everything squared away neat and proper. Once the votin' commences I don't figure we're gonna have much chance to get our heads together. Whatever's got to be ironed out, we'd best get to it now. Later we likely won't have time."

There was a moment of silence while everybody digested that. After a while Hazeltine cleared his throat. "I don't follow you. What's left to be done?"

"Well, Tonk, when we agreed to deputize these boys"—Spivey waved his hand in the general direction of McCluskie and Bailey—"we sort of thought you'd make good use of 'em. I kept waitin' but as of last night you hadn't said yea or nay. Seemed to me we oughta talk about it."

"What's to talk about?" The lawman gave him an indignant frown. "I'm the law here and I'll see that everything comes off the way it's s'posed to."

Spivey and Muse exchanged glances. Then the judge made a steeple of his fingers and peered through them at Hazeltine. "Deputy, we're not casting aspersions on you personally. Nothing of the sort. We're merely asking what your plans are."

"Hell, we don't need no plans. You talk like we was electin' a new President or somethin'. It's nothin' but a measly goddamn bond vote."

Spivey swelled up like a bloated toad. "Measly, my dusty rump! Just in case it slipped your mind, what happens today could put the quietus on this whole town. What's at stake here is Newton itself."

"Bob's right," the judge agreed hurriedly. "We're fighting for our lives. Now let me tell you something. Six months ago this town was nothing but a cow pasture. Today we have a bank, hotels, businesses. A thriving economy. And something more, too. The potential—"

McCluskie turned a deaf ear to the judge's harangue. The past month had left him with a sour taste in his mouth for the grubby little game being played out here. Wichita was trying to shaft Newton. The Santa Fe was shafting everybody. And he was caught squarely in the middle.

All because the head office brass wanted to squeeze a lousy two hundred thousand dollars out of Sedgwick County.

But then, that's how the rich got fat and the poor got lean. The big dog kept nibbling away, bit by bit, at the little dog's bone. Which didn't concern him one way or the other. Except that the brass acted like they had a case of the trots and couldn't find the plug.

They had ordered him to split Newton down the middle and that's what he'd done. Pony Reid and John Gallagher started talking it up and before long the sporting crowd had swung over to Wichita's side of the fence. All of which made good sense from their standpoint. Wichita was farther south than any of the cowtowns and was sure to attract a greater number of the Texas herds.

Then, out of a clear blue, the brass told him to lay off. They had decided, according to their last letter, to let Sedgwick County resolve its own internal affairs. Stripped of all subterfuge, it simply meant they intended to play both ends against the middle. Whoever won—Newton or Wichita—the Santa Fe would still wind up with all the marbles.

If it wasn't so infuriating he might have laughed. The fact that they paid him to waste his time and effort only made it more absurd. Like a dog chasing its tail, he had accomplished nothing.

Judge Muse brought him back to the present with a sharp rap on the table. "We're fighting for nothing less than our very lives! Everything we possess has been poured into this town. Speaking quite frankly, Deputy, I think that demands some added effort on your part also."

Tonk Hazeltine gave him a glum scowl. "I already said my piece. Trouble with you fellers is you're makin' a mountain out of a molehill."

"Like hell we are!" Spivey replied hotly. "This town'll be swamped with Texans today, and if I know them they won't miss a chance to hooraw things good and proper. It's our election, but odds are they'll use it as an excuse to pull Newton up by the roots."

"Which could disrupt the voting," Muse added, "and easily jeopardize whatever chance we have of defeating the bond issue."

Hazeltine said nothing, merely staring back at them. Spivey and the judge looked nonplused, but it was all the Irishman could do to keep from grinning. What he had suspected from the outset was now quite apparent. The lawman was all bluff, and he plainly wasn't overjoyed by the prospect of cracking down on the cowhands. Muse and Spivey had blinded themselves to the truth, staking their hopes on his much publicized reputation. Right now he was the only law the town had, and they couldn't see past the glitter of his tin star.

The silence thickened and after a moment Spivey glanced over at the Irishman. "What d'ya think, Mike? Isn't there some way we could keep the lid on till after the votin' is done with?"

"Why the hell you askin' him?" Bailey snarled. "The only thing he ever give Texans was a hard time, and you'd better believe they ain't forgot it neither."

Judge Muse raised his hand in a curbing gesture. "Mr. Bailey, may I remind you that you and Mr. McCluskie were deputized in an effort to even things out. You're a Texan, and you should be able to reason with them if things get out of hand. Mr. McCluskie, on the other hand, is versed in—shall we say, keeping the peace—and that, too, has its place. All things considered, it seems like a good combination."

"Like hell!" Bailey rasped, edging forward in his chair. "You turn him loose with a badge and I guaran-damn-tee you there's gonna be trouble. He's got it in for Texans and everybody knows it."

McCluskie pulled out the makings and started building a smoke. "There's only one Texan I'm on the lookout for, and you're sittin' in his chair."

"You're gonna get it sooner'n you think." Bailey half rose to his feet, then thought better of it and hastily sat down. "That goes for your snot-nosed sidekick, too."

The Irishman fired up his cigarette and took a deep drag. Then he tossed the match aside and smiled, exhaling smoke. "Bailey, you monkey with me and I'll put a leak in your ticker. Any time you think different, you just try me."

Spivey broke in before the Texan could frame an answer. "Now everybody just simmer down. Whatever personal grudge you've got is between you two. But for God's sake, let's keep the peace today. C'mon now, what d'ya say? Do I have your word on that—both of you?"

When neither man responded, the saloonkeeper hurried on as though it were all settled. "Good. Now, Mike, you never did answer my question. What do we do to keep the lid on?"

McCluskie puffed thoughtfully on his cigarette. "Where's the votin' booth? Horner's Store, isn't it?"

"That's right. What with it bein' just north of the tracks, we figured it was handy to everybody concerned."

"Yeah, that sounds reasonable." The Irishman took a swipe at his mustache, mulling some thought a moment longer. "Way I see it, the thing to do is to keep the cowhands from crossin' the tracks in any big bunches. Hazeltine could watch over Horner's, and me and Bailey could patrol opposite sides of the street down on the southside. That way if any trouble starts we could close in on it from three sides. Oughtn't to be that much of a problem if we handle it right."

Hazeltine stiffened in his chair and glared around at Spivey. "Who's callin' the shots here, me or him?"

McCluskie chuckled and flipped his cigarette in the direction of a spittoon. "Tonk, the man just asked for some advice. I wouldn't have the job on a bet."

Spivey nodded vigorously, looking from one to the other. "Course, you're callin' the shots, Tonk. Wouldn't have it any other way. But you'll have to admit, he's got a pretty good idea."

The deputy pursed his lips and shrugged with a great show of reluctance. "Yeah, I guess so. Probably wouldn't hurt none for me to stick close to that votin' booth."

McCluskie wiped his mouth to hide a grin. *Wouldn't hurt none.* What a joke! The sorry devil had been oozing sweat at the thought of patrolling the southside. Holed up in Horner's was just his speed. Likely what he had intended doing all along.

Judge Muse climbed to his feet, smiling affably. "Then it's all settled. Gentlemen, I'm happy to see we've reached an accord. I, for one, have a feeling this is going to be a red-letter day in the history of Newton."

The men pushed out of their chairs, standing, and Bailey's gut gave off a thunderous rumble. Someone suggested breakfast and the others quickly agreed. Despite Randolph Muse's optimistic forecast, they shared a hunch that it wasn't a day to be faced on an empty stomach.

Walking back to the hotel, McCluskie couldn't shake an edgy feeling about Bailey. The man was a loudmouth and a bully, but he was no coward. Not that he wouldn't backshoot somebody if that seemed the best way. He would and probably had. Yet even that took a certain amount of sand, and Bailey had his share.

The Irishman wasn't worried about himself. Characters like Bailey were strictly penny-ante, and there was a certain savor in beating them at their own game. But the threat against the kid was another matter altogether. It was very real, and Bailey had ample reason to want the youngster dead. Making a fool of a hardcase, who had set himself up as bull-of-the-woods, was a risky sport. It could get a man—or a boy—gunned down in a dark alley. Or in bed. Or just about any place where he least expected it.

Thinking of the kid made him chuckle, but it was amusement heavily larded with concern. These days the button was cocky as a young rooster. That he had shaded Bailey on the draw was only part of it. Mostly it had to do with a girl named Sugar, and the fact that she had become his regular girl. Not that she was his alone, but she came as close as she could. Sugar was one of Belle's girls, and Belle was a businesswoman first and last, and even for the kid her generosity had certain limits. After listening to McCluskie's arguments she had agreed to a compromise of sorts. Sugar could see the kid all she wanted on her off time, and so long as he made a definite appointment at night, Belle wouldn't use the girl for the parlor trade. Otherwise Sugar would work the same as usual, which meant that she was the boy's private stock, but only about halfway.

The kid wasn't exactly overjoyed by the arrangement, yet he couldn't help but strut his stuff the least little bit. Sugar had a knack about her, there was no denying that. She had convinced him that he was the only real man in her life, and every time they were together, he came away fairly prancing. What they had wasn't just the way he wanted it, but it was far more than he'd ever had before. Life had dealt him enough low blows so that having Sugar, even on a part-time basis, seemed like a stroke of luck all done up in a fancy ribbon. The way he talked it was as if the bitter and the sweet had finally equaled out. He was happy as a pig in mud, only he couldn't stop wishing the wallow was his alone.

When McCluskie entered the room, he found the kid standing before the mirror, practicing his draw. Every day the boy got a shade faster, but smooth along with it, as though somebody had slapped a liberal dose of grease on a streak of chain-lightning. The Irishman felt a little like God, profoundly awed at what he had wrought.

Kinch saw him in the mirror and turned, holstering the Colt in one slick motion. "Just practicin' a little. I been waitin' breakfast for you."

"Already had mine." McCluskie cocked his thumb and forefinger and gestured at the pistol. "You've got yourself honed down to a pretty fine edge. What's the sense if you won't shoot nothin' but tin cans?"

"Same song, second verse. You're talkin' about Bailey again, aren't you?"

"That'll do for openers."

"Mike, I done told you fifty zillion times. I had him cold. There wasn't no need to shoot him. He was froze tighter'n an icicle."

"There's some men that would've dusted you on both sides while you was standin' there admirin' how fast you were. You try pullin' a fool stunt like that again and the jasper you're facin' might just be the one that proves it to you."

"Okay, professor." The kid smiled and threw up his hands to ward off the lecture. "You don't have to keep beatin' me over the head with it. I got the idea."

"Yeah, but have you got the stomach for it? I've been tellin' you not to wear that gun unless you mean to use it next time. So far you've given me a lot of talk but you haven't said anything."

"Awright, I'm sayin' it. Next time I won't hold off."

McCluskie eyed him skeptically. "Sometimes I think it was a mistake to give you that gun. Might have saved us all a pile of grief."

"You lost me. Where's the grief in me packin' a gun?"

"I just came from a meetin' with the big nabobs." The Irishman hesitated, turning it over in his head, and decided there was nothing to be gained in holding back. "Bailey was there and he started makin' noises about nailin' you. Course, he's been makin' the same brag all over town, so it's not exactly news. But it's past the talkin' stage now. He'll have to make his play soon."

"Aren't you and him gonna be workin' together today?"

"Now what's that got to do with the price of tea?"

"Nothin'. I was just thinkin' I might tag along with you."

McCluskie grunted, shaking his head. "Bud, you're barking up the wrong tree. Bailey knows better than to mess with me. It's you he's after."

"Still wouldn't do no harm."

"Maybe. But we'll never find out. I want you to stick close to the room today. I'll have the cafe send up your meals."

"Aw, cripes a'mighty, Mike. I'm not a kid no more. If he's spoilin' for a fight it might as well be sooner as later."

The Irishman studied him a moment, weighing the alternatives. "No soap. I'll sic you on him when I'm convinced you won't hold off pullin' the trigger. Meantime, you keep your butt in this room. Savvy?"

Kinch spun away and kicked a chair halfway across the room. "Horseapples!"

McCluskie walked to the door, then turned and glanced back. "How's your cough today?"

The kid wouldn't look at him. "Why, you writin' a book or somethin'?"

"Keep your dauber up, sport. There's better days ahead."

The door closed softly behind him and an oppressive silence fell over the room. Kinch flung himself down on the bed and just lay there, staring at the ceiling. Then he felt the first tingle deep down in his throat.

He waited, knotting his fists, wondering what his lungs would spew up this morning.

Shortly after the noon hour Hugh Anderson and his crew rode into town. McCluskie saw them pull up and dismount before the Red Front Saloon, and his scalp went prickly all of a sudden. That explained it. Why things had been so quiet all morning. The Texans crowding the saloons up and down the street had been biding their time. Waiting for the big dog him-self to start the show.

Anderson and his hands were the bane of every cowtown in Kansas. They were wild and loud, ram-bunctious in the way of overgrown boys testing their manhood. Only their pranks sometimes got out of hand, and they had a tendency to see how far a town could be pushed before it stood up and fought back. Their leader was an arrogant young smart aleck, the son of a Texas cattle baron, and he had developed quite a reputation for devising new ways to hooraw Kansas railheads. Worse yet, he fancied himself as something of a gunslinger, and had an absolute gift for provoking senseless shootouts.

McCluskie knew what was coming and headed to-ward the tracks at a fast clip. Crossing Fourth, he scanned the street for Bailey, meaning to give him the high sign, but the Texan was nowhere in sight. Before he could reach the next corner, men began boiling out of saloons and Anderson's crew was quickly joined by another forty or fifty cowhands. There was con-siderable shouting and arm waving, and suddenly the crowd split and everybody raced for their horses. The Irishman jerked his pistol and took off at a dead run.

But he was no match for them afoot, and they thun-dered across the tracks even as he passed the hotel. Townspeople were lined up outside Horner's Store waiting to vote and the Texans barreled down on them like a band of howling Indians. Anderson opened fire first, splintering the sign over the bank, and within moments it sounded as if a full scale war had broken out. Glass shattered, lead whanged through the high false-front structures overhead, and above it all came the shrill Rebel yells of Texans on the rampage.

Most of the town had gathered to watch the balloting, and now they stampeded before the cowhands like scalded dogs. Women clutched their children and ran screaming along the street, while men scattered and leaped into nearby doorways seeking shelter. The Texans made a clean sweep up North Main, laughing and whooping and drilling holes through anything that even faintly resembled a target. Then they whirled their ponies and came charging back toward the tracks.

Tonk Hazeltine made the mistake of stepping out of Horner's Store just at that moment. Had he remained inside the cowhands would probably have kept on going, satisfied that they had taught the Yankee bloodsuckers a lesson. But the sight of a tin star was a temptation too great to resist.

Hugh Anderson skidded his horse to a halt, and the Texans reined in behind him, cloaked in a billowing cloud of dust. Hazeltine stood his ground on the boardwalk, watching and saying nothing as they walked their horses toward him. When they stopped, Anderson hooked one leg over his saddlehorn and grinned, gesturing toward the deputy.

"Well now, looka here what we caught ourselves, boys. A real live peace officer. Shiny badge and all."

The Texans thought it a rare joke and burst out in fits of laughter. Circling around behind them, McCluskie saw the lawman's face redden but couldn't tell if he said anything or not. It occurred to him that Hazeltine was probably too scared to draw his gun. Still, if he could just get the drop on them from behind it might shake the deputy out of his funk. Once they had the cowhands covered front and rear that would most likely put an end to it.

McCluskie raised his pistol but all at once cold steel jabbed him in the back of the neck. With it came the metallic whirr of a hammer being thumbed back and a grated command.

"Unload it, Irish! Otherwise I'll scatter your brains all over Kingdom Come."

One of McCluskie's cardinal rules was that a man never argued with a gun at his head. Slowly, keeping his hand well in sight, he lowered the Colt and dropped it in the street. Then he stood very still.

There was no need to look around. Bill Bailey's voice was one in a hundred. Maybe even a thousand.

With or without a cocked pistol.

ELEVEN

Bailey marched the Irishman forward, nudging him in the backbone every couple of steps with the pistol. The cowhands' attention was distracted from Hazeltine for a moment, and they turned in their saddles to watch this curious little procession. McCluskie looked straight ahead, ignoring their stares, and took his lead from the jabs in his spine. They circled around the skittish ponies and came to a halt before Hugh Anderson.

"What've you got there, Billy?" Anderson was casually rolling himself a smoke. "Another lawdog?"

"He's the one I told you about. Pride and joy of the Santee Fe. Ain't you, Irish?"

McCluskie kept his mouth shut, coolly inspecting Anderson. The Texan was older than he expected. Pushing thirty, with a bulge around his beltline that spoke well of beans and sowbelly and rotgut whiskey. A hard drinker, clearly a man with a taste for the fast life. But for all the lard he was packing, there was nothing soft about him. His face looked like it had been carved out of seasoned hickory, and back deep in his eyes there was a peculiar glint, feverish and piercing.

All of a sudden McCluskie decided to play it very loose. He had seen that look before. Cold and inscrutable, but alert. The look of a man who enjoyed dousing cats with coal oil just to watch them burn.

"McCluskie." The word came out flat and toneless. Anderson flicked a sulphurhead across his saddlehorn and lit the cigarette.

"You're the one that had everybody walkin' on eggshells back in Abilene."

"Yeah, that's him," Bailey crowed. "The big tough Mick. Leastways he thinks he is."

"Bailey, whatever I am," McCluskie observed softly, "I don't switch sides in the middle of a fight."

"He's got you there, Billy." Anderson smiled but there was no humor in his eyes. "Folks hereabouts are gonna start callin' you a turncoat, sure as hell."

"No such thing," Bailey declared hotly. "I just played along, that's all. So's you boys would get the lowdown."

He rammed McCluskie in the spine with the gun barrel. "You smart-mouth sonovabitch, I oughta fix your wagon right now."

Anderson laughed, thoroughly enjoying himself. "Hold off there, Billy. We can't have people sayin' we go around murderin' folks. Besides, I got a better idea." His gaze settled on McCluskie and the odd light flickered a little brighter. "You. Trot it on over there beside jellyguts."

The Irishman's expression betrayed nothing. He walked forward, mounted the boardwalk, and took a

position alongside Hazeltine. The deputy shot him a
nervous glance, but just then he couldn't be bothered.
His attention was focused on Anderson.

The Texans were also watching their leader, not
quite sure what he had in mind. But knowing him,
there was unspoken agreement that it was certain to
be a real gutbuster. Whatever it was.

Anderson just sat there, leg hooked over the saddlehorn, puffing clouds of smoke as he contemplated
the lawmen. People appeared from buildings along
the street and started edging closer, drawn in some
perverse way to the silent struggle taking place in
front of Horner's Store. At last Anderson smiled, nodding to himself, and flipped his cigarette at Hazeltine's feet.

"Let's see how fast you two can shuck out of them
duds." Idly he jerked his thumb toward the southside.
"We're gonna have ourselves a little race. Last one
to hit the town limits gets his head shaved."

The cowhands cackled uproariously, slapping one
another on the back as they marveled at the sheer
artistry of it. Goddamn if Hughie hadn't done it again,
they shouted back and forth. Come up with a real
lalapalooza! On the whole they looked proud as
punch, as if the sentence rendered by Anderson somehow reflected their own good judgment. The jeers and
catcalls they directed at the lawmen made it clear that
they wanted no time lost in getting the show on the
road.

Hazeltine began shaking like a dog passing peach
pits, and it was plain to everyone watching that he
was scared out of his wits. Without his badge to hide
behind, divested of even his clothes, there was no

telling what these crazy Texans would do to him. He
had thought to talk them back over to the southside
once they'd had their fun, but it was obvious now that
he would be lucky to escape with his life. The fear
showed in his face, and not unlike a small child being
marched to the woodshed, he started peeling off his
shirt.

McCluskie just stood there.

Anderson eyed him a moment, then grinned.
"Hoss, you better get to strippin'. Jellyguts there'll
outrun you six ways to Sunday if you try racin' in
them boots."

The Irishman met and held his gaze. "I guess I'll
stand pat."

"Cousin, you don't seem to get the picture. I ain't
offered you a choice. I only told you how it was
gonna be. *Sabe?*"

McCluskie did something funny with his wrist and
a .41 Derringer appeared in his hand, cocked and centered squarely on the Texan's chest. "Your boys
might get me, but I'll pull this trigger before I go
down. What d'ya say, check or bet?"

"Well now, don't that beat all? Got himself a hideout gun." Anderson was laughing but he didn't make
any sudden moves. At that range the Derringer would
bore a hole the size of a silver dollar. "I got to hand
it to you, cousin. You're bold as brass, damned if you
ain't."

"Yeah, but I get nervous when I'm spooked. You
talk much more and this popgun's liable to go off in
your face."

Anderson studied him a couple of seconds, then

shrugged. "What the hell? It wouldn't have been much of a race anyhow."

"Judas Priest, Hugh!" Bailey scuttled forward, waving his pistol like a divining rod. "Don't let him back you down. He's runnin' a sandy. Can't you see that?"

"Bailey, my second shot's for you." McCluskie's voice was so low the Texans had to strain to catch his words. "Keep talkin' and you'll get an extra hole right between your eyes."

"Back off, Billy!" Anderson's command stopped Bailey dead in his tracks. "Trouble with you is you never could tell a bluff from the real article. He's holdin' the goods."

Bailey kicked at a clod of dirt and walked off. After a moment Anderson's mouth cracked in a tight smile. "McCluskie, we'll just write this off to unfinished business. There's always another day. Now, why don't you make tracks before some of my boys get itchy?"

"What about Hazeltine?" the Irishman asked.

"What about him?"

"I thought maybe I'd just take him along with me."

"Don't push your luck, cousin." Anderson scowled and the feverish glow again lighted his eyes. "Our deal don't include him."

When McCluskie hesitated, he laughed. "Mebbe you're thicker'n I thought. You got some notion of gettin' yourself killed over a two-bit marshal?"

McCluskie glanced at the lawman out of the corner of his eye, then shook his head. "Nope. Just figured it was worth a try."

"So you tried," Anderson remarked, dismissing

him with a jerk of his head. "See you in church."

The Irishman stepped off the boardwalk and backed away, keeping Anderson covered as he circled around the milling horses. Once clear, he saw Spivey and Judge Muse standing in the doorway of the Lone Star and made a beeline to join them. Both men looked grim as death warmed over, and at the sight of the Derringer in his hand they paled visibly. While they had caught only snatches of the conversation between Anderson and the Irishman, there was no need to ask questions. It was all too obvious that a killing had been averted by only the slimmest of margins. McCluskie retrieved his pistol from the street and came to stand beside them in the doorway.

Tonk Hazeltine was left the star attraction of the Texans' impromptu theatrical. Accompanied by a chorus of gibes and hooting laughter, he skinned out of his clothing a piece at a time. Shirt, gunbelt, pants, and boots hit the street in rapid succession, and at last he stood before them in nothing but his longjohns and hat. Bare to the waist, he made a ludicrous figure, like some comic scarecrow being ridiculed by a flock of birds. Half-naked, humiliated in the eyes of the townspeople, he had been stripped of much more than his clothes. The reputation he had brought to Newton was gone, vanished in an instant of shame, and with it the last vestiges of his backbone.

He stood alone and cowering, a broken man.

The Texans gave him a head start and choused him south across the tracks at a shambling lope. His hat flew off as he passed the depot and every few steps they dusted his heels with a flurry of gunshots. All along the street the sporting crowd jammed the boardwalks watching in stunned silence as his ordeal was played out to its conclusion. Never once did Hazeltine utter a sound, but his eyes were wild and terror-stricken, and tears sluiced down over his cheeks even as he ran. The last they saw of him, he was limping aimlessly across the prairie, a solitary wanderer on the road to his own private hell.

Anderson and Bailey hadn't joined in the chase. They watched from in front of Horner's Store, seemingly content to let the cowhands share whatever glory remained in the final act. Now, grinning and thoroughly delighted with themselves, they became aware of the three men standing outside the Lone Star. Anderson reined his horse about, with Bailey walking alongside, and they crossed the street. Halting a few paces off, the cattleman gave McCluskie a gloating smile, then turned his attention to Spivey and Muse.

"Gents, it would appear your little metropolis needs itself a new marshal."

Judge Muse bristled and shook his finger at the Texan. "Anderson, you've brought yourself a peck of trouble. That was a deputy sheriff you ran off, which makes this a county matter. Tomorrow at the latest the sheriff himself will be up here with a warrant for your arrest."

"Is that a fact?" Anderson studied him with mock seriousness for a moment, as if amused by the jabber of a backward child. "What would you like to bet that the sheriff don't get within ten miles of Newton?"

Bailey laughed, plainly taken with the idea. "Yeah, he ain't comin' up here to pull your fat out of the

fire. Hell, we'd send him hightailin' in his drawers
the same as Hazeltine."

"Which come election time," Anderson added,
"might look real bad to the voters. Or don't you gents
agree?"

The logic of Anderson's argument was all too persuasive. Spivey and the judge exchanged bemused
glances, and in the look was admission of defeat.
Whatever help there was for Newton wouldn't come
from a sheriff whose bread was buttered by Wichita
voters. The town was on its own, and like storm
clouds gathering in a darkened sky, it was plain for
all to see.

"By damn, it don't end there," Spivey declared.
"We'll just hire ourselves a marshal of our own.
That's what we should've done in the first place."

Anderson leaned forward, crossing his arms over
the saddlehorn. "Now I'm glad you brought that up.
Fact is, I was thinkin' along the same lines myself."

Muse eyed him suspiciously. "I fail to see where
it concerns you."

"That's where you're wrong, judge. Case you don't
know it, me and my boys have got this town treed.
Just offhand, I'd say that gives us quite a voice in
who gets picked as lawdog."

"By any chance," Muse sniffed, "were you thinking of nominating yourself for the job?"

"You got a sense of humor, old man. I like that."
Anderson grinned and dropped his hand on Bailey's
shoulder. "No, the feller I had in mind was Billy here.
With him totin' that badge you'd have a townful of
the friendliest bunch of Texans you ever seen."

Spivey's face purpled with rage. "I'll kiss a pig's

tail before that happens. Newton's not gonna have any back-stabbin' jackleg for a marshal."

Bailey jerked as if stung by a wasp and started forward. "Swizzleguts, I'm gonna clean your plow."

McCluskie had been standing back observing, but now he shifted away from the door. "Bailey, you're liable to start something you can't finish."

The Texan stopped short and his beady eyes narrowed in a scowl. "Big tough Mick, aren't you? Think you're fast enough to take both of us?"

McCluskie smiled, waiting. "There's one way to find out."

Anderson had seen other men smile that way. Cold and taunting, eager somehow, like a hungry cat. The odds didn't suit him and he very carefully left his arms folded over the saddlehorn. Bailey glanced around, suddenly aware that he was playing a lone hand. After a moment he grunted, ripping the deputy badge from his shirt, and flung it to the ground.

"Jam it! I got better things to do anyway."

Everybody stood there and looked at each other for a while and it was finally Anderson who broke the stalemate. "Judge, you and Spivey oughta think it over. Not go off half-cocked, if y'see what I mean. You put that tin star on anybody besides Billy and I got an idea Newton's in for hard times."

Then his gaze fell on the Irishman. "You've braced me twice today. Third time out and your number's up."

McCluskie gave him the same frozen smile. "Don't bet your life on it."

Anderson reined his horse back and rode off toward the southside. Trailing behind, Bailey ambled along like a bear with a sore paw. From the doorway of the Lone Star, the three men watched after them, and at last Spivey let out his breath between clenched teeth.

"Christ!"

Late that afternoon nine men gathered in the small backroom office of the Lone Star. Among them were saloonkeepers, businessmen, one judge, and a blacksmith. They comprised the Town Board, and their chairman, Bob Spivey, had called them into emergency session. None of them questioned why they were there, or that a crisis existed. But as they stood around the smoke-filled room staring at one another, few of the men had any real hope of solving what seemed an insoluble mess.

When the last member arrived, Spivey rapped on his desk for order and stood to face them. "Men, I'm not gonna waste time rehashin' what's happened today. Most of you saw it for yourselves, and them that didn't has heard the particulars more'n once by now. The thing is, we've got ourselves a real stemwinder of a problem, and before we leave here we're gonna have to figure out what to do about it. Otherwise you can kiss the town of Newton good-by. That goes for whatever money you've got invested here, too. Now, instead of me blabberin' on about the fix we've got ourselves in, I'm gonna throw the floor open for discussion. Who's first?"

The men looked around at one another, hesitant to take the lead, and after a moment Randolph Muse cleared his throat. Rising from his chair, he studied each face in turn, as if in the hope of discovering some chink in their stony expressions. Though he had tussled with the problem all afternoon, he had yet to settle on the best approach. They were a disparate group, with conflicting interests and loyalties, and it would be no simple matter to hammer out an accord. Not a man among them could be bullied, and logic was an equation foreign to their character. That narrowed the alternatives considerably. Leaving perhaps only one appeal which might muster some solidarity in what lay before them.

"Gentlemen, what I have to say will be short and straight to the point. Where there is no law all values disappear. Whether on life or on property. Newton was founded on a cornerstone of greed, and I think each of us is honest enough to admit that to ourselves. We came here hoping to make our fortune, and for no other reason. Unless we restore law and order to this town there is every likelihood we will leave here paupers."

He paused, screwing up his most judicious frown. "Without restraints of some sort, the Texans will turn this into one big graveyard long before you can unload your business on some unwary sucker. If you don't believe that, you have only to wait and watch it happen."

Val Gregory lashed out angrily. "That's a lot of hot air. I say give the drovers their way. They're about the only ones that come in my place, and god-damnit, I don't mean to bite the hand that feeds me. You think about it a minute and most of you'll see that you're rowin' the same boat."

Perry Tuttle, the dancehall impresario, readily agreed. But the others evidenced less certainty, muttering and shaking their heads as they tried to unravel what seemed a very tangled web. Seth Mabry, still covered with grime from the smithy, pounded a meaty fist into the palm of his hand.

"No, by God, I don't agree. It's like the judge says. You give in to 'em, and make Bill Bailey marshal, and we'll wind up presidin' over a wake."

"That's right," Sam Horner growled. "Inside of a month they'd tear this town down around our ears."

Charlie Hoff and John Hamil, whose stores were south of the tracks, both chimed in with quick support. That seemed to shift the scales off center, and for a minute everybody just stood around and glared at one another.

Harry Lovett, who operated the Gold Room, finally sounded a note of moderation. "Seems to me we're all after the same thing. It's just a matter of how we get it. Hell, nobody wants to rankle the Texans. Most of my business is with highrollers, but I still turn a nice profit on the cowhands. The long and the tall of it boils down to one thing. We can't operate in a town where every store and saloon and dancehall has to be its own law. That'd be like fightin' a fire with a willow switch. There just wouldn't be no stoppin' it. What we need is somebody the drovers respect. Just between us, I don't think Bailey's the man."

The gambler had presented a convincing argument, and before anyone could object, Bob Spivey came out swinging. "Harry, you hit the nail right on the head. Only I'd take it a step farther. What we need is not so much a man they respect, but a man they're afraid of. We've got the same problem Abilene had, and everybody here knows how they solved it. Bear River

Tom Smith and Wild Bill Hickok. Texans are like any other jackass. You can't reason with 'em and being nice to 'em is a waste of time. You've got to teach 'em that every time they step out of line somebody's gonna get a busted skull. That's the only thing they understand."

The men stared back at him, somewhat dumbstruck by his heated tone. Spivey wasn't a violent man, and when he used words that strong it seemed prudent to weigh them carefully. None of them said anything simply because there was no way to refute his statement. It was all true.

After a while Val Gregory grunted and gave him a wry look. "I suppose you just happen to have a man in mind?"

Spivey walked to the door, yanked it open, and gestured to someone in the saloon. There was a brief wait and a slight stir of expectancy, but it came as no great surprise when McCluskie entered the office.

"Boys, I think you all know Mike McCluskie." Spivey slammed the door, and while everybody was still nodding, he gave them another broadside. "Mike, if we was to appoint you city marshal, how would you go about handlin' the Texans?"

McCluskie saw no reason to mince words. "Same as I would a mean dog. Educate 'em as to who's boss. That'd likely mean some skinned heads, and maybe even some shootin'. But it's the only thing that'd get the job done."

"What about the Santa Fe?" Perry Tuttle asked. "Wouldn't think they'd hold still for you gettin' mixed up in a thing like this."

"I cleared it with 'em this afternoon." The Irishman

nodded at Spivey. "Soon as Bob put it to me I got on the telegraph."

Sam Horner rubbed his jaw and looked thoughtful. "Where would you start? Educatin' the Texans, I mean."

McCluskie smiled. "Best way to kill a snake is to cut his head off."

The room went still and Spivey glanced around at the solemn faces. "Anybody opposed?"

When none of the men offered objection, he pulled out a badge and pinned it to McCluskie's shirt. Then he sighed wearily and a grave smile touched the corners of his mouth.

"Marshal, I guess you better get to killin' snakes."

TWELVE

McCluskie wasted little time. What he had in mind depended not so much on nerve or guts or even luck. It required mainly an element of surprise. The Texans had to be taken off guard, hit fast when they least expected it. But if it was to work he had to make his move before the board members scattered and spread the word. Otherwise the chances of taking Anderson and Bailey unawares would be pretty well eliminated.

While Spivey and the board were still hashing it around, he excused himself and made a hasty exit from the Lone Star. None of them expected anything rash on his part—they were the kind that believed in coppering their bets—and it would never occur to them that he might go the limit strictly on his own hook. That gave him an edge of perhaps a quarter hour, certainly no more. He meant to use it to best advantage.

His advantage.

Turning south, he crossed the tracks past the depot and began checking saloons along the street. His plan

was already formulated, had been since that afternoon, yet he wasn't fooling himself about the risks.
It boiled down to one of two things. Brace Anderson
outright or make an object lesson out of Bailey. The
latter alternative seemed the slicker move. Dusting
Bailey off would serve as warning, and it might just
avert a showdown with Anderson and his crew. That
was something he wanted to avoid if at all possible,
for Anderson had the men and the guns to turn Newton into a battleground. Still, the plan fairly bristled
with danger. There were simply too many unknowns.
If he had guessed wrong, and Anderson decided to
deal himself a hand, the fat was in the fire.

But in the end that's what life was all about. Get
a hunch, bet a bunch. Logic might make a man rich,
but it was no substitute for raw instinct. Not when the
other players carried guns.

A fellow either backed his hunches or he folded
his cards and got out. Yet a man who cultivated the
habit of running really wasn't worth his salt. To himself or anyone else.

Tony Hazeltine had proved that.

McCluskie found what he was looking for in front
of Gregory's Saloon. The hitchrack was crowded with
horses bearing the Flying A brand, and among them
was Anderson's chestnut gelding. Odds were that Bill
Bailey wouldn't be far from his Texan friends on this
night.

The Irishman paused outside the batwing doors and
surveyed the house. Anderson and Bailey were standing shoulder to shoulder at the bar, and the room was
jammed with cowhands. There seemed to be a contest
of sorts taking place. Whoever yelled the loudest got

the floor and tried to top the others with some whopper about the afternoon's chief sporting event. Though they had been at it for some hours, the stories seemed to get better the longer they drank, and there was no dearth of laughter. Apparently Hazeltine's one-man race was the favorite topic, with the stampeded voters running a close second, and every time someone launched into a fresh version it was greeted by raucous shouts from the crowd.

McCluskie slapped the doors open and walked in as if he had just foreclosed on the mortgage. Hardly anyone noticed him at first, but as he crossed the room a ripple of silence sped along before him. When he came to a halt in front of Anderson and Bailey the saloon went still as a graveyard.

Anderson leaned back against the bar and gave Bailey a broad wink. "Well, looka who's here, Billy. The holy terror hisself." Suddenly he blinked drunkenly and peered a little closer. "Goddamn my soul. Billy, I think that's your badge he's wearin'."

"Let's get something straight," McCluskie warned him. "I didn't come here lookin' for trouble with you or your boys. My beef is with Bailey. You stay out of it and we'll just chalk this afternoon up to one for your side."

"Sort of a Mexican standoff."

"Something like that."

"Maybe it don't suit me to let it ride. You're a feller that needs his wick trimmed, 'specially after today."

"Then we can settle it later. Right now all I want is Bailey. Course, you can step in if you like. There's nothin' I can do to stop you. But it's gonna start folks to talkin'."

Bailey finally caught the drift and got his tongue untracked. "Hugh, he's bluffin' again. Can't you see that?"

Anderson's gaze never left the Irishman. "What kind o' talk?"

"Why, the sort of stuff they're already sayin'. That one Texan hasn't got the sand to go up against a lawman by himself."

The saloon went deathly still. Anderson's face turned red as ox blood and for a moment he almost lost his steely composure. Then a tiny bead kindled back deep in his eyes and a crafty smirk came over his mouth. Turning sideways, he leaned into the bar and gave Bailey a speculative look.

"What about it, Billy boy? Think you can haul his ashes?"

Bailey swallowed hard. Every man in the room was watching him and he knew it. They had heard his brag for the past week, and Anderson's question now made it a matter of fish or cut bait.

"Hell, yes, I can take him. Won't hardly be no contest at all."

McCluskie moved while he had the advantage. "Bailey, you've got your choice. Get out of town or go to the lockup."

"Lockup? You're talkin' through your hat. I ain't broke no law."

"You were deputized and you broke your oath. That's good for about six months accordin' to Judge Muse."

Bailey's lip curled back and he launched himself

off the bar. Whiskey had given him a measure of false courage but it hadn't clouded his judgment. Somewhere deep in his gut he knew that if he touched his gun the Irishman would kill him. But in a rough and tumble scrap it might just go the other way. He was bigger and stronger and he'd never yet lost a barroom brawl. Nor did he intend to lose this one. Hurtling forward, he let go a haymaker that would have demolished a stone church.

Except that it never landed. McCluskie slipped under the punch and buried his fist in the Texan's crotch. Back in Hell's Kitchen, one of New York's grimier slums, Irish youngsters were educated at an early age in the finer points of survival. What he didn't know about dirty fighting hadn't yet been written. Though he would have preferred to kill Bailey, he felt a certain grim satisfaction that it was to be settled with fists.

The Texan jackknifed at the middle, and as his head came down McCluskie's knee met it in a mushy crunch. Bailey reeled backward, his mouth and nose spurting blood, but he didn't go down. He was hurt bad, blinded by a chain of explosions that felt like a string of firecrackers inside his skull. Yet, in the way of a wounded beast, the pain only compounded his rage. Spitting teeth and bright wads of gore, he waded in again, flailing the air with a windmill of punches.

McCluskie gave ground, ducking some of the blows, warding off others. But he was hemmed in on all sides by shouting cowhands and there was no way of avoiding the burly Texan altogether. The air suddenly seemed filled with knuckles and for every punch he slipped past another sledgehammered off his head. With no room to maneuver, he had little choice but to absorb punishment and wait for an opening. His eyebrow split under the impact of a meaty fist and blood squirted down over his face. All at once it dawned on him that he was in grave danger. If he ever went down Bailey would stomp him to death, and the longer the fight lasted the more likely it was to happen. He had to end it fast or there was every chance he wouldn't end it at all. Operating now on sheer reflex, he stopped thinking and let his body simply react.

Shifting and dodging, he feinted with a left hook and suckered the Texan into a looping roundhouse right. The blow grazed past his ear and he slipped under Bailey's guard. Setting himself, he put his weight behind a whistling right that caught the other man squarely in the Adam's apple. Bailey's mouth flew open in a strangled gasp and his lungs started pumping for air. Both hands went to his throat and he doubled over, wretching in a hoarse, grating sound as he sucked for wind. McCluskie stepped back, planted himself, and kicked with every ounce of strength he possessed. The heel of his boot collided with Bailey's chin and the big man hurtled backward as if shot from a cannon. Cowhands scattered in every direction as the Texan went head over heels through the batwing doors and collapsed in a bloody mound on the boardwalk. Like a great whale snatched from the ocean's depths, he gave a blubbery sigh and lay still.

He was out cold.

McCluskie retrieved his hat, jammed it on his head, and somehow made it to the door without fall-

ing. He slammed one wing of the door open and
leaned against it for support, inspecting the battered
hulk with the cold, practiced eye of a mortician. Then
he turned, glowering back at the crowd until his gaze
came to rest on Anderson.

"When he comes to, give him the word. If he's not
out of town in two hours he goes in the lockup."

The door swung shut behind him and he lurched
off in the direction of the hotel. Except that he was
walking, he would have sworn that somebody had just
beaten the living bejesus out of him. Even his hair
felt sore.

Kinch was stretched out on the bed with his hands
locked behind his head. When McCluskie entered the
room he gave him a sullen glance and looked away.
Then it hit him, and he sat bolt upright, staring slack-
jawed at the Irishman's eyebrow. The cut itself was
crusted over with dried blood and didn't look so bad.
But a knot the size of a hen egg had swollen his brow
into an ugly, discolored lump.

McCluskie gave him a tight grin and headed for
the washstand. "You're gonna catch lots of flies if you
leave your mouth hangin' open."

The kid's clicked shut and he bounded out of bed.
"Holy jumpin' catfish! What'd you do, butt heads
with a steam engine?"

"Just about. Closest thing on two legs anyhow."

McCluskie sloshed water into a washbowl and then
dampened one end of a towel. Inspecting himself in
the mirror, he understood why the kid looked so startled. The lump over his left eye was the color of rotten
squash and a jagged split laid bare the ridgebone

along his brow. It was a souvenir he wouldn't soon forget. The same as his busted nose and scars from other fights. From the looks of this one, though, it would turn out to be a real humdinger.

After squeezing the towel out he began scrubbing caked blood off his face and mustache. The wound itself he left untouched. It had stopped bleeding and the flesh seemed pretty well stuck in place. Washing it now would only start the whole mess bubbling again. Ugly as it was, it would have to do for the moment.

Kinch came around and took a closer look at the cut. For a while he just stared, saying nothing, then he whistled softly under his breath. "Mike, that's clean down to the bone. Doc Boyd's the one that oughta be workin' on it, not you."

McCluskie grunted, swabbing dried blood out of his ear. "I'll let him patch me up later."

"Yah, but cripes, that thing needs stitchin'. You're hurt worse'n you think."

"Bud, I can't spare the time now. It'll have to wait."

The boy glanced at him in the mirror, struck by a sudden thought. "It was Bailey, wasn't it?"

"All five hundred pounds of him."

"What happened?"

"He beat the crap out of me, that's what happened. I finally got in a lucky punch and put him to sleep."

"C'mon, I'll bet there weren't no luck to it at all. You could take him with one hand strapped down."

The Irishman met his gaze in the mirror. "Much as I hate to admit it, that's one bet you'd lose."

Kinch blinked a couple of times, clearly amazed. "Tougher'n you thought he was?"

"Well, let's just say he wasn't exactly what you'd call a creampuff. Fact is, if I had it to do over, I'd sooner fight a real live gorilla. Probably stand a better chance all the way round."

"Quit funnin' me. You whipped him, didn't you?"

"Just barely, sport. Just barely."

McCluskie stripped off his shirt and tossed it in a corner. Crossing the room, he opened a dresser drawer and selected a fresh shirt. His arms and chest were covered with splotchy bruises from the pounding he'd taken, and every movement was a small agony in itself. Slipping into the shirt even made him wince, but as he turned back to the kid he forced himself to smile.

"Never seen it fail. Clean shirt and a little birdbath and it'll make a new man out of you every time."

"Malarkey!" Kinch obviously wasn't convinced. "The way that eye's puffed out, I'd say you need a sawbones more'n anything else."

"All in good time, bud. There's a few things that still need tendin' before I call it a night."

"You mean Bailey? I thought you said you whipped him."

"Some folks might give you an argument on that." McCluskie finished buttoning his shirt and began tucking it in his pants. "Thing is, I posted him out of town. Now I've got to make it stick."

The boy gave him a look of baffled aggrievement. "You knew it was gonna happen, didn't you? Even before you went down and talked with Spivey and his bunch, you knew you was gonna take that badge and go after Bailey and then start cleanin' house on the Texans. That's the way you had it figured all along, wasn't it?"

"Yeah, I guess it was. So what, though? You're talkin' like it was some skin off your nose."

"Damn right it is! You got me locked up in this room instead of lettin' me pitch in and help. That ain't my idea of what friends are for."

"Don't say ain't."

"Aw, horseapples. I'm serious and you're standin' there grinnin' like it was some kinda joke."

"Nope, it's a long ways from being a joke. Fact is, things are gettin' sorrier and sorrier. Regular as clockwork, too."

"You're gonna go lookin' for Bailey tonight, aren't you?"

McCluskie smiled and shook his head. "Most likely he's already left town. I'll just sashay around a while and see what's what."

"I'm goin' with you," Kinch announced.

"Some other time, bud. Tonight's liable to get a little dicey."

"Goddamnit, Mike, you got no call to treat me that way. I don't need nobody to wipe my nose. That's what you said, wasn't it? Out here a man's got to look after himself. Well I'm as fast as you are and I'm near about as good a shot, too."

"There's more to it than that. I've told you before, tin cans don't shoot back."

"Yeah? Well what if you go lookin' for Bailey and them drovers back his play? Where'll you be then?"

"That's the luck of the draw. A man has got to play whatever hand he's dealt. But that don't change nothin'. Like it or lump it, you're still not invited."

Kinch's eyes went watery all of a sudden, like a scolded child, and it was all McCluskie could do not to reach out and touch him. The kid was right. He didn't need anyone to wipe his nose. But for all the wrong reasons.

The last couple of days had been the hardest of the Irishman's life. After considerable self-examination he'd decided he didn't like what he saw in himself. Or what he'd done to the kid. Before he got to Newton, Kinch had been a decent, God-fearing youngster. Raised up proper, taught right from wrong. Innocent as a lamb if a man got down to brass tacks. Now he had himself a gun and somebody had showed him how to use it. Worse than that, though, he no longer had any qualms about using it. That *somebody* had drilled him so good he was all primed and ready to pop. Like a puppy that had been fed raw meat and gunpowder till he just couldn't wait to bust out and kill the first thing that moved.

Not that he wanted to kill anybody. Or even liked the idea. But just so he could prove to his teacher that he was everything a man ought to be. Cold and unfeeling and pitiless. The badge of manhood that had been drilled into him by someone who saw life at its very elemental worst.

The quick and the dead.

McCluskie wasn't proud of himself. Not any longer. He hadn't done the kid any favors, and that was an itch he'd have to learn to live with. But it was no longer just a matter of the kid killing someone. It had worked down to someone wanting to kill the kid. That was the one thing he wouldn't allow to happen.

However much he had to hurt the boy's feelings.

Watching him now, McCluskie made it even stronger. "Let's get it straight. You don't budge out of this room tonight. Got me?"

"Aw, c'mon, Mike." Kinch's look changed from one of hurt to disappointment. "I got a date with Sugar."

"What time?"

"Eight. I set it up with Belle yesterday."

The Irishman flipped out his pocket watch and gave it a quick check. "Okay. Just to Belle's and nowhere else. I'll walk you down there, but I want you to leave that gun here."

"Cripes a'mighty, don't you never give up? How am I gonna look out for myself if you make me walk around naked?"

McCluskie was forced to agree. It was just possible that Bailey hadn't left town. That he might be laying for the kid somewhere, hopeful of settling at least one score before he made tracks. Even with a gun the kid would be in a bad fix. Without it he wouldn't have the chance of a snowball in hell.

"You got a deal. But remember, just Belle's. Nowhere else. Okay?"

Kinch grinned and gave him a shrug more elaborate than words.

After dropping the kid off at Belle's the Irishman headed for Hide Park. He hadn't spotted any of Anderson's horses along the street, which meant the Texan and his crew had probably adjourned to the sporting houses. Wherever they were that's where Bailey would be. If he was still in town. Oddly enough, he halfway wished Bailey had lit out for parts unknown. It would set his mind at rest about the kid.

But it wasn't a hope he meant to stake his life on. Wherever possible he stuck to the shadows, passing lighted windows quickly, without bothering to peek inside. Hitchracks were what interested him, and at the corner of Second and Main, he found what he was looking for. The same bunch of Flying A cow ponies, Anderson's chestnut included, standing hipshot in front of Tuttle's Dancehall.

Nearing the entrance, he slowed and moved up cautiously. If Bailey was inside he wanted to know precisely where, and more importantly, the best way to approach him. Otherwise, it was walk in blind and take a chance on getting his head shot off. Edging closer to the door, he stuck his head around the corner and slowly scanned the dancehall. Anderson's men were plainly visible, stomping and howling as they swung the dollar-a-dance girls around the floor. But Bailey himself was nowhere in sight.

Then, as his gaze swept the room once more, the door frame above his head splintered and an instant later he heard the snarl of a slug. Dropping and rolling, he came up on one knee as another shot chunked into the wall behind him. He saw Bailey across the street, scuttling along the boardwalk, firing as he ran. McCluskie drew a bead, waiting, enjoying it. The bastard had set him up like a duck in a shooting gallery. And it would have worked, slick as a whistle, except that the numbskull couldn't shoot worth a lick.

When Bailey silhouetted himself against the window of Krum's Dancehall, the Irishman opened fire. The first slug nailed him in his tracks, and the next two sent him crashing through the window in an explosion of sharded glass. When he collapsed on the floor inside only the soles of his boots were visible over the windowsill.

McCluskie uncoiled and came to his feet. There was considerable commotion inside Krum's and the thought of it made him chuckle. It wasn't every day that a dead man came sailing through the window. Not even in Hide Park. He was halfway across the street when the kid's voice rang out in a hard, businesslike growl.

"Hold it! First man that moves gets drilled."

The Irishman wheeled around, dropping low in a crouch as he brought the Colt to bear. Hugh Anderson and most of his crew were framed in the spill of light from the doorway of Tuttle's. Bunched together, they stood still as church mice, looking pretty sheepish in the bargain. Kinch had them covered from the side, over near the corner of the building.

McCluskie didn't know whether to laugh or curse. Somehow neither one seemed appropriate, so instead he just shook his head in mild wonderment. Plain to see, the kid had snuck out of Belle's and covered his back the whole time he was pussyfooting down the street. Like as not, the little wiseacre had it planned all along. But it proved one thing nobody was likely to question any more.

The kid had grit, clean through.

Chuckling to himself, McCluskie turned and started back across the street.

"Keep 'em covered, bud. I'll have a looksee and

make sure our friend is out of his misery."

Kinch just grinned and kept his pistol trained on the Texans. There wasn't any need to answer.

It had all been said.

THIRTEEN

McCluskie got the word over his second cup of coffee. Seated in the kitchen, watching Belle slap together some bacon and eggs, he was congratulating himself on last night's little fracas. It had been a nice piece of work. Bailey laid out on a slab and the Texans sent packing. That was one Anderson and his boys could paste in their hats and think about while they were out herding cows. Letting a slick-eared kid get the drop on them. They'd be a long time living that down.

Sweet Jesus! It was a sight to warm a man's heart. The way the kid had stood there, grinning, holding that Colt steady as a rock. Just like if someone had run up and primed his pump, he'd have hauled off and spouted a pail of ice water. Nervy didn't hardly describe it. The kid was ironclad and brass-bound. More guts than a bulldog with a new bone.

The thought brought his mind back to Belle. Last night had been something extraordinarily special. Maybe she was so glad he'd come out alive she just naturally put her heart into it. But whatever the reason, he felt like he'd been put through the wringer and hung out to dry. The lady knew what pleasured a man, and she flat turned into a wildcat once she came unwound.

Like this breakfast. Belle Siddons hadn't cooked a meal in all the time he'd known her. Hell, maybe never. But here she was, bustling around the kitchen, cursing every time the bacon grease spit the wrong way, determined to make this a very special day for him. All because he'd come through last night with his hide still intact.

He smiled and suddenly winced, reminded that his hide wasn't exactly intact after all. The swelling over his eye had gone down a bit, but he could scarcely stand to blow his nose. If he ever sneezed, he was a goner for sure.

That was more of Belle's doing. Pitching a fit till he'd agreed to let Doc Boyd stitch him back together. That old quack had the touch of a butcher, and with a needle he was nothing short of a menace. Still, the eyebrow was back in one piece, and seemed to be healing, so he had little room for complaint. Actually, he couldn't blame anybody but himself.

He should've learned to duck better.

Reflecting on that bit of wisdom, he had just started on a second cup of coffee when the kid burst through the door. He was breathing hard, as if he'd been running, and as he slammed to a halt before the table it suddenly caught up with him. He began to choke and a moment later his lungs gave way. McCluskie grabbed a bottle of whiskey and in between coughs forced a jigger down his throat. The liquor took hold slowly, trickling down through his system, and after a few more heaves and shudders, the spasm petered out. Gulping wind, blinking furiously to clear his eyes, the kid began sputtering in a hoarse, wheezing rattle.

"Slow down, goddamnit!" McCluskie barked. "The world's not comin' to an end. Just take your time, for chrissakes."

His gruff tone brought a withering look from Belle, but she didn't say anything. Bacon and eggs now forgotten, she moved around the table and eased Kinch into a chair. The boy nodded, still sucking air, and made a game attempt at smiling. Presently his color returned, and he seemed to have caught his breath, but his voice was still shaky.

"Mike, they're after you. It's all over town." He gasped and took another long draught of wind. "Soon as I walked into the cafe ever'body and his brother started givin' me the lowdown."

"Bud, you're not makin' sense. Who's after me?"

"The Texans. That's what I'm tryin' to tell you. They sent word in this mornin'."

"What d'ya mean, sent word? Who to?"

"I don't know. But it's all up and down the street. They aim to run you out of town or kill you. Cause of what you did to Bailey."

"Now is that a fact?" McCluskie tilted back in his chair and pulled out the makings. "Y'know, I always heard that pound for pound a Texan would assay out to about nine parts cowdung. Maybe we'll just find out before the day's over."

"You thickheaded Mick!" Belle squawled. "That's

just what you'd do, isn't it? Sit there and wait for them to come kill you."

"Cripes, Belle, what d'ya want him to do?"

Kinch gave her the look men reserve for hysterical women. "He can't back down or his name'd be mud."

"Sport, you hit it right on the head!" The Irishman slammed his fist on the table so hard his coffee mug bounced in the air. "Once a man runs he's got to keep on runnin'. You mark what I tell you. Them Texans are all hot air and taffy. Anybody that gets hisself in a swivel over that needs his head examined."

"Men!" Belle stamped her foot and glared down on them. "There's no end to it, is there? Just have to go on proving how tough you are."

McCluskie put a match to his cigarette and gave her a wry grin. "Belle, I don't like to bring it up, but you're burnin' my breakfast to a cinder."

Belle screeched and turned back to the stove. Kinch and the Irishman exchanged smiles as she commenced slinging smoking skillets in every direction. Just then the door banged open and Dora, the colored maid, came rushing in. The whites of her eyes were flared wide and she was waving a scrap of paper in her hand.

"Miz Belle! Miz Belle! Some man near broke the door in an' tol' me to give this to Mistah Mike. Said it was a mattah o' life and death."

Sugar raced into the kitchen before the others had time to collect their wits. "What's all the commotion about? Honest to Christ, Dora, you could wake the dead." All of a sudden she stopped and glanced around uneasily. "Well land o' Goshen, why is everybody staring at me like that?"

McCluskie took the piece of paper from Dora's hand and unfolded it. Inside was a scrawled message, and as he started reading the others scarcely dared to breathe. Finished, he flipped it on the table and let go with a sour grunt.

"Seems like Mr. Spivey has called a meetin' of the Town Board. Says for me to get up there pronto."

The room went still as a tomb and everyone just stared at him for a moment. Sugar gave a rabbity little sniff and wandered over behind Kinch. She leaned down and put her arms around his neck.

"Sweetie, what's going on? Everybody looks like they've just come from a wake."

Kinch took her hands and drew her down closer, but he kept his eyes on the Irishman. After a while McCluskie climbed to his feet and gave Sugar a grim smile. "Little lady, you're pretty close to right. Only thing is, the wake's just gettin' started."

"Sure'n begorra, the great Mick has spoken." Belle shot him a scathing look. "Now why don't you take a peek in your crystal ball and tell us who the corpse will be."

"Why Belle, that's simple," McCluskie grinned. "He'll be wearin' big jingly spurs and a ten-gallon hat, and after they kick all the dung out of him, they're gonna bury him in a matchbox."

"Very funny," Belle snapped. "I suppose you do song and dance, too."

"Just on request. Weddings and funerals and such. But in your case, I'll make an exception. Like tonight, maybe."

He chucked her under the chin, still smiling, and headed for the door. Then, struck by a sudden thought, he turned and looked back. "Say, you still keep a greener around the house?"

Belle stiffened and her eyes went wide with alarm. "What—what do you want with a shotgun?"

"Why, hell's bells, I didn't get no breakfast, that's what. Thought I might scare up a covey of birds on my way uptown."

"With buckshot?"

"There's all kinds of birds, honey. Some are just bigger'n others, that's all."

Belle moved past him without a word and stepped into the hall. She opened the door of a linen closet, reached inside, and pulled out a sawed-off shotgun. When she returned, McCluskie took it from her, broke it open, and checked the loads. Satisfied, he snapped it shut and thumbed the hammers back to half-cock. Looking up, he smiled, trying to lighten the moment.

"Jesus, I hope you never have to shoot this thing. With what you weigh a ten-gauge would knock you on your keester."

Her eyes went glassy with tears and she turned away. The others watched on in frozen silence, struck dumb by the Irishman's jovial manner. Sugar and Dora couldn't make heads or tails of the whole affair, but the look on Belle's face sent cold shivers racing through them. The girl clutched tighter at Kinch, as if some unseen specter might suddenly snatch him away.

The kid pushed her hands off and started to rise. Then he caught McCluskie's eye and slumped back in his chair. "I guess I don't have to ask. You want me to stay here and suck my thumb."

"Sport, you're gettin' to be a regular mind reader."

The Irishman smiled, but there was something hard about his eyes. "If that's not plain enough, lemme give it to you straight. You pull another stunt like last night and I'll swap ends on this scattergun and paddle your rump. Savvy?"

Without so much as a backward glance, he wheeled about and marched off down the hall. The sound of his footsteps slowly faded and moments later they heard the front door slam shut.

Kinch just sat there, grinding his teeth in quiet fury, while Sugar stroked his hair with the soft, fluttering touch of a small bird.

The shotgun didn't draw a crowd, but all along the street people rubbernecked and gawked as if the circus had come to town. McCluskie's appearance brought them out of stores and saloons like flies to honey, and as he strode past they gathered in buzzing knots to discuss this latest wrinkle. Word of the Texans' threat had spread through town only within the last hour, but already the gamblers were giving six-to-five that the Irishman wouldn't run. His tight-lipped scowl, and the double-barreled greener, seemed to reinforce those odds substantially.

Far from running, it appeared McCluskie had declared war.

The sensation created by his passage left the Irishman grimly amused. There was nothing quite like a killing, or better yet the chance of a massacre, to bring the fainthearts out of their holes. Not that they wanted to risk their own necks, or in any way get involved. They just wanted to watch. It spoke eloquently of man's grubby character.

But while he ignored the townspeople, Mc-

Cluskie's eyes were busy scanning the street. Oddly enough, the hitchracks stood empty and there wasn't a cowhand in sight. That in itself was a sign. More ominous, perhaps, than the warning delivered to Spivey.

Passing Hamil's Hardware, he noted that the doors were locked, and at the next corner Hoff's Grocery was also closed. Plain to see, the buzzards had come to roost at their favorite watering hole. Probably squawking and bickering among themselves while they waited for him to rout the bogeyman and lay all ghosts to rest.

Cursing fools and fainthearts alike, he crossed the tracks and headed for the Lone Star.

When he came through the door of Spivey's office the talk ground abruptly to a halt. The room was filled with smoke, and a sense of something queer, not as it should be, suddenly came over him. The men gathered there stared at him with eyes that were flat and guarded, and as his gaze touched their faces, he saw part of it. Apprehension and alarm and maybe even a little panic. Yet there was something more. Something he couldn't quite put his finger on. Mistrust, perhaps, or just a tinge of hatred. Whatever it was, it eluded him, and for the moment he set it aside. He shut the door but advanced no farther into the room. Someone coughed, and as if the spell had been broken, he nodded to Spivey, who was seated behind the desk.

"I got word you wanted to see me."

"Well, not just me, Mike." Spivey smiled and waved his hand at the others. "The boys here thought you ought to sit in on this. Sort of kick it around and see where we stand."

The rest of the men looked glum as undertakers, and Spivey's smile was far short of convincing. McCluskie felt the hair come up on the back of his neck. "Kick what around?"

"This goddamn mess you've got us in!" Perry Tuttle snarled. "What the hell'd you think we'd be meetin' for?"

The Irishman looked him over with a frosty scowl. "Mister, lemme give you some advice. Talk to me civil or don't talk to me at all. Otherwise you'll wind up with a sore head."

"Judas Priest, what'd I just get through tellin' you not ten minutes ago?" Val Gregory threw his cigar to the floor and glared around at the other men. "You can't say *boo* to him without gettin' your skull caved in. Or shot dead. Hell, it's no wonder the Texans are on the warpath."

"Gentlemen, please!" Judge Muse stepped to the center of the room, motioning for silence. "We have enough trouble on our hands without fighting among ourselves."

"You can say that again," Sam Horner muttered. "What beats me is why you go on jabbering about Texans. Newton's dead as a doornail anyway." His glance flicked around to the Irishman. "Case you haven't heard, we lost the referendum. Wichita will get its railroad."

Everyone fell silent, watching for his reaction. He let them stew for a minute, then pursed his lips. "Sorry to hear it."

"Yeah, sure," Perry Tuttle rasped, "we can see you're all broken up."

"Tuttle, I warned you once. Don't make me do it again."

"For Chrissakes, can't you fellas stick to one problem at a time?" Harry Lovett sounded as exasperated as he looked. "That railroad's a year down the line. Today's right now, and I'm a sonovabitch, it seems to me we ought to be thinkin' about the Texans."

"You're right, Harry. Dead right." Spivey looked over at the Irishman, but he was no longer smiling. "Mike, we got ourselves some powerful trouble this time. Anderson sent one of his boys in with a message. Short and sweet and to the point. Either you're on the noon train or they'll kill you and burn Newton down to the ground. I don't think they're foolin' either."

McCluskie shrugged, his expression wooden, almost detached. "Maybe. Leastways they might try. But they won't get very far."

"What makes you so sure?"

"This." McCluskie raised the shotgun, and in the closely packed room it was like looking down a cannon. "Double-ought at close range has a way of discouragin' a man."

"Who're you kiddin'?" Gregory inquired acidly. "Puttin' a couple of loads of buckshot into that crowd'd be like spittin' on a brush fire. Hell, there'll be a hundred of 'em. Maybe more."

"So you can hire yourself a new marshal. Thing is, they won't do nothin' to the town. That'd bring the army down on 'em, and not even Anderson's that dumb."

Judge Muse hawked and cleared his throat. "Mike, I'm afraid that's a risk some of these men feel they can't afford to take."

McCluskie sensed it again, the queer feeling that had come over him when he'd entered the room. "Care to make that a little plainer?"

"Yes, I suppose it's time. Understand, there is nothing personal in this. It's just that we have to consider what is best for the town."

Spivey broke in. "Mike, what he's tryin' to say is that we're between a rock and a hard place. If we keep you on, the Texans are gonna pull this town up by the roots."

McCluskie gave him a corrosive stare. "What you're sayin' is that I'm fired—"

"Now I didn't say that, Mike."

"—and if I don't hightail it you'll throw me to the wolves."

"Damnit, you're puttin' words in my mouth. Fact is, I don't know what we'd do without you. We're damned if we do and damned if we don't."

"If you wanted another Tonk Hazeltine that's what you should've hired." The Irishman tapped the badge on his shirt. "As long as I'm wearin' this it's up to me to pull the fat out of the fire. I'll handle Anderson and his bunch my own way. You boys just get yourselves a good seat and sit back and watch. It'll be worth the price of admission."

He turned to leave but the judge's voice brought him up short. "Mike, before you go, let me ask you one question. You have every right to get yourself killed. That's your privilege. But if you face that mob of Texans other people will get caught in the crossfire.

Now, do you really want the blood of innocent bystanders on your hands? Won't you agree that's rather
a high price to pay for one man's pride?"

McCluskie just glared at him and after a moment
the judge smiled. "I suspect you're too decent a man
to take that chance. And it's not like you were running. I mean, after all, once things have calmed down
there's nothing to stop you from coming back."

"Judge, that's the trouble with this world. There's
too many runners and not enough stayers. Looks to
me like it's time somebody drew the line."

The door opened and closed, and the men were left
to ponder that cryptic observation. Nobody said anything, but as the silence deepened they found it difficult to look one another in the eye.

Belle gave a little start and jumped from her chair as
he entered the parlor. Kinch and Sugartit also came
to their feet, but none of them said a word. The dark
rage covering his face was unlike anything they had
ever seen, frightening in the way of a man touched
by the sun. He stalked across the room and halted in
front of Belle, thrusting the greener at her.

"Guess I won't be needing this after all."

"I don't understand." She took the shotgun, staring
at him numbly. "What happened?"

"Spivey and the Judge just informed me that they
don't want a war. Seems like Anderson sent word for
me to be on the noon train and that bunch uptown
don't know whether to blink or go blind."

Belle clapped her hands with delight. "Then you're
leaving! You're really leaving."

"Hell, no, I'm not leavin'. Wild horses couldn't get

me out of here now. I'm just gonna give 'em a little war instead of a big one."

"Oh, God." She seemed to wilt and slumped back into her chair. "There's just no end to it. No end."

She let go of the shotgun and McCluskie grabbed it before it hit the floor. "That's where you're wrong. I mean to end it once and for all. Anderson's about to find out he treed the wrong town."

He hefted the greener, studying it a moment, then laid it across the table. "If I meet 'em without this, I've got an idea I can keep it between him and me. Thought it all out on the way back down here. That way Spivey and his bunch will just get that little war I was talkin' about."

"Mike McCluskie, you're a fool." Belle's lip trembled and she looked on the verge of tears. "Do you know that? A stubborn, thickheaded fool!"

Over her shoulder he saw the kid watching him intently and he smiled. "Well, it takes all kinds. Course, the nice part about being a fool—"

"—is that they walk in where angels fear to tread." Belle gave him a withering look. "Isn't that what you started to say?"

The kid blinked a couple of times, as if he couldn't believe what he was hearing. "Cripes a'mighty, he can't just take off like a scalded cat. Them Texans would be tellin' it all over that they scared him out of town. Then where'd he be?"

"Kinch Riley, you stop that!" Belle snapped. "He'd be alive, that's where he would be. If he doesn't get on that train they'll kill him. Is that what you want?"

"Stay out of it, Belle." McCluskie shot her a harsh look, then glanced back at the kid. "You're right, sport. Sometimes a fella does a thing just because it needs doing. That's what separates the men from the boys. Knowin' when to stop talkin' and get down to business. That's the kind of lingo Anderson will understand."

Belle uttered a small groan and sunk lower in her chair. "Talk never killed anybody. Or running either. If you weren't so pigheaded, you'd see that."

"Better a live coward"—McCluskie grinned—"isn't that how it goes?"

She turned away from him and began dabbing at her eyes with a handkerchief. Sugartit moved up behind the chair and laid a comforting hand on her shoulder. The Irishman stood there a moment, aware now that he'd gone too far with the jest. Then he glanced up and saw a look of fierce pride in the kid's eyes, and suddenly it was all right.

"Like I said, it's a thing that needs doing."

FOURTEEN

Newt Hansberry waited on the platform as the evening train rolled to a halt. This was the last train of the day, and the station master felt a weary sense of relief that it was only an hour late. All too often it was midnight or later before he closed the depot, and he was grateful for any small favors the Santa Fe passed along. Hansberry waved to the conductor as he stepped off the first passenger coach, then turned and headed toward the express car. Once he had the mailbag locked away he could call it a day and begin thinking about himself for a change. Heading the list was a good night's sleep, something that had been rare as hen's teeth since he took over in Newton.

Out of the corner of his eye Hansberry saw something that suddenly made him forget late trains and mailbags and even his weary bones. He wheeled around and peered intently toward the street. Just for a moment he thought his eyes were playing tricks on him. The flickering light from the station lamps was poor at best, and shadows often fooled a man into seeing things that weren't there. Then he took a closer look and grunted. What he saw wasn't imagination, and it had nothing whatever to do with shadows. It was the real article. A yard wide and big as life.

The station master couldn't seem to collect his wits, and he just stood there as the Irishman crossed the tracks and headed toward the southside. Before he could call out it was too late. McCluskie melted into the darkness at the end of the platform and vanished from sight. Hansberry blinked and rubbed his eyes, looking again. There was something spooky about it. Like waking from a dream bathed in sweat. Yet there was nothing unreal about this, or the sudden chill that swept along his backbone. It was just damned hard to accept, and perhaps frightening in a way he didn't wholly understand.

McCluskie got much the same reaction from people he passed on the street. Particularly the Texans. They stopped, hardly able to credit their eyes, and stared after him with a look of bemused disbelief. That he hadn't quit and run, boarding the noon train, they could accept. Some of them, the ones with gumption, liked to believe they would have done likewise. But that he was out prowling the streets—fully aware of what he faced—was beyond reason. The act of a man who had crossed the line separating foolhardiness from common ordinary horse sense.

Angling across Main, McCluskie hesitated before the hotel and then walked on. With everybody staring at him like he was some kind of tent show freak, he wasn't about to give them that satisfaction. They could guess and be damned, but his reasons for staying were his own. He meant to keep it that way.

The baffled expression of everyone along the street gave him a moment of sardonic amusement. Before the night was out they would have talked themselves dry trying to put a label on it. But they wouldn't even come close, and in a grim sort of way, it made everything easier knowing he had them stumped. Most of them would chalk it up to lunacy or pride, and they weren't far wide of the mark. Perhaps, after all, it did take a certain brand of madness to stand and fight. To shoulder the burden of an entire town and accept the responsibility of the cheap piece of tin pinned on his shirt.

But there was a simpler truth, one not so readily apparent, and only after considerable thought had he seen it for what it was. *Each man in his own way feared certain things worse than he feared death itself.* The lucky ones were never forced to take that close a look at themselves, and what it was they feared most went to the grave with them. The vagaries of fate being what they were, McCluskie hadn't been that fortunate.

He had found his secret fear in the eyes of a kid.

That revelation had come hard, after searching his innermost self with a fine probe. Somehow it was all jumbled together. The town and the kid. Since the war he hadn't given a tinker's damn for anyone or any place. A nomad answerable to no one but himself, with no ties to bind him and no obligations he couldn't sever on the whim of the moment. Now, after grappling with it most of the day, he knew that it was only partly pride, and an even smaller sense of duty, which had prompted him to goad the Town Board. To back them into a corner and force them to let him stay and fight their fight. Underneath it all, perhaps overshadowing his own flinty pride, was the kid. That was the part which had come clear and crystal bright.

Quitters finished last.

Kinch had proved that in the siege with his own special devil. After all that had passed between them, McCluskie could do no less. The look he'd seen in the kid's eyes, exultant at his determination to stay and fight, had made it all worthwhile.

Whatever happened.

Along with a fitful day, holed up in Doc Boyd's office, this newly acquired awareness hadn't given him much rest. Which struck him as neither odd nor unreasonable. Somehow it seemed merely fitting. Luckily, he wasn't forced to dwell on it any longer.

Approaching Third, he saw the yellow parlor house and his thoughts turned to Belle Siddons. While he had curbed the impulse to stop at the hotel, there was no reason to avoid Belle. She was the closest thing he'd ever had to a sweet tooth, and tonight seemed a little late in the game to start resisting temptation.

When he entered the parlor, Belle uttered a small gasp and the color drained from her face. Several Texans were lolling about making smalltalk among themselves, and the conversation fell off sharply as he stepped through the doorway. Apparently they were passing time, waiting, for there wasn't a girl in sight. Somewhat taken aback, the cowhands stared at him as if he had dropped out of a tree. None of them said anything, but they suddenly got very careful with their hands. Galvanized at last, Belle came out of her chair as if touched by a hot poker.

She grabbed his arm, raking the Texans with a

fiery glance, and marched him through the door and down the hall to the kitchen. Only after she had drawn the shade on the back door did she turn on him. Somehow, though it came to him only at that moment, McCluskie had always liked her best when she was angry. She was plainly in one of her spitfire moods right now and the look on her face made him smile.

"Mike, for God's sake, stop grinning at me like a jackass. Don't you know what's happening?"

"Yes, ma'am." He doffed his hat and gave her a half bow. "You see I heard stories about this lady that snorts fire like a dragon, and I've come to pay my respects. Queer thing is, them stories weren't the least bit exaggerated."

"Stop it! Stop it!" A tear rolled down over her cheek and her bottom lip trembled. "They're going to kill you. Do you hear me, Mike? Anderson and his men are in town right now. This very minute. Don't you understand that?"

He crossed the kitchen and took her in his arms, sobered by what he had seen in her face. She met his embrace with a fierce hug and buried her head against his chest. After a moment he raised her chin and kissed her, slowly and with a gentleness he'd never shown before. When their lips parted, she gave a small sniffle and he smiled, wiping a tear off her cheek.

"There's lots of things I understand better than I did this morning."

Belle kissed his hand, then blinked as the words slowly took hold. "Why do you say that?"

"Well, I guess because I had plenty of time to do

some thinkin'. I've been holed up in Doc's office all day, waitin' for things to cool down before I braced Anderson. Just sat there starin' at the wall for the most part, figuring things out."

"What things?"

McCluskie let her go and drew back. He pulled out the makings, trickling tobacco onto paper, and started building a smoke. There was something deliberate and unhurried about his movements, as if he was stalling for time, keeping his hands occupied while he collected his thoughts. Belle waited him out, and at last, when he had the cigarette going, he met her gaze.

"I was thinkin' about the kid."

She gave him a quick intent look. "Kinch? Why, there isn't any reason to worry about him. He's just a boy. Texans aren't even low enough to take their spite out on a boy."

"That wasn't what I meant, just exactly." The Irishman took a deep drag and exhaled, studying the coal on the tip of his cigarette. "I was thinkin' about the way he looked at me this mornin' when he heard I hadn't quit."

"My god!" Belle paled and her eyes widened with comprehension. "You stayed so he would go on thinking you're some kind of holy terror."

"Something like that. I'd already made up my mind anyway, but it came to me sort of gradual that I stayed for the kid as much as for myself."

"And you're going to hunt Anderson down just to prove it?"

"That's about the gist of it, I guess." McCluskie flicked ashes toward the stove and smiled. "Seems odd, don't it? Can't say as I've quite gotten used to the idea myself."

"Not odd, Mike. Insane. Do you hear me? Crazy mad! You'll get yourself killed for nothing." She waited for an answer but he just stared at her. "He's dying, Mike. Don't you understand? In a few months he'll be dead and whatever you proved to him won't mean a thing."

"That's the point I've been tryin' to make. It'll mean a whole lot." His brow wrinkled and he took a swipe at his mustache. "Funny thing is, it's hard to explain, but when you get it boiled down, it's real simple. The kid don't have much besides me. When his string runs out I'd like to think nothin' between us had changed."

"You're just kidding yourself, don't you know that? He's in Sugar's room right now. Does that sound like someone who's all busted up because his idol might wind up dead?"

"Belle, you've been in the business long enough to know better'n that. Sugar's like a toy, just something to keep him from suckin' his thumb. Case you don't know it, he spent most of the day searchin' all over town for me. Doc told me so himself."

He took a final puff and ground out the cigarette in an ashtray. "You say he's in her room now?"

"Yes, has been for the last hour. Why?"

"Nothin'. Just hadn't planned on seein' him, that's all."

"Well that takes the cake! I'll swear to God, it does."

"What's the matter?"

"Matter? Oh, nothing at all. Just that you're willing

to get yourself killed, but you can't face Kinch and tell him why. Doesn't that strike you as a little strange?"

"Depends on how you look at it. First off, it's not all because of him. Never was. And there's no sense makin' it out to be something it's not. Next thing is, I don't plan on gettin' killed. Likely there's some that could punch my ticket, but Anderson's not one of 'em."

He paused and gave her a tight grin. "Tell you the truth, there's an even better reason. Hell, you know how the kid is. If I told him what's up, he'd raise a fuss to go along. I want him kept out of it."

"You're crazy, Mike McCluskie, do you know that?" Belle stomped off a couple of paces and turned, glaring at him. "Just once in your life couldn't you stop being so bullheaded? Anderson isn't about to stick to some silly set of rules. He wants you dead, and he'll use every dirty trick in the book to make sure it comes out that way."

The Irishman shrugged and grinned. "I'm not much for playin' by the rules myself. Like the fella said, there's more'n one way to skin a cat."

"Whose cat you gonna skin?"

Startled, they looked around and saw Kinch standing in the hallway door. There was no way of knowing how much he had overheard, yet it was apparently enough. His eyes were fastened on McCluskie, and as he stepped into the kitchen, a wide grin spread over his face.

"You've been sorta scarce today. Everybody said you was hidin' out, but I told 'em they was full of beans. I knew you'd show up."

"Well you had me shaded there, bud. I wasn't real sure myself till the sun went down."

"Yeah, but I knew. I got to thinkin' about it after you left this mornin', and I told myself there wasn't nothin' on earth that'd stop you. I was right, too."

"Guess you were, at that." McCluskie smiled and punched him on the shoulder.

Kinch paused and eyed him steadily for a moment. "You're gonna go lookin' for Anderson, aren't you?"

The Irishman cocked one eyebrow and nodded. "Guess it's time somebody called his hand. Seein' as I'm still wearin' the badge, it might as well be me."

"You'll need some help. Like that night with Bailey, remember? Wouldn't hurt none a'tall for me to back your play."

"Not this time, bud. It's personal. Something Anderson and me have got to settle ourselves."

McCluskie expected the kid to sull up and start pouting. Oddly enough, it fell the other way. Kinch nodded, as if he understood perfectly, and for once showed no inclination to argue the matter. They stared at one another a while and the Irishman finally chuckled.

"Tell you what. You wait here for me and after I'm finished we'll go up and check the yards together. Fair enough?"

"Whatever you say," the boy agreed. "Don't make it too long though. I'd like to get back to Sugar sometime tonight."

McCluskie laughed and turned back to Belle. She was fighting hard, determined not to cry, and from somewhere, she dredged up a tiny smile.

"Take care, Irish."

He grinned and gave her a playful swat on the rump. "Keep the lamp lit. I'll be home early."

"I'll be waiting."

Her words had a hollow ring, and as he entered the hallway she couldn't hold back any longer. Tears sluiced down over her cheeks, and when the front door slammed her heart seemed to stop altogether. Behind her another door closed softly, eased shut with only a slight click of the latch. Somehow she knew even before she looked, and a spark of hope fanned bright as she spun around.

Kinch was gone.

McCluskie had thought it all out at Doc Boyd's while he waited for it to grow dark. The choice was between Gregory's Saloon and Perry Tuttle's Dancehall. Those were Anderson's favorite hangouts, and sooner or later he was bound to show. Tuttle's somehow seemed the more appropriate of the two dives. That was where he had killed Bailey, and it was only fitting that the big dog himself be accorded the same honor.

Striding along toward Hide Park, the Irishman amused himself with a wry thought. Chances were it wouldn't be so much a matter of him finding Anderson as it would of Anderson finding him. While he had been on the street less than an hour, it stood to reason that word had already spread through town. The Texan likely knew every move he was making, and by now any chance of surprise would have worn off. The fact that he chose to flaunt his decision by invading Tuttle's made it a challenge Anderson could hardly overlook. That was something he counted on heavily. Bait of sorts.

Only in this case it was a tossup. He hadn't quite decided whether he was the hunter or the hunted. Not that he would have too long a wait to find out. The question would be resolved soon enough.

Tuttle's was packed to the rafters and going full blast when he came through the doors. He swept the room with a slow look, assuring himself that Anderson wasn't present, but even that seemed more out of habit than any sense of caution. Tonight he didn't feel wary. Quite the opposite, he felt reckless and anxious to have it done with. He had come here to kill a man, and the sooner it could be arranged the better. Perhaps he wouldn't walk away himself, but that had ceased to trouble him. For an assortment of reasons, none of which he had bothered to explore, he was riding a crest of fatalism. It was a thing that needed doing and he had tapped himself for the job. That was explanation enough.

Spotting an empty table against the far wall, he began threading his way through the crowd. That was an edge of sorts—having his back against a wall—and it might just make the difference. At least they couldn't get him from behind. Approaching the table, he noted that the one next to it was occupied by two Santa Fe men. An engineer, Pat Lee, and his fireman, Jim Hickey. When they glanced up, he shook his head, warning them off, and slipped into a chair on the far side of the table.

He ordered a bottle and when it came, poured himself a single shot. Leaning back in his chair, he sipped at the whiskey and kept one eye on the door while he watched the mad whirl on the dancefloor. The trailhands turned the whole affair into one big struggle,

pushing and shoving and shouting, like a gang of
wrestlers who just happened to wear spurs and six-
guns. Their antics alone were worth the price of admission, and in passing, it occurred to him that
dancehall girls earned every nickel of their money.
After a night on the floor with the Texans, most of
them were probably nothing short of a walking bruise.

McCluskie was still nursing the same drink when
the doors flew open and Hugh Anderson strode into
the room. Behind him were five hard-looking cowhands, and they all came together in a little knot,
quickly scanning the crowd. One of the hands spotted
him sitting alone at the table and nudged Anderson.
The Texan's gaze jerked around, settling on him at
last, and an instant later the men separated. Anderson
came straight toward him, but the others fanned out
and moved across the floor from different directions.
The Irishman grunted to himself, smiling slightly, and
climbed to his feet.

Now he had his answer. It was the hunters who
had come for him. Which was just as well. He'd never
been one to bet short odds, anyway.

Anderson stopped before the table, his lip curled
back in a gloating smirk. "Mister, you got enough
brass for a whole herd of monkeys."

"Want to borrow some?"

"Come again?"

"Why, it's pretty simple, Anderson." The Irishman
jerked his chin at the five hands. They were now
spread out in a rough crescent that had him caught in
a crossfire from all sides. "If you had the starch to
fight your own fights you wouldn't need so much
help."

"You stupid sonovabitch. This ain't no church social. That plain enough, or you want me to draw you a picture?"

McCluskie started to answer but movement off to the left caught his eye. The moment his gaze flicked in that direction he knew he'd been suckered. The cowhand farthest down the line had shifted positions, distracting him for a crucial instant, and it had worked perfectly. Even as his eyes swung back he sensed it was too late.

The gun in Anderson's hand was out and cocked, pointed straight at him. It was as if time and motion had been arrested. He saw the hammer fall, glimpsed the first sparks of the muzzle flash, and then went stone blind as the pistol exploded in his face. The slug mushroomed through his throat, slamming him back against the wall, and he felt something warm and sticky splash down over his shirt. Then his knees buckled and he was suddenly gripped with the urgency of killing Anderson.

The trainmen seated at the next table leaped to their feet just as the other Texans opened fire. The shots were meant for the Irishman, but they were hurried and wide of the mark. Lee collapsed, drilled through the bowels, and Hickey screamed as a slug shattered the thigh bone in his right leg. McCluskie heard the gunfire and the terrified shrieks of dancehall girls, sensed the crowd scattering. But it was all somehow distant, even a little unreal. Blinded, falling swiftly into darkness, he willed his hand to move. To finish what he had come here to do.

Another bullet smacked him in the ribs, but like a dead snake, operating on nerves alone, his hand reacted and came up with the Colt. That he couldn't see Anderson bothered him not at all. In his mind's eye he remembered exactly where the Texan was standing, and even as he pressed the trigger, he knew the shot had struck home.

Anderson staggered backward, jolted by a fiery blow in the chest. His legs gave way and he started falling, but with some last reserve of strength he raised his pistol. The floor and his rump collided with a jarring crash, and in a final moment of consciousness, he shot the Irishman in the back.

McCluskie grunted with the impact of the slug and pitched headlong between the tables. His leg twitched and his hand slowly opened, releasing its grip on the Colt. Then his eyes rolled back, the sockets empty and sightless, and he lay still. A wispy tendril of smoke curled out of the gun barrel and disappeared. Afterward there was nothing.

Hurriedly, the five cowhands moved forward and gathered around their boss. The instant they came together the sharp crack of a pistol racketed across the dancehall. One of them clutched at his stomach and slumped forward, and the crowd again dove for cover. But the Texans seemed frozen in their tracks, unable to move, staring at the fallen man in a numbed stupor.

Standing just inside the doorway, Kinch thumbed the hammer back and fired again. There was nothing rushed in either his manner or in his soft feathering of the trigger, yet the shots thundered across the room in a staccato roar. Coolly, just as the Irishman had taught him, he spaced the shots evenly and drilled each one precisely where he meant it to go. Every time the worn Navy bucked, another Texan went down, and within a half-dozen heartbeats it was over. When the gun clicked at last on an empty chamber not a single cowhand was left standing.

The kid slowly lowered his arm and stood there a moment, looking at the tangled jumble of bodies. Something inside tugged at him, demanding that he cross the room and make sure. But he shook it off, touched by the grim certainty that there was no need. He had seen McCluskie go down, felt that last slug as if it had been pumped into his own back. Whatever the Irishman had been in life, he was just a dead man now. Nothing more. That wasn't the way Kinch wanted to remember him.

Backing away, he holstered the Colt and brushed through the doors. There was a sudden chill in the air and he shivered. Then he knew it for what it was and hurried on into the night.

FIFTEEN

❦

The kitchen was still as a crypt. Kinch sat slumped in a chair, elbows on his knees, staring at nothing. He hadn't moved in the last hour, as if he had retreated within himself, locked in some private hell all his own.

Seated nearby, Sugartit looked on helplessly. She wanted to touch him, take his hand, comfort him in some way. But she knew there was nothing she could say or do that would ease his grief. Years ago she had lost her own family, and she remembered all too well the cold, deadened sensation that clutched at a person's heart. Remorse came quickly, but it released its hold with infinite slowness. Only time would heal the feeling of rage and loss that gripped him now, and difficult as it was to remain quiet, the girl merely watched and waited. When he was ready, in his own fashion, Kinch would find some way to talk about it. However long it took, Sugar meant to be there when he needed her.

The only sound in the room was the soft shuffling

of Belle's footsteps. She circled the kitchen like some distracted ghost, wan and ashen-faced. She had long since cried herself out, and now she felt drained of all emotion and feeling. Her hands were icy cold, though the room was sticky with summer warmth, and she kept her arms wrapped around her waist. Somehow she couldn't bring herself to take a seat at the table. She felt some restless compulsion to keep moving, almost as if in her mindless pacing she could outdistance the dreaded truth.

That he was gone, lying dead at that very moment, she still couldn't accept. He had always been so charged with life, full of strength and wit and energy, and it just wasn't possible. Someone with his lust and vitality simply couldn't be extinguished that easily. Like snuffing out a candle. Whatever God watched over Irishmen wasn't that capricious or impersonal. To cut a man down in his prime, kill him needlessly and without purpose, was a waste she couldn't comprehend. A truth so appalling her mind simply wouldn't accept it as fact.

Yet she had known it the minute Kinch walked through the door. The sickly pallor covering his face, and the shock etched deep in his eyes, bespoke the horror of what she had feared most. Stunned, unwilling to believe, she had stared at him a long time, until finally he lowered his head. His words still rang in her ears.

"They got him."

That was all he said. Having spoken those simple words, a death knell sounded in a quavering voice, he slumped into a chair and hadn't moved since. A rush of tears stung her eyes, and something vile and thick clogged her throat. She hadn't questioned him then, and later, after she stopped crying, it didn't seem to matter. Whatever had happened, she chose not to hear it. Somehow, in a way she hadn't yet reconciled, if she didn't hear it then it couldn't be true. But even as she witlessly paced the floor, frantically seeking to elude the truth, she knew deep down that she was only fooling herself.

Mike McCluskie was dead, and all the King's horses and all the King's men couldn't bring him back again.

The nursery rhyme jarred her to a halt.

Humpty Dumpty sat on a wall. Humpty Dumpty had a great fall. *God, she must be going mad.* Reaching back into her childhood, dredging up some silly nonsense to cushion a blow she hadn't yet been able to accept. That's what it was. Some form of lunacy. Letting her mind play tricks on her. Turning a tall, sandy-haired hellraiser into a dumpy little innocent. Watching him tumble from the wall and shatter to pieces. It was a device. A childish game. Something conjured up from God knew where to convince herself that he really couldn't be scraped up and glued back together again.

Life didn't work that way. Only in fairy tales did the good guys win. Out in the harsh reality of the world it was the bastards who walked away with the marbles. They never died. Or perhaps, because there were so many of them, it merely seemed that their numbers never dwindled.

She turned and was amazed to see Sugartit sitting beside the boy. Though her mind seemed lucid and clear, she couldn't recall the girl entering the kitchen.

But obviously she had, and plain to see, she was wholly absorbed in the boy's sorrow. Then, in a moment of self-loathing, Belle realized that for the past hour she had dwelt on nothing but her own grief. She had given no thought whatever to Kinch. Wasted and sickly, dying by inches as some ravenous thing consumed his lungs, he sat there stricken with remorse. Not for himself, but instead for what he had lost. The one man who had befriended him, given him a reason to live, made him forget for a small moment in time that he was marked for an early grave.

All at once she felt an outpouring of pity that completely overshadowed her own misery.

She crossed the room and gently laid her hand on the kid's head. "Mike wouldn't like this. Do you know that? If he walked through the door and caught us moping around this way, he'd just raise holy hell."

Kinch kept his eyes fastened on the floor. "He ain't comin' through that door no more."

"No, I suppose not." Belle's stomach churned, queasy and fluttering, as if she had swallowed a jar of butterflies. She took a deep breath to steady herself. "But that's no reason for us to crawl off and call it quits. Mike lived more in thirty years than most men would in a couple of lifetimes. And he enjoyed every minute of it, too. Do you know what he would say if he was here right now? He'd laugh and then he'd say, 'Bud, it's nothin' but the luck of the draw. You pays your money and you takes your chances.' "

Sugartit placed her hand on the boy's arm. "Belle's right, honey. You mustn't blame yourself. These things just happen."

Kinch slammed out of the chair, jerking away from

them. "What d'you know about it? You weren't there."

The girl winced as if she had been slapped in the face and stared after him in bewilderment. He stalked across the room and stopped beside the stove, refusing to look at them. The heat of his words left them startled, and for a while no one said anything. Sugartit had plainly hit a nerve, and the boy's wretched look disturbed them in a way they couldn't quite fathom.

Presently Belle got a grip on herself and decided to have another try. Whatever was bothering him had to be brought out into the open. Left to fester and feed upon itself, it would only get worse.

"Are you blaming yourself, Kinch? Is that why you can't look at us?"

He still wouldn't turn around. "I waited too long. I should've gone in there with him. If there'd been two of us they would've backed down."

"Don't you think Mike thought of that?"

"I dunno."

"Yes you do. You know it very well. He told you to stay here because he didn't want you mixed up in this business."

"Yeah, but he was always sayin' that. I shouldn't have listened."

"That's just the point. You didn't listen. You followed him anyway. Nobody could have asked any more of you than that. Why should you expect more of yourself?"

"She's right," Sugartit blurted. "You did what you could, and that's the most anybody can do."

"Cripes, you two don't understand nothin', d'you?

I should've talked him into lettin' me back his play. He'd have let me if I just spoke up."

"You're wrong, Kinch." Belle's tone had the hard ring of certainty. "He would have tied you hand and foot before he let that happen."

"Don't be too sure. He knew how good I was with a gun."

"Yes, but there's something you don't understand. He thought the sun rose and set in your hat. Why else do you think he stayed here? You just think about it a minute and you'll see he would never have let you go along."

Belle realized her mistake only after the words were out. She damned herself for speaking out of turn, but by then it was too late. Kinch whirled around, his eyes distended and flecked through with doubt.

"What're you talkin' about? It was his job. He stayed here to get Anderson, didn't he?"

"Of course he did. I just meant he thought too much of you to risk getting you in a jam with the Texans."

"That's not what you meant. You're lyin' to me, Belle." The kid scrunched his eyes up in a tight scowl. "I got a right to know, and you got no right to hold back on me."

She just stared at him a moment, feeling helplessly trapped. "Maybe you're right. I suppose when a man does something like that it shouldn't be kept a secret." She faltered, trying to break it gently, but found herself at a loss for words. "I don't know how else to say it except straight out. Mike never ran from anything in his life and he probably wouldn't have this time either. But there was more to it. The reason he stayed, I mean. He was willing to take on Anderson and that bunch so you wouldn't think bad of him. I tried to talk him out of it, but he had his mind set."

"Oh, Jesus." Kinch seemed to stagger and his face went ashen. "He didn't have to get himself killed to prove nothin'. I would've understood."

"Mike thought it was important enough that he wasn't willing to take a chance. He did it the only way he knew how." The boy was badly shaken, worse than Belle had expected, and she tried to soften the blow. "Maybe it's not much consolation, but Mike was sure he could trick Anderson into making it a fair fight. I think he really believed he could pull it off and walk away without a scratch."

"Yeah, it was fair awright." The muscle at the back of his jawbone twitched in a hard knot. "Six to one. With him backed up against a wall."

There was a sharp rap at the back door and the room went deathly still. Kinch's arm moved and the Colt appeared in his hand. Stepping back beside the stove, he drew a bead on the window shade, then nodded for Belle to open the door. She threw the bolt and jerked the door open, moving quickly out of the line of fire. Dr. Gass Boyd stepped through the entrance and stopped, looking first at the two women and finally at the gun barrel centered on his chest.

"Youngster, it would be a serious error in judgment for you to shoot me. I'm about the last friend you have left in this town."

Belle slammed the door and bolted it. Something in Boyd's voice alarmed her, more the tone than the words themselves. But as she turned to question him,

Kinch holstered his pistol and stepped away from the stove.

"Sorry I threw down on you, Doc. Guess I'm a little jumpy tonight."

"Save your apologies, son." Boyd set his bag on the table and smiled. "After what you did tonight you have every right to a case of nerves."

"I don't understand." Belle shot him a puzzled frown. "What's Kinch done?"

The doctor looked from her to the boy and one eyebrow arched quizzically. "You mean to say you haven't told them?"

"Just about Mike." Kinch ducked his head. "Didn't see that it'd do any good to tell 'em about the rest."

"What do you mean, the rest?" Belle moved around the table and faced Boyd squarely. "Doc, will you please explain what's going on here?"

"Perhaps you ladies had better sit down. Our young friend seems to have omitted a few rather salient details."

Sugar obediently took a chair but Belle remained standing. "Quit hedging, Doc. Let's have it."

"Very well. I have just come from the hardware store, which is temporarily serving as a funeral parlor. As of this moment there are five dead and four wounded. In my opinion one of the wounded will die before morning. The others have a fair chance of pulling through."

"You're still beating around the bush. What does that have to do with Kinch?"

Boyd glanced over at the kid and his sober expression deepened. "Belle, it seems you are harboring a paragon of modesty as well as a fugitive. According to a hundred or so eyewitnesses, Kinch personally accounted for four of the dead and two wounded. One of whom is as good as dead right now."

"Oh, my God." Belle sank into a chair.

Sugartit stared unblinkingly at the boy, her eyes glazed over with shock. Belle was aghast, unable to get her breath for a moment, and finally she looked up at the little physician in complete bafflement.

"He didn't say a word."

"Precisely." Boyd treated the kid to a benevolent smile. "Along with unerring aim, he has the virtue of modesty."

"Five men." Sugartit's statement came in a dazed whisper.

"And a sixth wounded," Boyd noted in a clinical undertone.

Belle shook her head in numbed disbelief, and at last her gaze settled on the boy. "Why didn't you tell us?"

Kinch gave her a hangdog look and shrugged. "I figured you had enough on your mind. Hearin' about Mike, I mean."

"But how in God's name did you do it?"

"I dunno. It all happened so fast I ain't real sure." The kid mulled it over a little, trying to sort it out in his mind. "Mike and Anderson went down just as I come through the door. Then the rest of them Texans ganged around for a looksee and I started shootin'. Funny thing is, they just stood there. Didn't try to run or duck or nothin'. It was sorta like knockin' over tin cans, the way Mike showed me when we used to practice."

Silence descended on the kitchen, and for a moment everybody stared at him in dumbstruck wonder. Presently the doctor cleared his throat and tugged reflectively at his ear. "I'm not much of a shot myself, but offhand, I'd say you had a damned good teacher."

"Best there ever was," Kinch agreed. They exchanged glances and the boy frowned. "Something you said bothers me, though, Doc. I ain't no slouch with a pistol, but Mike never taught me how to get six men with five shots. Y'see, he believed in carryin' the hammer on an empty chamber, and I only had five loads. That's what throws me. There was only five of them Texans and I drilled ever' one of 'em dead center."

Boyd eyed him speculatively. "What about the trainmen?"

"What trainmen?"

"There were two Santa Fe men seated at the table next to Mike's."

"I don't know what you're talkin' about, Doc. All I saw was that bunch of Texans standin' over Mike and Anderson."

Belle gave the physician a keen sidewise scrutiny. "Doc you're hinting at something. That's why you snuck in the back door, isn't it? You didn't want anybody to see you coming here."

"I'm afraid so," Boyd admitted. "One of those killed was Pat Lee, a Santa Fe engineer." He paused and looked at the boy. "Anderson swears it was your shot that killed him."

"*Anderson?*" Kinch spit the word out, glaring thunderstruck at the doctor.

"Why, yes. Perhaps I forgot to mention it, but Anderson is going to live. Despite a very serious chest wound he'll make it with any luck—"

Kinch kicked a chair out of his way and headed for the door. Boyd surprised even himself by darting across the room and blocking the boy's path.

"Now wait a minute, son. Don't go running off in circles like a bee had stung you."

"Get out of my road, Doc."

"You're going after Anderson, is that it?"

"Damn right! He killed Mike, didn't he?"

"And I suppose Mike taught you how to walk in and shoot a wounded man while he's laid up in bed. Was that one of the lessons?"

The kid just stood there a moment, half mad with rage, then he wheeled around and started pacing the kitchen. Belle and Sugar looked at one another, unnerved and not a little frightened by what they had seen in his face. After a moment Boyd regained his composure and came back to the table.

"Kinch, the night Mike McCluskie carried you to his hotel room I promised him I would look after your health. In a way, that's what I'm still doing. Now suppose we all remain calm and I'll explain what brought me down here."

When no one objected, he went on. "There are a number of things happening in Newton at this very moment. First off, Bob Spivey has telegraphed to Topeka for a U.S. marshal. He means to put the fear of God into this town, and there is already talk that a swift hanging would be just the thing to turn the trick. Secondly, Anderson's statement against Kinch is backed up by one of his cowhands. The one who's going to live. Son, from where I sit, that makes you the prime candidate for a necktie party."

Kinch stopped pacing and glowered back at him. "I didn't kill no Santa Fe men. All I shot was Texans."

"I don't doubt that for an instant. But it's your word against theirs. Now, you're in no danger from the Texans. From what I heard at the dancehall they don't think much of the way Anderson and his crew ganged up on Mike. Unfortunately, the same can't be said for the townspeople. Or the U.S. marshal, for that matter."

"What about Anderson?" the kid demanded. "Hadn't somebody better charge him with murder for what he did to Mike?"

"Probably they will. But from the little I've overheard, I suspect his men intend to sneak him out of town before morning. That won't change a thing, though. Anderson's statement will still hold, and when the U.S. marshal arrives, he'll come looking for you. Whether or not you actually killed the engineer would be a moot question at that point. The townspeople are in an ugly mood. They want to make an example out of somebody, and I'm afraid you're it."

The logic of Boyd's argument was hard to dispute. Everybody looked back and forth at one another for a while and there was silent agreement that the boy had worked himself into a bad spot.

At last Belle turned to face the doctor. "What you're saying is that we have to get Kinch out of town before some drunk gets busy and organizes a lynching bee."

"That's correct," Boyd nodded. "The sooner, the better. Oddly enough, there happens to be a horse out back right now. With a bill of sale in the saddlebags."

Belle turned her attention to the kid. "Kinch, I'll try to tell you what Mike would say if he was sitting here instead of me. He was a gambling man, but he always knew when to fold a losing hand. That's what you're holding right now. It's time to call it quits and find yourself a new game. Otherwise Sugar's liable to be burying her man the same as I'll have to bury mine."

That struck home and the boy swallowed hard. "Maybe so, but I'd feel like I'm runnin' out on Mike. I sorta had it in mind to finish what he'd started with them Texans."

"You're not running! Get that out of your head. If you had it to do over, you'd have told Mike to leave. Wouldn't you? Well this is the same thing. Sugartit and me, we're asking you to go for our sake."

Sugartit flew out of her chair and rushed into the kid's arms. "Please, honey, do it for me. Just this once. Wherever you go, you let me know and I'll be there with bells on. I promise."

Boyd cleared his throat and looked away. "Son, I suspect there's little time to waste. You had best be off while you have the chance."

"Yeah, sorta looks that way, don't it?"

Kinch pulled Belle into a tight hug and afterward shook the doctor's hand. Then Sugartit threw herself in his arms again and gave him a kiss that was meant to last. Finally she let go and he headed for the door. But halfway out he turned and looked back.

"You want to hear something funny? I ain't never been on a horse in my life. This oughta be a real circus."

The door closed and they just stood there staring at it. Somehow the whole thing seemed a bad dream of sorts. A nightmare that would pass with the darkness and leave their lives untouched. But moments later the spell was broken and reality came back to stay.

Hoofbeats sounded outside and slowly faded into the night. Like a drummer boy tapping the final march, they heard a faint tattoo in the soft brown earth.

Kinch Riley would return no more.

SIXTEEN

〰〰〰

The kid often came to a grove of cottonwoods along the riverbank. There was something peaceful about the shade of the tall trees and the sluggish waters gliding past in a silty murmur. Yet it was only within the past week that the Red had settled down and started to behave itself. Spring rains had been heavy, and the snaky, meandering stream had crested in a raging torrent for better than a fortnight. A mile wide in some places, roiling and frothing in its turbulent rush southward, it had been a watery graveyard of uprooted trees, wild things dead and bloated, and a flotsam of debris collected in its wandering rampage.

Kinch hadn't cared much for the river in flood. It reminded him somehow of an angry beast, hungry and drooling, devouring everything in its path. Watching it had disturbed him, almost as if the river and the thing gnawing on his lungs were of a breed. Kindred in the way of things carnivorous and lurking and ever ready to fatten themselves on the flesh of the living. That the thought was far-fetched—a figment of the nagging fear which shadowed his thoughts these days—made little difference. It was no less real, and in some dark corner of his mind he was obsessed with but one thing.

He must not die. Not yet.

But as the flood waters receded, and the warmth of spring came again to the land, he found a measure of hope. The prairie turned green as an emerald sea, and overnight bright clusters of wild flowers seemed to burst from the earth. New life, borne in on soft southerly breezes, was everywhere he looked. He drew strength from its freshness and vitality, and with it, the belief that he might, after all, hold on till his work was completed.

While his thoughts still turned inward, he dwelled not so much on himself these days as on the happier times of a summer past. That brief moment when he'd had it all. The excitement and laughs, friendship and love. When the Irishman and Belle and Sugartit had given him something that neither time nor space could erase.

Seated beneath the leafy cottonwoods, soaking up the warming rays of a plains sun, his mind often wandered back. There, in a bright little cranny far off in his head, McCluskie still lived. Tall and square-jawed, alert and tough and faintly amused. Busted nose and all. Kinch could summon forth at will the tiniest detail. How the Irishman walked and talked and knocked back a jigger of whiskey. The hard-as-nails smile and the quick grin and that soft grunt of disgust. The deliberate way he had of rolling a smoke and flicking a match to life with his thumbnail. Every mannerism and quirk acquired on the long hard trail from Hell's Kitchen to the dusty plains of Kansas. It was all there, shiny bright and clear as polished glass, tucked neatly away in the back of his mind. Etched boldly and without flaw, indelible as a tattoo.

Still, the kid wasn't fooling himself. The image existed only in his mind's eye. Along with it persisted the certain knowledge that the man he summoned back so easily was dead and long buried. Mike McCluskie, that part of him which was flesh and bone, had been under ground some nine months now. The other part, what the preachers always made such a fuss over, was somewhere else. Though just exactly where, nobody had ever nailed down for sure.

Kinch had given that considerable thought. Particularly at night, when he came to sit beneath the trees and listen to the river. Head canted back, searching the starry skies, he wondered if there was a heaven. Or a hell. And if so, the further imponderable. Which place would the spirit of Mike McCluskie most likely be found? Somehow he had a feeling that the Irishman had made it to the Pearly Gates. Probably fighting every step of the way, too. Heels dug in and squawling like a sore-tailed bear.

The kind of people McCluskie had enjoyed most in life were the rascals and the highrollers. Being separated from them in the hereafter was something he wouldn't have counted on. If he had gone up instead of down, it had doubtless taken some mighty hard shoving on somebody's part.

Which way he had gone didn't mean a hill of beans, though. Not to the kid, anyhow. He himself wasn't all that hooked on religion, and so far as he could see, one way looked about as good as another.

Just so he could tag along with the Irishman when his time came, he didn't give a tinker's damn whether it was heaven or hell or somewhere in between. When he checked out for good, finally gave up the ghost, he meant to make himself heard on that score. Anybody that tried to punch his ticket a different direction than McCluskie was going to have a stiff scrap on his hands.

Kinch chuckled to himself and slowly climbed to his feet. For someone living on borrowed time, he sure had some powerful notions about the hereafter. Like as not, when a fellow passed on, they just gave him his choice, and there wasn't any big rhubarb about it one way or another.

Squinting at the sun, he made it a couple of hours before noon. Time he got off his duff and swamped out the saloon. Quitting the cottonwoods, he headed up the bluff toward the station.

The town wasn't much. Aside from the saloon, there was a ramshackle hotel, two general stores, and perhaps a dozen houses scattered about the surrounding prairie. While the township had been officially designated Salt Creek, honoring a nearby tributary which flowed into the larger stream, it was known simply and universally as Red River Station. Situated on a high limestone bluff overlooking the river, it was as far as a man could go and still say he was in Texas. Once across the Red, he entered Indian Territory.

The reason for the station's existence lay just west of town. There, a wide natural chute, boxed in by limestone walls, sloped down to the water's edge. Starting in late spring and continuing into early fall, herds of longhorns were driven down the chute and pushed across the river. A sandbar ran out from the northern back, and when the cattle reached it, they had begun the long haul up the Chisholm Trail. Some two hundred fifty miles farther north, after passing through Indian Territory, the trail ended at the Kansas railheads. Abilene, Newton, and the reigning cowtown this particular spring, Wichita.

Small as it was, it seemed likely that Red River Station would thrive and prosper forever. Though the cowtowns faded into obscurity as quickly as rails were laid south and west, the station depended on nothing but itself. It was the gateway to the Chisholm Trail, the only known route through the red man's domain, and this strategic location guaranteed its prosperity.

The trail herds passing the station had been sparse thus far this spring. Cattlemen were reluctant to ford the Red, and the latticework of rivers crisscrossing Indian Territory, until the flood waters had receded. But the billowing plume of dust on the southern horizon steadily grew larger, and over the past week, better than three herds a day had made the crossing. Soon, as many as ten herds a day, numbering upward of twenty thousand longhorns, would be stacked up waiting their turn. Red River Station made not a nickel's profit off the cattle themselves, but its little business community grew fat and sleek off the cowhands. After fording the river, the Texans wouldn't again see civilization for close to a month. The station was their last chance, and in the way of thirsty men doing dirty work, they made the most of it.

Kinch came through the back door of the Alamo Saloon and started collecting his gear. Broom and featherduster, mop and pail. Tools of the trade for a swamper. He didn't care much for the job, emptying spittoons and swabbing drunken puke off the floor, but beggars couldn't be choosers. The way he looked at it, Roy Oliphant had been damned white to take him on, and he felt lucky to have a bunk in the back room, three squares, and a little pocket change. More importantly, it allowed him to straddle the jaws of the Chisholm Trail while he watched and planned and waited.

Hugh Anderson would pass this way, as did all Texas cattlemen, sooner or later. When he finally showed, the kid had a little surprise in store. An early Christmas present, of sorts.

After sweeping the floor, he started mopping the place with a practiced, unhurried stroke. Nine months on the end of a mop had taught him that there was no fast way. Slow and sure, that was the ticket. It left the floor clean and his lungs only slightly bent out of shape. He was nearing the rear of the saloon when Roy Oliphant came down from his room upstairs.

The boy paused, breathing hard, and leaned on his mop. "Mornin', Mr. Oliphant. All set for another day?"

Oliphant stopped at the bottom of the stairwell and gave him a dour look. The saloonkeeper was a gruff bear of a man, widowed and without children, and early morning generally found him foul-tempered and vinegary. But in his own way, rough and at times blistering, he had a soft spot for strays. The ones life had shortchanged and left discarded along the wayside. There were occasions when he reminded the kid just the least little bit of McCluskie.

"Bub, ever' now and then I get the notion you haven't got a lick of sense. Look at the way you're huffin' and puffin'. Goddamnit, how many times I got to tell you? Slow down. Take it easy. The world ain't gonna swell up and bust if you don't burn the end off that mop."

Kinch grinned and took another swipe at the floor. "Aw, cripes, Mr. Oliphant. Workin' up a sweat is good for me. Gets all the kinks ironed out."

"Why sure it does," Oliphant observed tartly. "That's why you're wheezin' like a windbroke horse, ain't it?"

"Well, I always say if a job's worth doing it's worth doing right. Besides, you got the cleanest saloon in town, so what're you always hollerin' about?"

Oliphant grunted, holding back on a smile. "Don't give me none of your sass. This here's the only saloon in town and you damn well know it."

"Yeah, but it's still the cleanest."

"Real funny, 'cept I ain't laughin'. You're not foolin' anybody, y'know?"

"What d'you mean?"

"C'mon, don't play dumb." Oliphant headed toward the bar, talking over his shoulder. "You buzzsaw that mop around so you can get back down to the bluffs and start bangin' away at tin cans."

The kid blinked a couple of times, but he didn't say anything.

Oliphant drew himself a warm beer and downed half the mug in a thirsty gulp. He wasn't a man who liked riddles, and the boy had been a puzzle of sorts from the day he walked through the door. Looking back, he often wondered why he'd taken the kid on in the first place. He knew galloping consumption when he saw it, and a smoky saloon didn't exactly qualify as a sanatorium. Which was what the youngster needed. When he rode into town, he'd been nothing but skin and bones, pale and sickly and wracked with fits of coughing. The saloonkeeper would have laid odds that he'd never make it through the winter. But the kid had hung on somehow, and never once had he shirked the job.

Still, after all these months, Oliphant had to admit to himself that he really didn't know the kid. Like this deal with the tin cans. He had sneaked down and watched the boy practice a few times. What he saw left him flabbergasted. Kinch made greased lightning look like molasses at forty below. Moreover, he rarely ever missed, and he went through the daily drills as if his life depended on every shot. The saloonkeeper was baffled by the whole thing, plagued by questions that seemingly defied any reasonable answer.

Where had he learned to handle a gun that slick? Who taught him? And most confusing of all, why in the name of Christ did he practice so religiously, day in and day out?

But Roy Oliphant wasn't the kind to stick his nose in other people's business. He ruminated on it a lot, watching silently as the kid spent every spare nickel on powder and lead, yet he had never once allowed his curiosity to get the better of him. Not until today.

Kinch was still staring at him as he drained the mug and set it on the bar. "That's what I like about you, bub. You're closemouthed as a bear trap."

"You mean the gun?"

"Hell, yes. What did you think I was talkin' about?

You work at it like your tail was on fire, but I never once seen you wear the damn thing. Sorta gets a fellow to wonderin' after a while."

"Aw, it's just a game somebody taught me. Y'know, something to help pass the time."

Oliphant gave him a skeptical look, but decided to let it drop. He hadn't meant to bring it up in the first place, and why he'd picked this morning to get nosy puzzled him all the more. Live and let live was his motto, and he'd never lost any skin minding his own business. If the kid had some deep dark secret, that was his privilege. Most times, what a man didn't know couldn't hurt him, and it was best left that way.

"Well, I guess you'd better finish up and get on back to your game. Only do me a favor, will you? Don't wear out my mops so fast. Them goddamn things cost money."

Kinch grinned and went back to swabbing the floor. Presently he disappeared into the storeroom and after a while the rusty hinges on the alley door groaned. Oliphant listened, waiting for it to close, then smiled and drew himself another beer.

Some more tin cans were about to bite the dust.

The kid's routine varied little from day to day. Swamp out the saloon, put in an hour or so working with the Colt, then return to his room and clean and reload the pistol. Afterward, he would stroll around town, always keeping his eye peeled for horses with a certain brand, and generally end up back at the saloon not long after noontime. There, he took up a position at the back of the room, supposedly on hand in case Oliphant needed any help. But his purpose in being there had nothing to do with the job. Whenever a fresh batch of Texans rode into town they made straight for the Alamo, and he carefully scrutinized each face that came through the door. While the long hours sapped his strength, and breathing the smoke-filled air steadily worsened his cough, he seldom budged from his post till closing time. Sooner or later the face he sought would come through the door, and he wasn't about to muff the only chance he might get.

Time was running out too fast for that.

Hardly anyone paid him any mind. He was just a skinny kid with a hacking cough who cleaned up their messes. That was the way Kinch wanted it. He kept himself in the background, and since coming to town, he had made it a habit to never wear a gun. With the Colt on his hip, there was the ever present likelihood he might become involved in an argument and wind up getting himself killed. That was one chance he wasn't willing to risk. Not until he'd performed a little chore of his own.

Yet there were times when he despaired of ever pulling it off, and this was one of those days. His cough was progressively growing worse, and the only thing that kept it under control was the bottle he had stashed in the storeroom. It was something to ponder. Nine months he had waited, and unless something happened damned quick, he'd cough once too often and that would be the end of it. Which wasn't what he'd planned at all, and personal feelings aside, it seemed unfair as hell to boot. Justice deserved a better shake than that. But then, as the Irishman had once observed, life was like a big bird. It had a way of dumping a load on a man's head just when he needed it least.

This was a thought much on his mind as he returned from the storeroom. He had developed quite a tolerance for whiskey the past few months, and the fiery trickle seeping down through his innards right now felt very pleasant. With any luck at all it would hold his cough at bay for a good hour. Not that an hour was what he needed, though. The way things were shaping up he had to figure out a cure that would hold him for a month, or more. Maybe the whole damn summer. Then he chuckled grimly to himself, amused by the absurdity of it.

There wasn't any cure, and if that big bird didn't dump all over him, he might just luck out with a couple of more weeks. But as he came through the door the laugh died, and his throat went dry as a bone.

Hugh Anderson and his crew were bellied up to the bar.

Kinch couldn't quite believe it for a minute. After all this time they had finally showed. He stood there, watching Oliphant serve them, and it slowly became real. The waiting had ended, at last, and for the first time in longer than he could remember, he felt calm and rested and cold as a chunk of ice. Stepping back, just the way he'd planned it, he simply vanished in the doorway and headed for his room.

Moments later, he reappeared and the Colt was cinched high on his hip. Walking forward, he stopped at the end of the bar, standing loose and easy, just the way the Irishman had taught him.

"Anderson."

The word ripped across the saloon and everyone

turned in his direction. Somebody snickered, but most of the crowd just gawked. The hard edge to his voice had fooled them, and they weren't quite sure it was this raggedy kid who had spoken. Then they saw the gun, and the look in his eye, and the place went still as a church. Kid or not, he had dealt himself a man's hand.

Anderson took a step away from the bar and gave him a quizzical frown. The Texan had slimmed down some from last summer, but other than that, he looked mean as ever.

"You want somethin', button?"

"Yeah. I want you."

"That a fact?" Anderson eyed him a little closer. "I don't place you just exactly. We met some-wheres?"

"It'll come back to you. Tuttle's Dancehall in Newton. The night you murdered Mike McCluskie."

"Sonovabitch!" Anderson stiffened and a dark scowl came over his face. "You're the one that shot up my crew."

Kinch nodded, smiling. "Now it's your turn."

"Sonny, you done bought yourself a fistful of dai-sies."

"You gonna fight, yellowbelly, or just talk me to death?"

The Texan grabbed for his gun and got it halfway out of the holster. Kinch's arm hardly seemed to move, but the battered old Navy suddenly appeared in his hand. Anderson froze and they stared at one another for an instant, then the kid smiled and pulled the trigger. A bright red dot blossomed on the Texan's shirt front, just below the brisket, and he slammed sideways into the bar. Kinch gun-shot him as he hung there, and when he slumped forward, placed still a third slug squarely in his chest. Anderson hit the floor like a felled ox, stone cold and stiffening fast.

There was a moment of stunned silence.

Before anybody could move, Roy Oliphant hauled out a sawed-off shotgun from beneath the bar. The hammers were earred back and he waved it in the general direction of Anderson's crew. "Boys, the way I call it, that was a fair fight. Everybody satisfied, or you want to argue about it?"

One of the cowhands snorted, flicking a glance down at the body. "Mister, there ain't no argument to it. The kid gave him his chance. More'n he deserved, I reckon. Leastways some folks'd say so."

Kinch turned, holstering the Colt, and walked back toward the storeroom. His eyes were bright and alive, and oddly enough, his lungs had never pumped better. He felt like a man who had just settled a long-standing debt.

What the Irish would have called a family debt.

Late that afternoon Kinch stepped aboard his horse and leaned down to shake hands with the saloon-keeper. "I'm obliged for everything, Mr. Oliphant."

"Hell, you earned your keep. Just wish you'd have give me the lowdown sooner, that's all. Not that you needed any help. But it don't never hurt to have somebody backin' your play."

"Yeah, that's the same thing I used to tell a friend of mine." The kid sobered a minute, then he grunted and gave off a little chuckle. "He was sort of bull-headed, too."

"You're talkin' about that McCluskie fellow."

"Irish, his friends called him. You should've known him, Mr. Oliphant. He was one of a kind. Won't never be another one like him."

"Well, it's finished now. You ever get back this way, you look me up, bub. I can always use a good man." They both knew it wasn't likely, but it sounded good. Oliphant suddenly threw back his head and glared up at the boy. "Say, goddamn! I ain't ever thought to ask. Which way you headed?"

"Wichita. Just as fast as this nag'll carry me."

"That's a pretty fair ride. Sure you're in any kind o' shape to make it?"

"I'll make it." The kid went warm all over, and in a sudden flash, Sugartit's kewpie-doll face passed through his mind. "Got somebody waitin' on me."

Oliphant leered back at him and grinned. "Yah, what's her name?"

"Mr. Oliphant, you wouldn't believe me if I told you."

Kinch laughed and kicked his horse into a scrambling lope. Just as he hit the grade down to the river, he turned back and waved. Then he was gone.

One last time, he was off to see the elephant.